T.Davis Bunn

THE DREAM VOYAGERS

BETHANY HOUSE PUBLISHERS
MINNEAPOLIS, MINNESOTA 55438

The Dream Voyagers
Copyright © 1999
T. Davis Bunn

Cover illustration by Michael Carroll and Joe Nordstrom
Cover design by Dan Thornberg,
Bethany House Publishers staff artist.

Published by Bethany House Publishers
A Ministry of Bethany Fellowship International
11400 Hampshire Avenue South
Minneapolis, Minnesota 55438
www.bethanyhouse.com

Printed in the United States of America by
Bethany Press International, Minneapolis, Minnesota 55438

Library of Congress Cataloging-in-Publication Data

Bunn, T. Davis, 1952–
    The dream voyagers / by T. Davis Bunn.
      p. cm.
    ISBN 0–7642–2180–9
    I. Title.
PS3552.U4718 D74 1999
813'.54—dc21
                                                        99–6409
                                                         CIP

THIS BOOK IS DEDICATED TO:

Colin & Lia Bruce
Joseph & Jean-Claire Peltier
Mason & Brent Williams

Never stop dreaming

Books by T. Davis Bunn

The Quilt
The Gift
The Messenger
The Music Box
One Shenandoah Winter
Tidings of Comfort & Joy

*Another Homecoming**
The Dream Voyagers
*The Meeting Place**
The Presence
Princess Bella and the Red Velvet Hat
Promises to Keep
*Return to Harmony**
To the Ends of the Earth
*Tomorrow's Dream**
The Warning
The Ultimatum

The Priceless Collection

1. *Florian's Gate*
2. *The Amber Room*
3. *Winter Palace*

Rendezvous With Destiny

1. *Rhineland Inheritance*
2. *Gibraltar Passage*
3. *Sahara Crosswind*
4. *Berlin Encounter*
5. *Istanbul Express*

*with Janette Oke

Contents

PART I

Dream Voyager

PART II

Path Finder

PART III

Heart Chaser

T. DAVIS BUNN, a native of North Carolina, is a former international business executive whose career has taken him to over forty countries in Europe, Africa, and the Middle East. With topics as diverse as romance, history, and intrigue, Bunn's books continue to reach readers of all ages and interest. He and his wife, Isabella, reside near Oxford, England.

PART I

The
Dream
Voyager

CHAPTER ONE

Consuela was delighted when Rick could not come to pick her up, and it had nothing whatsoever to do with his reputation. She was happy because it meant he would not be able to see where she lived, or how she lived, or with whom. Consuela did everything she could to separate her school-life from her home-life.

Not even the girls on the cheerleading squad had ever visited her home. This was very odd, because the girls took turns inviting the squad over for Wednesday night meals. When it was Consuela's turn, she treated the group to dinner at the local hangout, saying her mother was down with the flu—though the extravagance cost her a month's wages. Which was another odd thing about Consuela—some afternoons and Saturdays she worked for the most expensive women's boutique in town. One of the girls discovered it only because her parents took her there for a sixteenth birthday ball gown, and who should wait on them but Consuela. When the other girls asked her about it, Consuela played it very casual and grown-up, saying it was easy work, she met a lot of interesting people, and it gave her money to buy clothes. Which was a strange thing for her to say, since Consuela had only a few outfits that any of them had ever seen, but she mixed and matched them so cleverly that it was really hard to tell. And none of the clothes looked expensive enough to have been bought where she worked.

Had Consuela been less attractive or friendly, it would have been easy to make her an outsider. Not that she was beautiful. Consuela's features were too strong for her to fit the modern view of beauty. Her black hair hung long and full and simple, without any of the curls or flounces or frosted layers that were popular with the other girls. She wore no jewelry and little makeup. But there was a mystique to Consuela, a sense of strength and depth that drew people to her.

"I feel like I can tell her anything," her best friend Sally told the others one lunchtime. "I mean, *anything*. I don't know why, but I bet if I told her I was hooked on drugs or moving to Morocco, she wouldn't bat an eye."

"She's seventeen going on ninety-seven," somebody else agreed.

"She is the most unshakable person I've ever met," Sally went on, trying to put into words what she really couldn't understand herself. "She just listens to whatever I want to tell her, like she's taking it all really deep inside. I never get the feeling she's out to put me down."

"I know what it is," another of the girls declared. "She has this mysterious past. She's been all around the world, seen it all, done everything, and she's just too modest to talk about it."

"I like her," someone else declared. Then she realized what she had just said and covered it with a laugh.

Had Consuela heard what they said about her, she would not have believed it. Her own feelings about herself were very different. To Consuela's mind, her life at school was one big lie.

But she didn't want to think about those things now. Not when she was rushing from the bus stop to the carnival entrance, where she was to meet Rick Reynolds, captain of the football team and the best-looking guy at school. Consuela turned the corner; up ahead the road was lit by the garish carnival lighting. Under the flickering sign stood Rick, and she felt a little thrill of excitement at the thought that he was waiting there for her. For *her*.

Now was certainly not a time to be worrying about all the stuff she kept hidden from the world. Consuela put on her very best smile and hoped he would look happy to see her. Then he turned and spotted her, and his own face lit up with a satisfied smile. Yes, things were certainly looking up.

———

Wander climbed down the bank as carefully as he could. He was still unused to wearing the scout's robe of pale blue and wished he could return to his everyday clothing. But scouts were required to wear their robes at all times, on and off duty. So Wander gathered up the folds,

tucked them into his belt, and tried hard not to slip on the icy embank-
ment.

The tree trunk brought back a flood of memories. So many hours he
had sat there, looking across the floodlit expanse at the great vessels
resting in their gravity nets, eager to be released to fly up, up, up and
away. Since his childhood, Wander had known only one dream, to fly
with them.

He checked his chronolog, a habit that was useful because it masked
his burgeoning abilities from those who did not share his sensitivity. But
here in the splendid isolation of a frozen forest, he had no need to check
the time. He could hear the pilot's droning count as clearly as if he were
still in the instruction hall, his headpiece plugged into the amplification
system.

The pilot gave the captain the formal two-minute warning. Wander
brushed snow from the trunk and seated himself just as the first glimmer
emanated from the ship's circular base. Four other ships awaited their
place on the thruster shield, all freighters bound for the Outer Rim. Passenger vessels used daytime departure slots while the port was fully active. At night things slowed down, and the port's two shields were given
over to freight and private vessels unwilling to pay for daytime slots.

A thrilling hum lifted the hairs on the nape of Wander's neck as the
ship's thrusters built up power. The charged smell of ionized air lifted
over the energy fence and sent Wander spinning back to earlier times,
but not for long. At the one-minute count, the power-up reached quarter
thrust, and the first faint shimmers of the gravity net came into view. This
was the part Wander loved best. The air became so charged that faint
blue tendrils of disconnected power drifted behind each movement of
his hand, while around him the frozen tree limbs glowed like living sap-
phires.

Thirty seconds, half thrust. The energy net shone all about the ship,
like interconnected weavings of light. The strain of holding the ship
earthbound caused the net to shoot off brilliant silver fire. Fifteen seconds, three-quarters thrust. The fire-net was now so fierce that Wander
had to squint to hold it in focus. His robe had become charged to the
point that it billowed slightly from his body. About him the entire landscape shone with an eerie luminosity. The humming grew so intense
that his chest vibrated. The final countdown began.

Seconds flowed more slowly through his mind. He remained connected to the pilot as the ship's power was extended outward, outward,

outward, and the heavens split open, a great whirling seam just above the ship, revealing the nothingness into which the ship would leap. Two seconds remaining now and the pilot's voice was as slow as the thrumming ship's chronographer, one second and the final destination was brought into tight focus. Time slowed to an almost frozen moment as the energy net was released and the ship began the stretching, reaching, flowing motion that extended it upward and into the seamed opening, through the void and to its destination.

Then it was over. One moment there, the next gone. To the world the time required was less than a second. To Wander it was a moment beyond time, his body registering earthbound time, his mind connected to the pilot and his search through the known universe for the destination, until the moment came for the stretching, reaching climb. Then his mind snapped back to earthbound focus, and he breathed for what felt like the first time in days.

He never grew tired of this experience.

Wander rose to his feet, brushed the snow from his robes, and struggled back up the slope. His control-tower watch began in less than an hour, and he had to make his way around the energy fence.

Still, there was an excellent vantage point by the water reservoir. If he hurried, he could stop and see one more freighter depart.

"Hey, Consuela, great, you made it!" Rick's smile was legendary, as were his looks and his accomplishments.

And his reputation.

Consuela found her resistance melting under the power of his smile and eyes. Earlier that week, after Rick had sauntered up to where Consuela sat studying in the school library and asked her out, Sally had described his reputation in detail. Rick had the habit of coming on strong, charming a girl, taking what he wanted, then dumping her. The story was, Sally told her, that Rick had fallen head over heels for a girl the year before. She had dropped him hard. Since then, Rick had played it cool and tough with every girl in reach.

"Hello, Rick." Her neatly pressed khaki trousers and stripped knit top had seemed fine earlier. But now, as she noted his expensive clothes and Italian loafers and gold watch, she wasn't so certain. "I hope I haven't kept you waiting."

"No problem. Come on, what do you want to try first?"

She laughed as his arm slipped possessively around her waist and drew her close. All the warnings were swiftly evaporating in the excitement of the moment. She could hardly believe it was happening to her. A date with Rick. Maybe it would be different with her. Maybe he would decide that they made a great couple. Maybe . . .

If only she could keep him from finding out the truth.

Rick took her laughter as a signal to draw her closer still. "You like roller coasters?"

"Sure." She had never been on a roller coaster in her life. She had hardly been anywhere or done anything. The depth that other girls noticed in her did not come from incredible experience—at least, not the kind of experience they imagined. Her strength came from simply having to cope.

Her mother was an alcoholic. Her father had left home so soon after she was born that Consuela had no memory of him at all. The social worker responsible for her case had come within a hair's breadth of taking her away and sticking her into foster care a dozen times or more. Consuela had survived because Consuela was a survivor. But inside, where only she could see, Consuela felt ashamed about her home-life and terrified that someday somebody would discover who she really was.

Her gaze caught sight of another young man who emerged from one of the dusty side lanes. Though his smile was as warm as his gaze, Consuela did not like this other man at all. There was too much challenge in that smile. Too much awareness of who she truly was.

Daniel waved, and the simple action was enough to make her stumble. Rick's grasp of her waist tightened. "You all right?"

"Yes." Consuela looked away. Maybe Daniel would not say anything. Maybe he would get the message.

But Daniel walked over and said, "Consuela, one of my favorite people. How are you?"

"Fine." But she was not fine. Not any more. She kept her gaze down. She felt as though the whole world could hear her heart beating, even over the carnival's tumult. Daniel knew too much. One sentence, one knowing look, and all her carefully constructed myths would come tumbling down.

Instead, Daniel turned to Rick and offered a hand. "Hi. I'm Daniel Mitchum. You're Rick, am I right?"

"The one and only." Rick's easy tone said he was very accustomed to having strangers know who he was.

"I'm youth pastor at First Community Church."

"Sure, across the street from school." Rick's arm started to steer them around. "Nice meeting you."

"Nice to see you again, Consuela," Daniel called after them. "Have a great time tonight."

Consuela waited until they were further down the causeway before she relaxed and took a deeper breath. Rick noticed the movement and said, "You go to his church?"

"No." Consuela hesitated, then added, "I've seen him around."

Rick led her down the midway towards where the roller coaster rose glittering and whooshing in the distance. "What's a preacher doing around here on a Friday night?"

"Daniel goes everywhere." Even to her apartment. She had met Daniel two years earlier, when she had arrived home from school one day and there he was. He had been sitting in the living room, smiling and nodding as her mother slurred through a discussion only she could understand. Daniel had walked into the kitchen with her, and explained that he had received her name from the social worker responsible for her case. Consuela had been absolutely mortified when Daniel had said where his church was, so close to the school that all he had to do was walk across the street and open his mouth, and her house of cards would come tumbling down. She had never even set foot in his church, yet once every few weeks he still stopped by.

Rick shouted a hello to some friends and stopped to trade insults. Consuela was content to stand and watch and listen, her habitual small smile hiding everything inside. To others, she appeared incredibly mature. To herself, she seemed the loneliest person on earth.

Rick refused their pleas to join the others and pulled away, but not before one of the other girls gave Consuela a knowing smirk. In that instant the thin veneer of calm that shielded her shattered. Once more Consuela faltered, and she was simply a scared young girl walking through the tawdry garishness of a cheap carnival.

"Hey, listen, if you want to go with them, it's fine with me," Rick said, misunderstanding her grave expression. "I just thought, you know, it'd be more fun to be alone."

"It's fine," she said, struggling hard to recapture the moment. "I'm glad you asked me out."

"Likewise." Rick Reynolds, senior class president, captain of the football team, and student most likely to succeed at whatever he decided to do with his life, smiled down at her. "I mean, when I saw you trying out for the cheerleading squad, I thought this was one babe I had to get to know."

Babe. It was the first time anybody had ever called her a babe. She wasn't sure she liked it, even from Rick. But before she could say anything, he stopped at the end of the line waiting turns on the roller coaster and said, "Wait right here. I'll go get us tickets."

She watched as another group stopped to talk with him. He turned and pointed back in her direction. She gave them the smile and wave they expected, although she knew none of them. But everybody knew Rick and wanted to be seen with him. Rick's dad ran some big company. He drove an almost-new Corvette. He dressed like an ad in one of the magazines Consuela saw around the shop—Armani jeans, Doc Marten's shoes, silk-and-cotton knit shirt, a bomber jacket slung casually across one shoulder. Last week his picture had been in the city paper with an article about his acceptance of a full football scholarship to the best university in the state. No question about it, Rick was a guy on his way to the top.

He came trotting back, all eagerness and charm. "Hey, I'm really sorry about not being able to pick you up. But like I said, the coach always keeps us late on Fridays."

"It was no problem, really," Consuela replied. "I got a ride." Right. With her friendly bus.

"Good. Where is it that you live, anyway?"

"Westgate," she replied, naming the nice development that bordered the tenement area where she lived. It was only by dint of a shadowy school borderline and her own excellent grades that Consuela was permitted to go to the Nathan Henry High School at all.

"Nice," he said approvingly. "I live in Northside."

"I know," she said quietly. Sally again. Her friend was a font of useful information.

For reasons Consuela could not understand, Sally had adopted her the first day of school. Sally was everything Consuela was not—vivacious, eager, happy, lighthearted. Her father was a doctor, her mother a dedicated nurse.

Sally had insisted that they try out for the cheerleading squad together. Consuela had agreed with her plan that either they would both be accepted or neither would join. Consuela had seen it as the perfect out; she had known there was no chance she would be accepted. When they both were selected, she found herself unable to back out, and then to her surprise found that she really enjoyed it. Yes, it was silly. But all kinds of people suddenly said hello to her in the halls, and she was accepted into a group of girls that she would never have dared speak with before.

And now a date with Rick. It was all happening so fast.

————

Rick was finding the night to be very rough going.

He was not used to having to work so hard. He was not used to having to force anything. Girls normally gushed over him. All he had to do was go with the flow. But not Consuela.

Whatever else this girl was, she was no conversationalist. As a matter of fact, Rick was not really sure why he had asked her out in the first place. Maybe it was the mystery that hung in the air around her like a veil. Yeah, that was probably it. Consuela had something about her that made her stand out from the other girls at school.

When they finally reached the head of the line, Rick let her slide into the roller coaster's padded seat first so he could watch her reaction. Most girls showed some kind of nerves. But not Consuela. She looked about and revealed nothing more than a sort of mild curiosity. Rick slid into the seat beside her and wondered if maybe the whole date was a total loss.

The car started off to a chorus of screams. Consuela's eyes widened slightly as they began to climb. The wind caught her long dark hair and tossed it so that it was flung into his face. She pulled it back. "Sorry."

"No problem. Have you been on this one before?"

She hesitated, then replied, "I've never been on a roller coaster in my life."

"You're kidding."

"Why would I kid you about something like that?" She seemed oblivious to the shouts and squeals rising before and behind them as the climb continued up above the entire carnival.

"I mean, aren't you a little scared?"

"Of what?" She seemed truly baffled by his question.

But before he could reply, they crested the ridge and plunged down. Rick cast a quick glance her way and was somehow extremely pleased to see her smile. For reasons he could not explain, it really mattered to him that he break through that impenetrable shell of hers. Then he turned back and gave in to the thrill of a three-second free fall.

A swoop at the bottom, an impossibly sharp curve, an upside-down loop, and then into the tunnel. Blackness surrounded them, and the air was filled with the sound of semi-fake fear. Then came the rush out of the tunnel, screaming around the final bend, and braking to a halt.

"Want to go again?" Rick asked, only half joking, his eyes still adjusting to the flashing lights. He turned to the seat beside him and felt his entire body go cold.

Consuela was no longer there.

Chapter Two

Wander sat on what he thought of as his own little mound and readied for the next two-minute countdown. No one else ever came out here, especially at night, so he was safe in laying claim to this spot. Certainly no one from the port came this way. All the roads led back in the other direction, toward the city. The unfortunates who lived in the hovels beyond the woods considered the area to be haunted.

Before him the water reservoir lay frozen solid and frosted with snow. Wander liked watching the seasons reflect the power of a launch. In summer the lake reflected launches in mirror stillness, as though a second ship was being fired toward the center of the earth. In winter the ice sparkled blue and alien with discharged kinetic energy.

Wander had been coming here since he had learned to walk, drawn by the voices and the power that he then thought everyone could hear. Now he knew better and was learning to live with the loneliness that his special abilities created.

Suddenly he sensed that he was no longer alone.

He whirled and found himself facing a girl. A *beautiful* girl. Dark hair, sharply defined features, tall and poised, with dark wide-open eyes. Eyes that spoke of total incomprehension.

And she wore a scout's robes.

She looked at him with a gaze that only half saw, and asked, "Where am I?"

He had to laugh. For a scout to ask that question was just too funny.

Then he remembered something from the morning's class. "You're the newcomer, aren't you?"

"What?" She gave another start as she looked down at herself, lifted one fold of palest blue, and asked, "Am I dreaming?"

"The mind-lag must have hit you really hard," Wander said sympathetically. "I hear it can be rough the first few times you make a jump." He hesitated, then made the embarrassed confession, "I've never been off-world before, so I wouldn't know."

The girl made a genuine effort to draw him into focus. "Who are you?"

"Wander. I'm in your scout class," he said patiently. "That is, if you're the newcomer. Where are you from?"

"Baltimore," she replied, looking down at her robes again.

"Never heard of it," he said, "but there are so many worlds, I guess that's no surprise."

"So many what?" Then the ship's pilot droned the formal two-minute warning, and the girl gave a little gasp and jumped a good foot off the snow. "What was *that?*"

Wander stared at her. "You heard it?"

She was still searching the surrounding fields. "Heard *what?*"

"They said the newcomer was supposed to be really something. I guess you'd have to be, if they let you skip the first cull." He slid over, trembling in the excitement of suddenly not being the only one. The odd boy out. The lonely kid who heard what others refused to believe truly existed. "Come sit down. The show's starting."

In dazed confusion, the girl walked over and sat beside him. Then the first hazy impressions of the gravity net appeared about the ship, and she cried aloud.

Ninety seconds, came the pilot's drone, and again she gasped, and Wander felt a chill go through his entire frame. She had indeed heard it.

The icy landscape spreading out before them began to pick up the energy discharge caused by the ship's thrusters straining against the shield's gravity net. Wander risked a glance her way, saw eyes impossibly wide and a slightly opened mouth, and suddenly realized she had never seen a launch before.

He raised his hand and said quietly, "Look at this." With a gentle loose-limbed motion, he extended his arm and flung his hand outward. A cloud of bluish energy wafted out and over the lake. He turned back and was rewarded with a look of utter disbelief. But no fear. Wander was sure of it without really understanding why. Although the scene was utterly new, the girl showed no fear.

He turned back, unable to stop grinning, and waited for the launch to continue. For some reason, having her here beside him made it feel as though he were seeing it all for the very first time.

She gasped when the first tendrils of snow lifted from the field and began their ghostly dance. As the energy friction grew in power, breaths of azure light passed from one dancing cloud to the next, and the entire frozen vista glowed as though lit from beneath.

Then the fifteen-second interval was marked, and time began to stretch, and the girl reached over and took his hand. Wander could scarcely believe it was happening, nor understand what it meant, that here beside him sat another person who required neither headset nor amplifier to tie into the moment of transition. The moment stretched out, granting him the thrill that he had known a hundred thousand times and never tired of, feeling his body count the normal seconds while his mind was let loose to know an endless instant's freedom.

Almost.

Perhaps it was because of the training he had begun. Perhaps it was the heightened sensitivity he felt, having this girl seated beside him holding his hand. Whatever the reason, Wander found himself able to search out the niggling impression that he had always known but not identified. The moment of blissfully being freed from time's chains was not complete. The bonds were stretched, but not broken. Yet his heart yearned for something more, and in that stretched instant of heightened awareness, Wander knew that a true freedom was possible. He *knew* it.

Then the swirling lightning-flecked clouds opened to reveal the maw of nothingness, and in his heightened time-sense Wander watched the gravity-net dissolve, permitting the ship's thruster to rise from the shield, a brilliant ball of pulsating force, transforming the vessel into a lance of molten gold that stretched higher and higher and higher into the maw, through the infinite nothingness, to touch the shield at its final destination, for a moment shorter than the smallest measurement of earthly time resting on both planets simultaneously. Then the ship departed, the maw closed, the energy dissipated, the snow flurries settled, time returned to its normal boundaries, and the night drew in about them.

It was a very long moment before the girl took a ragged breath and sighed, "Wow."

The feeling was so glorious Wander felt free to say anything he wanted. His own shackles of shyness were momentarily gone. "That was your first launch, wasn't it?"

"Yes." Her response was a breath, a cloud of sweet air wafted out so softly he could barely hear it.

"I'm glad I could share it with you." He looked down to his hand, which still held hers, wishing it could stay there forever, knowing she would come alert in a moment and take it back.

She looked about, then called to the night, "Rick?"

"We're alone," Wander replied. "Nobody comes here. If any of the other scouts heard we did this, they'd scorn us."

"The other what?" Still she searched around her. "Have you seen a carnival around here?"

"There are no people around here," he replied questioningly. "There haven't been since the port became operational." He examined her face. "The mind-lag really has affected you, hasn't it?"

"I guess so," she sighed, then shivered. "It's cold."

"Is it not winter where you came from?"

She shook her head. "Autumn."

"Here spring is less than two months away. This is the time of the hardest frost. What is your name?"

"Consuela."

When she shivered again, he stood and said, "We'd better go back. I'll have just enough time to help you find your quarters before I go on watch."

Consuela rose unsteadily to her feet, but did not release his hand. "Where did you say we were?"

He gave her slender fingers a gentle squeeze and said quietly, "Come on, try and walk a little faster. Everything is going to be all right."

CHAPTER THREE

"Gone? Whaddaya mean, gone?" The carnival manager was a fleshy jowled, cigar-chomping little man in his late fifties. His office smelled of ashes and burnt coffee and old sweat. "Nobody can get outta those seats when the ride's going. You saw that padded bar. We had it specially made. It goes down automatic, stays down 'til the ride stops. You can't stand up, much less get out." He leaned heavy forearms on the paper-strewn desk. "You trying to make trouble?"

Rick drew himself up to full height. "Of course not."

"You look like a trouble-making punk to me."

"Look," Rick protested, "I'm telling you the truth. She did get out. In the tunnel."

"Sure, sure." Thick, rubbery lips sneered around the mangled cigar. "She dumped you, so you gotta come in here and give me a hard time."

"Now look. I'm Rick—"

"I know who you are. I seen you and punks like you all my life." The sneer turned ugly. "You don't get outta here, I'm calling the cops and let them search those fancy pants pockets of yours. See what it is you got in there, find out how you got the money to buy them clothes." The man half rose from his chair and pointed one stubby finger at the door. "It ain't enough you gotta come around here selling your stuff. Now you wanna give me trouble? Go on, get outta here, or I'll show you what real trouble is."

Fuming with rage and embarrassment, Rick stumbled out the door and down the rotting stairs. He walked across the mushy ground lining the back sides of the tents, following the path around to where it intersected the central grounds.

The carnival was winding down. People wandered in little clusters, their gaiety sounding forced and tired, like revelers who refused to leave a party that was already over. Rick walked under the garish lights, searching for a girl he no longer believed he would find, feeling like an idiot.

The carnival manager was right, he knew it in his gut. Consuela had made a fool of him. She was probably already back in her bed, giggling into her pillow at how silly she had made him look. Three solid hours he had searched the grounds, until his third argument with the roller coaster operator forced the harried man to send him back to the manager's office. Rick kicked angrily at an empty popcorn box, wheeled about, and headed for the exit. He had never been so humiliated in his life.

He took his anger out on the car, pushing the massive engine up to redline, taking turns in full four-wheel squeals, hitting insane speeds on the straights. It was not until he pulled into the driveway that he realized just how crazy he had been. He cut off the motor, sat in the car listening to the engine clink, and felt his anger give way to the same shaky nerves that always followed his outbursts. What if the cops had picked him up? What if his parents had been called down to the station to bail him out? What if he had wrecked and been injured, couldn't play ball, lost the scholarship, lost the good life?

The good life. That was his dad's expression. Rick sat in the car and heard the words echo through his brain. "You're destined for the good life, son. You've got it all. Looks, brains, build, backing. Just remember how lucky you are and behave. Make us proud."

Make them proud. He heard them say that endlessly, even when they didn't really say anything at all. It was with him all the time. Their expectations were constantly pushing him to strive, work, measure up, achieve.

Rick left the car and walked up the cobblestone path, climbed the wide brick stairs, passed under the tall two-story columns, unlocked the door, entered the front hall, fingered the code into the alarm system, heard the safety peep, and turned on the lights. His parents weren't back yet. They seldom were in before him on the weekends. They were local movers and shakers and were invited everywhere. Friday afternoons were times to avoid being at home. His mother was always in a whirl-wind of frantic preparations, shouting orders to anyone who came within reach. His dad would rush in from work, shout back, change clothes, and then together they would put on their polished outside masks and leave.

As usual, Rick tried to make it down the domed entrance hall without giving the full-size family portrait a glance. He hated that painting. Rick stood between his seated parents, an arm on each of their shoulders, his number one fake grin firmly in place. The perfect son. Never any trouble to his folks, always tops at whatever he did, always polite around his parents' friends, always popular, always successful. Always measuring up.

His room had one wall of shelves, all filled with trophies. The maid had strict instructions to polish everything once a week, more often if they were entertaining. His dad liked to bring his cronies up, show off everything, point to the school banners he had ordered Rick to nail onto the wall—all the schools that had offered him a full scholarship. Sometimes when he had to stand there and listen to his dad boast, Rick felt as though he himself were just another trophy.

Not bothering to take off his clothes, Rick stretched out on his bed. His anger at Consuela was giving way to bafflement. Why would she go to all that trouble? Had she accepted the date just to make a fool of him? He went back over the evening in his head, but recalled nothing that might hint at sarcasm or derision. No, Consuela was not the type to make fun of somebody—at least, he didn't think so.

He checked his watch, decided it didn't matter whom he woke up, and reached for his phone. He called directory assistance, asked if there was a listing for Consuela Ortez, and struck out. She did not have her own phone. He went back downstairs, checked the directory, and found over twenty Ortez families listed, none of them living on a street that he recognized as being in Westgate. He checked his watch. After one. Too late to start calling around at random.

Rick walked back upstairs, debating which of the girls on the cheer-leading squad he should call the next morning. He just needed a reason, something that would throw them off the track, and not leave them thinking that one of their friends had made him look like a fool.

———

The port building gleamed silver and yellow in the night. It was utterly lacking in corners; the walls curved and flowed like great metal ribbons, one stacked upon the other, crowned by a vast circular copper dome. Balls of light suspended high overhead splashed the entire area with radiance almost as strong as day. Wander walked beside Consuela and watched her examine everything with wide-eyed wonderment. The robotaxis, the automated street cleaner, the bulbous freight carriers, the vast stretches of almost empty parking for ground cars—everything was new to her. Twice she stumbled and would have fallen save for the grip she kept on his hand, once when a hovercraft alighted, and once when a senior cargo captain passed them with a perfunctory salute. Wander saw the questions in her eyes and had a thousand questions of his own, but for the moment was content to walk alongside this remarkable girl and feel her soft hand cling to his.

The doors sighed back, and Consuela passed through, her eyes never seeming to blink. Inside, the spaceport was open spaces and burnished marble floors and sparkling surfaces. The info-voice whispered its habitual, "Greetings and welcome to the Hegemony Spaceport. State your needs, and the way will be shown."

From the look on her face Wander realized, "You weren't even shown the spaceport?"

"No, I . . . " Consuela pointed to the triangular column rising in front of them. "Was that what spoke?"

"Scout Wander entering grounds," Wander said toward the waist-high column. Then to Consuela he said, "State your name as I did."

"Scout Consuela entering grounds," Consuela said, her voice stumbling softly over the words.

"Greetings and welcome, Scouts. Your presence is noted and Grade-C clearance granted."

"You have to say this every time you come in," Wander said. "Your voice is checked against records, and security flashes your image. Then if you don't know where to go, you speak like this." He turned back to the column and said, "Request guidance to private quarters of Scout Consuela."

"Follow the yellow path," came the instant reply. At Wander's feet a light appeared and shot out across the hall, disappearing around a corner.

"That's great," Consuela cried, so delighted by the simple spectacle that Wander had to laugh.

He said, "Not really. It's fine when you only have a few people looking for something, but when the port is busy, the floor looks like a spider web and everybody gets mixed up. Last week we had some Hegemony bigwig get so lost we had to hold up the vessel outbound for—"

"Scout Wander, are you not on duty?"

Wander stiffened to full alert, gave an instant to hoping that his handholding with Consuela had been hidden by the folds of their robes, and without turning replied, "Twenty minutes still, Pilot."

"Don't leave your arrival to the last minute," snapped the reedy voice behind them. "And who, pray tell, is this?"

"Scout Consuela, sir."

"Scout who? We don't have any Scout Consuela. . . ." The tall, gaunt man stepped in front of them. He wore the midnight blue robes of a full pilot, his shoulders flecked with the stars of seniority. His head was utterly void of hair—no eyebrows, no beard, no nothing. It granted his eyes an even more piercing quality than they already had. He lifted the noteboard from its waist pouch, keyed in, then nodded. "Ah, yes. The newcomer. The name escaped me for a moment." Frosty gray eyes peered at her. "I suppose Alena checked you in?"

Consuela gave a hesitant nod. Wander winced at the coming storm, but the pilot was too miffed to notice Consuela's lack of proper reply. "I thought so," he groused. "Typical of her sloppy work. No details noted whatsoever. I am amazed you were even outfitted. Did she manage to show you your quarters?"

"No, sir," Consuela said meekly.

"No, Pilot," he corrected automatically, his eyes still on the noteboard. "Sirs are passengers and other cattle." He shook his head. "Just look at this. Alena didn't even manage to note your homeworld. I would castigate her severely were she not already outbound for her new assignment. Well, that is certainly no loss." He gave an exasperated sigh. "At least this is the last mess of hers I shall have to clear up. All right. Where are you from, Scout?"

"Baltimore," came the timid reply.

"Baltimore?" A hairless brow furrowed in concentration. "That is a world unknown to me."

"I believe it is beyond the Rim, Pilot," Wander offered.

"Ah. An outworlder. Of course. There are few ships out your way, I suppose, and thus you were granted entry at this late date." He peered at her over the board, his gaze openly curious, before murmuring, "Remarkable. Well, once again talent is shown to have no borders."

"If you are busy, Pilot Grimson," Wander volunteered, "I could show her around."

"Yes, I suppose the outworld newcomer will be needing a guide. Very well, Scout, but I caution you not to shirk your other duties." He glanced at his chronolog. "Which include reporting to the duty officer immediately."

"On the bounce, Pilot," Wander replied and motioned with his head for Consuela to follow him. Once they were out of earshot, he told her, "That wasn't too bad."

"He is important?" Consuela asked.

"Senior Pilot Grimson is responsible for the scout training course," Wander replied. "And he has a reputation that reaches through the Hegemony. The first day I was on the course, my guide told me the reason you never saw scouts with more than ten downchecks on their record was that Grimson ate them for breakfast. Sometimes I almost believe it."

Consuela hesitated at the entrance to the Plexiglas chute. Grateful for the chance to take her hand once more, Wander assured her, "It's easy. Just grasp one of the rails and let it guide you up. Come on, we can take this one together, if you don't mind being a little cramped."

She shook her head, then stepped in with him, and when the gravity diminished to one-tenth G, she let out a little, "Ooooh."

He found her innocence delightful. "The first time I stepped into a gravity chute—I was only twelve or thirteen—I thought the idea was to climb. I got all tangled up with this woman in a long veil, and the only thing that saved me from serious trouble was that I screamed so loudly she was glad to let me go."

She followed his example, locking her arm into the support-rod so that her twelve-pound weight was kept stationary. She asked him, "Are you from beyond the—I forgot what he called it?"

"The Rim," he said, suddenly ashamed. "I'm sorry. Outworlder isn't a nice thing to call you. The way people say it around here, it means primitive."

"I suppose it's true," she said, looking at the grand vista of the spaceport. "Compared to this."

"I'm from right here," Wander said, for some reason feeling able to tell her anything. "The reason I had never seen a gravity chute is because there aren't any in the barrio. And I was twelve before I ever left it, except when I would come over to the field to watch the ships take off and land. That's how I got my name. From what my family says, I started wandering off as soon as I learned how to walk. There's this busy highway between the barrio and the port, but I found a drainage tunnel that was just high enough for me to walk through."

She was watching him with grave dark eyes. "You were born in a barrio?"

"The worst in the Hegemony," he stated. "My dad was a miner until he lost his leg in a phaser accident. My mom worked as a servant in a rich pilot's house. She used to tell us stories about how the man lived, but we didn't really believe her. Nobody could live like that, we thought."

Her gaze did not flinch at the shameful truth, so he asked, "What about you?"

"I never knew my father," she replied calmly, her gaze locked in on his. "My mother drinks."

He felt a sense of harmony so strong it filled his chest to bursting. "My dad hits the bottle hard too. Here we are, this is our level. Okay, step out, that's it, keep your legs loose until the gravity stabilizes, great, you've got it." He pointed to the tall bronze doors. "This is the Control Tower. You can come in if you like, but I'll be pretty busy. They keep the scouts running errands and playing the mind games."

"Mind games?"

"You'll see." He pointed down a corridor behind them. "Your quarters will be along there somewhere. There's another info column just around the corner. Ask for directions. Tell your name to the door, that will give you entry. My room is thirty-four, the last on the hall. If you have any trouble, come down and state your name, and I'll code it for you to have entry. Are you hungry?"

She seemed to search for the answer. "Yes."

"The room controls are voice coded. Say 'lights' and they'll switch on or off, whichever they are not at the moment. Same for bed, desk, chair, shower, and so on. We work odd hours, so there's a meal chute in each room. Just ask for menu. Okay?"

She squeezed his hand and dredged up a smile. "You've been really nice to me. Thank you." She hesitated, then said, "I really appreciate your sharing the spectacle with me. If I don't see you again, I just wanted you to know that."

"What do you mean? I'm your guide. We'll be seeing a lot of each other."

She remained unconvinced. "Anyway, I think you are a really nice person."

"I have watch for three hours," he said, finding it hard to get the words out. "Then I'll go to bed, unless you want to come by."

She shook her head. "I'm pretty tired."

"Sure. Oh, and one thing. Don't mention mind-lag to the pilot. He thinks a scout should be able to control things like that, and you'll get a downcheck."

"Thank you, Wander," she said quietly, and something in her voice made it sound as though she were saying good-bye.

"You're welcome," he replied, unable to mask his grin. "If you like, I'll come by and collect you for class."

Again there was the hesitation, then, "That would be fine. Good-night."

He watched her make her way down the hallway, pausing to take in everything from the view out over the ship fields to the circular illumi-nation-sculpture poised near the ceiling. Wander had the momentary impression that she was trying to imprint it all on her memory, as though seeing it for the first and last time. Then he shook his head. Mind-lag did strange things to people. In his few weeks here, he had already heard a number of travelers' stories.

He turned and announced himself to the security doors, then bounded up the curving ramp leading to the tower, a sense of gaiety leaving him weightless.

CHAPTER FOUR

The next morning, Consuela lay in her bed for a long time after awakening. The darkness which surrounded her had been her most secret shield for as long as she could remember. Her tiny bedroom was a sort of afterthought, placed in the exact center of the tenement apartment, and had no windows. When she was little, she would retreat from the bad times by coming in and turning off the lights and sliding under her bed. With her cheek pressed against the cold hardwood floor and her arms cuddling the blanket's scratchy warmth, she would give herself over to dreams.

Now she was older, and reality did not scare her as it once had. The loneliness she had known as a child still remained her constant companion, but she was no longer frightened. Now she knew she possessed an inner strength that would help her through the toughest trials. As she had grown up, she had also grown determined.

Consuela saved every cent she could toward college. She was going to study computer software and graphic design. She had read that this was the coming wave and that companies could not find enough qualified people. Salaries were good, and work was plentiful. That was why she was so set on college, to find a good job. At the ripe old age of seventeen, Consuela had already gained enough experience of poverty and hardship to last a lifetime.

Now she lay in the darkness of her closet-room, and wondered at the strange half-memories which lingered from the previous night's dreams. Stranger still was how she could not remember leaving either Rick and the carnival. As far as she could recall, one moment she had been on the roller coaster, the next she had been dreaming those strange and powerful dreams. She wondered if perhaps Rick had put something in her drink—but no, she had not had anything to eat or drink, at least not that she could recall. She lay on her bed and stared up into the pitch black. The slender line of light which otherwise would have told her day had arrived was blocked from coming in under her door by the rug she always jammed in place before lying down. Consuela found herself reluctant to get up and start this day, for it would mean letting this particular memory go.

And Wander. She rolled over, hugging her pillow to her chest. He had the saddest eyes she had ever seen. She would remember those eyes for a very long time to come.

Consuela sighed long and deeply, wishing there were some way to have spent more time with him. In Wander she had felt a kinship, a bonding that went beyond time and space and the borders of dreams. She had sensed a depth that mirrored her own, a harmony of hearts. She remembered how he had held himself there beside her in the chute and said with that calm sorrowful strength of his that he had been born in a barrio. Yes, it was as though the dream and Wander's calm confession had been meant as some sort of dreamtime lesson, found there in the beautiful sadness of Wander's eyes.

Sally. As Consuela sat up and swung her feet to the floor, she decided that one person she could tell was her best friend, Sally. At least Sally would not laugh at her.

Then her feet touched the floor, and Consuela cried aloud.

Instead of a scuffed hardwood floor, she felt soft carpet. She reached out, moving blindly until she touched the wall, and cried again. The warm-smooth surface tingled slightly under her fingers, as though the power required to produce the articles upon demand could be felt.

"Light!" she gasped, and cried a third time when the illumination revealed the alien room, her pale blue robe lying crumpled on the floor where she had flung it.

"Bed!" Silently her bed retreated back into the wall, melding into the bland, smooth surface. Now the room was utterly bare, save for a small plaque by the door. There were listed, in a strange language which somehow she could read perfectly well, all the commands that the room understood.

"Mirror!" she called, and when the reflecting surface was revealed, Consuela stared into the sleep-tousled face of a scared young woman.

The doorchime caused her to leap completely clear of the floor. A disembodied voice announced calmly, "Scout Wander requests entry."

"Just a minute." Frantically she plucked up the robe and slipped it on, grasped the long feather-light stocking-boots and pulled them up. She moved back to the mirror, brushed her hair with her fingers, then straightened, took a deep breath, and said, "Door."

Wander was there, smiling in such a way that even the usual sadness of his eyes was muted. The sight of him touched her so unexpectedly that she had a sudden urge to rush up and hug him close. Instead she smiled and said, "I'm still here."

"So I see. Mind-lag better?"

"I think so."

"Excellent. Have you eaten?"

"Not yet." Wanting him to know how great it was to see him again, she said, "I was sort of waiting for you."

A flush of pleasure crept out of his collar and spread across his features. "We'd better hurry, then. Class starts in less than an hour."

————

Sally was totally astonished, when her mother called her downstairs Saturday morning, to greet Rick at her front door.

He stood there looking foolish, trying to hide it behind a big smile. "Hey, Sals, how's it going?"

"Rick!" She pulled her overlong T-shirt down straight and wished she could slam the door, shout at her mother for not giving her fair warning, and race back upstairs for makeup and other clothes. "What are you doing here? I mean, would you like to come in?"

"No thanks. Look, I'm sorry to come by so early, but I talked to Cindy this morning, and she said you might know where Consuela lives." Cindy was head cheerleader and the girlfriend of Rick's best buddy. "She said Consuela gave her some story about their redoing the exchanges in her neighborhood or something, she wasn't sure. Anyway, she didn't even have her telephone number."

"I don't either," Sally said, both relieved and jealous that the reason for Rick's visit was Consuela and not her. What was it about that girl? "I kept asking her for it, and she always gave me one excuse or another. I guess I finally just gave up."

Rick looked skeptical. "You're her best friend, and you don't have her number?"

"I know it sounds crazy, but Consuela is real mysterious about a lot of stuff." Sally shrugged. "I don't even know where she lives."

"But her telephone number? Come on, you've got to be kidding."

"I don't have it. Really. Why, is something the matter?"

Instantly Rick's attitude became overly casual. "No, of course not. We just had a sort of crazy end to the night, you know, and I wanted to talk with her. That's all."

They had a fight. Sally could not totally hide her smirk. He tried to put the moves on her, and Consuela gave him the brush-off. Way to go, girl. "Gee, I wish I could help, Rick. But unless Consuela calls me, I've got to wait and see her at school."

"Hey, it's no big deal. I'll talk to her Monday." Another of the patented Rick smiles. "Have a great weekend, okay?"

"Thanks, Rick. You too."

"If you hear from her, ask her to give me a call." He skipped lightly down the stairs and walked toward his car. "See you around."

CHAPTER FIVE

It was all his fault.

Wander did not mean to make their arrival so late. But talking was so easy with Consuela. At breakfast he lost all track of time, until he happened to look up and realize they were the only scouts left in the residence hall. He glanced at the wall chrono and leapt to his feet. "Come on!"

"What's the matter?"

"Class is starting right now. Hurry!"

Together they raced down the corridors and entered the room just as Pilot Grimson stepped onto the podium. Bad, but no downcheck.

The pilot frowned in their direction. "You are setting what unfortunately is coming to be the expected example from you, Scout Wander." He silenced the snickers that rose from the room with a single frigid glare, then turned his attention back to the pair. "Scout Consuela, you must appear more promptly from now on."

"Yes, Pilot," she said quietly.

"Very well. You will take the seat corresponding to your chamber number. This will apply to all training rooms and lecture halls." As Consuela walked to where he pointed, Grimson continued to the class as a whole, "I ask you to join me in welcoming the newest addition to this scout squadron. Consuela's arrival was unavoidably delayed by a lack of transport to the Hegemony."

From beside the podium, Wander heard the boy seated next to Consuela's station mutter, "Another outworlder." He felt great shame for her until he saw her settle into her place, turn, and fasten the boy with a fathomless gaze. The boy held it for a moment, then wilted.

Wander turned back to the podium and felt his pleasure mount when he saw Pilot Grimson's thin lips curve into a small smile of approval. Wander cleared his throat and said quietly, "Pilot, I believe—"

"Your place awaits you, Scout Wander," the pilot replied coldly. "If you have business with me, I suggest you arrive before the entire class has gathered."

Wander knew he was taking his life in his hands, but he had to try. "Pilot, if you please—"

Grimson swiveled, looked down from the dais, and froze Wander with his glare. The scout had no choice but to retreat to his seat.

"Now then," Pilot Grimson said, his scowl following Wander into his seat before dropping to the podium's controls. "Today we begin the second phase of your training. As many of you have already surmised, the first three weeks have primarily been a time of culling. It is not enough for you to have talent. You must also have the ability to direct, to focus, to orient both yourselves and the ships that will one day be placed under your care."

Wander sensed the sudden change which swept the room. Spines stiffened, bodies leaned forward in anticipation. They had made it. Over two-thirds of those who originally entered the scout squadron were now gone. But the culling was over. Port scuttlebutt had predicted this would happen. A point was reached when each scout squadron was deemed ready. Those remaining were the ones not only sensitive to the higher energies, but able to *use* them.

From this point on, they were almost assured of a position. Some would become port communications officers, directing incoming and outgoing ships. Others would be assigned permanent duty as interstellar communicators, manning stations throughout the Hegemony and beyond the Rim. Others with greater clarity might act as backup navigators. Some would escort passenger vessels flying the permanently channeled inner-Hegemony spaceways. A few might have the abilities required to direct the flight of long-distance freighters. And perhaps one candidate in three or four squadrons might have the abilities required to rise to the highest honor of all—Senior Pilot, Navigator to Starfleet Command.

"All of you have demonstrated the ability to draw upon the power placed at your disposal and identify what remains unseen to the physical eye," Grimson droned on, watching his panel lights flicker to green as the hall's amplifiers reached full power. "Now begins the process of learning control. You must learn to override the physical senses and focus entirely upon the data being obtained through your headsets. You must set aside all distractions, all random thoughts, all outside sensations, and *focus*."

He scanned each eager face in turn, then nodded. "Very well. Attach your headsets and connect."

Wander watched as Consuela grappled with the unfamiliar equipment. When she finally looked his way, he raised his own headset and slid it around his forehead like a padded headband, fitting the two cushioned points to his temples. She followed his example and gave a smile of thanks. He pointed to the single black switch set to the right of the writing pad and thumbed it to the "on" position, but when she did the same, he felt a rising sense of alarm. He reached under his desk and fingered the override switch, which only his desk had. As he did so, he hoped fervently that his premonition was wrong. And just as strongly hoped that he was right.

"For the next few days," Pilot Grimson continued, "there will be no downcheck given to anyone who wishes to withdraw from the lesson. If you feel yourself losing touch, withdraw, re-orient, then continue. Therefore it is suggested that you rest your hand near the power switch. I urge you, however, not to retreat unless absolutely necessary. Five days from now, when we enter our first simulation exercise, you will be downchecked for retreating."

He checked the controls set in the curved podium and went on, "Today you will be expected to find your way through a maze, charting your course on paper. This means that you will no longer be able to keep your eyes closed at all times. You must begin to learn to see visually while focusing. Marks will be given both for finding the quickest route to the goal, and for doing so in the shortest amount of time."

Grimson flickered a glance toward Wander, who understood perfectly. He was not to be the first to finish. Wander swallowed his qualms over Consuela and replied with a minute nod.

"One important clue," Pilot Grimson offered. "It is possible to reorient your perspective and see the entire maze from above, but only if you are able to reach beyond the perspective of barriers and first identify the goal."

Wander risked a glance around the chamber. The squadron's study hall was a domed structure, shaped like a broad shell, with curving half-rings of tables rising up before the pilot's dais. Wander saw many confused looks among the forty or so scouts. He knew a moment's sympathy.

Up to now, their most difficult task had been to correctly identify some item that was not visible with the physical eye. Now they were to be presented with a maze that they could not even see, and not only were they expected to find their way through it but to identify the goal before they started. Wander understood the purpose behind this task, but knew that few others would be able.

A pilot was required to focus upon both the starting point and the destination at all times. It was only when both were held in tandem that a safe interstellar transport was possible.

"Are there any questions?" The class had by now learned that the offer was symbolic and obediently remained silent. "Very well." Pilot Grimson reached down and began coding in. "Prepare for vision. I will begin the countdown from five, four, three, two, one."

Instantly the silence was shattered by a bloodcurdling scream.

Before he was even consciously aware that he had moved, Wander was on his feet and tearing off his headset. Consuela fell writhing to the floor, shrieking so loudly the student beside her toppled from his chair. Wander fought his way around the circle, shoving other scouts out of the way.

"*Make it stop! Make it stop!*" Consuela screamed. Wander leapt over the neighboring student and ripped the headset from Consuela's head.

She gave a final cry, whimpered, and fainted in his arms.

Pilot Grimson tumbled down beside him. He pressed two fingers into the pulse-point at the base of her chin, concentrated, then permitted his shoulders to slump slightly in relief. But not for long. Swiftly he collected himself and rose to full height. "I want to know who did this," he said, his voice an ice-bladed knife. "I *demand* to know who sabotaged this scout's controls."

The class remained frozen in gaping silence. Wander struggled to his feet, holding Consuela's limp form in his arms.

"Can you manage?" Grimson asked.

"Yes, Pilot." He could not stop his voice from trembling. It was all his fault.

"Straighten up," Grimson snapped. He turned back to the room.

"Very well. If the culprit refuses to give himself up, you may all consider yourselves downchecked. You will remain here until I have returned, and you will remain *silent*." He wheeled about. "Come with me, Scout."

Wander followed the pilot from the room. Once they were outside and the door closed, Grimson hustled down the hall. "To the infirmary. Quickly. Do you wish me to help?"

"No thank you, Pilot. She's not so heavy." And it was his fault. He could not release her.

"Did you suspect this?"

"Yes, Pilot."

"And was this what you wished to tell me about?"

"Yes, Pilot."

His hairless face blazed with cold fury. "Your habitual tardiness has almost cost us the life of a Talent."

"Yes, Pilot, I know." Wander's misery could not have been greater.

Grimson keyed the infirmary door, snapped for lights, then helped Wander settle Consuela's inert form on the padded stretcher. Harshly he ordered the communicator to locate the duty medic and send him up on the bounce. He checked her pulse once more, peeled back one eyelid, seemed relieved to hear her moan.

When the white-robed medic popped through the door, the pilot growled, "What took you so long?"

"Pilot, I—"

"Never mind. This girl has suffered an extreme amplified mental shock. For the record, someone tampered with her headset."

The medic's eyes widened to round moons. "A Talent?"

Grimson hesitated, then nodded. "Perhaps. But you are ordered to keep this strictly confidential. We have not yet confirmed anything."

"Yes, Pilot, I understand."

"I want a report as quickly as possible. You will find me in the squadron's training hall." Pilot Grimson motioned toward the door. "Come with me, Scout."

The infirmary door sighed shut behind them. Wander felt hollowed and weak, capable only of the thought that it was all his fault.

The pilot finally said, "I see that you are punishing yourself far better than I ever could."

Wander swallowed. "Do you think she's all right?"

"You suffered a similar shock, if my memory of your records is correct."

"When I was eleven."

"Then you know what she is feeling, and what will happen when she awakens." His tone was surprisingly mild. "Tell me why you suspected her abilities."

"Last night we watched a transport launch together."

"Where?"

"Beside the reservoir." Wander could not take his eyes from the door. "I think she could hear the countdown with me."

There was a long silence, then, "Look at me, Scout."

Wander tore his eyes away, looked into Pilot Grimson's penetrating gaze. The man searched his face for a long time, as though seeking something only he could see, before asking, "You can follow ship communications without amplification?"

Wander started, realizing he had finally let go of his long-held secret. Then he decided it really did not matter, not with Consuela unconscious inside the infirmary. It was all his fault. "Yes, Pilot."

"Without amplification?"

"Yes, Pilot." The man's eerily soft voice helped him focus. "But not through a shielded structure like the port. I have to be outside somewhere."

The hairless face inched closer. A trace of the customary coldness returned to his voice. "You had best not be trying to trick me, boy."

"I've been going out there and watching ships depart and following them in my mind since I was five years old," Wander said, not caring anymore. All the years of scorn and derision, all the shouts of laughter when as a child he would respond to voices only he could hear. The punishments, the scoldings, the accusations by teachers and family that he was imagining, lying, insane, that he was a troubled little boy. All the anger came rushing to the surface. "It's all I know," he said, his voice as hot as his face. "It's all I've ever done."

Surprisingly, the pilot seemed unfazed by Wander's outburst. "Your record mentioned this ability when you were young. It is rare, but not unheard of, in children. I recall seeing no indication of this in your later tests, however."

"I lied," Wander replied flatly.

"I see," Pilot Grimson said slowly, then straightened. The gray eyes showed no reaction whatsoever, they just continued to hold him fast. "Can you hear Control Tower from here?"

"Whispers," Wander replied. "The tower doors are shielded. I hear the whispers all the time. If I concentrate, I can make out the individual voices. But I try not to. It's hard enough when I'm on duty."

"Why haven't you told me this before?"

"I haven't heard of anyone else being able to hear like this. I know the others can't. The highborns give me a hard enough time as it is." Wander took a breath. "And to be honest, Pilot, I'm scared of you."

"And well you should be," the man replied, but without menace. "So how do you work on tower duty?"

"I rewired a training headset," Wander replied, glad to have it all out in the open. "My father was a miner. I cut strips from his lead-lined protective garment and pasted it to the headset. With my temples covered and the band across my forehead the noise is cut down to a level I can stand."

"I see," the pilot said again. "Did you know there is an attachment available to Tower amps called a desensitizer?"

It was Wander's turn to stare. Slowly he shook his head. So there were others. There were others *like him.*

"No, of course not. But had you not been so secretive, you might have saved yourself and the young lady inside a great deal of distress."

The infirmary door slid back. "She appears to be okay," the medic announced. "All vital signs check out. I've given her something, and she's resting peacefully. But if she's a Talent, you know how disoriented she's going to be when she wakes up."

"Thank you, Medic," the pilot said, and stopped Wander's forward motion with one upraised finger. "We will join you momentarily."

"Yes, Pilot." The medic stepped back, and the infirmary door slid shut behind him.

"Very well, Scout. I want you to remain by Scout Consuela's side until she is fully recovered." A glint of frosty humor surfaced in those probing gray eyes. "I assume that will not be too harsh a duty."

"No, Pilot. Thank you."

"We will discuss all this further once the incident is behind us. For now, I have a class I must see to." Grimson granted him a slight nod before striding down the hall.

Wander turned back to the infirmary and called the door open. His heart twisted at the sight of Consuela's pale form. The medic stood and dropped his magazine. "You been assigned watch over the patient?"

"Yes."

He walked to the door, then turned and smirked down at the sleeping girl. "Pity those looks have got to be wasted on a Talent."

"They're not wasted," Wander replied.

"She'll be locked up like all the others," the medic told him. "A waste, just like I said."

Wander raised his gaze. "Like what others?"

Suddenly the medic realized with whom he was talking, and his smirk slipped a notch. "Just rumors, Scout."

"You know something," Wander insisted. "Tell me."

Consuela chose that moment to moan softly. "Better see to your patient, Scout." The medic sidled toward the door. "That's a lot more important than bandying rumors about."

Wander waited until the door had slid shut, then took Consuela's hand. Her hair looked impossibly dark, strewn as it was across the white covering. Wander tucked the blanket around her shoulders, then sat back, his gaze fixed upon her face, and gave himself over to memories of the past and yearnings for the future.

CHAPTER SIX

When Consuela did not show up for school on Monday, Rick could calm himself no longer with vague hopings that all was as it should be. One minute he was angry with her for making a fool of him. The next he was worried that something really bad might have happened. One minute more and he was completely baffled.

He stopped by the principal's office before lunch and used charm by the bucketful on the school secretary. By the time he was finished, the poor woman no longer knew whether she was coming or going. She made not a whimper of protest as he scribbled down Consuela's home address from her permanent records.

After football practice he drove straight to the Westgate subdivision. But the first three people he stopped had never heard of Loden Boulevard. Then one old geezer out walking his dog told him, "Sure I know Loden. But you won't find it in Westgate."

"That's where my friend said she lived."

"Then either your friend is lying or she don't know the name of her street," the old guy said, stooping down to quiet his dog. "I've lived in these parts all my life, and the only Loden in Baltimore runs right smack dab through the middle of Sutton Park."

Rick reached over and turned off the engine. In the sudden silence he felt things falling into place. Sutton Park was one of the city's worst neighborhoods. It bordered on Westgate, and the locals were always after the city to either clean the place up or tear it down. Yes, it was making sense.

He turned back to the old man, who was watching him with a shrewd gaze. "Girl made herself out to be something more than she was, did she?"

Rick found himself unable to let that one pass. "She's one of the finest people I've ever met."

"Then you better grab hold, sonny," the old man replied, not in the least put out. "Anybody who can pull themselves outta Sutton is a prize. She pretty?"

"Yes," Rick said, his face growing hot. "She is."

"That'll have made it all the more hard for the young lady." The old man nodded sagely. "Yessir, if I was the one driving that fancy car, I'd make a beeline over to that gal's house and put a padlock on her heart."

"How do I get there, please?"

"Turn yourself around and head down this very road about a mile to the first major intersection. That's where Westgate ends. Go through that light, and your next road is Loden. You got a street number?"

"Twelve seventeen."

"Then you'll want to go right. It's bad up there, but not as bad as it is down southward." The old geezer grinned at him and patted the Corvette's roof. "Gal from those parts, she's gonna think you're her knight in shining armor."

Rick found the street and paid to park his car in a guarded lot, which was a lot cheaper than having to buy a new radio, side window, and four new tires with rims. He walked the cracked and buckling sidewalk past tawdry shops with barred windows and loud rap music thumping through open doors. It seemed as if every corner had a liquor store. The people were a mixture of white and black and Latino and Asian. His height and his clean-cut features and his nice clothes earned him a lot of looks, none of them kind. Rick picked up his pace almost to a trot, counting off those house numbers he could spot, and vowed to be out of the area before nightfall.

The stairs leading to Consuela's front door were crumbling, and the rusting bank of doorbells had a spaghetti of disconnected wires dangling from their base. The old door complained loudly as he pulled it open. He walked across the broken mosaic floor and pushed through canted inner doors, their broken windowpanes repaired with cardboard and masking tape. The inner hall stank of old refuse and rang with the sounds of screaming children and blaring televisions. The walls were mildewed, and the only light was a bare bulb hanging high overhead.

Rick checked the paper in his hand, then started for the stairs.

The woman who answered his knock was no doubt once very beautiful, but now her features were as blurred as her voice and her eyes. "Yeah? Whaddaya want?"

Rick was not used to speaking to somebody through a cracked door with two chains holding it from opening farther. "Mrs. Ortez?"

"The name's Johnson. Who're you?"

"Oh, I'm sorry. I was looking for the apartment of Consuela Ortez."

The woman made an effort to focus. "Consuela's sick. I called you people this morning. How come you can't just leave us alone?"

Rick stared. "You're Consuela's mother?"

"Why do I have to go through this every time you assign someone new?" Her voice rose to a habitual whine. "My husband was Puerto Rican. He left us soon after Consuela was born, and I've never heard from him since. Consuela has his last name on her birth certificate. I changed my name back. It's all legal and down in black and white, if you'd just take time to check your records."

"I'm not from the school, Mrs. Johnson. I'm a friend of Consuela's. May I speak with her, please?"

Watery green eyes squinted in concentration. "You sure you're not from the office?"

"I'm just a friend, honest. We had a date Friday and, well, to be honest, I'm not exactly sure what happened. I'd just like to talk with her and make sure everything's okay."

Mrs. Johnson tucked strands of grayish blond hair back into her unkempt bun. Rick saw that her fingers were red and chapped raw, the fingernails bitten to the quick. "Well, if you're sure you're her friend."

"Really, Mrs. Johnson. Please."

"Just a minute." The door closed, and he heard chains being ratcheted back. The door opened once more to admit him as the woman backed up on unsteady legs. "You're really her friend?"

Rick nodded, trying hard not to stare around the threadbare room. From the woman's unkempt appearance, he guessed Consuela was the one responsible for the place being so clean. But nothing could hide the poverty. "Yes, ma'am. Could I speak with her, please? I won't be a minute."

"She's not here," she replied, and for the first time a hint of worry showed through. "She hasn't been home since Friday night."

"What?" Rick felt his knees grow weak.

"She went off to see some friends. I think that's what she said. Something about bowling."

"She had a date with me, Mrs. Johnson."

"Consuela didn't say anything about a date," her mother replied, more certain about that than anything since opening the door. "It was a couple of girlfriends. But I can't remember their names. My memory is a mess."

Rick felt insulted. Why would she not want her mother to know she had a date with him? "Could I maybe check her room? Maybe there's something there you missed."

Mrs. Johnson hesitated, then said, "I suppose it's all right. First door down the hall. You're sure you're not from the office?"

"Just a friend." Rick crossed the living room and entered the stubby hallway. The first door opened into a cramped windowless room.

Consuela's bedroom was utterly spotless. Everything had its place, a place for everything. The bed was neatly made, the few books stacked along shelves made from raw planks and concrete blocks. The walls were covered with advertisements for past orchestral performances and ballet and art exhibits. At the corner of each were tagged single tickets. Rick glanced at the books. Most were classics—Shakespeare, Milton, Thoreau, Conrad, Joyce—and all were dog-eared from heavy use. Several had their bindings taped to keep the books from falling apart. For some reason, seeing those books made him feel ashamed.

As he searched her room for something, anything, that might suggest where she had gone, Rick found himself thinking back to the year before, and the girl who had dumped him, and what she had said. He shook his head, trying to drive away the memories, but they would not go. The recollections added a frantic note to his search.

A flake. That was what Audrie had called him. A total flake. A year later, the words remained etched in his brain.

She had been a senior and a cheerleader, he the first guy ever to be made captain of the football team his junior year. The year's difference in age had been a challenge to him and a joke to her. It had been far more than puppy love, at least to him. After dating a month, she had wanted nothing to do with him. But the harder she pushed him away, the more he wanted her.

Finally she had taken him aside and talked down to him. To *him*. As if he were some unruly little brother who had to be shown his place. "I won't go out with you anymore because you're a flake," she had told him bluntly, "and with your looks there's a good chance you'll make it all the way through school without ever having to grow up."

Rick had been so stunned by the words that it was only when his anger boiled over that he could speak at all. "You're crazy. You just wish you had it so good."

Her reply had been as curt as her tone. "I don't know if I can put it in words of one syllable, and even if I could, I doubt if you would listen. Someday something is really going to shake your world and force you to grow up. I only hope it won't be too long in coming."

All Rick could think of as he searched Consuela's room was, what if the time had come? What if this was what would shake his world? The darkness of unknown dangers rattled him to his core. But try as he might, he could come up with nothing that suggested where Consuela might be.

Rick felt himself driven from the room by mysteries and unfounded fears. As he walked down the hallway and passed the kitchen door, his eye was snagged by several business cards tumb-tacked to the wall. Rick hesitated, then ducked inside the kitchen. It was as spotless and barren as the rest of the apartment. He ran his eye down the cards, searching for someone who might know where Consuela was—doctor, ambulance, dentist, social security office, police, everything neat and orderly.

Then he spotted a newer card stuck down at the bottom. It was not held with a thumbtack like the others, but rather with an enamelled gold cross. Rick bent over. Sure enough, the card was held in place by a lapel pin, as though someone had hastily tagged it into place with the only thing at hand. The card itself had a cross in the corner. The name rang a vague bell in Rick's mind. Reverend Daniel Mitchum, youth pastor at the First Community Church.

Rick worked the little pin free and carried the card out to the living room. Mrs. Johnson was seated at the dining table with a glass in her hand.

He thrust the card forward and asked, "Do you think he might know where Consuela is?"

"Huh?" Her head moved like a puppet on a loose string.

"Daniel Mitchum," Rick insisted. "His card was by the phone."

She struggled to focus. "Oh. Danny is a good boy. A real gent. He makes me smile." She nodded, a bumpy motion that took her chin al-

THE DREAM VOYAGERS / 47

most to her chest. "He comes by from time to time. Say, you want something to drink?"

"No, thanks." Rick hesitated, then said, "I think maybe we better call the police, Mrs. Johnson."

That brought her around. Raw fear appeared in her eyes. "Don't," she pleaded. "They're always making trouble for me. Don't tell them she's not here."

"But Mrs. Johnson—"

"You're her friend," she begged. "You find her. Call Danny. Maybe she's there. Yeah, that's it. She's gone to visit Danny. He's a good kid. You just call the number on the card. Everything will work out fine."

CHAPTER SEVEN

It was almost dusk when the church van pulled into the parking lot. Daniel saw off his vanload of teens with a smile and a kind word, then turned to where Rick stood waiting by his car. Rick was growing weary, but still tried hard to put on a good face. "Hey, Dan. How's it going?"

"Hello, Rick." The dark-haired young man wore a Red Sox warm-up jacket and a very tired expression. "Nice to see you again. That your car?"

"Yes."

"Let's go." Despite his evident fatigue, Daniel set a rapid pace. "Do you think the carnival's still open?"

"Hey," Rick said, slowing down. "I told you on the phone, I checked that place from top to—"

"Then one more time won't hurt anything." Daniel grasped his arm and urged him forward. "Never can tell what we find if we check it out together."

"Then, you believe me?"

"Let's just say," Daniel replied, hustling through the main entrance, "I'm sympathetic to what you've been going through."

When they had piled into Rick's Corvette, Daniel said, "Run through the story one more time, all right?"

Rick did so, feeling the affair become more real as someone finally took him seriously. "I searched all over the place, spent almost three hours looking. Believe me, I did everything but climb back into the tunnel."

"I believe you," Daniel said quietly.

When they pulled into the carnival parking lot, Daniel was up and running even before Rick cut off the motor. Rick raced to catch up with him and demanded, "What's the hurry?"

"I'm not sure. I just have the feeling that the answer we're looking for is at the roller coaster."

"But I told you, I've talked to the manager and walked all around the place!"

Daniel did not bother to reply. He ran down the gaudy thoroughfare, his haste and his serious demeanor attracting stares from the remaining fun-seekers. He bought two coaster tickets, then motioned for Rick to join him in the line. He reached into his jacket, brought out a pen and a piece of paper. He scribbled hastily, then handed it to Rick. "If something happens and I don't come out, call this number. It's my home. My wife's name is Bliss."

Rick stared at him. "What do you mean, if something happens?"

Impatiently Daniel waved it aside and pushed the pad and pen at Rick. "Now do the same for me."

"What are you talking about?"

Daniel gave him a grim stare. "Listen to what I am saying. I just think it would be a good idea if we knew a contact for each other."

"Not me," Rick replied numbly. "The last thing I need is for my folks to know what's going on."

"Hey!" The barker brusquely waved them forward. "You jokers want to ride, get a move on! I ain't got all night."

Together they moved forward and allowed themselves to be seated. When the bar crashed down, Daniel settled back and sighed, "Here we go."

Rick's query was cut short by the horn sounding, announcing that the ride was pulling out. The climb to the top seemed endless, the swoop downward uninteresting. Rick sat beside a grim-faced Daniel, allowing himself to be thrown back and forth by the centrifugal force, wondering what the guy had been talking about, wishing he could just make it all go away.

Somehow the tunnel ride felt as though it lasted a lot longer than the first time. Rick decided it was just nerves, especially when the light reappeared and he glanced to his left, and Daniel was still there. The feeling of relief was so strong he had to laugh.

But Daniel remained thoughtfully silent as they stepped from the car.

He pulled Rick back around to the front and said, "Wait here." Then he stepped forward and bought another ticket. When he returned, he was pulling pen and paper from his pocket once more. "You need to write out a little note to your folks."

"No thanks. Uh-uh. No way."

"Just tell them you're going to be away for a couple of days, so they won't worry. Or at least, not worry too much."

Rick could scarcely believe what he was hearing. "Are you crazy?"

"Hurry, there's not much time," Daniel gave him an assessing gaze. "This isn't my trip. You need to go yourself. Alone."

"Go where?"

"Look, do you want to find Consuela, or don't you?"

"Sure, but—"

"Then every second counts. Write out the note and put your address on this second page. I'll drop your car and the note off." When Rick still did not move, Daniel leaned forward and said forcefully, "I can't do this, Rick. If you want to help Consuela you've got to believe me and do what I say."

Feeling cut off from the garish sights and sounds that surrounded him, Rick did as he was urged. When he handed back the scribbled message, Daniel read it and grunted, "It will have to do." He grasped Rick's hand, guided him forward, and said as they walked, "Will you take some advice?"

"I guess so, but—"

"When you find yourself growing lost or confused, search out the light that remains unseen. Remember that the answer does not lie in strength or power or anger, but in love. Open yourself up to the Lord's higher call, and know that you will always be protected."

Daniel patted his shoulder and handed the barker the single ticket. As Rick climbed into the seat, Daniel called out from behind the wire barrier, "Tell Consuela that we'll be praying for your safe return."

CHAPTER EIGHT

Consuela awoke with a gasping exclamation that sounded as if it had been torn from her throat. Wander squeezed her hand, pressed another upon the soft skin where neck joined shoulder, and soothed, "Easy, easy. It's going to be all right."

"Ooooh, my head. Everything keeps spinning around," she said, her voice barely a whisper.

"You've had a psychic shock." Wander's voice was calm despite his racing pulse. "Your amplifier was tuned up too high."

"Wander? Is that really you?" She struggled to open her eyes, but they swam unfocused until she groaned and closed them once more.

"It's me," he said softly.

"I'm still here," she murmured.

He had to smile. "Why do you keep saying that?"

"Don't leave me, okay? Don't let go. I feel like I'd go spinning out of control if you didn't keep hold."

"I'm here," he said quietly, daring to stroke the tiny thread of hair falling before her ear. "I'm right here."

"What happened? I know you told me already, but I don't think I understand."

"Let me tell you a story," he replied quietly. "You just lie there. It's better if you're quiet."

"Lights," she said softly. "They keep flashing in my head."

"I know. It will pass," he quietly assured her. "Listen. When I was eleven, a specialist came to my school. He was some big doctor, volunteering time to work with the barrio kids. All the teachers made a big fuss over him. They made me go see him. The doctor inspected me and said, 'There's nothing wrong with this child except he hasn't had enough to eat.' The head teacher prodded me in the shoulder and said, 'Tell the good doctor about your voices.' I will never forget how ashamed I was. I couldn't look at the doctor after that, even when he ordered me to.

"When I wouldn't say anything, the head teacher started telling him stories. About how when I was younger I would go off into these spells—that's what she called them, spells. One minute I was there, the next I wasn't. I just drifted off and away, then I would snap back and have no recollection of where I was or how I got there or why the teacher was shouting at me and why the kids were laughing."

Wander leaned back in his chair, drawing her hand closer to the edge of the bed so that he could hold it with both of his. "She told him how sometimes I would answer voices that no one else could hear, or ask questions that made no sense, or speak words that no barrio child had any way of knowing, like gravity shield release, or transition approach, or thruster station. She made me stand there while she told him how, when the kids kept laughing at me, I stopped talking about the voices. How I stopped talking at all. How for over a year I did not speak to anyone. But how I would sometimes still have these spells. And how other kids would talk about how I spent all my free time wandering around the port, sitting for hours in the haunted fields that everyone else refused to walk through.

"I had to keep standing there, terrified that all my secrets were coming out. I knew they were going to do something to me. I just knew it. I stood there and tried to shut out her voice and wished the floor would just open up and swallow me whole."

Slowly, gradually, inch by inch, Consuela turned her head. She opened one eye at a time, her brow furrowed with the effort of trying to focus on Wander. When both of those beautiful dark eyes were fastened on his face, he asked, "Feeling any better?"

"I think so. This will really go away?"

"Yes. Are you thirsty?"

"Very."

When he brought the cup over, she opened her mouth, accepted the straw and swallowed, holding her head as still as she could. "Thank you."

Wander settled back and went on, "The doctor made the head teacher leave the room. He then took hold of my shoulders and guided me over to a seat and forced me to sit down. I can still remember how his hands smelled, clean and a little soapy. He had a very deep voice. He told me that he was going to sit there for as long as it took for me to stop being shy and speak with him. But until I was ready, he was going to talk, because he didn't like wasting time. He was not a volunteer as the school thought. He was paid by the Hegemony. There, he said, he had told me a secret. One he knew a silent boy like me would keep. But because he was being so honest and open with me, he hoped I would think about talking to him.

"Then he said that his job was to look for sensitives, had I ever heard that word? When I did not answer, he told me that there were different stages, and almost everyone was at least a little sensitive. But for reasons no one could explain, some people had more sensitivity than others. A lot more. These people were called Talents. And one of the first signals of a Talent child was that they heard voices."

Wander stopped, stroked her arm, and said, "Am I boring you?"

"No," she said softly. "Go on."

"How do you feel?"

"Better. The spinning isn't so bad. Go on."

"All right. The doctor asked me, did I ever hear the voices talk about countdowns?" Wander smiled at the memory. "I could scarcely believe my ears. Here was somebody who not only did not laugh at me but knew what I was hearing. I raised my head, and this seemed to please him very much. He asked me, 'Can you remember what the pilot says when he starts his own counting?' And I said, very quietly, 'Two minutes.' The doctor became extremely excited, and it scared me, but not too much, because somehow I got the impression that he was also very pleased. He had trouble opening his case, his hands were trembling so bad. He pulled out this steel-backed pad that had a questionnaire attached to it. He scribbled something across the top, and then looked back at me. I remember his hair was almost as dark as yours, but his eyes were pale blue. He had a mustache and thick, dark hair on the back of his hands. I remember the room smelled dusty, and there was sunlight coming in though the window. I remember that day as clearly as this one. I will never forget it. Never. My life started on that day."

Wander felt he was looking into two worlds at the same time. The one before him was filled with the beauty of Consuela's open gaze. The other was the one in his mind, made more real than ever before by the chance to share it with someone. "Then he asked me, 'What is the word for the opening a starship passes through?' and I said in my very small voice, 'The vortex.' Then he asked, 'What did the Control Tower say just before the ship's thrusters were started?' 'Gravity net on full.' 'And what were the words for where the ship went?' 'Coordinates of the planetary destination.' On and on the questions went, with the doctor growing more and more excited. Finally he put his questionnaire down and asked me if I would like to play a game. A mind game. He would attach me to a little portable amplifier he carried and show me things I couldn't see with my eyes. I let him put the headset on my temples, then he hit the switch, and my whole world exploded."

She grimaced in shared pain as Wander continued, "I remember screaming, but not much else. It seemed as though it took him hours to turn it off and get the headset off my head."

"Hours and hours," Consuela agreed.

"I must have fainted, because the next thing I knew, I was in a hospital bed, and my mother was leaning over me, stroking my forehead and crying. When I opened my eyes and felt the world spinning, she made it a lot worse by screaming to the doctor, who was still with me, that he had destroyed my brain. Finally he quieted her and leaned over me and said that he was very sorry, that somehow the amplifier had been turned up too high, it was a terrible mistake, but there should be no permanent damage. After an hour or so things were a lot better, and my mother calmed down, and she let me speak with the doctor alone. He told me that there was a good chance that I was a Talent, and he would need to give me more tests. There was a problem, though, and because he had hurt me he wanted to tell me about it.

"He said that all children lost some of their sensitivity as they passed through puberty, did I know that word? More than nine-tenths of all children who tested positive at earlier ages lost it completely. And the more sensitive the child, the greater the likelihood that the loss would be total. So the Hegemony did not do anything except register sensitive children. Doctors like him were working on the problem night and day, but they had not discovered either the reason or a cure. I listened to what he said and decided I didn't mind. Well, I did, but not too much. I liked watching the ships take off, but other than that, Talent had done nothing but make my life miserable. I had no friends. Most people, including my family, thought I was crazy. No, I decided I wouldn't mind it all that much if my Talent disappeared."

"But it didn't," she said quietly.

"No," he agreed. "On my fifteenth birthday I was taken to a big hall and tested again. There were a *lot* of people there. Most of the children came with their families, and almost all the families were rich. They were different from me. They wore nice clothes and they spoke with different tones. They looked down their noses at me. So did a lot of the teachers. So I did what I did best. I retreated inside and tried to disappear."

"I know the feeling," Consuela said, her eyes calling out their sympathy.

"I learned a lot that day," Wander continued. "It's amazing what you can hear and learn when people think you're of no account."

"They ignore you and forget that you're even there," Consuela agreed.

"I learned that some children could receive special training as they passed through puberty, training that helped them hold on to their sensitivity," Wander continued. "I learned that it was only privately available, and that it was *extremely* expensive. I learned that the government kept it that way, because they preferred to develop sensitivity in people whose station taught them to use it responsibly. Those were the exact words I heard: To use their sensitivity in a responsible manner for the good of the Hegemony."

"The field," Consuela said. "You sat out there and watched the ships. That was your training."

"Maybe." Wander leaned forward, his voice intense. "I learned something else. Something other than the fact that most of the highborn people despised me, and felt I had no business being there. Something other than the fact that entry into scout training was extremely competitive. I learned that these rich kids, with all their special training, were not all that sensitive. I could run rings around them."

"So you hid your abilities," Consuela said, giving her head the barest of nods. "Smart."

"Yes," he agreed, drinking her in. "I showed them only enough to pass their tests. I scored well, but not *too* well. And they sent me here, to the scout's academy. And here I learned that a Talent is someone who has what they call hypersensitivity, which means the ability to 'hear' with only a small amount of amplification. This is the first sign that the person can be trained to guide a starship through null-space. A couple of times I read about people who can 'hear' without any amplification at all. They're talked about like they were freaks."

"Have you talked to Senior Pilot Grimson?"

"I've been afraid to," he replied quietly. "When I arrived here, I discovered that Talents only come through here once every couple of years, so rare that a lot of people aren't even sure what they are. Then I started hearing strange rumors. Frightening ones. Of scouts who came here and then partway through training just disappeared. Rumors say they're taken somewhere for experimentation. Never heard from again. I worried that maybe these were people like me, and the scientists used them to see if they could breed for Talent." Slowly Wander shook his head. "I don't want to let anything come between me and going into space."

Consuela released his hand and began softly stroking his wrist. Her touch sent electric tingles through his body. "So Wander has remained the lonely little boy."

"I've had a lot of experience," he said. "Can I ask you a question?"

"Anything," she replied. "Anything at all."

"Have you ever been tested?"

"Never."

"Then how did you wind up here?"

"I have some secrets of my own, and when I'm feeling better I want to tell you about them." She hesitated, then added, "If I'm still here."

"They won't be letting you go, that's for certain," Wander assured her. "I need to ask you something else. When we were out there on the field, did you hear the countdown?"

"Yes."

He could scarcely keep his voice from betraying his excitement. "When the fifteen-second mark was hit, did you notice anything?"

"It felt," she groped for words, "like time was being stretched."

Wander felt the band of pressure tighten across his chest. "Where did the ship go?"

She searched her returning memory, then said in confusion, "Antari. I know where it is, but I've never heard of it before. How is that possible?"

His voice shaky, he said, "You don't know how long I've dreamed of this."

She looked at him a long moment, and for some reason her eyes brimmed with sorrow. "Oh, Wander."

"Someone to talk to," he went on. "Someone who understands."

"If only," she bit her lip, then sighed the words, "if only I could stay."

He laughed with relief. "They'd never let you go. Not if you painted yourself green and ran screaming down the halls at midnight."

"Not much chance of that," she said and to his great joy smiled a second time. "Thank you for sharing your story with me."

"I haven't ever told anyone about it before," he confessed.

"I know," she said. "Come here."

He leaned forward. "What?"

"Closer," she said, raising her face to meet his, guiding him down with one cool hand on his neck, and kissing him with lips that were soft and warm and tasted just as he thought they should.

CHAPTER NINE

"Up and at 'em, Ensign," barked a voice near his head. "Captain Arnol wants you."

Rick opened bleary eyes and focused on a barrel-shaped man blocking the doorway. "What?"

"Down with mind-lag? Tough. On this ship, what the captain wants, the captain gets. And right now he wants you. Flight deck. On the bounce."

Rick rolled out of his bunk, only to find that his legs would barely support him. A hand twice the size of his own gripped his upper arm.

"Still suffering, are you? Don't worry, I've seen worse, and they always get better. Nobody ever dies from mind-lag. They just wish they could."

Rick struggled to focus on the man who held him upright. He was dressed in a flashy uniform, the dark green shoulders piped with gold braid and the sleeves bearing numerous gold slash marks. Something triggered in the recesses of his foggy brain, and he asked, "Chief Petty Officer?"

The barrel-chested man grinned. "Name is Tucker. I heard they boarded you on a stretcher. Don't worry about it. First time in null-space hits a lot of people hard. You're an outworlder, I hear. Where do you call home, son?"

"Baltimore," Rick mumbled.

The grin broadened. "Now that must have been a journey from the back of beyond. I've been shipping more than twenty Standard years, and I've never come across that name before." Experienced eyes checked his appearance. "Well, your uniform doesn't appear too much the worse for wear, seeing as how you've slept in it across the Hegemony. Come along then, and easy does it. Just put your weight on me until your legs get to working."

Uniform. Rick cast a glance down at his form and would have lost his footing save for Petty Officer Tucker's strong grip. He was dressed head to toe in palest gray, cut like the petty officer's, except without the slash marks. The material caught the light and shimmered in faint rainbow hues. His trousers were tucked into boots of the same material. Two rows of small gold buttons paraded up the front of his shirt, and his cuffs were trimmed with a single thin line of gold braid. He craned and saw that each of his shoulders bore a tiny gold pip.

A *uniform*.

The information was there in his mind. How, he could not explain. Yet still he knew. Ship's officers wore uniforms of gray—the higher the rank, the darker the uniform. Ensigns stood upon the bottom rung. Noncoms and flight technicians wore green—chief petty officers and senior scientists were top of the list. Scouts wore pale blue robes, communicators royal blue, pilots midnight blue.

But what was a pilot?

While Rick was still busy examining himself, Tucker guided him into the chute. It was only when his weight dropped away that he glanced up and gasped.

The petty officer was vastly pleased with the reaction. "Now that's what I like to see. A youngster who's not above showing a little pride in a ship of the line. Grand, isn't she?"

Dumbly, Rick nodded. Grand indeed she was. The chute tracked itself up one wall, while below extended a vast surface of bustling activity. Great sparkling machinery and strange-looking equipment were monitored by numerous personnel in uniforms of pearl white. The words popped unbidden into his mind: specialist technicians assigned off-world duty.

"Ah, coming around, now, are you? Good." Nothing escaped the chief petty officer's perception. "So tell me, Ensign, what is it you're looking at?"

"Outer cargo hold," Rick said, bemused. He could not say how he knew, but know he did. "Used for oversized freight and consignments requiring preparation while in shipment."

Tucker grunted his approval. "What's that contraption over in the corner, then?"

The enormous multi-sided globe was all polarized windows and energy reflectors, with various arms and drills and scoops sprouting at odd points. It shone like a polished bronze sphere. Rick said in confused wonderment, "A three-man mining pod, designed for solar-proximity worlds."

"And that tin can there at your feet?"

Rick looked down, saw a massive steel-gray canister being inspected by a score of technicians, and felt the information click into his consciousness. "A retrievable drone for surface studies under extremely adverse conditions such as corrosive atmosphere, ultra-high atmospheric pressures, or hostile inhabitants."

"You'll do," the chief petty officer decided. "Straighten up now, we're on final approach."

The chute continued through several upper levels before emerging into the flight deck's antechamber. Rick stepped out after his guardian, felt gravity resurge, and followed him through doors marked with strange signings that he somehow knew read "Flight and Comm Deck. Authorized Personnel Only." He stepped through the portal and gasped a second time.

"Here's your fresh meat, Captain Arnol," the petty officer announced.

"Two arms, two legs, a head, all limbs still intact," a hatchet-faced man said, swiveling his chair around. "You were gentle on the lad, Tuck."

"There's time for paring him down if the need arises," the petty officer replied. "Right now the boy's barely got the strength to hold himself upright."

Rick felt an elbow nudge him, and he dragged his eyes away from the vista spread out before him. Somehow he knew what was expected. "Ensign Richard reporting for duty, sir."

"Richard, Richard. Don't believe I've come across that one before. What sort of label is that, Ensign?"

"It, ah, belonged to a famous king, Captain. He was known as the Lionhearted."

"Your land has kings, does it? Ah yes, now I recall. You're an outworlder. Well, we don't hold a shipmate's origins against him, not on this ship. What counts is performance."

Captain Arnol was a taut man, his actions measured and swift. He plucked a form from the pouch attached to one arm of his chair. "Your record is impressive, Ensign, as far as it goes. But book learning and athletic skills interest me only if they can be transferred to ship duty. That's why the Hegemony requires ensigns to serve aboard ship before beginning their final tour at the academy. You with me?"

"Yes, Captain."

"Your uniform says ensign, but in reality you are junior to every bo-sun's mate on this ship. The reason is simple. They are experienced spacers, and you are a raw recruit. Nothing will earn you a downcheck faster in their eyes or mine than putting on airs you don't deserve."

The captain tossed the sheet aside. "Over the next ten weeks, you'll be serving on every level of this ship. There is no duty that you can re-fuse, nothing that is beneath your station. If the chief petty officer orders you to scrub the main cargo deck with a toothbrush, I expect you to carry out your orders with a smile. You follow?"

"Yes, Captain." Rick could not help it. His eyes tracked upward as though drawn on their own will. He was looking at it and still could not believe what he saw.

When the silence dragged on, he glanced back to find the captain smil-ing thinly. "Never been on a flight deck before, have you, Ensign?"

"No, Captain," he replied weakly. "First time."

"Ever spaced before?"

"No, Captain," he said and let his eyes coast back up.

"You mean the trip from your homeworld was your first time out-bound?"

A lean little man in the seat next to the captain gave a chuckle. Rick recognized the position as belonging to the helmsman. "Raw isn't the word for this one, Skipper."

"Quiet," Captain Arnol said mildly. "I suppose it wouldn't hurt for you to join us for the landing, Ensign. Understand, though, you'll make up all duties the chief petty officer may have for you before going ashore."

"Look at the poor guy," the helmsman said. "He's all eyes and mouth."

"Quiet, I said. All right, son. Take a seat, no, not that one, that's the pilot's chair. Remember that. This elevated position at the height of the Signals station is reserved for the pilot, whether or not the ship carries one. Which we don't, since we're on planetary duty inside Hegemony boundaries."

"And good riddance," muttered the other officer. The captain allowed this to pass without comment.

Rick let himself be steered into an empty seat by the inside wall. He nodded when ordered to report to Chief Petty Officer Tucker after they touched down, yet he scarcely gave it conscious thought. All he could see, all he could take in, was the vista in front of him.

The flight deck was split into two segments. The lower half was one unbroken mass of instrumentation and switches and flickering lights and complex read-out systems. Each chair spun on its own free axis and had a series of banked instruments that slid up alongside each arm or glided on transparent wings up and over the chair's head. Rick found himself aware that each seat was called a station, and that each station had a name—Captain, Watch Commander, Communications Specialist, Pilot, Helmsman, Weapons, Assistant Watch Officer, Power Technician, and so on around the room.

But the growing sense of unbidden knowledge could not take away from what stretched out above him.

The other half of the chamber was a solid sheet of unbroken horizon. Rick knew that in truth it was a great series of interconnected screens joined to ultra-precise cameras set in the ship's nose. But this did not affect his awe for a second.

The ship was inbound for a planet that was already so close the blackness of space was limited to an encircling border. To his left, a small orbiting moon was spinning up and away behind them. The sun was just cresting the planet's upper horizon, crowning the hazy atmosphere with a broad sweep of flame. Directly before him, a brilliant blue sky was flecked with swatches of white cloud.

"Might as well switch on his seat," the captain instructed. "Give him the full effect."

"Aye, aye, Captain."

For a third time, shock punched the breath from his body. Rick felt as well as saw a golden ribbon race out from the ship, connecting it to a pulsating beacon located down below the clouds. It was the ITN, he knew without knowing how—the interplanetary transport network. In shipboard slang, the ITN was called a lightway. Ships transversing the inner Hegemony locked into the appropriate target-route and rode on semi-automatic the entire way.

Yet his awareness of these facts was buffeted by the other effect which was now coursing through his mind and body. The seat was now connected to him, and through this coupling came a sensation unlike anything he had ever known.

Power.

Chapter Ten

The next morning found Consuela standing on the highest of the seven balconies that looked out over the vast spaceport arena. She felt she could spend days watching the scene. Behind her, the field itself was visible through thick shielded windows, but for the moment she was content to ignore the ships' comings and goings. There was simply too much else to take in.

Directly in front of her rose an unbroken wall of polarized glass eight stories high and two hundred yards wide. Through it she watched hovercraft descend, deposit passengers and personnel, and silently depart. Beyond the unloading bay stretched a vast surface filled with personal vehicles the likes of which she had never even imagined. Part wheelless car and part glider, their stubby wings retracted as the carriers slowed and settled to earth.

Seven stories below her stretched the bustling port's colorful panorama. Wander had been correct—the floor's directional lights did look like a multicolored spider web. Consuela watched as people entered, stated their business to the information column, and then haughtily ignored the pulsating ribbons of light. From her lofty position she could stare with abandon at their obvious wealth and station. Highborn passengers wore beautiful clothes and bored expressions, as though determined not to be impressed by anything they saw. Every few moments the entire structure hummed with the power of departing spaceships. Consuela was the only person who paid the slightest notice.

"Ah, there you are."

Consuela turned to confront a slender boy who eyed her with disdain. The boy went on, "Watching the animals go through their paces, are we?"

"I've never seen anything like this," she replied honestly.

The boy's air of superiority strengthened. "Yes, we hear all sorts of ghastly tales about primitive outworld societies. How did you survive?"

"I kept my spear sharpened at all times," Consuela replied calmly. Maybe it wasn't so different here after all.

An angry glint surfaced. "Pilot Grimson has chosen me to be his errand boy. He wishes to see you in the Tower."

"Where—"

The boy raised one haughty eyebrow. "Don't tell me an exceptional sensitive like yourself can't even find the Tower. Tsk, tsk. How shameful."

"I've just arrived," she replied, her cheeks burning.

"Yes, so I heard." He turned around and sauntered off, tossing a parting remark over his shoulder. "I suggest you just reach out with all these powers of yours and find it for yourself."

———

She was still hot when she found the pilot waiting impatiently at the Tower entrance. "What took you so long?"

"A little snit of a scout who couldn't be bothered to show me where to go," she replied angrily.

"Ah," Pilot Grimson said, nodding his understanding. "Only to be expected."

"Maybe to you."

"Put yourself in his position," he said, for some reason showing her patience. "Child of a good family, given every opportunity to develop what sensitivity he has, only to arrive and discover that an outworlder, who is not even required to go through the horrors of culling, shows a sensitivity he shall never know."

"It still doesn't excuse his bad manners," Consuela retorted.

"No, in a perfect world, it would not. But as we must deal with what we have, I suggest we move onward. How are you feeling?"

"Better. Still a little shaken, but better."

"Very well." He slipped back into his mantle of frosty control. "All scouts are required to stand training watches. For most it is a period of observing and learning and trying to hone their abilities through mind games. Scout Wander has shown a remarkable level of skill, however, and today will begin actual Tower Watch. As you have shown Talent potential, I want you to stand to his schedule."

"Fine with me," Consuela said, and could not suppress her grin of pleasure.

Grimson's eyes narrowed. "I also suggest you learn from Wander the correct manner in which to deport yourself with your superiors."

Still rankled by the scout's snipes, Consuela found that the pilot's lofty attitude struck a spark to dry tinder. "Wander is afraid of you."

He had clearly not expected that. "And you are not?"

"Wander lives for space. It's all he's ever wanted to do." Consuela forced herself to meet the pilot's probing gaze. "He's terrified that a downcheck from you would hold him back."

"Remarkable how close you have become in such a short period," Grimson murmured.

Consuela felt her face go red, but stood her ground. "Maybe what he really needs from you is a compliment and a kind word."

The pilot studied her thoughtfully. "A scout who on her third day presumes herself ready to advise a pilot . . . Let us hope your Talent is sufficient to excuse such behavior. Come along."

She followed him through the great bronze portal. Immediately her mind was beset with a hundred buzzing voices. She entered a circular room perhaps fifty paces across, where several dozen people staffed complex consoles rising in curved rows. The globe's entire upper surface was transparent, granting an uninterrupted view of the fields and the ships and the spaceport roof.

His headset already in place, Wander stood at nervous attention on the right-hand dais, a broad elevated platform that looked down and out over the Tower activities. A young woman in robes of royal blue sat beside him, operating a half-moon console of bewildering complexity. Two additional chairs with smaller consoles stood behind her, unmanned.

Pilot Grimson started for the side stairs, but was immediately halted by a graying man with a dark brown uniform and a very irritated manner. "Just a moment, if you please, Pilot."

"Can it wait?" Grimson asked testily.

"No, it cannot." The man stepped directly in front of him. "As watch commandant, I formally protest this action."

"Your protest is noted. Now if you will please step aside—"

"I insist that my protest and your response be formally logged," the man persisted.

Grimson gave an exasperated sigh. "Very well, Commandant. Lead on." To Consuela he said, "Wait here, Scout."

As the pilot moved off, Consuela tried to give Wander a reassuring smile, but the noise in her head was as persistent as a dentist's drill.

The watch commandant stepped to a solitary console set on the central dais, separated by a valley of stairs from Wander's platform. He touched a switch and said, "Tower Log official entry. Watch Commandant Loklin speaking. I wish to officially protest granting the Scout Wander full watch status. Having only completed two months of the training program, the scout is not qualified for such responsibilities. I believe this places the activity of the entire port in serious jeopardy."

Consuela saw Wander's jaw drop open. She wanted to rush to him and share in the moment even though she was not sure exactly what it meant, but she was held captive by the infernal buzzing voices.

Meeting the commandant's angry gaze, Grimson replied, "Senior Pilot Grimson responding. I hereby officially override the commandant's objection and assign the Scout Wander to full watch."

The commandant viciously punched the switch and snapped, "You are making a grave error, Pilot."

"And you are in for a very big surprise," the pilot responded.

"I hope so," the commandant said, glaring at Wander. "For all our sakes, I very much hope so."

Grimson came back around the curving walk, and as he drew close he noticed Consuela's distress. "What is the matter?"

"Voices," she said. "They won't stop."

A blaze of triumph lit the pilot's features. "Voices?"

"In my head," she replied, struggling not to wince. "It *hurts*."

"Follow me." He turned and walked up the side stairs to where Wander stood by the platform's polished railing. He extracted a small apparatus from his belt pouch, picked up a headset, and attached it just above the temple pad. He fitted it to Consuela's forehead, then stepped back. "How is that?"

"A little better," she said, so relieved that the painful buzzing was diminishing she even smiled at the frosty old man.

"But still there?"

"Yes."

For some reason, her response increased the pilot's triumph. He took her hand, guided it up to the little box, said, "There is a dial recessed into the surface. Feel the edge? Good. Now turn the dial until the sound disappears."

Consuela spun the little dial, and as the buzzing voices faded into silence, she let out a grateful sigh. "They're gone."

"Excellent." Pilot Grimson pointed to Wander's headset. "This is the one you have altered?"

"Yes, Pilot."

"Take it off."

Still bemused, Wander did as he was ordered. Shaking his head, the pilot inspected the headset. Then he set it down, picked up a different set, extracted a second apparatus from his pouch, and fitted it on. He handed it over and said, "Try this. Use the dial as I instructed."

To Consuela's surprise, Wander gave a blissful smile. "Amazing."

"You heard them too?" she asked him.

"All the time," he replied. "Until now."

"How could you stand it?"

"It was hard. Very hard."

"Enough," the pilot ordered. He pointed to the communication console and said to Wander, "You must adjust the amplification so that all directed signals are clearly audible. I assume this is what you have been doing all along?"

"Yes, Pilot."

"Very well." He raised his voice so that it carried through the Tower. "Scout Wander, you are now assigned full watch duty."

From his central station, the commandant released an angry snort. Grimson turned so that he watched the back of the commandant's head as he continued, "You have for the past two weeks been acting under the direct guidance of a senior communicator who has done nothing but monitor your activities."

Slowly the commandant swiveled his chair about and looked at Wander in surprise. Grimson went on, "You have performed faultlessly. I expect you to continue doing so. The safety of this port is now in your hands."

"Yes, Pilot," Wander managed. His look of ecstasy was almost painful to Consuela.

The pilot nodded and walked back down the side stairs. At the portal he turned and addressed the Tower as a whole, "For the sake of harmony within the new trainee-scout squadron, I ask you all to say nothing of this development."

The Tower remained frozen, all attention focused on Wander, until a voice called, "Incoming."

The Tower sprang back to life. All but the watch commandant, who kept his gaze fastened on the scout.

Wander turned and nervously said, "I relieve you, Communicator."

"Eleven Hegemony ships," the communicator droned, "all in proper ascendance-descendance, channels two, seven, four. Three starships approaching transcendence, note the channels."

"Noted," Wander said, his eyes luminous.

The woman stood. "There are fourteen listed departures for the next hour. All on schedule, plus-or-minus the acceptable limits."

"Noted," Wander repeated.

"Very well." She keyed the console and stated, "Specialist Communicator Evana logging out."

"Scout Wander logging on," he said, his voice strengthening.

The auburn-haired woman inspected Consuela, gave them both a minuscule nod, and said, "Good luck."

His hands already busy on the controls, Wander motioned Consuela into the seat to the right and behind his own. She sat and watched as he reached over her console, pointed to the central pulsing dial, and said, "Amplifier. Raise it to where you can comfortably hear me and the incoming messages." Hastily he hit three keys, said, "I have locked your channel onto mine. Just sit and watch. It will all begin to make sense in time."

Commandant Loklin gave her a hostile inspection, then dismissed them with a shake of his head and swung back around. Consuela felt other gazes on them from about the room but was determined not to respond. Very slowly she swung the amplifier dial until voices became audible in her head. But this time they were single voices, and held to a comfortable level.

And Wander's was one of them.

"Starship Excelsior, this is Hegemony Port. You are scheduled for transition in six minutes and counting."

"Port, this is Excelsior," came the droning reply. "Six-minute mark noted."

Wander thumbed a switch on his chair's arm and said more quietly, "Can you hear me?"

"Yes."

"There's no need to talk out loud. Just move your lips. It helps shape the words. I know this is all very confusing, but there is no other way to learn."

She found herself thrilling to the intimacy of this contact. "Congratulations."

He angled his chair her way just long enough to show his grateful smile. "This is a dream come true."

"I know."

"Just a minute." He ran through a series of switches, and with each she heard a different voice. Wander did not speak until keying the final switch, when he droned, "Watch notes quarter-hour sweep, all in order and on schedule."

He then keyed his chair and said, "When you see me hit this switch, we can talk. Otherwise you need to just watch and listen."

"I understand."

"Most of watch is oversight. Sensitives are the only ones capable of interstellar communication, unless a drone is sent through null-space carrying something too confidential for the normal relay. Normal communication bands are held to the speed of light. You've probably heard this before."

"None of it," she confessed.

"Don't worry, it'll come soon. Sensitives are assigned watch duty to check a ship's transition and confirm that everything is in order." He paused as a vast beehive of burnished metal lowered itself onto a brilliant platform of fire. "Hegemony vessel. They travel along lightways, or ITN target-routes. Lightways traverse Hegemony planetary systems and punch through n-space on short patterns in constant use. For all other routes, a pilot is responsible for ship's transition."

Things became increasingly busy then, and Wander had scarce moments to speak with her. She did not mind. Consuela was happy to sit and watch the harried bustling take on a tight sense of order. Wander monitored all incoming and outgoing vessels, communicated with all ports either receiving or dispatching ships. Tracking codes were accepted by other staff, who barked back landing and takeoff instructions, which were passed on by Wander. The watch commandant said little, but his eyes missed nothing. Each time he glanced her way, Consuela felt his searing frustration scorch her where she sat.

In a quiet moment, she asked, "Why do they look at us like that?"

Wander did not need to ask what she meant. "Nobody much likes a pilot."

"But why?"

"Passengers call us the ship magicians. When you go out in public in your robes, you'll be addressed as 'wizard'. People say we speak with ghosts and control dark forces. The staff have other names for us. Freakos, pointy heads, amp junkies—those you'll hear a lot."

"That's a lot of nonsense."

"Get used to it," he replied. "There's nothing else you can do. I hear it's the same shipboard. Captains don't like sharing power and having to rely on us for the transitions. I heard one say the Hegemony would be better off finding another way to chart their vessels, one that fits to the proper scheme of things."

In the far lower corner, opposite the main tower entrance, a second set of doors opened into the staff compound. Every time a flight landed, Wander explained, a formal transfer was made to the ground crew who occupied the bottom two rows of consoles. They assigned the ship to a free terminal, directed refueling and mechanics and cleanup and staffing and the myriad of tasks that prepared the ship for its next departure. An officer entered the lower door after each landing, saluted the crewperson staffing the first console, and handed over the ship's documents. They were distributed, inspected, stamped, coded, and returned.

Beyond the transparent globe, four thruster shields were spaced equidistant about the central field. Peripheral fields were given over to ships awaiting transition, freighters being loaded for night departure slots, ships undergoing major repairs, storage sheds, private vessels in longer-term storage, and military craft. Every few minutes an internal Hegemony vessel would lift off or arrive in smoothly humming precision.

Once every quarter hour a brilliant gravity net would peel open in an awesome display of barely controlled power, releasing a ship into the swirling nothingness of null-space. Timed in similar cadence, a vortex would suddenly appear above an empty thruster shield, and suddenly a ship would appear in a white-gold flash of light. Consuela noticed how Wander would key them both out of direct contact with the ship just before the fifteen-second count was coded. She understood him perfectly. He had other duties that would not give him the interval necessary to recover from having time stretched.

After two hours of almost constant activity, Wander's robe was growing damp spots under his arms and at the small of his back. His voice was steady but hoarse. Several times he paused long enough to wipe the perspiration away from his eyes.

A few minutes later the main portal opened to admit a heavy-set woman with a head of tightly clenched curls. As she treaded up the stairs to the communicator's platform, she did not bother to cover her astonishment. "You are standing watch?"

"Yes, Communicator," Wander replied.

"A scout handling full watch?" Her cheeks sprouted two red spots. "Who authorized this?"

"Senior Pilot Grimson," Commandant Loklin said dryly, swiveling his chair around to face Wander. "You may tell the pilot that he was correct. I have indeed been surprised."

"Thank you, Commandant," Wander said, rising to his feet.

The woman demanded, "How long have you been in training, Scout?"

"Two months." Wander pointed to the flickering console. "Fifteen Hegemony vessels, all coded on channels seven and nine. Four—"

"Get off my platform," she snapped. "Now."

Wander bowed his head in weary acceptance. He coded the message board and stated quietly, "Scout Wander logging out."

"Communicator Zenna logging in," she stated in fury, and kept her hand on the key as she continued, "What utter mess have you left me with?"

Wander motioned with his head for Consuela to follow him down. As they approached the portal, Commandant Loklin called out, "Scout Wander."

Wander straightened. "Yes, Commandant."

"You may tell the senior pilot," the commandant replied, "that you are welcome to stand duty on my watch at any time."

It took Wander a moment before he could reply. "Thank you, Commandant."

Consuela turned to toss a gloat back toward the outraged communicator, when she caught sight of something out of the corner of her eye. She seized Wander's arm. "Wait a second."

"What's the matter?" He followed her eyes and said, "It's just another ensign logging in his ship."

"No, it's not," she cried. "That's *Rick!*"

CHAPTER ELEVEN

They did not like each other. That much was clear even before introductions were made.

No question about it, Rick looked incredibly dashing in his uniform. As the three of them walked the crew's passage back to his gate, every female crew member who passed granted him frankly assessing glances. Consuela would have enjoyed the questioning attention that consequently landed upon her, except for Wander. After the excitement she had shown over seeing Rick, Wander had retreated into his silent shell and had not emerged.

The passage forked, one way leading through customs and out into the port proper, the other back toward the eastport terminal gates. Wander stopped and announced, "I think I should report back to Pilot Grimson."

Consuela found herself reluctant to let him go. "Can't you leave it for just a little while?"

"I can see you want to speak with your homeworld friend," he said quietly, refusing even to look in Rick's direction.

"Yeah, look, I don't have much time," Rick agreed. "My ship's scheduled to lift off, soon as we onload a shipment."

Consuela found herself hurting from the look of sorrow in Wander's eyes. "He's just a friend," she said softly.

"Of course," Wander replied. He gave them a stiff nod and walked down the outgoing passage.

Consuela stayed where she was, watching his retreating back, until Rick pressed, "I've got to be getting back. They keep me on a short leash."

"Okay," she said and walked on, trying to collect herself. "What are you *doing* here?"

"What do you think?" Rick flashed his famous grin. "I came to rescue you."

She felt herself growing hot. "I can take care of myself."

"Sure, sure." Under the gaze of three attractive crew women, Rick's walk took on a swagger. "Anyway, do you want to hear what happened or not?"

"Tell me."

As she listened to his story, Consuela found herself thinking more of Wander than of the world she had left behind. Rick finished with, "The craziest thing is how I know all this stuff. Everything about the ship, you name it, I know it. Has that happened to you too?"

"No. But I have," she hesitated, then settled on, "some new abilities."

"Yeah, you're wearing a scout's robes. That means you're a sensitive, right?"

"Yes." But she was thinking of how sad Wander had looked when he had left them. Consuela gazed up at Rick, comparing his easy strength and unshakable confidence with Wander's quiet reserve. No, there wasn't any question whom she preferred.

"See what I mean? There's no way I could know anything like that." He pointed down a branch passage. "This is my gate."

Consuela tried to push her heart's concerns aside. "So do you want to go back home?"

"Yeah, sure. I mean, I've got to, right?" Then he turned and looked down the branch passage. "Do you think all this is real?"

"I don't know what to think."

"Me neither. Sure seems—"

"Ensign, is your captain on board?"

Consuela started at the sound of the voice echoing down the passageway and turned to see Grimson and Wander rapidly approaching. She watched Rick come stiffly to full alert and reply, "Should be. We're scheduled for lift-off soon."

"Find him, please. Tell him that Senior Pilot Grimson urgently needs to speak with him."

"Yes, Pilot."

"No, better still, we will follow you on board. This matter cannot wait." Brusquely the pilot motioned him forward. "Lead on, Ensign. Come along, you two."

Consuela fell into step alongside Wander. As the other two pulled ahead, she whispered, "What's going on?"

Wander shook his head. "He was looking for me. I've never seen him run—"

"Silence," Grimson rapped out.

The passage jinked and opened into a broad loading platform. Landing crew entered through the cargo passage. They manipulated hand controls to guide wheelless handcarts up the ramp and through the broad ship's portal. Two of the ship's crew inspected documents, checked each item off their noteboards, and assigned a hold number before permitting passage. When Grimson came into view, both crewmen snapped to startled attention.

"Ensign Richard with visitors for the captain," Rick announced, and the change in his voice caused Consuela to look at him anew.

The senior crewman raised his noteboard. "Names?"

"Senior Pilot Grimson and two scouts," the pilot snapped.

"I'll call him downside," the crewman said.

"You'll do no such thing. The matter is most urgent. I demand immediate entry."

Clearly the crewman had no interest in a confrontation with an irate pilot. "He's in the top outer hold with the supercargo."

"Notify him of our arrival. Lead on, Ensign. Hurry, man, hurry." Grimson motioned for Consuela and Wander to follow.

Consuela caught fleeting glimpses of vast holds, incredibly strange machinery, bustling technicians. As she rode the chute alongside Wander, she was gratified to see that the excitement of being in a ship had erased his earlier sorrow.

She took the moment of relative privacy to whisper, "Everything's all right, Wander. Really."

Wander tore his gaze from the vista beneath them. His face took on somber lines as he said, "The ensign is very handsome."

"Very," Consuela agreed.

"And he is from your homeworld. You must have a lot in common."

"Some. But we are still just friends."

"Why are you telling me this?"

She tried hard to open her gaze. "It's important to me that you understand, Wander. Rick is not a threat to us."

"To us?" he repeated softly.

"That's right," she said. "Us."

He started to speak, then glanced up. "Get ready to disembark."

Consuela turned away, stepped out, adjusted to the gravity change, and followed the pilot and Rick across the deck toward a pair of stout hold doors. But before they could push through, a hatchet-faced man emerged. The sharp-edged officer wore a uniform of darkest gray dressed with numerous gold insignias. "Senior Pilot Grimson?"

"Captain Arnol." The pilot gave a little bow. "Thank you for seeing me."

The captain maintained his cold rigidity. "I understand the matter is so urgent you could not obey proper procedures."

"That is correct. I would ask a favor."

That startled him. "A pilot asks a favor of a Hegemony freighter captain?"

"I understand that you are outbound and due to return here again in nine days' time."

"All that is a matter of record."

"I would ask that you take these two scouts with you on a training run."

Wander gasped aloud. Captain Arnol eyed him, then turned his attention back to the pilot. "This is most unusual."

"Indeed. So are the circumstances." Grimson held himself stiffly erect. "I would consider myself in your debt, Captain."

The captain studied him. "I have heard that Senior Pilot Grimson is a man of his word."

"You need but name your request, Captain."

"You are perhaps aware," Arnol replied slowly, "that I am up for consideration as captain of a new outbound passenger vessel."

"I was not," Grimson replied. "But I shall make it my business to become fully involved in the matter."

The captain unbent enough to nod once, then turned his attention to the two scouts. "How long have they been in training?"

"Scout Wander for just over two months. Scout Consuela for less than one week."

"A *week?*" The captain's ire mounted. "You are saddling me with a novice?"

Pilot Grimson hesitated, then said quietly, "They are both Talents."

Rick mirrored the captain's astonishment. "You're sure?"

"Absolutely certain."

"Two Talents based at this port?"

"Two Talents in the same scout squadron," Grimson replied. "And I have just received word that a diplomat is arriving this very afternoon."

"Ah. I understand your dilemma." Arnol hesitated, then said, "I must warn you, Pilot, that our destinations are Solarus and Avanti."

The pilot was clearly rocked by the news. "I wondered why the destinations were not stated on your manifest."

"As you can see, we have reasons for secrecy."

Grimson thought his way through a deep breath. "I have no choice. Yours is the only vessel scheduled for a swift return that departs before the diplomat's arrival."

"Very well." Captain Arnol turned to Rick and ordered, "Take them to Chief Petty Officer Tucker. Have him assign berths. Then get below and prepare for lift-off."

"Aye, aye, sir."

"You have earned a pilot's gratitude," Grimson said solemnly.

"No small matter. You must excuse me now, Pilot. We are approaching the final countdown, and I have a ship to run." Captain Arnol returned the pilot's bow, then said to Wander and Consuela, "Follow whoever gives you instructions. Stay in your berths until either I or the chief petty officer sends for you. A novice scout carries no authority on this ship. Step out of line, and you'll stand punishment detail like any other shipmate. Understand?"

"Yes, Captain," they chorused.

"I see they have landed in the correct pair of hands," Grimson said, then turned to the pair and ordered, "I have taken on a debt because of you. Repay me with correct shipboard service. I will give Captain Arnol's report my most careful scrutiny." He inspected them for a long moment, then walked to the down-chute and disappeared.

"All right," the captain barked. "Departure stations. On the bounce."

CHAPTER TWELVE

Consuela found the wait incredibly boring. Her cubbyhole had the same featureless quality of her room at port, only smaller. There was a limit to the amount of time she could nap, especially when she knew she was in a ship under power.

After what felt like days, the door opened to reveal Rick. He grinned and said, "The chief petty officer wants you on deck, Scout."

"Finally." She leapt from the seat, checked her hair in the mirror, and followed him into the passageway. "I never thought space could be so boring."

"Get used to it," he replied, stopping in front of Wander's door.

"What do you mean?"

"I'll let Petty Officer Tucker tell you." Rick made no move to open the portal. "Who is this guy, Consuela?"

"Wander is a friend. A good friend."

"Wander," he snickered. "What a name."

"He is the finest person I've ever met."

"That so?"

"Yes," she replied. "It is."

Rick did not show the jealousy she had half expected. Instead he seemed positively thrilled. "So you're falling for the guy."

"What if I am?"

"Hey, don't get me wrong. I think that's great."

"You sound relieved."

"Maybe so." Rick hesitated. "Last year I got burned by this girl back at school. I don't know, for some reason I was worried about you doing the same thing. But I haven't fallen for you, see, so everything's great. Really." He looked at her. "You don't think I'm a flake, do you?"

She started. It was exactly what she had been thinking. "I think you are too handsome for your own good," she said slowly. "And I think life is too easy for you."

Anger flared in his eyes. "That shows how well you know me."

"There's no need to get mad. You asked me what I thought."

"Yeah, well, thanks for nothing." He punched the door pad and watched Wander scramble to his feet. "Show time, sport. The chief petty officer doesn't like to be kept waiting. And watch yourselves in there. Something's got him in a bad state."

As they walked down the gently curving passageway, Consuela bumped up against Wander, swiftly grasped his hand, squeezed and released it. She felt a warm spot blossom in her heart with the delight that sprang to his face.

Still miffed, Rick asked as he walked, "You really think it's wise to get involved when we don't know how long—"

"Stop that," Consuela snapped back. "Right now."

"Just asking," he said, pleased to find a weak point. "I mean, you can't tell—"

"I'm warning you," Consuela declared.

Wander looked at her. "Is this the secret you wanted to tell me about?"

"Yes," she replied.

Rick stared over his shoulder. "You're going to try and explain it to him?"

"Lead on, Ensign," Consuela replied. "This is between Wander and me."

Rick snorted his derision. He stopped in front of a portal, keyed the intercom, and said, "Ensign Richard reporting with the two scouts."

"Enter."

The door sighed back to reveal one of the largest men Consuela had ever seen. He glanced up from his cluttered work station. "Scouts Wander and Consuela, do I have that right?" From beneath bushy eyebrows he gave them a dour inspection. "Neither of you have worked flight duty before, is that not also true?"

"I have never been on a ship before," Wander replied.

He glowered at them. "We ask for Starfleet help," he groused. "Every outbound voyage. We hear nothing for years on end, and now this?"

Consuela followed Wander's lead and said nothing.

"I am Chief Petty Officer Tucker, Tuck to my friends, which you two are most certainly not. I won't make any secret of it, I don't have much time for sensitives, nor do my crew. You'll be well advised to stay in your berths except when you're standing watch. Ensign Richard here has offered to escort you to and from flight deck and to deliver your meals."

"But that's like being in prison," Consuela protested.

"Not at all," the petty officer replied with vast satisfaction. "Ship's company have no right to order sensitives about; I know that as well as the next man. You're welcome to go anywhere you want, any time you want. But don't come crawling to me if some mate decides to let you have it. I guarantee your protection only if you obey my rules." He settled massive forearms on his paperwork and leaned forward. "Stay in your quarters if you know what's good for you."

"But why would they want to hurt us?" Consuela demanded. "I've never even seen the inside of a ship before."

"More's the pity," Tucker barked. "Let's just say that your kind has let us down one time too many." He glowered at them a moment longer, then picked up a form and said, "Now then. Captain Arnol says he wants to have you train together. Save him the need of repeating things. You sensitives are limited to a four-hour shift each Standard day, so—"

"I'd like to volunteer for more duty," Wander said and swiftly passed a look Consuela's way.

"Me too," she piped in.

He dropped the duty roster. "What's that?"

"I would like to go for watch and watch," Wander said.

The barrel-chested man leaned back in his chair and gave Wander a hard look. "You're telling me that we've got us a pair of sensitives who are volunteering for four hours on, four off?" He glanced at Rick. "Have you ever heard of a sensitive volunteering for anything, Ensign?"

"Chief Petty Officer, I—"

"Never mind." He lumbered to his feet. "This is one for the captain. Come along, all of you."

The hostility that flanked them between decks was as searing as a blowtorch. Consuela felt eyes burning into her from every direction. Clearly the crew had been alerted to their presence, and those they passed slowed and stared with undisguised loathing. She struggled to follow Wander's example and ignore them all.

She gasped at the star-flecked vista that greeted her inside the control room, but Captain Arnol granted them little time for relishing the view. He received the chief petty officer's report, then turned his knife-edged features their way and demanded, "Well? What have you got to say for yourselves?"

"Nothing, Captain," Wander replied. "We just want to volunteer for extra duty."

"None of your kind ever volunteers for anything," he snapped. "I'd rather play nanny to a shipload of dowagers than spend one watch with most sensitives. Your Pilot Grimson is an exception, I'll grant you that. Did he put you up to this?"

"No, Captain."

"If this is somebody's idea of a prank, they'll be scrubbing the thruster tubes while we're still under power, and before this watch is over, I can promise you that." A snicker rose from the chamber's far corner, until the captain whirled about and lashed out, "Quiet!"

He then turned back and demanded, "Let's have the real reason, and right smart, mister. And mark my words, I won't stand for nonsense from you or anybody else."

"I've waited all my life for this moment," Wander said quietly.

The few heads still bent over instruments rose and joined the others staring their way.

"What's that?" Arnol said.

"Going to space is all I've ever dreamed of," Wander replied.

The captain's gaze narrowed as he searched Wander's face. "You're telling me you *want* to stand watch on a Hegemony freighter?"

"It's still space," Wander replied. "I want to learn."

The attention swung to bore into Consuela. "You have anything to add to that?"

"I wouldn't give most of the sensitives I've met the time of day," Consuela said.

"You don't say," the captain said slowly. "Chief Petty Officer, have you ever heard the like?"

"Never in all my born days, Skipper."

The captain backed two paces and settled into his chair. He pointed to his right, where a seat stood isolated behind a separate console, and said, "Observe, if you please. That is the pilot's chair. How long have I skippered this freighter, Tucker?"

"Going on five and a half years, Captain."

"And how often have you seen that chair occupied?"

"Not the first minute, Skipper. Not the very first."

"Signals," he barked.

"Aye, aye, Captain."

"How many requests have you sent during this voyage for a sensitive to give us a hand?"

"Same as every voyage for the past seven months," the signals officer replied, his eyes never leaving the pair of them. "Once every Standard day."

"And what does our message book log in?"

"Same as what we've got outside our ports, Skipper," Signals replied. "A lot of nothing."

"So what happens," the captain went on, "but in the middle of a stop-over, a senior pilot rushes up, asks me to do him the favor, the *favor*, of taking two Talents on board?"

There was a unison of indrawn breath around the room. From behind them, Chief Petty Officer Tucker asked, "So the scuttlebutt was true? They really are Talents?"

"So the senior pilot said. Mind you, he also told me that the boy here has had a grand total of two months' training, and the girl somewhat less. How much was it again, Scout?"

Consuela lifted her chin and replied, "Three days."

"Three days," Captain Arnol replied, nodding slowly. "So they are what you might call novices. Still, the pilot sounded very definite about their abilities. Either of you ever spaced before?"

"No, Captain."

"So how did you know to volunteer for watch and watch?"

"I stood it in the Control Tower," Wander replied.

"Under a communicator's supervision, I take it."

"One watch I stood alone," Wander replied. "The one before we were brought on board."

The captain permitted himself a wintry smile. "Let us hope it was not so disastrous a watch that the pilot decided he had to be rid of you."

"The watch commandant said he would be happy to stand watch with Wander again," Consuela announced proudly.

"Did he now?" His eyes still on Consuela, Arnol said, "You ever heard of that one before, Tucker?"

"Definitely another for the books, Skipper."

The man next to the captain intoned, "Ten minutes to the first attack zone, Skipper."

"Thank you, Helmsman." He resumed his steely calm. "Chief Petty Officer, see if you and the ensign can swing a second chair behind the pilot's console."

"Aye, aye, Captain."

"Mind you disconnect the power supply," the captain said, swinging back around. "Hate to think what would happen if they had the mind amp and power chair on together."

"Maybe an improvement," suggested someone from the room's corner.

"Enough of that. Weapons team, power up."

"Weapons powered and full on, Captain."

"Signals?"

"Tracking and all clear."

"Thrusters?"

"One-third power, ready to redline on your command."

"Chief Petty Officer, the men are prepared?"

"All stations manned and ready, Skipper. They won't be boarding this vessel."

"Standard watches, Tucker. Can't have the men jumping at shadows the whole voyage."

"As you ordered, Skipper," the burly man replied, muscling a chair in behind the pilot's console. "But they'll be sleeping with one eye on the ready-light, believe you me."

"You two settle in," Captain Arnol ordered. "I have little experience in training sensitives—none at all, in fact. So for the time being I expect you to watch and listen and learn what you can. Know how to power a ship's amp?"

"I think so," Wander said hopefully, seating himself and running one excited hand over the console. "It looks a lot like the Tower controls."

"Five minutes, Skipper."

"Signals, ready to alert?"

"On your command, Captain."

"Everybody, stay awake."

Rick spoke up tentatively, "Request permission to remain on deck, Captain."

"Any objections, Tucker?"

"None, sir."

"Then seat yourself and power on, son."

"Three minutes, Skipper."

Wander reached into his belt-pouch and brought out two headsets. "Grimson gave them to me back when he found me in the port passage," he whispered. "Turn the damping mechanism on full. I'll start the amp on low, and power up slowly. Tell me when you're ready."

Consuela checked the dial, fitted her headset in place, and whispered, "Go ahead."

"Two minutes, Captain."

Slowly, very slowly Wander spun the console's central dial. "Feel anything?"

"Not yet. What's got everybody in a lather?"

"I don't know, but—" then he stopped. He had to. His attention was captured by the transformation in the vista overhead.

Consuela followed his gaze upward. Stretching out from the nose of the ship was a broad ribbon of golden light. She breathed, "What is *that?*"

"A lightway," Rick said quietly from behind them.

"Sixty seconds and counting," intoned the signals officer.

Consuela's heightened sensitivity gave her the feeling of stretching out beyond the flight deck, reaching out to every aspect of the ship. She reveled in the sensation of tracing her way through the myriad of passages, racing at the speed of thought from nose to powering thrusters.

"Fifteen seconds."

The ship was a chorus of signals and images, far too complex for her to take in, but wondrous in the sense of not just riding in a ship, but joining with it. Flying through space, intimately connected with the vessel and its power—

Then she leapt out of her seat with a shriek of disgust, and flung the headset across the room. Wander shouted and writhed and sent his headset spinning directly into the captain's back.

"Skipper, look!"

Consuela tore at her robes, flinging them about, then convulsively shook her head and body. She had the fleeting image of a million metal insects crawling all over her body, and she shrieked again.

Then it was gone.

She stood on shaky legs, her chest heaving. Wander raised himself from where he had been rubbing his body across the decks. He gasped, "Is it over?"

"Signals!" The captain's steel gray eyes gleamed with excitement. "Mark the spot!"

"On target, Skipper. To the decimal point."

"I was right!" Captain Arnol pounded the armrest, his gaze glued to the pair of scouts who struggled to gather themselves. "The shadow-lanes are real!"

CHAPTER THIRTEEN

The atmosphere in the officers' mess was heavy with suspicion. Captain Arnol was held in too much esteem for the gathered officers to voice outright objections, yet they clearly resented having two young scouts granted entry, and resented eating in their company. Several of the more senior veterans shoved their plates aside untouched and fastened the pair with hostile glares.

Rick sat in the chair closest to the outer door and said not a word. His post was known as the Ensign's Corner, and he was placed there to do the bidding of whichever officer spoke in his direction. He stared as frankly as the others at Wander and Consuela. Their resolute calm had a disturbing effect on him. They seemed so *connected*. He could see from the briefest of glances that Consuela cast in Wander's direction that she was truly smitten with the guy. There was such love in her eyes, such admiration. But what she saw in the slender kid with the sad eyes was utterly beyond Rick. Especially since this whole world might just disappear at any moment. And especially when she could have had him.

The doorchime sounded, and the chief petty officer appeared. "You sent for me, Skipper?"

"That I did, Tucker. You've been telling me about our new ensign's encyclopedic knowledge."

"Aye, Captain. That's right, I have." Tucker shot a worried glance Rick's way.

All Rick could do was shrug in reply. He had no idea what this was about.

"Fine, fine." Captain Arnol seemed entirely at ease, but it was the quiet of a tensely coiled spring. He curled one hand about his steaming mug and said, "I thought you might like to be here for the examination."

Rick froze as all eyes turned his way.

"Draw up a chair, Tucker."

"Aye, aye, Captain." The chief petty officer looked as troubled as Rick felt. "But the lad has only been on board for a few days now."

"I know, I know. But I just wanted to acquaint myself with what you've been talking about." He cast a frosty glance down to the table's end. "The chief petty officer has been telling me that he has yet to come up with a question that you can't answer."

Rick swallowed.

"I was wondering, Ensign, if you would tell our two guests a little about the freighters working the internal Hegemony spaceways."

Petty Officer Tucker did a double take as he glanced down the table and spotted the two scouts. "Skipper, I—"

"Let the lad speak, Tucker," the captain said easily. "What do your friends call you, Ensign?"

"Rick."

"As you have observed, Rick, we like to keep our mess on an informal footing. You can refer to me as Skipper, if you like. That is, unless you have earned my wrath, in which case it would be wise if you did not speak at all."

A ripple of amusement ran down the table. From his previous times at mess, Rick recognized this pattern of questions from the captain as a time-honored tradition. It granted the most junior officers an occasion to speak, when otherwise they would be forced to sit and listen to their seniors dominate the conversation.

Captain Arnol went on, "Now let us see just how far your band of knowledge extends."

Rick found that his throat had suddenly become as dry as cotton. He sipped from his glass, and in that instant felt the knowledge surface. "There are two types of freighters traveling the Hegemony lightways," he replied, wondering if his surprise registered on his face. "The licensed Free Traders and us, the Hegemony's own fleet. We carry all government-issue freight, as well as supplies destined for government bases, outposts, monitor-stations, and Hegemony mining asteroids. We also supply the military. There are private companies who also use our services, especially in some areas."

Arnol nodded. "And why, pray tell, would a private company wish to use us for carrying freight, when the Free Traders are known to be far less expensive?"

"Because the Free Traders avoid the danger zones," Rick replied, and wondered how he could feel so certain about something when he had no idea where it sprang from. "In some areas we are the only vessels that ply the route."

"And what constitutes a danger zone?"

"Three or more vessels lost on a target-route within one Standard year."

"What did I tell you?" Tucker exclaimed. "Not bad for a lad who's never been inbound before in his life."

The captain was less easily impressed. "What reason can you give for these losses?"

The answer, when it came, shocked him so that Rick had difficulty replying. "Pirates."

"What can you tell us about their operations?"

"They are almost impossible to catch, even detect," Rick said, his response slowed by the import of his words. "We know they are active because ships have sent final communiques before contact has been lost. By measuring these contact break-points, we have found that the attacks take place at certain spots along the lightways. Transporters and freighters are beginning to call them strike-points."

Captain Arnol demanded, "Have you been granted access to classified documents?"

"No, Skipper," he replied.

"Then how—" He turned to his chief petty officer. "You were quite right in your assessment, Tucker."

"Thank you, Skipper."

The captain swung his attention back to Rick and demanded, "Have you in your studies ever come across the term shadowlane?"

"Rumors only, Skipper," he replied, gaining strength from the approving looks about the table—especially those of the pretty young assistant signals officer stationed at the room's far end. "It is thought that there might be decommissioned lightways, routes set in the dim recesses of space history."

The captain nodded his approval. "Well done, Rick. You may now breathe easy."

"Thank you, Skipper," he said and permitted himself a grin. Then he caught sight of Consuela's knowing gaze, and for some reason he found the moment losing some of its glory. As though he hadn't earned it. He found himself becoming angry. Maybe the others were right after all. These sensitives just didn't belong.

"Before we move on," the captain said, "do our guests have any questions?"

"I do," Consuela offered. "What is a lightway?"

The power control lieutenant, a sharp-jawed woman whose glances made Rick's skin crawl, snorted her derision. He was not overly sorry when Arnol shifted about and glared her way.

The captain demanded, "What is our policy toward honest questions?"

The lieutenant straightened and intoned, "Ignorance in areas other than a shipmate's expertise is excused, and honest questions are welcomed." She shot an angry glance toward the scouts, as though the reprimand were their fault.

"Remember that." He turned his attention to the junior helmswoman, a brilliant former ship's ensign who, according to ship gossip, was slated for bigger things. "Perhaps you would be willing to explain the target-route we follow, Irene."

"Captain," Tucker interrupted, "if you'll not be needing me—"

"Bear with me a moment longer," the captain said, and then to the helmswoman, "Go on."

"Lightways were developed in an earlier spacing era," Irene began. "They are carefully measured routes that the Hegemony used to connect major world systems. They run between Hegemony systems and derive their power from the suns to which they are anchored. At the time of their development, ships would power out from an orbital system, accelerating along the lightway, punch through n-space, then decelerate and enter planetary orbit. Lightways are limited in length to twenty-five parsecs, and in earlier times they essentially defined the Hegemony's size. Then you sensitives were discovered, and about the same time the system of vortex transport was developed."

"And now the limits are very different," the captain took over. "Stand down, Irene. Well done."

"Thank you, Skipper."

"Our limits are your limits," Captain Arnol went on, his attention now fully on the scouts. "There are never enough pilots, and they are always assigned to outbound starships. The number of starships is restricted to the number of active pilots. The few Talents that surface are assigned to

Starfleet Command or conscripted into the Hegemony's diplomatic service. And there are never enough Talents, never enough pilots, never enough communicators, never enough sensitives of any kind.

"Exercising control over pilots is one way Starfleet holds the reigns of power. Which means that an urgent request from some inbound freighter for a pilot to help track down rumors goes unheeded. Three lost vessels per Standard year on certain routes is a small price to pay, when the Hegemony struggles to control outworld regimes with too few ships. The empire is constantly fraying along the edges, and there are never enough sensitives to staff every point. Am I getting through?"

"Yes, Captain," they intoned.

"Not to mention the fact that pilots scorn inbound duty. They consider it beneath them, even when their absence means that my ship is at threat every time we traverse a danger zone. Every one of my shipmates has friends who have been lost to the pirates, killed, or sold into slavery. So perhaps you can now understand why your presence is not so welcome."

He dipped a finger in his cup, and drew a straight line of coffee across the table. He then stabbed the line's midpoint and said, "Many of us have wondered why it is that these pirates attack only at certain points along the lightways. And why our inbound police vessels have had such difficulty in tracking them. What if, we ask, it was because they did not use the lightways at all. What if they had their own routes which only *intersected* ours."

He drew a second diagonal line across the table. "What if they were forced to remain upon their shadowlanes just as we must upon our lightways. We have rumors that this is so."

"Rumors," spat the senior weapons officer. "Rumors and lies and the tales of paid informants who would swear the lost golden moon of Altinthor has appeared above my homeworld, if only I would pay to hear it said."

"Yet rumors are all we have," Captain Arnol replied. "It is said that tribes of thieves have burrowed deep into rogue worlds, sunless balls of ice which in eons past escaped from solar orbit." He moved his cup to one side and leaned across the table. "We and other ships who think there might be something to these rumors have been begging Hegemony for Talents to see if the shadowlanes can be detected. We find nothing suspicious on our instruments, nothing at all. And this is why we who think the rumors might hold truth are opposed by many who think otherwise."

"I for one," the weapons officer said. "The pirates must have learned a way of shielding their ships, nothing more. We know for a fact the slavers have stunners strong enough to break through our shields without cracking our skins. Their cloaking devices are a new technology, I warrant, and nothing more. They stay clear of our detection until they attack, and they attack only when we're too far from help." He looked scornfully across at the pair. "I for one say keep the sensitives off our ship, and good riddance to the lot of them. What we need is to stop spending time on these overbred overspoiled prima donnas and build ourselves better ships with more powerful weapons."

Rick nodded his agreement. That made sense to him. The guy sounded like his coach giving the same pre-season speech year after year—strive for strength, sweat for guts, go for glory. Besides, maybe this would wipe that superior attitude off Consuela's face.

The senior weapons officer's gaze flickered in Rick's direction, but all he said was, "We don't need to analyze these pirates, Captain. We need to have Starfleet build us better weapons so we can blast them out of the sky."

The captain calmly waited until the senior weapons officer was through, then said, "Any officer on this ship is welcome to voice his or her opinion at mess, as long as the captain's decision is fully obeyed and his orders willingly carried out. Is that clear, Guns?"

"Aye, aye, Skipper," came the growled reply.

"Very well." He turned back to the pair. "Now tell us what you felt at the zero mark, Scout."

"Like a hundred metal fingers were digging under my skin," Wander replied.

"It was horrible," Consuela agreed.

The captain turned and gave the senior weapons officer a very long look. Then he asked, "Signals, when is our next suspected strike point?"

"Five hours, plus or minus." He automatically checked his chrono, then continued, "We have our first null-space crossover in one hour and fifty-one minutes. Following that, we start the countdown. But it's a questionable, Skipper. One freighter missing, no communications prior to loss."

"Scouts, I cannot order you to stand another watch," the captain said, his eyes still locked with the weapons officer's. "But I would ask you. Could you endure the experience again?"

Wander exchanged glances with Consuela, then replied for them both, "If it would help the ship."

"It might," the captain replied. "It very well might." He released the weapons officer and turned to the chief petty officer. "Do you see why I asked you to stay, Tucker?"

"Yes, Skipper," the burly man replied, his astonished gaze flickering back and forth across the table.

"See that word spreads through the crew. Let them know we have a couple of sensitives who are standing double watch to help us out."

"They won't believe it."

"Perhaps not. But it may give them pause before making trouble." To the pair he said, "Watch yourselves between decks. I am hereby ordering all my officers to assist you, and granting you full access to the officers' quarters. You are also granted temporary pilot's status on the flight deck, which means you may come and go as you please."

"Thank you, Captain," Wander replied, the exultation clear in his voice.

"Skipper," the senior weapons officer interrupted. "I'd be willing to take the ensign here under my wing for a spell."

That brought a smile to Captain Arnol's face. "This is indeed an officer's mess I won't soon forget. Does the offer pass muster with you, Tucker?"

"It's a bit early in the game, Skipper, but as I've said, this lad shows all the makings of a good officer."

"Very well, I approve." The captain turned to Rick and said, "You should know, Ensign, that you are being accorded quite an honor. First of all, Chief Petty Officer Tucker is known through the Hegemony as a tough taskmaster, and he's had nothing but praise for you—something that has little to do with your book learning."

"Thank you, Captain," Rick said, glorying in the fact that Consuela was there to hear it.

"And secondly, this is the first time in my memory that our senior weapons officer has volunteered to work with any ensign on this ship. He is known as the best marksman riding the inbound lightways, and I am constantly fighting off attempts by other ships to lure him away. You will do well to listen with care and obey with alacrity."

"Aye, aye, Skipper."

Arnol glanced at the wall chronolog and rose to his feet. "All but those whose watch begins now are dismissed until T minus fifteen minutes."

Chapter Fourteen

"I take it you don't have any more time for these sensitives than I do."

"No, Senior Weapons Officer."

"Call me Guns." The senior weapons officer marched down the passage with all the grace of an impatient bull. He was not a big man, but Rick would not want to tangle with him. Muscles corded up taut under every square inch of exposed skin. His knuckles were as knotted as gravel, his nose looked twice broken, and a pouch of scar tissue split his left eyebrow.

Guns was a man who liked to fight, with or without his weapons. "Sensitives, pah! Wouldn't give a barrel full of space for the whole lot of them. They can't even sit in a powered chair, you know. Saw it happen once when I was about your age. Novice sat down without disconnecting, the skipper powered up for takeoff, and next thing anybody knew the sensitive was fried. Wouldn't shed a tear if it happened to the whole lot of them."

Rick felt as though he were barely touching the deck. He was still junior officer on the ship, but here he was, being treated like one of the crew. It reminded him of how he had felt when he had finally made the varsity team.

There were still vague whispers circulating through his mind and heart, questioning where he was and what he knew. But this place was real. He no longer doubted that. Real as anything he had left behind in Baltimore. He could not explain what was going on, and to be honest was caring less and less about the hows and whys with each passing hour. The challenge was great, the action fast, the opportunities tremendous.

Rick was having the time of his life.

The senior weapons officer cast him a canny glance. "You look like a fighter to me, lad. Am I right?"

"There was a sport I played before—" Rick stopped and corrected himself, "Back home. It was called a contact sport, but it was really a stylized battle. I loved it."

"Thought so," Guns said. "Others mighta been fooled by that pretty face of yours, but I know a warrior when I see one."

A *warrior*. Rick thrilled to the sound. "I really appreciate your giving me a chance."

"Earn the privilege," Guns replied. "Do well and make me proud."

The flight deck was structured as four pyramids of platforms set like great steps. Chromed railings and curved flight consoles separated each dais. The captain's chair stood isolated upon the central and highest dais. Before and below him were the helmsmen's three chairs. Engine, Power, and Signals claimed the three other pyramid bases—curving embankments interconnected by joined consoles like petals of three flowers grown together into one. At the crest of the signals platform was the pilot's chair. At the top of the power pyramid stood the weapons console.

Guns relieved the duty officer, then maneuvered the dais' second chair up close to his own, clamped it down, and flicked the power switch. "You won't be sleeping much these next few weeks," he warned. "I'll be expecting you to spend your off-duty hours on your hands and knees, getting to know our weapons better than your mother knew your father."

"I can do without sleep, Guns."

"That's the spirit. I'll be assigning you a gunner's mate who'll walk you through the lovelies. You'll come to know them by name, or I'll know the reason why." He pointed at the two arm-consoles and the three-tiered structure, which could be raised over the chairback. "Next few days we'll do some dry-firing runs, let you get a feel for the triggers. But first we've got to see if there's a match here."

Consuela and Wander chose that moment to enter the flight deck. Although she did not look his way, Rick found himself acutely aware of her presence. She spoke to Wander in the low tones of two people concerned only with each other. He found himself growing hot with anger.

Guns noticed his reaction, glanced over, and grunted, "Aye, they get under my skin too. But they've got the captain's blessing, so you'll do well to ignore them. Arnol's not a man to brook an officer going against his bidding." He patted the arm of Rick's chair. "Now set yourself down."

The chair conformed to Rick's contours as he settled, then extended two bands that Guns pulled up across his shoulders and fastened to the chairback. "We don't normally bother with the straps unless we're on alert."

"What are they for?"

"You'll see." He settled into his own chair. "Weapons can't be learned from a book. Either you've got what it takes to be a gunnery officer, or you don't. Ready?"

Rick shrugged as far as the shoulder straps would allow. "I guess so."

"Watch my actions." He keyed in his console. "Green light for all systems. But they're separate. We call this resting at arms. Standard ops for non-alert."

"What do you mean, separate?"

Instead of replying, Guns flipped his comm switch and demanded, "If that was a snore I just heard, I'll have you swabbing down the outer hull while we're under power."

"No need to talk that way, Guns," came back the laconic reply. "You know I don't snore."

"That you, Simmer?"

"Now who else would it be, this watch?"

"I'm taking a new boy through a dry run. Stand by with power."

"Power standing by," came the droned response. "Hope you singe his eyebrows for waking me up."

"What should I call you, Ensign?"

"Rick."

"All right, Rick. Grab hold of your socks." With both hands Guns pushed up two parallel series of levers.

Rick gripped his armrests in an uncontrollable spasm as the power flooded in. But it was not power as he had known in the ensign's duty chair. This was power with focus. Power with purpose. Power with *menace*.

His awareness coursed through the ship, directed by the instruments under Guns' control toward the four great chambers flanking the ship's thrusters. The weapons were situated beside the thrusters, he realized, because they drew from the same power source. Shield, thruster, and weapons, all powered by the same miniature star burning fiercely at the ship's heart.

"Shield," Guns said softly, and Rick could scarcely see his hand touch the controls. He was drawn inexorably out to the force-field that surrounded the ship, watched it mount from standard power to full attack status, and felt the power surge through himself as well. He *felt* it.

"Tracking systems," Guns intoned, and Rick felt himself connect to the signals station, then move outward, sniffing the boundaries of space for incoming threats, anything that he could fasten onto and attack.

"Weapons," Guns said, and Rick bucked against the straps as the spasm locked his muscles. The power was *enormous*. The dampers were lifted, and a shining arm of the ship's star reached out to awaken the dormant might. Rick felt the same strength course through his own limbs, and he wanted to roar with the primeval lust for battle. He was no longer a puny human, formed of mere flesh and bone. He was a warrior knight of old, encased in battle armor, shielded and armed and *ready*.

"Enough," Guns said, and swept the levers back toward him.

The power and the image faded. "What did you do that for?"

Guns inspected him carefully, then nodded. "Just as I thought," he said approvingly. "I've got myself a natural on my hands."

But Rick was not ready to let it go. "Can't you just—"

"One step at a time, lad. One step at a time. Can't be having you hooked to weapons through a n-space push. Not 'til you're good and trained." The weapons officer flicked the console to standby. "Release yourself from the straps and go fetch me a mug of coffee. You'll find the makings in the alcove beside the portal."

Rick fumbled for the catches, then raised himself with difficulty. His legs were as weak as after the first practice of the season. But the sensation of power stayed with him. He walked to the alcove, surrounded by the mantle of force that he had at his command.

A dulcet voice behind him asked, "How is Guns treating you?"

Rick turned to find himself facing the assistant signals officer, an auburn-haired beauty whose feminine form could not be disguised by the austere uniform. "That was the most incredible thing I've ever known in my life."

She smiled with eyes the same burnished shade as her hair. "Maybe we could meet after watch and you can tell me about it."

The surging might awakened by the weapons system took on a different focus. Rick felt his entire being vibrating with the strength of his desire. It enflamed him. "I'd like that," he said, his voice as shaky as his legs. "Very much."

The young woman noted the change with a welcoming smile. "I'll come by your cabin," she said softly, and turned away.

When Rick returned to the weapons station, Guns accepted his mug and said, "She's a pretty young thing, that one."

Rick slumped back down in his chair and mumbled, "Don't tell me that's off limits."

"You are ordered to keep up with your duties and learn the weapons systems backward and forward. If you've still got the strength to do anything besides sleep after that, then what you do off watch is nobody's business but your own." The weapons officer took a sip, then grinned, exposing teeth worn to flat stumps by constant grinding. "Gunnies have a reputation to uphold on and off the flight deck, Ensign. Remember that."

———

"Ten minutes to null-space transition," droned the helmsman.

Wander watched Consuela settle into the chair beside him, and asked, "Did you notice how it felt with the amp on before we hit the shadowlane?"

"As if I were expanding," Consuela replied. She picked up her headset and fitted it on. No one paid them any attention. The countdown to null-space transition kept everyone on the flight deck fully occupied.

"Right. That was less than one-tenth power, and with the headset damping mechanism on full." Wander scanned the flight deck. "But there won't be any noise here on the sensitive level until after we make transition."

"So?"

"So I'd like to stay hooked on while we make the passage through n-space."

"Do you think that's wise?"

He shrugged. "It's the first time I've ever been in a ship, and the first time I've been someplace where it's *quiet*. I want to try out this amping system, see what it does. How else am I going to learn how to guide a starship through uncharted null-space?"

Consuela thought it over and decided, "Then I want to do it with you."

He grinned. "I was hoping you'd say that."

"Then we'd better hurry." She fitted on her headset. "One tiny bit of power at a time, okay?"

"Don't worry." He unfastened the damping box from both their headsets, fitted his headset to his temples, and switched on the pilot's console. "If you start feeling anything unpleasant, tell me and I'll power down. Ready?"

She settled back in her chair. "Yes."

"Here goes." He nudged the amp dial.

"Oh, my." Immediately her senses were extended to the ship and beyond.

Wander turned the dial back to zero just as the helmsman chanted the five-minute call. "That was pretty strong, wasn't it?"

"How much did you give us?"

"Less than one percent."

She gaped. "The dial goes to one hundred?"

"Look for yourself." He leaned out of the way so she could see. "The normal range runs up to sixty percent. The top portion is what Senior Pilot Grimson called the Stellar range, that's handled by the override here. Then there's the redline." He traced a finger around the stable control meter. "You have to remember, this was developed to work with sensitives who don't hear *anything* without being hooked up to the amp. I've never seen directions for how it works with a Talent."

"Two minutes," intoned the helmsman.

"What do you think we should do?"

He thought it over. "Let's take it one step at a time. This first transition, we'll stay undamped but with no amp power, and see how we feel. Maybe go a little higher on the next transition, and see if we can chart our way."

The captain completed his final station-by-station check just as the helmsman began chanting down the seconds. Despite Wander's calm confidence, Consuela felt a thrill of nerves. "I wish I could hold your hand."

Reluctantly Wander shook his head. "I don't think that'd be a good idea. Not on the flight deck."

"Ten," chanted the helmsman. "Nine, eight, seven, six . . . "

And then time began to slow.

Gradually Consuela's attention was stretched in two, a physical portion linked to the steady chanting, and a mental which began to slow and stretch like taffy. Except for Wander's calm presence there beside her, she would have been terrified.

The ship continued along the carefully charted and computed course, barreling down the lightway, increasing speed at a steady rate until the final second, the final nudge, and the instantaneous push through nullspace. Beyond time, beyond physical reality, in and out in the span of no time at all, not even a microsecond.

Yet there had been something. Between the elastic final second and the return to the first stretched second after transition, her sense of awareness moved beyond the vastness of space. There was an instant beyond time, and at that point something called to her at the very deepest level. Something so powerful and yet so comforting that sensing it created an answering voice in her heart. A soundless, wordless keening, a yearning for that which she somehow felt she had known all along, yet never truly known. Something she had lost, yet never had.

The helmsman's chant began counting back up the seconds, the power officer intoned the gradual braking reduction in force, and little by little the sense of physical time and mental time meshed back together for her. Wander rose unsteadily to his feet. His voice trembled slightly as he said, "I need a break."

Consuela needed both hands to pull off her headset. "Did you hear it?"

"I'm not sure what I heard," he replied and pushed himself to his feet. "Let me take a moment's rest, then we'll talk."

CHAPTER FIFTEEN

"I don't like it," Consuela whispered. "It's too dangerous."

"Less dangerous than the ship going into a possible strike-point cold," Wander replied. "The captain has already said he's going to place the ship on full alert. All they have to go on are records of a couple of ships that disappeared between standard communication checks."

They had been arguing since transition. Wander's idea was to try to extend their awareness beyond the ship, and see if the shadowlane could be identified in advance. Knowing Wander was right did not make it any easier to accept. "But what if—"

"You know we're going to try," Wander told her, settling into his seat. "We can keep arguing, or we can just go ahead and start."

His calm resolve robbed her of the will to resist. She settled into her own chair, said, "Promise me you'll take it easy."

"The first sign of trouble," he assured her, "and we retreat immediately."

The flight deck was quiet, each station staffed by only one crewman. But it was a tense calm, a time of waiting. The fifteen-minute checks were done with voices clipped and strained by what all knew lay ahead.

"That transition reminded me of something. When I was little," she began, then hesitated, caught by the look he gave her as he turned from his controls. "What is it?"

"That is the first time you have spoken of your childhood," he said. "Go on. What happened?"

"I went to a church around the corner sometimes. It was safe there, and quiet, and people were nice. Sometimes I had a sense of being connected with, I don't know, something *beyond*. But as I grew older I thought it was childish, and I needed to put it aside. Now I'm not so sure."

Wander watched her for a moment, then said softly, "I would like to know all about when you were young."

"It was not a happy time."

"No," he said, his eyes deepening with compassion. "Perhaps that's why it seems so special to share the memories."

She reached over, squeezed his hand, not caring who noticed or what they thought. Her heart was simply too full to let the moment go without some act of sharing.

He let the moment linger, a bond growing between them, then finally said, "Ready to start?"

"If you are."

"Okay." Reluctantly he released her hand, turned back to the dials, said, "We will take this one small step at a time."

Consuela adjusted her headset, leaned back, and sighed as the power began surging, granting her that sense of expansion. With the first nudge of power, she felt her awareness pushed beyond the flight deck to encompass the entire ship. Not touching anything, not belonging anywhere. Another notch up the power-scale, and she felt herself extending beyond the ship itself, moving into the toneless depths of neighboring space. Another nudge, and she grew able to travel up and down the lightway, moving ahead of the ship, holding on to the security of her chair, feeling the ship anchoring her physically as her heightened senses reached out farther and farther.

"Can you hear me?" Wander whispered.

"Yes."

"Do you want to go on?"

"Maybe just a little."

A fourth nudge, and she found herself better able to focus if she closed her eyes. A fifth, and she knew if she wanted she could alter her mental course and begin searching space in every direction. Yet she did not reach out. She could not. It was hard enough to remain anchored in the speeding ship, her attention stretched outward along the lightway, without reaching through the vastness of empty space. She was afraid if she moved too far from the lightway's established path she might never find her way back.

A sixth notch up the power scale, and her awareness shot forward, flying down the lightway that she measured her distance in time the ship would take to travel, like inches along a golden ruler. And there it was. A second shadowlane. Much smaller than the previous one, a dark ribbon etched into the fabric of space, empty and lifeless.

A seventh nudge, and she flew further still. Then she became aware of something else. Something *more*.

————

"There isn't anything I can teach this lad," Simmers announced to the senior weapons officer. Simmers was a lanky gunner's mate whose laconic air belied a mind as sharp as a knife.

In their first few moments together, Rick had quickly surmised that Simmers loved his machines and would brook no slacking when it came to learning the tasks at hand. Which made the sudden appearance of the required knowledge that much more pleasing.

"He musta memorized the entire ship's weapons manuals," Simmers reported. "Even knew the wiring and circuitry patterns."

Guns bore down hard on Rick. "You told me the truth about your background?"

"Yes, Senior Weapons Officer."

"Never seen anything like it in all my born days," Simmers declared.

"I have ways of checking this out," Guns warned. "Changing your name won't help you in the end."

"I've never spaced before in my life, honest," Rick said.

"We'll see about that," he growled. Then his gaze flickered to the other side of the flight deck. "What's this, what's this?"

Rick turned to see Captain Arnol climb to the pilot's dais and lean against the console as Wander spoke low and urgently.

"Those the sensitives Tucker was going on about?" Simmers asked quietly.

"Aye, and there's trouble a'brewing, you can bet your back teeth on that," Guns rumbled. "Wonder what mischief they're scheming up over there."

The captain checked the chrono read-out, then demanded, "Signals, we still on target for our next danger zone?"

"Aye, Skipper. Such that it is." The junior signals officer coded in her console, then replied, "A highly questionable strike-point a half-parsec from here. One freighter missing and presumed, two Standards ago."

He looked back to Wander. "You notice anything that close in?"

Together they nodded. "It was another shadowlane," Wander replied. "Smaller than the other one. But nothing else."

Captain Arnol turned back to the signals officer and demanded "What's our travel time to the next one after that?"

"Ninety-six minutes and counting, Captain." The officer did not need to check her notes. "A code red, high alert. Seven vessels unaccounted for, two broken transmissions. One mentioned attack."

The captain turned back to Wander and demanded harshly, "That it?"

"It must be," Wander replied.

Consuela nodded agreement. "The distances fit."

"Are you sure?"

Wander hesitated. "No, Captain. But I think this is real."

"You can't expect me to throw the entire ship into a panic because of a guess, Scout," Arnol snapped.

"Just as I said," Guns muttered. "Trouble's on the rise."

"Captain, it's all too new for me to say for certain what—"

"Well, I can," Consuela declared defiantly. "Two of us can't be totally wrong. It's definitely another shadowlane."

Rick watched the captain glare at her, but she refused to back down. His eyes still on Consuela, he snapped, "Helmsman!"

"Yes, Captain."

"Inform the chief petty officer that the ship is to move onto full combat footing."

An electric current shot through the flight deck. The captain wheeled about and demanded, "Guns, who is on weapons station duty?"

"I am, Captain," Simmers replied.

The captain frowned. "What are you doing away from your station, mister?"

"I ordered him up to flight deck, Skipper," Guns replied. "We're planning the lad's training."

"Training will have to wait. Are we ready for full power to all weaponry?"

"Aye, Captain," Guns replied. "I ran through the gamut myself not two hours ago."

"Very well. Simmers, you have precisely ten seconds to return to your station and prepare for attack mode."

"Mind if I ask what's amiss, Skipper?" Guns asked.

"The scouts have detected not one but *two* more shadowlanes," Captain Arnol replied, speaking to the flight deck as a whole. "The first they say is empty."

"And small," Consuela added, seemingly fearless, even when confronted with the captain's stern glare.

The captain scowled at her, then continued "They claim there's activity on the next lane down, and well within cannon range."

"Pirates?" Guns said doubtfully and glared at the scouts. "Skipper, do you really think these novices can be trusted—"

"Don't bother me with questions I can't answer, Guns. Simmers, you have your orders. Helmsman!"

"Chief Petty Officer Tucker has been informed, Captain."

"Very well." The captain hesitated long enough to cast another glance toward his scouts, then said, "All crew, stand by for action stations. This vessel will enter red alert status in one hour. Mark!"

"Red alert, sixty minutes and counting," intoned the helmsman.

"All senior officers to my cabin in five minutes." Arnol focused on the scouts and said ominously, "You had better be right."

———

Curiously, neither Consuela nor Wander felt ensnared by the feverish excitement that captured the rest of the ship. Consuela willingly accepted Wander's suggestion that they return to his cabin until they approached the next shadowlane. The passages were filled with crew who went hurtling by, pausing only to flash an incredulous glance their way. Word had already spread throughout the vessel. Two young scouts, utter novices to space, claimed to have detected two more shadowlanes. The same shadowlanes which, up to now, had been little more than speculation. They also claimed to have identified pirates lying in wait. The same pirates who, up to now, had been little more than rumors. And on the basis of their unsubstantiated claims, the captain had ordered the ship to be readied for combat.

"Hey, youngsters!" A gray-headed swabbie stopped them with an upraised hand. He had the look of a veteran tomcat, scarred and beat up and still full of life. "This challenge for real?"

"We think so," Wander replied.

"We know so," Consuela corrected. "Something's out there where it shouldn't be. Whether it's a pirate or not, your guess is as good as mine."

"Ain't nothing else could be hanging about in the middle of deep space," the swabbie replied and eyed them shrewdly. "They's laying ten-to-one odds that you're wrong and the whole thing ain't nothing but smoke. Think I should take some of that?"

Consuela grinned and replied, "Bet your back teeth."

The swabbie laughed and slapped his thigh. "Gal, I like your spirit. Anybody on lower decks tries to make trouble, you come find old Tinker."

"Thank you, Tinker," Consuela said, putting as much feeling as she could into the words. "It's good to know we have friends like you."

Ancient eyes sparked with pleasure. "Aye, missie, friend it is. Like I say, any of these swabbies stand in your way, give me a shout. We'll fix 'em good."

As he keyed open his door, Wander asked, "What was that all about?"

"Oh, he reminded me of some of the geezers back in my old neighborhood." She eased her neck muscles. "Now that we're off the deck, I really feel tired."

"Me too." Wander called for chair and bed. "You can lie down, if you like."

"Come sit down beside me," she said, settling down and patting the mattress. "I need to tell you something."

"I think I know," Wander said.

"You can't. It's not possible." Suddenly she was nervous. Not so much about his reaction. Wander was the most accepting person she had ever met. But bringing it up forced her also to consider beyond the moment. To face the threat of tomorrow.

"You don't come from an outworld," Wander said quietly, his eyes returning to the sorrow of earlier days. Days before they had met. "Not the way we think of it."

She showed her astonishment. "How did you know?"

"I've been thinking a lot about it," he said. "Little things keep coming up, things even an outworlder had to know. And something else. It wasn't until I was here alone after takeoff that I realized what had bothered me about that night when we met on the field." He looked at her. "There was only one set of footsteps in the snow coming out from the port."

"I wanted to tell you," she said. "From the very first moment. I just didn't know how."

He took her hand in both of his. "Tell me now."

CHAPTER SIXTEEN

Rick thought it felt a lot like the run-up to a big game.

He sat in the far corner of the weapons platform, grateful for the chance to stay. He was almost completely ignored. The first team had been called in. Guns manned the primary console, his numbers two and three tucked in to either side. Rick's chair was squeezed up to the back railing, but he didn't mind—he was still able to sit and feel a part of the rising tension.

Then Wander and Consuela returned, and Rick found himself minding very much.

The entire flight deck turned, and all activity stopped momentarily as attention focused on the pair who had brought them to ready status.

"I believe we have a countdown to red alert," the captain barked, and activity resumed. But attention was continually cast their way.

Rick found himself reaching a slow burn. He wasn't used to being sidelined while someone else played the star.

He watched movement slow once more as the next shadowlane was approached. He saw the pair huddle together, as though drawing support from one another, although only Wander wore the headset. Rick heard Signals chant down the seconds to the next possible shadowlane. He and all the flight-deck crew saw a shudder rack both Wander and Consuela.

Rick watched Wander struggle to push off the after-effects, then announce, "It's another one, Captain. Smaller than the first one, but there just the same."

The captain snapped, "Mark!"

Signals responded, "Right on target again, Skipper."

The flight deck responded with a murmur of astonishment, which only the senior weapons officer and his crew did not share. "Aye, all right for some," Guns muttered and coursed his stubby fingers across the weapons console. "But it takes guts to handle *real* power."

From his central station, Captain Arnol asked the scouts, "Can you still function?"

"I can," Consuela said quietly, and stilled Wander's protest with a hand on his arm. "I didn't wear the headset. You did. Let me check."

"But I can't monitor," he protested.

"You don't have to listen in to set the amp level." Consuela slipped on her headset, settled back and said, "Ready."

An electric stillness held the flight deck as Consuela closed her eyes and frowned in concentration.

Rick whispered to no one in particular, "What is she doing?"

"Listening to space," Guns muttered back. "Aye, takes a vacuum between the ears to do it, too."

Rick turned to the veteran. "Why don't you like them?"

"You haven't been around like I have," Guns replied, his gaze leveled like a missile tracker on the pair. "Having a pilot on the flight deck is like taking a plague on board."

Consuela opened her eyes, struggled to focus, and announced, "They're still there, Captain."

"You're sure?"

"I can't say what they are," she replied, her voice quiet yet confident. "But there is definitely a ship waiting down the next shadowlane."

"Any ship in this quadrant that is standing poised off a lightway can be presumed to be enemy." He turned to the lower deck. "Any communication traffic?"

"Nothing in the sector at all except our vessel and the port," Signals replied.

He turned back to Consuela. "How far off the lightway are they lying?"

When she hesitated, Wander replied for her, "About two minutes at our present speed."

"Guns?"

"Aye, Skipper," the veteran groused. "Well within stunner range."

"Very well." He keyed his own console. "Chief Petty Officer, is the ship ready?"

"Battened down tight, Captain." The flight deck's intercom carried Tucker's bundled agitation loud and clear. "The crew's raring to go."

"Very well." He keyed a second switch and said, "All hands, this is the captain speaking. An unidentified vessel has been tentatively identified lying off the lightway approximately"—he checked his console—"sixty-one minutes ahead of us. No communication traffic has been detected. According to Hegemony law, a vessel not directly upon a lightway and not sounding a distress call may be presumed to be enemy and fired upon. In the case that the vessel is a slaver and this ship is hit by stunners, all crew are ordered to remain suited and shielded, with arms at the ready, until the all-clear is sounded. Marine units, prepare for possible boarding. Good luck and good hunting. Captain out."

He looked down at the upturned faces before him, checked the shipboard chrono, hesitated a long moment, then nodded. "Hit it."

A thrumming tone sounded over the ship's intercom. "Battle stations. Battle stations." The signals officer droned the words, yet nothing could keep the excitement from spilling over. "This ship is now on red alert. Battle stations."

"I want you scouts to check the vessel every five minutes," he ordered. "Alert me immediately to any change in status."

"Aye, aye, Captain." Wander slipped on his headset.

The captain swung around. "Guns, I have decided to go ahead as discussed in my quarters."

"But, Skipper—"

"You will not raise the shields," he ordered, overriding his weapons officer. "You will arm yourself, but you will not draw your weapons."

"I have to protest," Guns replied. "That puts us at a desperate disadvantage."

But Arnol was not finished. "You will track at your absolute limits. You will hold yourself fully ready to draw and strike. At the first forward move, you will attack. You will not wait for my command. I want you to try to take out their shields without cracking their skin." He let the orders sink in, then continued. "I wouldn't dare try this maneuver with anybody less skilled than you, Guns. Think you're up to it?"

Clearly the captain had hit the correct key. The weapons officer swelled visibly. "Give it our best shot, Skipper."

"Cripple an attack vessel, but leave those aboard alive." The captain swung about to ensure that the entire flight deck's attention was turned toward the weapons station. "I've never heard of such a maneuver."

"Aye, it'd be one for the books, that's a fact," Guns replied, basking in the attention.

"I ask this only because no one has ever captured a pirate vessel."

"Always wanted to be a bit of history in the making, Skipper."

"You realize, of course," the captain went on, "we are placing this ship and the lives of all within her in your hands."

"Split-second timing," Guns replied, planning out loud. "Blast her shield, hit them with a stunner bolt, melt the guts of her weaponry, go for the drive system. A four-step attack faster than you can blink your eye. That's the ticket."

"Very well, Guns, you have convinced me. I hereby authorize you to fire at will. But if the plan does not appear to work at first blow, I want you to annihilate her, is that clear? No time for inspection or hesitation, man. The risk is too great."

"The instant it even appears that they might either still have drive or secondary weapons," Guns promised, "that vessel will disappear, Captain. Mark my words."

Captain Arnol's features were more sharply drawn than ever. He nodded his acceptance and ordered, "To your weapons, then."

CHAPTER SEVENTEEN

Weapons Lieutenant Valens was a taciturn young man with the slender yet muscular build of a gymnast. He had done little more than nod in Rick's direction since arriving. When Guns swiveled back around to his console, however, he asked, "You want a trainee up here in the middle of a fight?"

Guns glanced in Rick's direction, hesitated, and for an agonizing instant Rick thought he was going to be taken out of the action.

The senior weapons officer caught a hint of Rick's distress, and humor flickered across his features. "Not just yet."

The lieutenant shrugged, as though it was of no great concern. "Might get awful busy later."

"Maybe our Rick here might serve a purpose."

"A trainee?"

"The boy's a natural, mark my words." Guns mulled it over for a long moment, then turned to his number three, a long-time weapons officer who clearly was not concerned with rising farther up the ladder of authority. "How'd you like to arm a second ferret?"

Experienced eyes cast themselves over Rick's form. "You really think he's got what it takes?"

"Set him on the power bank, have him hunt with our secondary weapons. Never can tell, an unknown vessel might have a little derringer up its sleeve." Guns nodded at the sound of his own decision. "I'll take the shield, that's the trickiest bit because I'll have to give it a glancing blow. Straight shot might leave us with a cloud of nuts and bolts."

"I'll hit them with a stun bolt soon as the shields are down," the number three offered. "Then go for the drive tubes."

"I'll take weapons," Lieutenant Valens said.

"Aim well back," Guns ordered. "Stay clear of the upper decks. I'll put a second shot on the nose and take out their control systems soon as the shield's cracked."

"You sure it's wise to leave a novice on the deck during action?" Valens asked once more, his gaze coming nowhere near Rick.

"Can't hurt," Guns replied. Clearly his mind was made up. "We three are seeing to all the known targets. Let him hunt about on his own, play the extra ferret. Lad's got to have his first taste of battle sometime."

Rick felt his entire system drenched in adrenaline when the two assistant gunners nodded their acceptance. "Thanks, Guns."

"Make me proud, lad," the grizzled veteran replied, understanding him fully.

Rick searched his memory, and when nothing came up he decided he had to ask. "What's a ferret?"

The officers exchanged glances, and the number three explained, "It's what we call a tracker in hunt-attack mode," he replied, as the other two bent over the weapons console. "You heard the captain give us the right to fire at will?"

"Yes."

"This means that as soon as the target is identified, we attack. Weapons officers assigned as ferrets search for unexpected threats." He motioned to Rick's overhead console. "Draw down your systems console and code in."

Instantly Rick knew what was required. He keyed the lever situated at the end of his right chair arm, and the console smoothly swung up and over and into place at chest level. A second key drew up the two side consoles, so that he was now situated at the center of an electronic cocoon. He scanned the elaborate array and felt the sweep of sudden understanding rise with the tide of his mounting excitement. The checklist was there, ready and waiting in his mind. He poised his hands over the incredibly complex pattern of levers and keys and readouts, and began. He announced, "Connectors keyed and coded."

"Power up."

He reached for the central dials and with both hands swept the levers forward. "Powering." As the levers rose, so too did the soaring sense of reaching out, joining with a force of incredible magnitude. "Power at full and holding."

The lieutenant paused in his work long enough to glance Rick's way. He then turned to Guns and raised an eyebrow.

"What did I tell you?" Guns replied proudly.

"Power to tracking," Valens ordered.

The side consoles were his tracking units, intended to be set in motion, then followed with gentle nudges of the two control sticks rising from their flexible mountings at hand level. Rick directed the power now set at his control to both tracking mechanisms. "Tracking alerted."

"Ready your weapons."

The top-central console drawn down over his head was his weaponry. Phasers, neutron missiles, strafers, stun bolts—they and the close-hold defense weaponry called energy lances could at the press of keys be armed and directed to his control sticks. Tracking would be guided and locked, then with a press of the red-light buttons capping his control sticks, the weapons would be fired. Rick ran through the weapons-power keys, then intoned as calmly as his quaking chest would permit, "Request weapons arming code."

"Listen to the lad," Guns exclaimed, turning to give Rick his flat-toothed grin. "How does it feel?"

"Incredible," he said, willing his hands to remain steady.

"Know what it is that's firing the flame in your gut?" The weapons officer's eyes held a knowing gleam. "It's the coming battle, lad. You can *smell* it, can't you?"

"I think so." Rick could not help but grin so hugely it felt as though his face were splitting. "Thanks for letting me stay, Guns. Don't worry, I won't let you down."

The veteran laughed and slapped the boy's shoulder. "That you won't, lad. That you won't. I'll be holding your final controls in my hands, mind, so there won't be any chance of firing early." He nodded to his number three. "Code his arms. Let the lad flex his muscles."

"Coding in."

Something then caught the senior weapons officer's eye, and the vast good humor slipped from his face. "Just look at those two over there, would you," Guns muttered. "Their heads together, practicing their mumbo-jumbo. Who'd have thought the captain would place a ship of the line in the hands of two novices like that."

Without looking up from his own monitors, Lieutenant Valens replied, "At least they've given us a chance to fight. You've got to grant them that."

"I'll grant them nothing," came the growled reply. "Witches is all they are. Witches and wizards run this Hegemony. It's a sad day when real men have got to bow and scrape to the likes of them."

Rick took advantage of the companionable atmosphere and asked, "What happened to you?"

Guns swung his way. "Eh?"

"Why are you so bitter about sensitives?"

There was a moment of grinding teeth before Guns muttered, "When I first started spacing I came up against a monster in midnight robes. A pilot who didn't like my attitude. Kept me a midshipman on a moon bus for five stinking years before I could shake off his curse and prove my worth. Five years I lost because I refused to suck up to the pompous fool."

Rick ventured, "Maybe those two are different."

All three weapons officers turned his way. Guns demanded, "What's it to you, then? You fancy the lass?"

"Not at all," he protested. Under the veteran's fiery gaze he confessed, "I knew her back home, that's all."

"You're both from the same homeworld?"

"Same town."

"Is that a fact." He looked bemusedly back toward the pilot's station. "I always figured them to have sprung up full blown from under rocks, like other vermin."

The lieutenant snorted a laugh but did not speak up.

"Stay away from them, lad," Guns warned. "You've got the makings of a top-flight officer. Don't let their kind destroy your chances like they did mine. Not a sensitive's been born that wasn't pure poison to good and decent folk."

Chapter Eighteen

To Consuela's great relief, she and Wander were left alone, an island of calm in a turbulent sea. With each five-minute course mark from signals and the helmsman, the flight deck's frenetic pace rose one notch. Yet the two of them remained isolated on the pilot's station, separated by an immeasurable gulf from the remainder of the flight deck.

Each five minutes also meant reaching out, connecting with the approaching shadowlane, following its course and touching briefly upon the silent vessel. It was a harrowing experience.

The shadowlane vibrated with a power that was as forboding as it was dark, a nemesis that left them feeling unclean. The closer they drew, the less amplification it required to reach forward and monitor, and the stronger the brooding menace sounded in their minds. It was an infernal buzzing, a hissing of unclean energies that tainted their innermost beings.

Evil.

They traded off the monitoring duties, one reaching outward every five minutes while the other leaned close and gave comfort. Consuela did not know which was worse, having to sit and watch Wander flinch as he drew into contact or doing so herself.

"Twenty minutes and counting," intoned Signals.

"Status unchanged," responded Wander, peeling the headset from his temples and discarding it upon the console. To Consuela he murmured, "I'm down to amp level five."

"We know what to look for," she agreed.

He nodded. "It's strange. When I'm out there, I can feel you."

"I know," she said, wishing she could touch him. "Just knowing your love is there with me—" She stopped with the sudden realization of what she had said.

He turned to her, his gaze soft and full and deep. "My love," he whispered.

She felt a swelling pressure push up from her chest and lock her throat tight. "I'm so scared."

"Not about the threat up ahead."

"No." She willed herself to steady. "Thank you for believing my story."

His brown eyes were great pools of yearning. "How long can you stay?"

"I don't know. It's the hardest part of all, not knowing."

"Do you want to leave?"

"No," she said, definite now. "I think of home, I wonder how my mother is. But my place is here now." She had to stop and swallow. "With you."

They sat in silent sharing until the monitor chimed.

Wander said, "Let me do it this time."

"No." She stopped further argument by fitting on her headset. "All right. Amp up."

Reluctantly he acquiesced. "I'll go to four unless you say more."

"I'll be fast," she said, and as the amp level rose, she reached outward, a tightly focused beam of concentration, racing down the lightway, unfettered by time or physical bonds. The shadowlane appeared and she veered off, anchoring herself to the lightway as she searched down the unclean way, feeling the buzzing vibratory patterns course through her mind. She flitted to the darkened vessel, saw it holding to its stationary pattern, and returned in a flash.

Yet even at her rapid and focused pace, she could not deny what she almost heard.

"Fifteen minutes and counting," droned Signals.

"Status unchanged," she replied, setting down her headset.

Wander asked. "Are you all right?"

She nodded. "I'll be glad when this is over."

"Me too."

Consuela looked up and out at the star-flecked expanse. In the far right corner, a nebulous gas cloud extended one purple-flecked tentacle out over a thousand stars. A supernova blazed almost directly overhead, outshining the two galaxy swarms that flanked it. "I wish I knew I could stay."

They sat in intimate silence until the monitor chimed once again. Wander sighed and fitted the headset back on. "Be there with me," he asked.

"For as long as I am able," she whispered, her gaze only for him.

————

At the ten-minute count, Guns passed on shield control to the on-board computers and to the captain, while keeping a third key directly under his left hand. The triple backup was established in case the vessel came under attack before one or more of them could react. Waiting until the pirates committed themselves before shielding to full strength, in order to reduce risk of their detecting the battle shield and safely fleeing, was the riskiest part of the whole plan.

That done, Guns ordered, "All right. Let loose the ferrets."

His heart hammering, Rick followed the number three's lead and keyed in the circuit that connected him to the wider-ranging signals' tracking units. The ship's outer tracker spread indiscriminately in all directions. It was the weapons tracker's function to wait and listen while the signals officer filtered through all incoming sensory data, until the foe was identified. At that split second, the tracker homed in, locked on, and attacked.

"Five minutes," Signals announced, his voice crackling with tension.

"Status unchanged," Consuela repeated, her calm utterly at odds with the flight deck atmosphere. When Guns snorted his derision, Rick had to agree. How could she remain so unaffected by the coming battle?

"Better make sure nobody's dropped off," Captain Arnol announced. "Helmsman, give them another blast."

"Red alert. Red alert. Battle stations. Attack in three minutes and counting."

Rick allowed himself to sink down in his seat, as though melding with the yielding surface and drawing directly into the power circuitry. As the signals officer searched, he sensed as well as saw on the monitors the outer reaches of the equipment's capacity, finding only empty space.

"Two minutes."

Rick's console squealed an alert, and his weapons circuits blinked ready to be locked, as Signals shouted, "We have a lock. A definite lock."

"Identify!"

"Shielded vessel, silenced and not under power, one minute ten seconds off the lightway."

"Weapons!" Guns shouted. "We confirm an armed vessel, Skipper! Their phasers are armed!"

"On my command!"

"In range in fifteen seconds and counting!"

"Shields on fu—"

Then they were struck, and struck hard.

CHAPTER NINETEEN

Perhaps it was because Rick did not know enough to keep careful hold of his weapons station. Perhaps it was his youth. Perhaps it was because of who he was and where he came from. Whatever the reason, Rick managed to fend off the stunners for the single instant required.

Barely.

A blinding flash of crackling energy exploded through the flight deck. Flickering blue tentacles of lightning raced up the consoles and passed through every body. The weapons lieutenant was blasted clear of his straps and halfway over his console. The number three screamed in agony and covered his eyes. Guns bellowed and went slack. Rick was aware of an awful pain searing his brain and locking his muscles down tight, yet still he somehow managed to hold his focus.

The moment before being struck, he had been glorying in the thrill of a surprise attack. His tracking system was focused down tightly on the alien ship, and as he monitored his tracking controls he was also extended outward, the warrior creeping up toward the enemy, weapons at the ready. In the span of two heartbeats he saw how the lieutenant honed in on the band of power that belted the ship's lower base, locking his weaponry on target, waiting for Guns to fire his neutron cannon and blow the shield. He saw how the number three had his weapons trained on the vessel's silent trail, where only a thin stream of emitted energy gave notice that the vessel was powered up to full, ready to move in for the kill.

But just as Guns prepared to blow the shield, Rick saw a bluish ball of energy race across the distance separating them and strike the nose of their own ship. In his convulsion, Guns fired off one cannon, and as the pain mounted in Rick's skull he saw the missile strike the shield a glancing blow, exactly as Guns had intended. The pirate's shield exploded in a fiery cloud of sparks, and the kinetic energy sent the vessel spinning slightly, so that the pirate's second stunner shot up and over their ship's nose.

Rick did not give it any conscious thought whatsoever. Screaming his rage and his determination not to give in to the pain, he locked in his controls to the lieutenant's tracking and weapons, and fired.

Their vessel shuddered under the backlash from firing three massive phaser bolts at once. Rick shouted his defiance as the bolts blasted their target, melting a glowering red belt around half of the pirate ship's lower base.

Guns heaved a heavy groan and struggled up in his seat.

"The controls! Get the controls!" Rick screamed, scarcely hearing himself as he worked to pull over the number three's tracking and weapons. As the pirates fired their thrusters, Rick's second batch of missiles smashed in and melted the tubes closed.

"They're rotating!" Guns roared, his fingers stabbing at his own power deck.

"Got 'em!" Rick shouted, racing against the menace of undamaged weapons being rotated into firing position. As the pirate ship's other side came into view, Rick fired a third volley, in sync with the stun-bolt blasted off by Guns. They shouted their defiant glee as the molten belt extended fully around the enemy's weaponry, and glimmers of angry lightning raced up and down the ship's surface.

"Firing second stunners!" Guns shouted, and again the blue-white powerball blasted the pirate's nose, sending the lancing light-traces along and through the ship.

"Hold your fire," Arnol ordered hoarsely. "Helmsman."

"He's still out, Skipper."

"Take over, Lieutenant. Retrace to the near point and hold position. Guns, train all weapons on the vessel."

"Aye, aye, Captain."

"Skipper," the junior signals officer announced, "we are receiving a distress call."

"Order them to surrender. Keep alert, Guns, this may be a ruse." He stabbed his console. "Chief Petty Officer, are you there?"

"Partly, Skipper. Only partly. What happened?"

"We took a stun-bolt direct amidships, but it looks like we survived and conquered. How's our battle readiness?"

There was a longish pause, then, "Couldn't muster more than half the main force, Captain. Maybe not even that."

"Captain," the junior signals officer announced, "they accept our surrender demand."

"Hold to your weapons, Guns."

"Finger's on the trigger, Captain."

"What's their attack status?"

"No sign of power to any weapons system."

"Order them to power down, suit up, open all bay doors, and bring all uninjured personnel into the outer holds where they are visible." He keyed and demanded, "You hear that, Chief Petty Officer?"

"Aye, Skipper." Life and strength were returning to Tucker's voice.

"Ready what men you can muster, weapons and suits." Arnol looked down and ordered, "Signals, inform me the instant their power is fully damped. Helmsman, at that point, I want you to extend the gravity net and draw them close enough for us to fasten a line."

"Power damped, Skipper. Bay doors opening."

"Gravity net extending, Captain."

"Full shield, Guns. Defense perimeter on attack."

"We're ready, Skipper."

"All right. Tuck, prepare to board and take prisoners." He glanced around. "And have a medic sent to the flight deck. We've got seven, no eight, wounded up here."

"Ten," Rick corrected, his gut clenching at the sight of Wander and Consuela sprawled motionless half-on and half-off their dais, their limbs intertwined. Even unconscious, they remained together.

CHAPTER TWENTY

The lean, dark man and the wizened, old crone both wore the black robes of diplomats, with shoulders and sleeves chased in the silver filigree of senior rank. They gave the scarcest of bows before the Prince Commander's desk and announced, "We have news."

"I assumed nothing less," the Starfleet commander replied dryly, "given the fact that you insisted on seeing me without delay, despite the fact that we are currently engaged in three major conflicts."

Ignoring his sarcasm, the man stated, "Our monitors report that someone seeks to invade our most secret ways."

The Prince Commander leaned back in his seat. "This is not what I wish to hear. Especially now."

"They have not yet found the door," the crone reported. "Yet they seek."

The Prince Commander, distant heir to the Hegemony throne and Commander of His Majesty's Primary Battle Fleet, rose from his seat and began pacing the cold stone floor. He positively loathed this Starfleet monitoring station, for that matter, and was immensely glad that he did not have to appear more than once or twice each Standard year. The only reason he came at all was because it housed the Talents.

This fortress world possessed the charm and ambiance of a deserted tomb. The walls were thick and overly high, constructed of close-fitting, reddish gray stone. Interior and exterior were totally unadorned. The hallways were long and windowless and winding and narrow, filled with the anguish of all Talents who had been trapped and tortured there in eons past. The Prince Commander did not object to the years of rigid discipline forced upon all Talents. He merely objected to having it under his command.

To make matters worse, the senior diplomats who were assigned liaison duty between the Talent station and his own command positively made his skin crawl.

From the relative safety of his office's most distant corner, he demanded, "So these forbidden ways do truly exist? I always thought they were the stuff of legends."

"That a man of your rank and station might consider them mere legends," the crone replied, swiveling upon a cane whose handle was carved from a single jewel, "is a testimony to the thoroughness with which we serve the Hegemony."

"Of course," the Prince Commander acquiesced. "So we are faced with the threat of a renegade Talent."

"Perhaps," the crone corrected. "It appears so."

"Appears? You're not sure?"

"We have lost contact with one of our ally vessels. And now we are picking up strange news. Rumors of a freighter inbound for Avanti with a captured pirate vessel."

"Impossible."

The other diplomat was a shrewd and ambitious man who ruled the planetary station with an iron fist. He tolerated the foul conditions only because his future advancement was at stake. "My monitors claim that it is so."

"Then your monitors have made a mistake."

"Doubtful," the crone quavered. "Most doubtful. These Talents guard their right to utilize the system's most powerful mind-amps with great zealousness."

The Prince Commander inspected his appearance in the full-length mirror. The tailored white robe hung most attractively over his corpulent form. The belt of woven gold managed to draw in his distended belly, and the high jeweled collar hid his chin's multiple folds. "If that is the case—"

"Then it is only a matter of time before the door is breached and the forbidden ways trod once more," the crone droned ominously.

"I suppose I must alert Central Starfleet Command," the Commander muttered, shuddering at the thought of bearing such news to the Prince

Regent. Then he had an idea. "But you say that these are mere rumors?"

"That is so."

"Then perhaps the renegade can be eliminated before confirmation has been received. That is, if he exists at all."

"Difficult in the extreme," the male diplomat protested.

"Yes, or captured by other pirates," the Prince Commander went on happily.

"We have done as ordered," the lean man retorted. "We have come to you with news of possible renegade Talents. What you do with this news is up to you."

The crone wheeled to face her associate and protested, "But this is a Talent we are discussing!"

"A *renegade* Talent," he countered.

"Yet a Talent just the same. No one else could have detected the forbidden way and done so without monitoring equipment!"

"If it was done at all," he responded.

"Whether or not the rumors are true must be checked out thoroughly," the crone snapped back. "But if they are, such a Talent must be brought to us and utilized!"

"Your report is duly noted," the Prince Commander said cheerfully, delighted at the sight of diplomats quarreling among themselves. They and the sensitives were the scourge of the empire, the lot of them.

He returned to his desk and seated himself. "Naturally, I could not take such a report to Starfleet Command without further verification. But in the meantime, I want you to use all powers at your disposal to eradicate this threat, if it exists at all. Yes. Then I should be able to report that the threat was identified and eliminated. Is that understood? Very well. Then, you are dismissed."

Chapter Twenty-one

Rick keyed the door and announced, "Ensign Richard reporting as ordered."

"Enter."

He walked in and stood stiffly at attention. "You wanted to see me, Captain?"

"That's right." Flanking the captain were the senior helmsman, his head swathed in bandages, the senior weapons officer, and the acting signals officer, and power control officer—their superiors were still laid up. "Have a seat, Ensign."

"Thank you, Captain."

The captain's quarters were both large and sumptuous, compared to the rest of the ship. A polished table extended the length of the carpeted front room, a console flanking the captain's head position. Two side alcoves contained softly glowing light-sculptures. Rows of framed commendations rose above the bookshelves. Ornate panels separated this room from the captain's private quarters.

"Guns has been relating to us your actions, or as much as he can remember. I want you to tell me what happened."

Rick swallowed. The stern visages facing him gave no indication as to whether they meant to reward him or demand his summary resignation. "It's all a little fuzzy, Captain."

"Take your time. Try to make it as complete as you can."

Rick struggled to make sense of the flurry of images. So much, so incredibly much had been packed into a battle that had scarcely lasted twenty seconds. He finished lamely, "I've probably forgotten something important, but I think that's everything."

Captain Arnol nodded once and glanced back down at the papers before him. "Your records indicate that other than your inbound transport, this is your first voyage into space. And that up to now you have received no formal training, as it was not available on your homeworld."

"I guess that's all pretty much true, Captain," Rick replied feebly.

"This beats all I've ever heard," the helmsman muttered.

"I agree," the captain said. "Yet nonetheless we must accept the fact that we are all alive and here today because of this young man's swift actions. Ensign, I am entering into your permanent records that your handling of this emergency saved the life of every man and woman on this ship."

"Thank you, Captain," Rick managed.

"Furthermore, as soon as we dock I am sending a message to Starfleet Command recommending that you be put up for the Medal of Valor. The recommendation will bear the signature of every officer on this ship."

To that Rick could find no reply.

"On behalf of all who serve under me, I extend to you my heartiest thanks and congratulations." The captain rose to his feet, and all followed his lead. "I am hereby granting you a temporary battlefleet promotion to lieutenant, and assigning you full watch status as Fourth Weapons Officer. This ship normally does not hold such a position, but I want you to go on record as a watch officer, and Guns says he would be willing to add you to his group."

"Proud to stand with him," the veteran growled. "Very proud."

"I have searched the records and found nothing to suggest that an ensign has ever been granted a battlefleet promotion even before cadet training, and there is every likelihood that this decision will be overturned when you return to Fleet Command. But nonetheless it will remain on your record. And if I have anything to do with it, your actions will go down in battlefleet history as an example which other ensigns should strive to follow."

"I found these among my own articles, thought you might care to use them." Arnol stood, picked up a small wooden box from his console, walked over, and handed it to Rick. "Your bars of rank, Lieutenant. Wear them with pride."

Rick looked down at the shining silver bars, and for a moment they seemed to shimmer before his eyes. He struggled to mouth the words, "Thank you, Captain."

"You have earned them." The captain marched back to his place, and still at attention, announced, "Dismissed, Lieutenant."

In a daze, Rick walked back out into the passage. He leaned against the wall and felt a sudden surging desire to run and share the news with someone, anyone who could share the thrill and make it real.

Almost without realizing it, he found himself walking down the corridor and entering sickbay. The medic gave him a friendly nod, noted the bars on his shoulders, and grinned. "The skipper did it, then. Congratulations."

"The whole crew knows about it?"

"Everybody who can walk and talk. You're the hero of the hour." He sobered as his glance shifted to the door behind him. "You and the pair of sensitives in there."

"How are they?"

"Hard to tell. The girl's from your homeworld, I hear."

"That's right."

The medic walked over, keyed the door, motioned Rick forward. "Hard to know exactly what's up with a sensitive who's been power fried, so I've let them sleep and just kept a careful watch."

The sickbay was crammed with beds and patients. Rick craned through the doorway, saw the two motionless forms lying in beds set side by side, both surrounded by softly beeping monitors. "She looks so pale."

"Deep sleep," the medic said calmly. Clearly he was not worried. "Done a little checking. Best thing that can happen under the circumstances, or so the books say. They both woke up a couple of times and drank some water, with my help of course. Even said a couple of words to each other. Almost as though each came back just to make sure the other was doing all right." The medic smiled a second time. "Never thought I'd see the day when I would care about a pilot's health."

"Scouts," Rick corrected, and for some reason felt a pang of jealousy. Not at the attention given these two, but rather over the feelings they showed for each other, even here, even now.

"Not anymore," the medic replied. "Not in my book. Anybody who's done what they've done deserves the full ranking." He gave the pair of beds a confident nod. "Give them time, they'll come around. They're

strong, they're sharp, and they've got the greatest reason of all to recover."

"What's that?"

The medic's third grin was the biggest of all. "Love."

———————

Consuela drifted in and out of sleep, moving back and forth in a rushing surge of waves. Steady and deep, carrying her away and then returning. She heard the calm voices, did not care to focus and listen, because to do so would mean rising to full consciousness. And she was
not ready for that. Not yet.

She felt the reassuring return of strength to her limbs, and the gradual easing of the pain in her mind. The shock had been staggeringly
powerful, but the memory of her experience in the training hall helped
her cope. That and Wander's presence. She had woken up several times,
managed to turn her head and see that he was there and resting easily,
even spoken to him once. For the moment, it was enough.

She heard a voice she recognized as Rick's, and took comfort from
his presence as well. Then she was away, swept back into the sea of
sleep. But this time there was a difference.

The flowing up and out and away was stronger this time, carrying her
farther and farther from the bed and the sickbay and the voices. Farther
still, a current so powerful she was helpless to resist, sweeping her back
in calm and fluid power.

Toward home.

PART II

Path Finder

CHAPTER ONE

Consuela did not have much time.

The realization struck her as soon as she stepped into her living room. She could not say how she knew, but the certainty was there, and it sped her actions. Not to mention attaching wings to her heart.

The entire time she tried to talk through her mother's alcoholic fog, part of her mind remained fastened upon the thought that she would soon be back with Wander. The surging thrill lifted her beyond her mother's muddled bewilderment, beyond her own pain of loss and departure. For this time there was a sense of belonging elsewhere, tied to this new mysterious place by her love for a man. A sensitive, openhearted, gifted young man. One who truly cared for her.

The last thing she remembered, she and Wander had been counting down their ship's approach along the lightwave. A pirate ship had been hovering just down the shadowlane, powered up and ready to pounce. Then the first ball of deadly blue energy had been flung across the space dividing them, and her world had exploded into a billion painfully shimmering bits.

There had come a scattering of glimpses through the pain of her recovery, a few words spoken with Wander. Then a sense of being pulled away.

Then she had woken up in her own bed, at home in Baltimore.

"Mama, are you listening to me?"

"Of course I am. Don't ask silly questions." Her mother's words were slurred, and her eyes remained glued to the television.

The bland voices of soap-opera stars mouthed lines that made no sense whatsoever to Consuela. She resisted the urge to walk over and turn off the set, knowing from experience that it would only start an argument. "I'm going away for a while. I have to. There's something important I need to do."

"She goes off and leaves me, doesn't say a word," her mother mumbled, drink and self-pity oiling her voice.

"That's why I came back, Mama, to tell you." Consuela spoke to her mother as to a little child. She knew this was required. Part of her mind felt the unexplained pressing need to hurry, to finish here and move on, to get the message through her mother's self-imposed fog. Another part registered the fact that it was earlier in the day than usual for Consuela's mother to be this far along, and that her complexion was pastier than normal. Consuela felt a stab of guilt. Maybe this was her mother's way of dealing with Consuela's absence, by drinking even more than usual.

She grasped hold of her mother's arm, said softly, "I had to come back, Mama. I had to tell you how much I love you."

A bleary gaze turned her way. The glass was shifted to her lap, and a hand patted her own. "You always were my good little girl."

"I've tried hard to do right, Mama," Consuela said. "That's why I need to be going."

"Go and leave me all alone." Her mother's self-pitying tone returned as she fumbled for her glass. "Doesn't matter what happens to her own mother."

"It does so matter, Mama. It matters a lot." But Consuela was forced to watch as her mother subsided into disjointed mutterings, her rheumy eyes glued to the television screen. Consuela remained kneeling beside her mother's chair until her legs ached, talking softly from time to time. But her mother did not respond.

Finally Consuela rose to her feet and walked into the kitchen. To her surprise, the card she was looking for was not there. She had no idea why she had let Daniel's card stay where he had pinned it. The little gold cross had drawn her attention every time she had glanced its way. But it was no longer there, nor the card for Pastor Daniel Mitchum. Consuela poked her head back through the doorway and called, "Mama, did you take down Daniel's card?"

As expected, there was no answer. Consuela picked up the telephone directory and looked up the number for the First Community Church.

After she asked for the youth pastor, she stood there wondering why she felt it was so important to speak with him.

But when his voice came on the line, she felt an overwhelming sense of affirmation in the man's calm strength. "Daniel Mitchum."

"This is Consuela Ortez. I don't know if you'll remember me, but—"

"Consuela!" Relief and joy sounded across the wires. "How are you? No, wait, where are you?"

"Back home," Consuela said, finding enormous comfort in not being alone. Why a man who was little more than a stranger would leave her feeling that way, she could not explain. Nor at that moment did she care. "I just came back."

"This is great," Daniel gushed. "I've been praying for you. And for Rick."

The information jolted through her. "How do you know about Rick?"

"When he couldn't find you, he called me. He said he found my card over at your house. Didn't he tell you?"

"No." Consuela let the news sink in. Rick had been here. Rick knew where she lived. She should have been mortified to hear this. Devastated that her carefully constructed myth had been demolished. Yet somehow it did not matter. And not just because she was returning to that other place. No. Something had happened. She was changing, and her attitude towards the outside world and other people's perception of her, all this was changing too. "We haven't really had much of a chance to talk."

"But he's okay?"

"Rick is fine." Consuela took a breath. "The reason I'm calling is, I have to go back."

There was a long pause on the other end, then Daniel spoke, more subdued now. "Where exactly is 'back'?"

"I'm not sure. But it doesn't seem to matter that much. Not now. There's so much happening. Our ship got hit by pirates, and that was awful. It felt as if my mind were going to explode. And I need to make sure Wander is okay."

There was a long pause, then, "Can we take that all from the top?"

"It wouldn't make any difference," Consuela replied. "Believe me."

"No, I suppose not," he said, speaking slowly. "So you think you should go back?"

"I *have* to."

"What do you want me to do?"

The simple question flooded her with relief. Here was someone she could trust. "I'm worried about Mom," Consuela said, and hastily described her mother's state. "Could you stop by and check on her?"

"Consider it done," Daniel replied.

"Thanks. Thanks a lot." Thunder rumbled through the kitchen window. For some reason Consuela felt the tingling pressure to move. "I've got to go."

"What's the rush?"

"I'm not sure, but I feel as though I've got to *hurry*."

"Then you probably do," Daniel said. "Think you can spare a moment for prayer?"

Consuela bowed her head, listened to Daniel intone the words, and felt an answering call within her heart. One that echoed the same sense of awe and silent longing she had experienced during transition. A silent voice spoke to her heart with something far beyond mere words. An invitation so gentle she could have ignored it if she wished, and yet granted with such power that her entire being resonated.

When Daniel stopped speaking, Consuela remained silent and still, feeling the comforting need without understanding what it was. Then the thunder rumbled once more, and the tingling sense of pressure brought her back.

"I have to go," she said quietly.

"We will be praying for you," Daniel said solemnly. "Each and every day."

———

Consuela had never been in a house that big before.

Under other circumstances, she would have loved to walk around and gawk. But there was no time for sightseeing, and the treatment she was receiving was bringing her to a slow boil.

To begin with, the maid had left her standing alone in the front hall until Rick's mother had appeared and looked her up and down and asked her how she happened to know Rick. The news that Rick had dated her before his disappearance was greeted with a disdainful sniff.

"I know all of my son's little friends," Rick's mother replied. "I am positive I have never heard him mention you before."

Consuela tried to hold her rising temper. "I assure you, Mrs. Reynolds, I had a date with Rick."

"Be that as it may," the woman replied, "Rick did not disappear over the weekend as you say. It was on a weeknight, a Monday to be precise."

"Of course," Consuela said. "He told me he went back to the carnival after I didn't show up at school."

The woman's glacial gaze sharpened. "How did you know about the carnival? Have you spoken to the police?"

"I told you, I was there."

The woman gave her another up-and-down inspection, then spun on her heel and started up the curving stairway. "Wait there."

Consuela stood and listened to the woman go from room to room, calling for someone named Henry. She stared up at the glistening chandelier, then inspected the life-size family portrait with its oh-so-proper dress and smiles and postures, and decided maybe Rick didn't have it all so perfect after all.

When the woman returned, she was accompanied by a tall, heavyset replica of Rick. Consuela watched them descend the double-bannistered stairway as though on parade. "This is the young woman I was telling you about."

The man's tone was rich and resonant and very condescending. "What's this about you and Rick and that carnival?"

The thunder boomed again, echoing through the vast hall with its lofty ceilings and marble flooring and sterile unloving atmosphere. Consuela felt as though the approaching storm was calling to her, urging her to finish her work and leave. "I just came by to tell you that I've seen Rick and he's fine."

"Now look here." The man stepped forward close enough to tower over her and bear down. "If you know anything about my son's whereabouts, I want you to tell me, and tell me *now*."

"Perhaps we should call the police," the woman suggested.

"Plenty of time for that." Her husband was growing increasingly red in the face. "First I intend to get to the bottom of this myself."

Consuela stood her ground. "I can't tell you where he is because I don't know. Not exactly. But I can tell you he's doing fine."

"Then why doesn't he come home?" the woman demanded. "Has he been kidnapped?"

Consuela inspected Rick's mother. There was far more irritation than concern in her features. "Rick is fine. He is just caught up in an adventure. He'll be home as soon as it's over."

"Nonsense," the man snapped. "He has made an absolute shambles of his responsibilities around here. How could our son embarrass us this way? How could he let down the family name? Doesn't he have a shred of decency?"

Thunder boomed outside, and the sense of urgency grew so strong Consuela felt as though she no longer had any choice.

"Rick is fine," she said, turning and making for the door. "That's all I can tell you. He doesn't want you to worry. He'll be home as soon as he can."

Consuela fled out the great entrance, their cries of protest tossed skyward by the growing wind. She raced across the road and through a broad park. Overhead the trees waved their branches, urging her to ever greater speed.

At the park's other side was a wide intersection, and beside it a bus stop and telephone booth. The instant she spotted the booth, Consuela realized there was one last bit of unfinished business she needed to resolve. She bounded inside, closing the door against the dust and wind and rumbling thunderclaps. Lightning sparked across the cloud-swept horizon as she looked up the school's number, deposited the coins, and dialed with fingers made clumsy with haste.

When the school secretary answered, Consuela deepened her voice and pretended to be her mother, as she had been forced to do on many other occasions. She assured the school secretary that everything was all right, that her daughter was fine now; yes, she had indeed been ill, but she was doing much better, and they had decided that she should take a trip to stay with friends for a while to recover fully. How long? Consuela hedged and promised that as soon as the girl was back to full health she would be returning to school. Yes, of course, she understood that a letter and doctor's report should have been sent, but she had been so very busy with work and tending to her sick daughter that the letter had slipped her mind. Yes, of course, she would give her daughter everyone's best wishes for her speedy recovery.

Consuela set down the phone just as lightning blasted down so close that the light and the sound struck her almost at the same moment. Urged on by pressures she neither understood nor questioned, Consuela flung open the door and raced back into the park. Another bolt of lightning blasted close behind her, urging her on.

At the park's center clearing, a blast of wind struck her with such force that she had no choice but to stop. She squinted through the swirling cloud of dust and leaves and saw that the clouds seemed to be encircling her, looming bigger and closer and darker, their gray-black surface illuminated by great internal sparks. Thunderbolts roared on all sides, splitting the air with such force that little answering flickers of static electricity began glimmering from her arms and legs and clothes. The lightning seemed to stalk her, moving ever closer, and yet the closer it came, the dimmer the sound became, as though the light and the concentrated force were pushing her away, farther and farther away until even as the lightning bolt crashed down right where she thought she had been standing, she was no longer there.

CHAPTER TWO

Consuela awoke with a gasp. Her first thread of awareness grew into a shocking world of white and stringent smells. She shut her eyes, took a shaky breath, felt the alien odors biting at her nostrils. Opening her eyes once more, she forced the room into focus and saw herself surrounded by instruments and dials and softly beeping noises.

A hospital. Although nothing she saw looked familiar, still there was no mistaking the overly clean environment, the soft erasing of all outside noise, the absence of any personal touches to the room. Consuela struggled up on one elbow, looked about the windowless chamber, felt panic rising with her wakefulness.

She was back, and she was alone.

"Wander?"

The room swept up her voice along with all other sounds, replying only with a soft sibilant sigh. Consuela struggled upright. She ignored the faint pinging from a machine on her headboard when she stripped off the band of wires attached to her wrist. She swung her feet to the floor, found a pair of disposable slippers there waiting for her.

"Wander?" Slowly she rose to her feet, grasping the bed's side rail with both hands. Her legs seemed barely able to support her weight. "Can anybody hear me?"

She felt a faint draft, reached behind herself with one hand, and groaned with frustration. There she was on the back of beyond, and they still had not come up with anything better than a hospital shift that left her backside exposed. Consuela forced her faltering legs to carry her over to the narrow closet, where to her vast relief she found a terry-cloth robe.

She had barely slipped it around her when the door slid back to admit a bright-eyed young woman who could not have been much older than Consuela. "It is not permitted for the young lady to arise," she said, her voice carrying a lilting accent.

"Where is Wander?" Consuela demanded, her strength too meager to permit small talk. "For that matter, where am I?"

"You are on Avanti," the white-clad nurse replied. "Welcome to my home. As for this Wander, I am sure if you kindly wait in bed for the doctor, he—"

"Was there a young man brought in with me?"

"There were several brought off the ship." Her eyes glimmered with admiration. "All Avanti knows of your battle with the pirates. You are heroes."

Consuela started for the door, but her legs chose that moment to falter. She would have collapsed if the nurse had not been there to catch her. "Please, you must return to bed," the nurse urged her. "You must show a kindness to your body. You have been unconscious for six days."

So long? Consuela allowed her fears to surface. "A man my age, a scout. Slender—"

"Tall and fair with most handsome features," the nurse gaily agreed, gently guiding her back toward the bed. "Of course I know this Wander. He and you are the only two who have not fully recovered."

Consuela used the last remaining fragments of her strength to halt her progress toward the bed, grip the nurse's arm, and plead, "Take me to him."

The nurse inspected her with excited eyes. "He is your special man?"

"Very special," Consuela agreed.

Clearly the idea of furthering a hospital romance met with the nurse's approval. "You will please sit. I will find a coaster and return."

Confused by the unfamiliar words, but relieved by her evident agreement, Consuela permitted the nurse to guide her down. She watched the nurse then turn and leave, too tired to even protest at being left alone.

Soon enough the nurse returned, pushing in front of her what appeared to be a wheelchair without wheels. "Here, you are to please sit," she said, drawing the floating apparatus up alongside the bed. With an expert efficiency of motion, she eased Consuela off the bed and onto the chair.

"Oooh, wonderful," Consuela sighed. Not only did the chair take her weight, but it actually took weight from her. She felt light as a feather, barely heavy enough to remain in the chair and not float away.

"Yes, is very nice. Sometimes when I am tired I use the coaster for little restings," the nurse agreed. She spun the chair about and pushed her through the doorway.

Outside, the hallway was fairly crowded, and everywhere faces greeted Consuela with smiles. The attention left her feeling very uncomfortable. When they passed through an empty space, she said, "Does everybody around here know who I am?"

"All Avanti knows," the nurse cheerfully agreed. "Every day is report on newscast of how you progress. I come off duty and meet hundreds of reporters. All want to hear how beautiful scout lady and handsome scout man are progressing." She gave an excited little sigh. "And now we are finding that he is your special man. Whole world will want to hear how you sleep for six days, then cannot even wait for doctor before seeking the handsome scout."

Consuela felt her cheeks growing red. "Is he all right?"

"Oh yes, monitors show all normal signs. But still he sleeps." The nurse's bright face leaned into view. "Perhaps he wakes for you, no? Oh, is all so romantic!"

The nurse stopped before a door marked with a yellow warning shield and pressed in a code on the numerical lock. When the door had sighed open, she pushed Consuela inside.

Consuela could not help herself. When Wander came into view, she gave a little gasp, partly of relief over seeing him again, and partly over how pale and still he looked. With his closed eyes and color only barely deeper than the starched sheet, Wander looked like a little boy, helpless and frail and utterly in need.

The nurse pushed Consuela over. She leaned forward and grasped his hand. "His skin is so cold."

"Six days he sleeps," the nurse agreed. "The pirate attack, it was terrible, no? And you, a *sensitive* attached to the ship's amplifiers, it was a wonder you survived."

Consuela turned to her in confusion. "You know all about that?"

"All Avanti knows," the nurse repeated. "My world, we suffer for years from pirate attacks on the shipping lanes. Some years, only two or three ships come through. Slowly, slowly we are strangled. We plead to the Hegemony for help, and they do nothing." Her dark eyes scattered thrilling sparks about the room. "And suddenly in our skies appears a ship, and with it comes news that they bring with them a captured pirate ship! And the captain tells how they carry sensitives who find the shadowlanes, and tell of ship waiting to attack. So all Avanti waits to hear of scouts' recovery."

Consuela turned her attention back to Wander's sleeping form. She leaned forward, traced a finger down the side of his cheek. She was embarrassed by the nurse's closeness and her melodramatic interest. Still, she kissed his cheek and whispered, "Wander, it's Consuela. Can you hear me?"

The slumbering young man emitted a soft groan.

All concern for the nurse's unbridled interest vanished. Consuela raised herself up, although it was hard, for moving from the chair meant taking on her full weight. She leaned forward and kissed his forehead, his cheek, his lips. "Wake up, Wander. Please, for me. Open your eyes."

And he did.

Wander blinked and focused, seeing her and sighing with the pleasure that flooded his face. He whispered, "I dreamed you had left me. Gone back."

"I did," she said, matching his gentle tone. Raising his hand to cradle it against her chest, her other hand resting featherlight against his cheek. "But I came back."

Wander licked dry lips, managed, "For me?"

The wings of her heart fluttered against her ribs as she nodded and softly replied, "For you."

"Ooooh." The sound of the little nurse clapping hands together under her chin turned them both about. "Is just toooo wonderful. All Avanti will sing of this love. Wait, wait, I must go and find doctor." With that, the nurse spun around and was gone.

Wander returned his gaze to her and asked, "What was that all about?"

"Later," she said. She brushed the hair from his forehead, etching the memory of each feature on the surface of her heart. "Can I get you something?"

"Water."

She helped him drink, then drank herself. Consuela felt energy course through her with the liquid. She drained the cup, set it down, asked, "How do you—"

The door sighed open, and a familiar voice said, "Here they are. Just as I suspected. Planning more mischief, no doubt."

Consuela spun about. "Captain Arnol!"

The nurse squeezed past the captain and attempted to bar the doorway with her small frame. "No, no, is forbidden!"

"Silence," the captain snapped, and brusquely pushed the squawking nurse to one side. He stepped in, then turned and motioned for a stern black-robed figure to enter. "If you please, Diplomat."

"This room is off limits," the nurse squawked, her arms making frantic motions, trying to shoo the pair back out and away. "Only with doctor's orders can you enter here."

"Oh, do be quiet, that's a good little girl." The silver-maned diplomat swept into the room with the air of one long used to regal command.

"I am going for doctor," the nurse announced hotly, and fled.

"An excellent notion," the diplomat drawled. He bent over the bed and examined Wander with the coldest eyes Consuela had ever seen. "So this is the renegade scout."

"I assure you, Diplomat," Captain Arnol began from his post by the door. "I had no idea whatsoever—"

"Quite, quite." His eyes lifted to fasten Consuela with a gaze that held no pity, no compassion, no life. "And whom do we have here?"

"Oh, the girl." Arnol shrugged his unconcern. "Grimson sent her along as a trainee. Goodness only knows why. Her ability is scarcely measurable."

"Not another Talent then," the diplomat said, showing a trace of regret.

"Her?" Captain Arnol clearly found that humorous. "Whatever gave you that idea?"

"Yes, of course. Two Talents found together would be impossible, even for Senior Pilot Grimson." The glacial eyes swung back to the silent figure on the bed, and the tone sharpened. "What is your name, renegade?"

"My name is Wander," he replied, as hotly as his weakened state would allow. "But I am not a renegade, and I resent you calling me one."

"Resent, do you?" The diplomat sniffed his amusement. "Have you any idea with whom you speak?"

"I do not, nor do I care."

"You will show proper respect when addressing the diplomat, Scout Wander," Arnol barked.

"Peace." The diplomat raised one languid hand in dismissal. "The gallant scout will have ample time to learn respect and a myriad of other things once we have him properly settled."

Consuela shifted so that she came between the diplomat's gaze and Wander. "Where are you taking him?"

Eyes the color of a frozen sky rose to meet her own. Consuela struggled not to show the fear she felt. Something must have been revealed, however, for the diplomat replied with frosty amusement, "And what might your name be, Scout?"

"Consuela," she replied, taking great comfort from the steadiness of her voice. "And yours?"

Captain Arnol broke in, "She is an outworlder, Diplomat. Clearly she has never heard that those who represent the Hegemony pay the ultimate price of giving up their own identity."

Something in the captain's voice lifted her gaze. She saw a clear warning in his eyes, and something more. Fear?

"A pity that the senior pilot did not include proper manners in your training, Scout," the diplomat said.

But Consuela's gaze remained on Captain Arnol, as he gave his head an imperceptible shake, then from behind the diplomat lifted one open hand slightly, in caution.

The door sighed open to admit an angry gray-bearded man in white. "What is the meaning of this?"

The diplomat did not bother to look around. "And who, pray tell, are you?"

"Doctor Alvero, head of this clinic." He stepped to one side and allowed the diminutive nurse to enter the room. "I am personally responsible for the scout."

"Very well, Doctor." The head turned a fraction. "I hereby relieve you of your duties in regards to this patient."

But the doctor was not so easily cowed. "Your robes mean nothing to me, Diplomat." He almost spat out the last word. "It is your kind who have strangled our fair world. You and the Hegemony you serve have stood and watched as the pirates brought us to our knees."

The diplomat raised one hand toward his face. The robe slipped back to reveal a bright metallic band around his wrist. He spoke the single word, "Guards."

Instantly the door slid back; this time six stern-faced men cradling snub-nosed guns shouldered through, pressing Arnol and the doctor immediately toward the side wall. When the doctor protested, one of the soldiers lifted his gun and jammed it into the base of the doctor's skull. The man grew still.

The diplomat ordered, "Lift this one into the coaster."

A pair of soldiers reached for Wander, while another grasped Consuela's arms and pressed her up against the wall. She cried, "Where are you taking him?"

The one holding her asked, "What of her?"

"She is an outworlder, and of no importance whatsoever," the diplomat sneered. "Now that she can no longer rely on this sensitive's abilities, she'll soon be scrounging for passage back to her dirty little globe."

"You won't get away with this," the doctor threatened, then groaned when the guard's nozzle jammed his face up hard against the wall.

"Ah, but I already have," the diplomat replied. He motioned for Wander's coaster to be pushed out, then ordered, "Search them, destroy the communicator, and seal the room. That should give us ample time." As he passed the captain, he paused and said, "I regret that I shall be forced to detain you with the others."

"It is an honor," Arnol replied grim-faced, "to serve the Hegemony."

"Indeed," the diplomat said dryly. "Your assistance in this matter will be duly noted." He turned and swept from the room.

Consuela felt brusque hands pat her down, then press her hard against the wall before releasing her entirely. She turned just in time to be blinded by a scorching blast from one gun, transforming the bed's headboard into a smoldering hulk. The last guard backed from the room. The door sighed shut, then glowed rosy-red as it was struck by a second bolt from the outside.

Consuela flung herself against the door, cried in frustration and pain when the unyielding portal scalded her. She turned to Captain Arnol and demanded, "Where are they taking him?"

"I did what I could," Arnol replied, his eyes on the closed door.

"Answer me," she demanded shrilly.

He turned slowly, like a man pushed beyond the limits of his strength. "I do not know for certain. But there have been rumors . . . "

"No!" the doctor gasped. "It is too terrible to imagine that there is such a place."

"What place?" Consuela pleaded.

"A bleak world," Captain Arnol replied. "One unfit for humans, home to an ultrasecret bastion of the Hegemony."

"But why do they want Wander?" Her heart felt lanced with the sword of despair.

"That I cannot say. All I know is the Dark Couriers never relinquish what falls within their grasp." Captain Arnol looked at her with eyes reflecting more sorrow than she would have ever thought possible. "It is best you forget him," he said gently. "I did what I could. I saved you at least from their clutches. They thought you innocent, naive, a parasite on his powers with none of your own."

She could hold back the tears no longer. "You mean Wander is gone?"

"You are free. Take solace in that now in this moment of loss." Arnol turned back to the door. "For the young man, there is no hope at all."

CHAPTER THREE

The double moons graced a star-studded sky. The larger globe glowed soft and golden, the smaller a ruddy red. A broad silver river of stars stretched from horizon to horizon, with three supernovas sparkling like heavenly beacons in their midst. The evening was warm and sweet scented, and the breeze was mild. Below the balcony where she stood, a night bird sang a plaintive melody, a sound unlike anything she had ever heard before.

Consuela had never known the meaning of loneliness until that moment.

Soft movement heralded the arrival of another. "Are you all right, Scout Consuela?"

"How could I be," she softly replied, not turning around, "when I don't even know where I am?"

"You are on Avanti," the pert little nurse replied simply. Her name was Adriana, and she had attached herself firmly to Consuela's side.

When the hospital door had been forced open, the news of Wander's disappearance had raced through the staff and out into the city. Within minutes an official convoy had arrived, led by a stately matron who said she represented the chancellor, who was offering Consuela a place within the official guest house. Urged on by all, including Captain Arnol, and too confused to think clearly for herself, Consuela had accepted.

On the way through a city she scarcely saw, Adriana reported that the spaceport confirmed that the Hegemony vessel carrying Wander and the diplomat had blasted off. It had departed against express orders and for an unknown destination. Consuela had allowed herself to be led into a spacious apartment, half heard the matron's assurances that she was utterly safe here, closed the bedroom door, and cried herself to sleep.

A gentle hand on her arm brought the night back into focus. "I know it is hard," Adriana told her. "But life must go on, yes? And you have an audience with the chancellor in an hour."

"I can't," Consuela said simply.

"You must." For once the nurse's gay chatter was absent. "The chancellor rules our land on behalf of the Three Planets Council. His requests are commands, and he has said that he will see you this night."

Adriana took her hand and led her back into the large bedchamber. "Look. I have laid out your scout robes."

Consuela's heart tolled the passing moments with the hollow note of a cracked bell. "What am I supposed to say to him?"

"Nothing, if you wish." Her voice remained gentle but firm. "He knows of your loss, as does all Avanti. But meet him you will. Who knows, perhaps he can help you."

A faint tug of interest lifted her gaze. "Help me do what?"

"Do whatever you must." Dark eyes met hers with shared sorrow. "At times like this, even the slenderest of hopes can offer a reason for life, no?"

When they departed an hour later, the night embraced their passage with a warm, perfumed breeze. Because the evening was so pleasant, they traveled by open floater. To Consuela, it appeared to be nothing more than a slab of illuminated sidewalk. Adriana led her toward the white square framed by soft light. They stepped on board, and polished railings swiftly rose to surround them. Adriana leaned down and spoke the words, "Palace, main entrance." Instantly the floater lifted and started away.

The floater traveled smoothly and silently at just over treetop level, taking them toward the grandest building on the horizon, surrounded as it was by a brilliant ring of light. From every peak and turret flew great flags, which appeared to shimmer with their own illumination.

Something at the corner of her vision caused her to turn around. "We're being followed."

"Guards," Adriana replied, not bothering to look. "They will be with you everywhere. It is necessary until we are sure the Hegemony takes no interest in you."

"We?" Consuela looked at her escort. "Just who are you, anyway?"

"I am a nurse," Adriana replied. "But I also serve the Three Planets and the ruling Council."

"Serve who?"

But further explanations were cut short by a brilliant shaft of light shifting around and pinpointing them. Momentarily blinded, Consuela raised her hand to shield her eyes and heard an enormous roar of noise rise up from the ground below. "What is that?"

"As I said," Adriana replied simply. "All Avanti knows."

Her eyes adjusted to the glare, Consuela leaned over and risked a glance as their floater began settling downward. Stretching out in three directions as far as she could see was a great mass of screaming, shouting, waving people. All with faces upturned. All looking at her.

At *her*.

The floater settled into a tiny island of calm. Great gold-embossed gates rose up behind them, while in front, uniformed soldiers cordoned off the crowd. A trio of larger floaters settled down alongside and in front of theirs, and a dozen stiff-faced guards joined those already flanking the crowd.

Consuela allowed Adriana to guide her off their own floater, but she could not take her eyes from the people. A forest of arms reached over the soldiers, all accompanied by faces shouting and laughing and crying. For *her*.

Consuela offered them a timid wave, and the noise became even more fervid.

Adriana touched her arm, and she turned as a cortege of guards in sharply creased uniforms passed through the open palace gates, flanking a pair of elderly statesmen in flowing robes. The guards formed a tall helmeted wall on either side of her as the statesmen approached and bowed. Because the crowd's noise overwhelmed them all, they simply motioned for her to take a station between them as they turned back toward the palace.

Only when Consuela had taken a half-dozen steps did she realize that Adriana was no longer with her. She turned back to see her new-found friend smile from her place by the floater and motion Consuela onward.

Reluctantly she turned back and allowed herself to be guided up broad steps surrounded by yet more guards, through the tallest doors she had ever seen, up a long sweeping set of broad inner stairs, through

more doors, and into a vast hallway whose painted ceiling seemed truly
to be as high as the sky itself. The statesmen introduced themselves with
more formal bows, then began introducing her to an endless line of people. The men were groomed and polished, the women wore a spectacular array of colors and jewels. All the faces were smiling, all the people
eager. To meet *her*.

Consuela allowed her hand to be taken by each person in turn, for-
getting the names and titles as soon as they were spoken, scarcely seeing the faces as belonging to individuals at all. The entire scene was too
overwhelming, especially coming as it did so swiftly upon the heels of
all the other shocks.

Then her attention was caught and held by a tall young man who
stood at the line's very end. Consuela stopped so suddenly that the
statesman following bumped into her. She did not feel it.

The man wore pilot's robes.

He made a deep and sweeping bow, the gesture adding to the majesty
of his looks and his robes. "Pilot Dunlevy at your service, noble sister
Scout. I am on temporary assignment to Avanti's main spaceport. Might
I have the honor of accompanying you?"

The pair of statesmen began an officious protest, but Consuela cut
them off by offering her arm and replying, "Gladly."

He moved in as close as decorum allowed and spoke in a voice
meant for her ears alone. "We have a good deal in common, you and I,"
he told her. "I too studied under Senior Pilot Grimson, and since then
have piloted ships beyond the Rim. Where is your home?"

"Baltimore," she said faintly. She glanced up at his face, guessed his
age in the late twenties. A tall and striking man. If she were not suffering
so from the pain of loss, she would even have called him handsome.

He shook his head in bewilderment. "Never have I heard of that one,
but perhaps I know it by another name. No matter. Avanti was my birth-
place, and my first allegiance is here. What has happened to this world
and her sister planets is a disgrace." His voice grew heated as he leaned
even closer. "I must warn you, sister Scout, there are Hegemony spies
everywhere. It is for this reason that I chose to approach you here."

Something in his voice clutched at her. "You have news?"

"Move along, lest we draw unwanted ears," he said, and forced a
smile to his face. "Can you laugh for the people?"

"No."

"Smile then. Not all the eyes upon us are here in this room. Nor are all those you see here your friends."

Consuela made do with a thin grimace. "Tell me."

"The chancellor himself asked me home to Avanti. He knows my family, and through them asked me to vacation here and see if I could help in solving the mystery."

"What—"

He gestured her to silence. "Later. We have only until those doors up ahead. I was at the spaceport when the Hegemony vessel blasted in earlier today, unannounced and uninvited. I was there too when it left."

Consuela stopped and wheeled about. "You saw where it went?"

"The quadrant only." His face stretched taut in a smile that cost him much. "Alas, I am not a Talent." He backed away and into another sweeping bow, then raised his voice so that it carried to those who sought to cluster close. "An honor to make your acquaintance, sister Scout. Perhaps you would do me the esteem of joining me at the spaceport tomorrow."

"Of course," Consuela replied, trying hard to match his formal manner.

"Excellent. Shall we say at noon?"

CHAPTER FOUR

The chancellor's inner sanctum was not as grand as the formal hall, but in its own way was just as elegant. The great oval-shaped chamber was surrounded by tall pillars supporting a domed ceiling colored like a sky at dawn. The carpet was embossed with what appeared to be three planets forming a triangle, with a pair of brilliant stars gleaming from their epicenter.

"Scout Consuela, what an honor and a privilege." The chancellor was a gray-haired gentleman who required neither height nor girth to grant him the stature of power. He wore his office like an invisible mantle, and authority shone from his clear gray eyes. He turned to the hovering statesmen and said, "Thank you, gentlemen, that will be all."

Clearly this was not what they expected or desired. "But sire—"

The chancellor needed only to raise his head a fraction and glance in their direction for both to bow and scurry from the room. When the great portals were closed behind them, he said with quiet solemnity, "All Avanti grieves with you at this time of loss and sorrow."

Consuela found herself losing control beneath the power of this man's genuine kindness. She stiffened her chin to stop it from quivering, took a long breath, managed, "Thank you."

He took note of her struggle for control with a single nod of approval. "Come over here and sit down. We shall not have much time to speak alone today. Avanti clamors for you. Later, perhaps, but not now. So you will excuse me if I do away with protocol."

Consuela allowed herself to be guided into a brocade chair with gold-embossed arms and made do with a nod.

"The good Captain Arnol tells me that you are a practical and level-headed young woman. And that you are indeed a Talent. Is all this true?"

His abrupt manner startled her into an equally direct reply. "Yes."

"Then I will come right to the point. We have long suspected that the Hegemony monitors the reaches available only to you Talents. How, we do not know, but we suspect that they must have amplifiers, the powers of which we cannot begin to imagine. Amplifiers so enormously potent that they can reach to the very borders of the empire. And they use these to constantly search out the sensitives who might have escaped them."

"But why?"

"I was hoping you could tell me that for yourself."

Consuela inspected the strong stalwart face and decided that here was a man she could trust. "I did not even know I was a sensitive myself until a few weeks ago. To be honest, I still find it a little hard to believe."

"I am sorry to hear that." The chancellor showed genuine disappointment. "Well, I suppose I should take comfort in the fact that your freshness no doubt explains how you managed to escape their clutches. Nonetheless, I am disappointed not to have an opportunity to have some of the mysteries encircling the Hegemony's use of Talents resolved."

"I don't understand," Consuela said. "Aren't you a member of the Hegemony?"

"In word and on paper, yes," the chancellor replied, his face settling into grim lines. "But in truth, less and less with each passing day. You see, we who make up the Three Planets were growing daily in power. Up until ten years ago, we pledged our unswerving loyalty to the Hegemony, and did so willingly. Still, they did not trust us. We were rich and growing richer. Other nearby star systems began forging stronger and stronger links, turning to us in times of trouble, rather than to the Hegemony. Our industrial might was unsurpassed. Our academies turned out the finest minds in the empire. Then everything changed."

Then he stopped and looked at her, as though willing her to find the answer for herself. It dawned with blinding suddenness. "Pirates."

"Precisely," the chancellor said approvingly. "Whether or not the Hegemony is behind their stranglehold, we cannot be sure. But what we do know is that help has not been forthcoming. Furthermore, on one point the Hegemony's rule is unbending; no single system is permitted its own military force. We may not arm ourselves beyond what is required to police our own internal borders. The Hegemony is responsible for all might and military presence beyond our own system. Yet we on Avanti have long felt that the local Emissary has orders to do nothing but stand aside and watch us suffer."

"It has been hard for you," Consuela observed, for the moment drawn beyond her own loss by the chancellor's gravity.

"Worse than that, my dear. We are a trading system. It is another reason why the Hegemony is jealous of our wealth, for we compete directly with their own traders. Or did. Now we are cut off. And as a result, the Three Planets are slowly dying."

Consuela studied the man's open gaze, realized that someone of his power and position would take the time to speak with her only if something important was required from her. Despite the fog of her heavy heart, she understood what he was driving at. "Your goals and mine are the same."

"I am most glad to learn that Captain Arnol's assessment of you is correct," the chancellor approved. "You want to find your special man. We want to know where the Hegemony has taken him. And why."

My special man. Just hearing the words warmed the night with hope. "I met a pilot outside. He says he may have found something."

"Yes, I have read the pilot's report." Clearly the chancellor was less than optimistic. "I know Dunlevy's family. They are good people. It was a long shot, requesting that he return. But to identify a possible segment of the empire, one which contains several hundred systems . . . " He gave a grim shrug. "In any case, tell him that anything he requires, anything at all, shall be placed instantly at his disposal. And yours."

"Thank you," she said, moved despite her own heartache by the man's noble strength.

"Adriana knows how to reach me at any time of night or day. If you find something of even possible use in our quest, do not hesitate to contact me."

A quest. *Our* quest. "You know my nurse?"

"Adriana is my own niece. She also happens to be one of a very special breed," he replied, rising to his feet. "Above all else, she is a patriot. Come, my dear. We must hold further talk for another time and give the people their due."

He led her across the chamber, pulled back heavy drapes embossed with the emblem of what appeared to be two suns, and revealed a tall glass portal. It was only as Consuela followed him through the doorway that she realized he walked with a slight stoop, as though weighed down by the invisible burdens he carried.

The balcony had been prepared for them, and was draped in bunting and flowers. Consuela stepped outside, waited while her eyes adjusted to the spotlights' glare, and felt the waves of sound crash over her.

The chancellor permitted the tumult to continue for a short time, then raised his hands high and waited until the hubbub had eased. "My friends and fellow citizens of Avanti," he declared, his voice amplified by a hidden microphone so that it rang out through the surrounding night. "It is with great joy that I stand here and proclaim with you the first sign of hope that we have known in ten long years."

The rejoicing below carried a sense of renewed hope, so strong that even Consuela's wounded heart knew a moment's relief. So it was with a smile that she met the chancellor when he turned toward her, and from a wooden case brought out a shining gold medallion hung from a ribbon of rainbow colors.

"Scout Consuela," the chancellor said, his voice booming through the unseen speakers, "while you lay, still suffering from the wounds received in our defense, your shipmates have already been so honored. Now it is your turn to be declared a Knight of the Three Planet Realm. All Avanti is in your debt."

Consuela bowed her head and allowed the chancellor to place the ribbon around her neck. She then turned to the crowd and raised the medal toward them, the smile still coming easy. When the clamor had run its course, once more the chancellor raised his hands for silence. He then lifted a second slender box high over his head. "One other should also be standing here, sharing in the glory, and receiving his well-earned acclaim."

The words were carried out and echoed back over a suddenly silent crowd. Their abrupt stillness caused her to realize what enormous risk the chancellor was taking, speaking thus in public. It was an unequivocal and direct challenge to the Hegemony.

"Scout Consuela," the chancellor went on, turning back and extending to her the box. "I charge you with delivering this tribute, along with our heartfelt thanks, for the part that Scout Wander played in our triumph."

Consuela accepted the box, turned to the crowd, lifted the box over her own head, and spoke for the first time since walking out on the balcony. "I will deliver this," she said. "You have my word."

CHAPTER FIVE

The Avanti spaceport was a massive affair, made enormously depressing by its emptiness.

Consuela arrived well before noontime, unable to wait any longer to learn what she could of Wander's destination. Nothing could have prepared her for what she found.

As usual, she was accompanied on the floater by Adriana, surrounded by a sweeping phalanx of guards. The day was overcast, the air so heavy with approaching rain that it felt thick in her lungs. Thankfully, the trip was not long, as the spaceport lay on the same side of the capital city as the consular palace.

The port was void of activity. She could see that long before they landed. The vast space set aside for ground transport was almost empty. And there were no people at all. No movement around the empty thruster pads or the long line of colossal warehouses or the terminal itself. None.

Throughout the entire time of their approach, a single ship glided in, small and scarred and clearly intended for little more than lunar transport. Beyond the terminal, Consuela saw how weeds were pushing up between segments of the cracked and pitted concrete surrounding the launch pads.

"Ten years," Adriana said quietly as the floater came to a halt. "Ten years we have watched as our world has slowly been strangled."

Consuela peered through the sweeping expanse of glass and saw only vast, empty spaces adorned with chrome and polished surfaces and gleaming artwork. But no people. "This is terrible."

"Before, it was said that Avanti lived and died by trade. Can the Hegemony truly not see what the pirates are doing here? I and most others think not." She motioned toward the door. "Come, let us enter."

The main hall was even grander than the spaceport where she had met Wander. The walls were rose-colored stone streaked with what appeared to be real gold. They changed colors dramatically as the sun finally emerged from behind the heavily overcast sky. Consuela looked up through the polarized ceiling glass and gasped.

Not sun. *Suns.* Plural. Two of them.

One great and orangish red, the other smaller and bright as an arc-lamp even through the glass. She shielded her eyes, saw how twin strands of brilliant power flowed from the top and the bottom of the larger sun, like ribbons of light tying the suns together. "Incredible," she breathed.

"Careful," hissed Adriana at her side, and from the corner of her eye she saw the guards stiffen to full alert. "The Emissary."

Consuela lowered her head, saw an obese figure in flowing multi-colored robes approaching them. He was flanked by stern-faced warriors with weapons at the ready. Despite the evident danger, she was far from frightened. Her growing anger left no room for fear. Besides, the fat man looked as though he were dressed in an over-bright bathrobe.

"Well, well, what have we here?" The silken voice carried undercurrents of dedicated cruelty. "If it is not the glorious scout. Or perhaps I should say, Knight Scout. Ah, but has she neglected to wear her well-earned medal of honor?"

Consuela squeezed down tight on her fury, focusing it with the precision of aiming down a rifle barrel. She walked straight up to him, so close that he not only stopped talking but jerked back a half step in surprise. Her eyes only inches from his, she said, "I want to know where you've taken him."

Eyes slit down in calculated coldness. "Missing our little Talent, are we? How sad."

"What you and your people did to Wander was as evil as what you're doing to this planet."

He drew himself up and back, then gathered his dignity with a sweeping motion of his robes. "You would be well advised to watch your brazen tongue."

Her gaze did not budge. "I'm not afraid of you."

"Ah, but you should be." He started to say more but glanced uneasily at Consuela's guards, tensed and close at hand. Eyes hard as marbles turned back to her, and with a little mock bow he said, "We shall meet again, Scout. Of that I am certain."

Only when the outer doors had sighed shut behind him did Adriana murmur, "I am not sure that was wise."

"I don't care," Consuela replied stubbornly. "I'm in no mood to play games with a worm."

"He is that," Adriana agreed. "Come, the pilot is waiting."

Like everything else about the spaceport, the control tower was twice the size of the only other she had seen. There were two half-moon control-mounds, set at an angle to each other so that they faced out over two separate collections of thruster pads. All this only made the emptiness even more aching. There were a total of four people on duty when they entered, all of them gathered in a cluster around the Watch Commandant's station and ignoring the barren fields outside.

Pilot Dunlevy detached himself from the little group, walked over, spoke a greeting to Adriana, then bowed to Consuela. "It is indeed an honor to meet you again," he said formally. "All the staff here are friends, and are to be trusted. Before we go on, allow me to say for all of us here how sorry we are over your distress. I hope you believe me when I say that this is truly all Avanti's loss."

The words and the genuine concern behind them were almost enough to shatter her fragile hold on control. Mentally Consuela pushed aside his words, drew herself back from the brink, and said, "What I'd like to know is how they got in so easily. If you were so concerned about their plotting against you, you'd have thought to put a couple of guards out there."

"The hospital was *surrounded* with guards," he responded defensively. "Top to bottom, the place was *sealed*. But they were warned to bar entry to strangers, not to officers of the Hegemony. Even the toughest of guards would think twice about questioning a diplomat."

"So they just walked in," Consuela said, sorrow welling up once again. "And took him."

"Never for a moment did we think they would operate so openly," Dunlevy said. "It is a first, and demonstrates just how desperately they wanted him."

"But *why*?"

"I wish I knew," Dunlevy replied grimly.

His helpless frustration pushed at her, forcing her once more toward the edge. Her eyes brimmed over with the same burning loss which seared her chest, and she had to turn away.

Dunlevy noticed her distress and changed the subject with, "You out-worlders don't have much time for us from the privileged classes, do you?"

She made a rapid swipe of her eyes and hedged, "I'm not sure I know what you mean."

"Yes, you do," he replied. "Did you ever stop to wonder why we were given such preferential treatment? It's because we're more easily con-trolled."

"By the Hegemony?"

"Training young people to be pilots is a two-edged sword," he went on, his voice cutting like raw acid. "They need us in order to guide their ships and hold their empire together. But handing such power to young people who have not come up through the proper Hegemony ranks is dangerous business. So they cull those they can from the landed gentry, families with the most to lose. Their hope is that the parents of these young people will have instilled in them a sense of loyalty to the He-gemony. But if not, then these are people whose families they can get to easily and hold for ransom or worse."

She inspected his finely chiseled features, asked, "Are they doing this to you?"

"Not yet," he answered. "After an absence of almost three years, I have every right to come and visit my family. But the emissary was not here to see you. Not just, anyway."

"What did he say?"

"Nothing much." Bitterness stretched his features taut. "Just asked about my sister's health. She requires a medicine that isn't available on Avanti. Without it she wouldn't last a week."

"He would do that?"

Dunlevy's eyes remained on the control tower's closed portals. "He knew and I knew. The message was clear. I must do the Hegemony's bidding or my family suffers."

Consuela took a long mental step back, then said in a subdued voice, "I can't ask you to take that risk."

He looked down at her. "What are you talking about?"

"Trading your sister's life for information about where Wander might have been taken," she replied. "I couldn't live with myself."

For the first time since they had met, Dunlevy showed genuine humor. "If they even suspected I had followed the diplomat ship's departure, you would be talking to a little pile of ashes."

Hope sprang anew in her heart. "Then you'll help me?"

"You still don't realize how big this matter really is, do you?" He turned and took the stairs to the pilot's chair in long strides. "Come up here and hook up."

Consuela followed him slowly, slid into the chair next to his, looked at the headset he jammed into her hands, and hesitated. Then it hit her. She was sitting unshielded in a control tower and was hearing no voices. She looked out through the main windows at the empty vista before her and realized for the first time just how cut off Avanti really had become.

She handed back the headset. "I can't use this."

He looked up distractedly from his adjusting of the amp controls. "Why, what's the matter?"

She studied his face a moment, then replied, "I think it's time I trusted you."

His hands became utterly still. "What are you talking about?"

"If I plugged myself into that amp with this," she said, indicating the headset in his hands, "you'd have a screaming idiot on your hands in no time flat. I know. I've done it."

The blaze of triumph came and went with the speed of a lightning strike. He leaned forward and hissed, "You're a Talent?"

"Just so you understand, let me tell you exactly what I am," Consuela replied. "I am somebody with exactly zero training on watch, and with precisely one space trip under her belt."

Quietly she outlined her days at the port, leaving out her unexplained arrival, but little else. How she collapsed at the onset of her first class, and had scarcely recovered when Senior Pilot Grimson had shuttled her up to the tower, reacted just as Dunlevy did when she complained of voices—

"Without amplification?" Dunlevy's agitation was so great he could scarcely hold himself in the chair. "You heard the control tower's communications even when you weren't hooked in?"

"Not only that," she said, and told him of watching the ship's departure with Wander, feeling time slow with the countdown, until she felt connected to the moment beyond time when the gravity shield was released and the ship departed.

With that, Dunlevy appeared to stop breathing. He swiveled around to face out over the empty field and stared at nothing for the longest time before whispering, "I had heard rumors. We all did. That there really were sensitives whose abilities broke all the known boundaries. I thought they were legends."

"There's more." Consuela waited until he had swung back around, then told him of Pilot Grimson's sudden appearance, and how they had been rushed into Captain Arnol's ship. How on the voyage she and Wander had been simply experimenting with the mind-amp controls, trying to extend their senses out as far as they could without losing shipboard contact, when they had found the shadowlanes.

"Arnol mentioned this," Dunlevy murmured. "I had trouble believing him, though." He inspected her. "Another legend come to life."

"You have spoken with the captain? When?"

Dunlevy waved it aside. "Finish your story, then we will move on to other things."

"There isn't much else. We tracked down each shadowlane as we approached, and on the third we found the pirate ship. Captain Arnol planned to attack first, but I guess they got in one shot, because the next thing I knew I was here in the hospital."

Dunlevy sat in silence a moment longer. "Two Talents in the same class, and a diplomat's ship suddenly appearing out of nowhere," he said to himself. "No wonder Grimson panicked and rushed to get away."

"How is he?"

"Worried, of that I am sure." He raised himself with difficulty from his reverie. "He should be made aware of what has transpired. Would you like to speak with him?"

Suddenly Consuela found herself missing the stern-visaged teacher. "Very much."

A second hint of genuine humor surfaced. "I understand your sentiments perfectly. He is a fright to study under, but whenever I am faced with the unsolvable, I try to do what I think he would expect of me." Dunlevy bounded to his feet. "But first we shall find you a damped headset, second I shall show you the quadrant where they took your Wander, and then you will see what our dear Master Grimson has to say for himself."

He left and returned with impatient swiftness. He plugged her in, then sat and watched her adjust the headset's damping effect. He leaned over, read the dial, and sat back with a bemused expression. "You can truly detect the amplifier's power at this stage?"

"Any more and I'd be climbing the walls," Consuela replied.

"Then perhaps there is hope after all." Agitation sped his movements

PATH FINDER / 159

as he bent over the amp's controls and said, "Just relax and follow my lead."

"I don't—" Consuela stopped as her focus was drawn first out to the nearest thruster shield, then out and up. And up. And farther still. "Oh my."

"Relax," he said, his hands busy, powering them together farther and farther away. "Stay alert."

Here was the power of a pilot on watch, she realized. Here was what her lack of training kept her from both doing and fully understanding. Not simply communicating with oncoming and outgoing ships. Not simply sending messages and directions out across the vastness of space. But *connecting* with space. Reaching through the limits, and beyond, yet all the while resting steady and in control there in the tower.

Consuela felt herself sitting and breathing and feeling her racing heart, yet at the same time found herself being guided farther and farther out through the heavens, remaining steady only because she was fastened firmly to Dunlevy. Farther and faster she moved, and knew that here was one skilled and trained and truly in control.

"There," he finally announced, the whispered word resounding out in the stars where her mind was reaching. "This is as far as I managed to follow. I do not know if they were cloaked in some way, or simply passed beyond my ability to track them. But this is the quadrant where they were headed."

Even under his steady direction, all she saw was a limitless field of unknown space. She felt as much as saw him draw barriers that limited the range to a sort of distended cone, yet even here the expanse was enormous. "So many stars," she whispered.

"Two hundred and forty inhabited systems," he agreed dismally. "Not to mention twice as many that are not yet charted, or have no known planets, or simply are not thought to hold anything of worth."

With a sweep of his hand he drew them back, the instant of her return so shocking she was forced away from the seeming hopelessness of their challenge, and back into the relatively safe confines of the tower. Consuela took a breath, said, "That was incredible."

"The tricks of our craft," he said deferentially. "Had it been you up here, perhaps we could have identified precisely where they landed."

"Had it been me up here," Consuela replied, "I would never have left the field."

If he realized she was paying him a compliment, he did not show it.

"And now to see if our dear Senior Pilot Grimson is available."

Again there was the sweeping outward, this time focused into a beam that followed a tightly controlled path. Consuela allowed herself to be swept along. She recognized even more clearly that having extra talent did not in any way make up for a lack of training.

There was a sense of planetary approach, then the call from Dunlevy, *This is Avanti Spaceport, Watch Communicator calling with a message for Senior Pilot Grimson.*

He is off watch, came the droned reply. *Report and I will pass on.*

Negative. This message carries priority one, code red.

You had better be right, Communicator, came the laconic reply. *Grimson hates to be disturbed when he is teaching.*

This is urgent, Dunlevy stubbornly repeated. *I take full responsibility.*

Hold on, came the response, and the contact ended.

Consuela waited with the patience of one who could scarcely comprehend what she was sensing. There she sat, safe and calm in a chair which molded to her in a comfortable support, looking out through tower windows at the broad expanse of empty field. And yet at the same time she was suspended in space, in contact with a world so distant she could not have found it on the clearest of nights, even if she had known where to look. Aware of the world about her, and still able to see out and through the endless night of space.

Grimson here, came the familiar icy voice. *This had better be good.*

Dunlevy reporting, Senior Pilot. I have a colleague of yours here with me.

Consuela found it possible to extend her thoughts better if she whispered softly. *Hello, Senior Pilot.*

Instantly came the sharp response, *Hold!* Then nothing.

Consuela drew back and looked toward Dunlevy, but he remained motionless, save for the lifting of a single finger. Wait.

A few moments later Grimson returned. *All right. This is as secure a channel as I can arrange on short notice. What news?*

Very little positive to report, Senior Pilot. Swiftly Dunlevy sketched all that he knew—starting with their discovery of the shadowlane and the pirates, ending with Wander's forced disappearance. Dunlevy spoke with the terse compactness of one accustomed to giving official reports. When he finished he simply stopped and waited.

I knew it was too good to be true when the diplomatic vessel departed from here so swiftly, Grimson said finally. *They were headed your way.*

Are you under suspicion?

*If so, it is nothing more than that. For the moment, in any case. My re-*cords show clearly that a training flight was arranged for two gifted stu-dents. *Nothing more, nothing less. What they may surmise, when given time to reconsider, is anyone's guess.*

Consuela could stand it no longer. *Where have they taken Wander?*

That I cannot tell you. A trace of sympathy crept into Grimson's disci-plined calm. *It is one of the Hegemony's most closely guarded secrets.*

If it exists at all, Dunlevy added.

Of that I have no doubt whatsoever, Grimson responded. *Wander is not the first Talent I have lost to the diplomats.*

Of course, Dunlevy said slowly. *That was why you took immediate steps to send this pair away.*

To no avail, I fear, Grimson said. *For Wander, at least.*

But Consuela refused to accept the note of hopelessness, even for a moment. *Dunlevy watched the diplomat's ship depart.*

A keenness surged across immeasurable distances. *You tracked the ship?*

To the quadrant only.

Tell me.

Vector Nine.

So far. The senior pilot was silent. *There was once a Hegemony battle station out that way. Before my time, but my own teacher had apprenticed there as a newly released scout. A terrible place, he said, one so horrible not even battle-scarred troops could stand it for long. Then the empire's borders were extended outward, and to everyone's relief the station was moved.*

And the planet?

Abandoned. Grimson hesitated, then offered, *Or so they say.*

This could be it. Dunlevy's own excitement remained barely under control. *You have the coordinates?*

Somewhere. I shall scour the records this very day.

This is news the chancellor must hear, Dunlevy said. *Does the planet have a name?*

Indeed, Grimson answered. *Taken from a time beyond time, or so leg-end has it. They called it Citadel.*

CHAPTER SIX

Rick found himself growing enormously bored.

He would have never imagined such a thing possible. But he missed the stringent challenge of combat, of being tested to his limits and beyond.

No question about it. Having a life of wine, women, and song grew stale faster than he would have ever thought possible.

News of their having captured a pirate vessel arrived before their ship did, as Arnol's first report had been broadcast all over the planet Avanti. They landed at a spaceport full not of ships, but of people. Rick would never forget that sight as long as he lived, a mass of people stretching out in every direction as far as he could see.

It was only with time that he and the others began to understand why they had received the greeting they did. How for ten years the world had begged and pleaded with the Hegemony for assistance against the pirates, and how the Hegemony had replied time after time, "What pirates are these?" For the Hegemony's official position was that, yes, of course, there were the occasional villains. But as to an organized band waging war for profit in space? Inside the Hegemony's borders? Absolute nonsense. And since nobody had ever encountered pirates and lived to tell the tale, all they had to go on were snatches of cut-off conversations and rumors of outworld slavers fattened with the product of pirate attacks.

But now they had captured a pirate vessel. Intact, with crew alive. And done not by a Hegemony battle fleet, bristling with men and weaponry. No, by a single trader traversing the Hegemony lightways, alone and outfitted with a grand total of four weapons officers and two trainee scouts.

Truly this was the stuff of legends.

Rick found himself singled out for special attention. For when the full account was heard, the world learned that it was he who had saved the ship by overcoming the effects of the stunner blast and firing off three well-aimed bolts of his own. The chancellor himself mentioned his actions at the reception honoring the crew before awarding him the same knighthood medal that they all now wore.

Things started heating up that same night.

Scarcely had he recovered from the spotlight's shock when the first women approached him. Their manners and their speech left no room for doubt. And it was not just one. Lady after highborn lady had drawn near and made him offers that had set his ears aflame and left him unsure whether to laugh out loud or pinch himself to make sure he was not dreaming. By the end of the night he felt ten feet tall and loaded for bear.

But to his utter amazement, within a week the adoring fans who followed them everywhere, the adulation and everything that accompanied it, all began to fade. Rick found himself yearning for the relative simplicity of space.

That very morning Captain Arnol noticed the change, and approved. At breakfast he had observed Rick seated glumly in the kitchen of their palatial quarters and remarked, "There's hope for you yet, Lieutenant."

"Captain?"

"I have accepted a somewhat irregular request from the local Chancellor, one that will have to remain confidential for a while longer. To be perfectly honest, I know little of the details myself. But I have decided to trust the chancellor and respect his need for secrecy. I'm sending the ship onward under the command of my number two." Arnol inspected him over the rim of his coffee mug, then said, "I've decided to keep you here with me."

Rick scrambled to his feet. "If it's all the same with you, Captain, I'd rather get back into action."

"I see that you would," Arnol said approvingly. "That is precisely why I have decided to hold you over. You and Guns will be my weapons contingent."

"For what, Captain? We won't have a ship."

164 / T. DAVIS BUNN

"At the moment. Things are brewing beyond the horizon, that's all I can tell you." Arnol set down his cup. "I have a meeting this morning with the chancellor. Perhaps there will be more to report later on."

Glumly Rick had spent the morning watching most of his crewmates pack up and set off. No matter what the captain said, he genuinely wished to be among them. And Guns was no help. The grizzled weapons officer had not stirred in almost two days. He had the ability to store up sleep and food as a camel did water.

"Ten-hut!"

Rick bounced to his feet, then realized the sound had come from far down the corridor. The captain. Arnol must have returned. Swiftly he donned his uniform and scurried to the front gallery.

"Ah, Lieutenant, good. Is Guns with us?"

Rick found himself unable to respond, his attention captured by the entourage accompanying Captain Arnol. The chancellor was there, along with a pair of statesmen, plus a tall man in pilot's robes, plus guards. Lots of guards.

And Consuela.

She entered the room and brought a shadow with her. Although she held herself erect, it was with effort. Her features looked hollowed out by some pain so deep he could only guess at it. It was strange, seeing so young a face locked in such grief. Yet it was real. He only had to look at her eyes to know that she was truly in agony over Wander's kidnapping.

They had all heard of it, of course. Even Guns, the harshest critic of the pilot class, now classified these two as a breed apart. When they had heard how the diplomat had broken into the hospital, kidnapped Wander only moments after he had been revived, blasted the room's controls, sealed them all inside, then made their escape with warriors guarding their exit, they had all wanted vengeance. It was a matter of pride for them, that and the desire to hunt down more pirates—and for that they needed Wander's abilities.

But this was something entirely different. Rick stared at Consuela, and somehow the sorrow etched on her face made the women and the celebrations and his experiences of the past few days seem even more hollow.

"Lieutenant."

He snapped to alert. "Captain, Guns is still asleep, far as I know."

"What about the others?"

"Tucker is about. I believe that's it."

"Go and rouse Guns, will you. Tell him to get out here and be swift about it."

But evidently the weapons officer's internal tracking system worked even in sleep, for he was already up and dressing when Rick arrived. "What's up, mate?"

"Captain wants you on the bounce."

"Let's be at it, then." As they passed back down the corridor, Guns asked, "Any idea what's behind this?"

Rick shook his head. "But the chancellor's here. And Consuela."

To his surprise, Guns actually brightened at the news. "Lass is up and about, is she? Good. That's real good."

They entered the vast main gallery to find Chief Petty Officer Tucker seated among the gathering, which had requisitioned the chamber's far side and now been cordoned off by alert guards. Tucker, a tall burly officer, was another of the crew ordered to remain behind when the ship had blasted off that very day. His response had blistered paint at thirty paces, but only after the captain had left the room.

Now he wore a different expression entirely. He sat in formal alertness, no surprise given the presence of both the captain and the chancellor, not to mention the other silent statesmen. But there was no disguising the battle gleam in his eyes.

"Ah, Guns, good of you to join us. You remember the chancellor."

"Aye, Captain." He saluted the chancellor, then turned and gave a formal bow of greeting toward Consuela. "Knew you were too tough to keep down for long. Nice to see you up and about."

Consuela managed a fleeting smile. "Hello, Guns."

"No need to worry, lass. We're going to bring the boyo back," Guns promised quietly. "You can take my very oath on that one."

"A worthy sentiment," the chancellor stated.

Consuela was forced to turn away for a moment, but not before the raw edge of her grief was exposed. Tucker reached over from the chair beside hers and enveloped her hands in one hairy paw. She took a breath, gave him a look of genuine gratitude.

"I need not tell anyone," the chancellor began, "that anything discussed at this or any other time is to be held in strictest confidence. Your dwelling is as safe as anywhere on this planet, but outside these portals you may assume to find Hegemony spies lurking everywhere." He scanned the group to ensure that his message had struck home, then nodded toward the captain.

"Now that we are all present," Captain Arnol said, "allow me to introduce Pilot Dunlevy, a man claimed as friend by our scout and vouched for by the chancellor. He has news that may interest us."

Dunlevy leaned forward and swiftly sketched his tracking of the Hegemony vessel and then his contact with Senior Pilot Grimson. "I have just come from communicating with him. To his utter astonishment, Grimson could find no record anywhere of a planet known as Citadel."

The chancellor tensed. "This is true?"

"I know this Grimson," Captain Arnol interjected. "Both by reputation and in person. He is a man of unquestioned integrity. If he says something, you can rest assured it is true."

"Grimson was up the entire night," Dunlevy went on, "checking through all records held by the spaceport library, going back to the original Hegemony mapping ships. Because they are a scout training station, they also hold numerous duplicates of master archive files. He found nothing. And yet the more he searched, the more he became convinced his own teacher had specifically told him of this world."

There was a moment of stunned silence, then the statesman seated beside the chancellor breathed, "Then we have found the target."

"Found it and lost it all in the same moment," muttered his compatriot.

"Not necessarily," responded the chancellor. "All we need to do is have a reason to go to that quadrant and make inquiries."

Tucker shifted uncomfortably in his seat. "Begging the master's pardon, but I'm afraid I've been lost somewhere out beyond the outer orbit."

The chancellor's smile came and went with fleeting swiftness. "Your pardon, Chief Petty Officer. I shall start at the beginning." He nodded toward Arnol and said, "I asked your good captain to remain behind and to hold this chosen few with him for a reason that I could not at the time explain to anyone else. First, I needed to receive permission from the Three Planet Council, which was finally granted this afternoon. It is a measure of your captain's loathing for our common enemy that he agreed to assist me, even to the point of giving up his command and perhaps his standing within the Hegemony fleet."

"I lost my allegiance to the Hegemony," Arnol replied implacably, "when I saw undeniable evidence that Starfleet Command and the pirates are truly linked."

"They are indeed, as we have long suspected," the chancellor re-plied. "Your capture of the pirate vessel pointed clearly in this direction, and our questioning of the pirate captain has confirmed it. Despite the best efforts, I might add, of the Hegemony's emissary to pluck the pirate crew from our custody."

"Not to mention confirming location of a pirate hideout in our vicin-ity," a statesman added.

"Indeed." The chancellor again paused to look about the gathering, then continued, "And now, my friends, it is time to attack."

Tucker responded for them all. "Begging your pardon, sir, but with what?"

"For over a year," the chancellor replied, "a contingent of my ground forces has been working in top secret conditions preparing a response to these pirates."

"A warship." Arnol leaned forward in his seat. "Just as I had hoped."

"More than just a single warship, Captain. And in the guise of a min-ing vessel."

Guns cleared his throat. "Pardon, sir, but the Hegemony has not heard of this?"

"The fact that I am still here speaking with you indicates that we have managed to keep this a secret," the chancellor replied. "But at such a cost that I cannot begin to describe. We declared to all and sundry that we were building this mining vessel. We then placed our workstation in an environment so hostile that no official would care to make more than a cursory inspection. We even made public offers for its eventual sale. But of course there were no takers. We were once known throughout the empire for the quality of our wares. Now few are interested in even talking with us, for goods ordered from our factories never arrive."

The chancellor leaned back, his face etched with both determination and fatigue. "Throughout the period of this ship's assembly, all workers and their families have been isolated from outside contact. Only the most trusted of garrisons have been involved in transport of materials. You have heard me say that Hegemony spies are everywhere. Still, de-spite all odds, we have accomplished this task through a combination of stern discipline and strict diligence and unselfish patriotism shown by many."

Captain Arnol inquired, "What had you planned to do with this ves-sel?"

"Attack," the chancellor repeated. "Where, we were not sure, but *what* we knew from the outset. If the Hegemony refused to stop the pirates, then we were going to have to try ourselves."

"In utter secrecy," the statesman added.

"This was our plan," the chancellor stated, leaning forward and lowering his voice. "We wanted to strike a blow not just against the pirates, but against the Hegemony itself. Let them know that they were not invulnerable. Nor could they continue to crush our lands without retribution."

"In utter secrecy," the statesman repeated.

"Precisely. Done in such a way that they would never know who it was behind it, not for certain. Sowing doubt among their own people. Demonstrating in the clearest way possible that if they do not govern with fairness, enemies they have made for themselves can and will strike at their very heart."

"And what better way to demonstrate this," Arnol finished for him, "than to attack pirates which the Hegemony claim do not exist, and then destroy a pirate stronghold for which there is no record."

"And rescue a man the Hegemony has kidnapped," Consuela said quietly, speaking for the first time.

The chancellor turned to her. "On you there must be placed a special burden. For the attempt to rescue Scout Wander, we ask you to promise us five years of service. Whether or not we are successful, with or without him, if we in turn give you our joint oath to do all within our power to bring him out."

"Five years," she murmured. "So long."

"We must have a network developed that protects us from pirate attack," the chancellor went on intently. "We *must*. It would be foolish to assume that one blow will be enough to ensure our safety. Only a Talent can help us by watching both lightways and shadowlanes for our transports." He stopped, then corrected himself, "Or Talents, if we are successful."

"I don't even know if it would be possible." Consuela thought a long moment, then squared her shoulders and said quietly, "But if I am able, I will stay."

Rick looked at her in astonishment. It was incredible that she would feel so deeply for the young man. Here she was committing herself to five *years* in a place that could not be any farther from her home. And for what? For somebody whom she scarcely even knew. As he watched her, he found himself growing angry. Why should she care so much for this Wander? Why did she not even bother to look at him anymore? Rick stared at her, consumed by sudden jealousy.

The chancellor turned to Captain Arnol and went on, "You have heard me describe how our own spacebound forces have been decimated. All our merchant fleet, all our trained officers and able-bodied spacemen, all gradually drained off through forced conscription. We have trained some of our ground forces in secret, but we need a captain." The chancellor looked from one to the other. "We need flight officers who will shape these soldiers into a cohesive fighting force. We need warriors who will take the battle to the enemy, and who will return to us with victory in their grasp."

————

Rick found Consuela standing alone in the archway separating the residence's main doors from the wrought-iron outer gate. She was shielding her face with one hand and staring up at the dual suns. "Sure is a long way from home, isn't it?"

She dropped her hand and turned around. "How have you been, Rick?"

Her solemn visage, her ethereal beauty, left him feeling uncomfortable and unsure of how to react. He gave his best grin and shrugged. "Not bad. Tired of being cooped up in these quarters."

"They've given you a palace and everything else you could ask for." Her sorrow lent her an almost regal dignity. "You're a hero. Aren't you enjoying that?"

"Sure." He felt unsettled. She had somehow grown older and wiser than he. "But it's sort of like cotton candy, all fluff and no substance."

She turned back to the sky. "I went home the other night."

"You mean, real home? Back to earth?"

She nodded. "My mother is sick."

Rick did not know how he felt about it. Home. Did he want to go back to Baltimore? Having the option become suddenly possible left him uneasy. "How did you do it?"

"I don't know. But I went. It was while I was still in the hospital." She looked at him. "I went to see your parents."

"You did? Why?"

"I felt as though they should know you were all right."

He felt ashamed then, without understanding why. And touched. She had done something for him, something he would never in a million years have thought of doing for her had their positions been reversed. "I bet they rolled out the old red carpet for you."

"They were horrible," she said, her voice empty of bitterness. "They didn't even invite me to sit down. They left me standing in the front hall under that huge portrait, and they grilled me."

"Yeah, that sounds like dear old Mom and Dad," Rick said. "I can just hear them now." He lowered his voice to a parody of his father's. "I cannot comprehend what would cause that boy to shame the family name like this."

"I don't recall his actually calling you a boy," Consuela said. "But you have the rest of it pretty straight."

"Incredible," Rick said bitterly. "They make me feel like some employee brought in to make them look good."

The sympathy and compassion that showed in her eyes came straight from the heart. "Poor Rick," she said quietly. "To have so much, and yet to suffer from the same loneliness as me."

Her words moved him deeply, as though she had reached out and touched his heart with her own. He started to speak, to tell her that he was there, to ask her to remember this if Wander was not found. But before he could open his mouth, another set of footsteps approached, and he heard Captain Arnol say, "Ah, Scout, excellent. Would you care to change quarters and join the rest of my crew?"

To Rick's relief and pleasure, Consuela read Arnol's words as the polite order that they were. "That would be fine, Captain."

"Excellent. Like to have all my personnel under one roof when there's a concern over security." He looked back at the vast palace set in its own grounds, said, "I imagine we can find quarters for the scout here, don't you, Lieutenant?"

"Aye, Captain," Rick said eagerly. "I'll see to it myself."

CHAPTER SEVEN

To Rick's profound disappointment, Consuela proved no easier to approach once housed within the crew's palace.

The manor was a genuinely grand affair, with two great wings opening off a broad central gallery. Consuela and the local girl called Adriana took chambers with the other female crew in the wing opposite his own and stayed very much to themselves even when gathered for dinner.

Rick went to bed that night frustrated and confused. An entire planet of women to choose from, and here he was longing after a girl in love with someone else. It made absolutely no sense whatsoever.

————

The change started even before he was fully asleep.

There was a sense of being drawn away, detaching himself from the bed and the quarters and the palace and the world. Not of going somewhere else, but rather of first no longer being *there*, and then of *being* elsewhere.

An instant of fog-bound confusion, then he knew. He was back.

But before the panic could set in, before he could protest that the choice had been taken from him, Rick realized that the return was not permanent. He did not know how he knew, but he was sure just the same.

He arrived at that pleasant hour just before an autumn dusk, when the world was cooling down from the day's heat, and the sky was lit with a glorious display of sunset colors. Rick looked about himself, realized he was standing in the park directly across from his house. He took a breath and did what he knew had to be done.

"Rick!" His mother's voice caught him before he had passed over the threshold. She came rushing up, her high heels tapping impatiently across the polished floor. "Are you all right? Where on earth have you been?"

"I'm fine," he replied. "It's hard to explain—"

He was cut off by a voice booming down from upstairs. "Who is that, Doris?"

"Your son!"

"Rick!" A tall and aging replica of himself came thundering down the stairs. "I've a good mind to . . . What insanity possessed you to go off on your own like that?"

For the first time in his life, Rick did not back away from his father's wrath. He did not give his best smile, he did not ease things by agreeing and giving in and going along. He stood his ground, he met his father's angry gaze, and he replied, "I've been involved in something important."

"Important!" The elder Reynolds blasted his ire. "Important! What on earth could be more important than meeting up to your responsibilities?"

"A lot of things."

"Why, do you realize the trouble I've had trying to calm down Coach . . ." His son's words finally sank home. "What's that you said?"

"I have other responsibilities right now, Dad. Important ones."

"Oh, I knew it, I knew it," his mother wailed. "He's gotten that girl pregnant."

"Mom—"

His father wheeled around. "What girl?"

"That trashy thing who came around not long ago, you know the one. She claimed she had been on a date with Rick."

"Consuela is one of the finest girls I have ever known," Rick said firmly. "And she's not pregnant."

"Then she's gotten you mixed up in something bad," his mother accused, her tone rising. "Is it drugs?"

"Good grief, no."

"Now you listen to me," his father ordered. "I don't know what shenanigans you've gotten yourself into these past few days, and I don't care. I want you to hightail up to your room, mister, and get ready for school on Monday. After you call Coach, that is, and apologize for all the trouble you've put that poor man through. You've got the good name of this family to uphold, and don't you forget it."

"I'm not staying," Rick replied quietly. "I just stopped by to let you both know I'm doing fine. I'll be home as soon as I can. Right now I have to go." He turned to the door, then stopped, held by a strong feeling that something was left undone. He turned back and added quietly, "Just know that I love you, and I'm doing fine. Really."

It was the image of his parents standing there, openmouthed and shocked into stillness by his quiet determination, that brought a smile to his face as he raced across the park and flagged down a passing taxi. He gave the driver the address, then panicked until he felt his wallet there in his back pocket. Rick settled back, the smile still in place. Whatever had brought him back had shown the good sense to return him to his own clothes, and not left him in the uniform of a lieutenant on a Hegemony vessel.

Consuela's apartment building was just as ratty and dismal as he remembered. He mounted the stairs two at a time, pressed forward by a strange sense of urgency, which he could neither explain nor disregard. To his surprise, he found an envelope pinned to the apartment door, marked for Consuela. After a moment's hesitation he pulled it down, opened it, and read:

"Dear Consuela, your mother had a bad attack on Wednesday. The doctor says it is nothing to worry about, but he has kept her over at Providence General for observation. I try to visit her every evening. The number is listed below. Your mother's room number is 238. In Christ, Daniel Mitchum."

Rick refolded the letter and pinned the envelope back in place. Then he raced back to the waiting taxi and ordered the driver to hurry over to the hospital.

At the door to room 238, he hesitated. What was he going to say to her? Then he heard the muffled sound of a man's voice. He knocked and pushed through to find Daniel there and seated beside the bed.

Daniel looked up, his eyes widened, and he waved Rick inside. "This is a friend of Consuela's, Harriet. Do you remember Rick?"

Rheumy eyes turned his way. The slack muscles of her face tensed as she squinted and tried to draw him into focus. "Maybe. I'm not sure."

"Your daughter is fine," Rick said, following Daniel's hand signals and drawing up a chair. "She's doing something very important and asks you not to worry."

"There, see," Daniel said, his voice infinitely gentle. "Consuela was so concerned about you she sent Rick all the way back just to let you know everything was going to be all right."

"She's a good girl," the woman mumbled.

"Consuela is a gem," Daniel agreed. To Rick he went on, "We shouldn't stay much longer. The nurse will soon be in to give Harriet her medication." Turning back to the bed, he said, "We were just talking about something, though, weren't we?"

The woman lay as though uncomfortable with her own skin, shifting about, never still. Her words were a rambling monotone. "Something nice. You talked about something real nice."

"It is nice, isn't it?" Daniel agreed, smiling with genuine pleasure. "I was telling you how God continually sustains the universe. It is a constant, never-ending gift. Were He to stop for even a moment, everything around us would collapse into chaos."

Perhaps it was the quiet assurance with which he spoke, perhaps the strength that radiated with his words. Whatever the reason, he had a calming effect on Consuela's mother. Her erratic motions slowed, then stopped. Her eyes ceased their endless search and settled upon Daniel's face. Her forehead scrunched into furrows with the effort of concentrating upon him and what he was saying.

"Think of a hot air balloon," he said. "Without the gas to hold it aloft, it collapses into a useless heap. What is true in the outside world is also true within us. We have been given the freedom to choose for ourselves, but without God our internal world is chaos. A universe of distraught emotions and conflicting aims."

Rick watched the woman nod slowly. Here was something she could understand. An internal chaos. She clearly knew it well.

" 'My father has never yet ceased his work. And I am working too,' " Daniel said from memory. "Those were the words of Jesus, when He was questioned about His doing good deeds on the Sabbath. It means that if we allow Him into our lives, He will work within us *continually*. Without ceasing, without holidays, without moments alone when old despairs might slip in and overwhelm us."

Rick could not help watching the woman on the bed. She looked awful and smelled worse. Yet Daniel sat there, pleasant and gentle and seeming to enjoy himself. Amazing.

As he watched, Rick found himself feeling as though Daniel's message was meant not just for the woman, but for him as well. This unsettled him tremendously. What could he have in common with a bedridden old lady?

"The old order has passed away," Daniel went on in his gentle way, "not just now and then, but for good. The new order is brought into being. This is Christ's work, granting all of us living in our fallen internal universes to become transformed. We are born anew, into a universe ruled by eternal love, eternal peace, eternal healing, eternal order."

———

Soon the nurse entered and to Rick's relief asked them to leave. He promised Consuela's mother to take good care of her little girl, then allowed Daniel to usher him outside. But the unsettled feeling did not leave. As they walked down the hospital corridor, Rick was struck with the vivid impression that this hospital visit and Daniel's message were the real reasons behind his being back.

They stopped in the hospital cafeteria for a cup of coffee. Daniel sat across from Rick and listened with singular intensity as he sketched out all that had happened since the roller coaster ride. To Rick's surprise, Daniel showed no consternation over the tale, and all his questions indicated that he believed Rick entirely. When he had finished, Rick asked, "Don't you find all this a little hard to accept?"

"Yes and no." Daniel eyed Rick over the rim of his cup. "I think we all have stories left unspoken. Tales the outside world would find impossible to believe. How is Consuela holding up with Wander being taken?"

"All right, I guess." Rick squared his shoulders. "I'm helping her out all I can."

There was a piercing quality to Daniel's gaze as he sat and watched Rick, but he said nothing. Not, that is, until Rick swayed and reached for his forehead, and then came close to sliding from his chair. "What's the matter?"

"I'm not sure." Suddenly Rick felt infinitely weary, more tired than he had ever been in his life. It felt as though all the hours of all the nights when he had done anything other than sleep were all gathered together, pressing him down and enveloping him in vast crushing waves of fatigue.

Daniel leaned across the table and gripped his arm. "Are you all right?"

"I don't know. All of a sudden I feel so *tired*."

He understood instantly. "Maybe this is your callback."

Rick yawned so wide his jaws popped. "My what?"

"It's as good a name for it as any." Daniel lifted him from the chair and half led, half supported him through the cafeteria and out into the lobby. "Come on, let's go to my car."

"Why?"

"If you're leaving, we've got to get you into a place where you won't be noticed going away." Daniel hustled him through the glass entrance doors, across the road, and through the parking lot until they came to a white Buick. He fumbled with his keys. "Slide into the backseat. There's a blanket on the window ledge, pull it up around you."

Daniel stood and watched as Rick used every last vestige of his strength to settle onto the seat, then leaned over and said, "Be sure to tell Consuela that I have spoken to the church's prayer circle. We surround you both with our prayers."

Consuela had so much difficulty falling asleep that she scarcely realized it when it finally happened.

All the pains she had faced in her life—the poverty, the loneliness, her mother's drinking problem—nothing compared with this. It was not so much that this pain was worse. Yet somehow all the others had been *outside* her, at least in part. This one was totally within. Totally hers. Missing Wander was an ache that sealed her heart in a sheath of stone.

This time, there was no way she could run away to some other place. No matter where she went, this sorrow would go with her. Her love for Wander was etched into every cell of her being. She found herself wondering sometimes, if she had it all to do over again, knowing that this would come, would she still want to give her heart away? The answer was an unswerving yes. This love now defined her world, for better or for worse.

For hours and hours that night she lay in her bed, exhausted by all that had transpired, made worse by the nervous strain of missing Wander. There in the darkness she discovered that the loss and the hurt had another effect, one she had never thought possible. All the lies and the shields within herself were stripped away. Everything she was had been

laid bare. She felt open and utterly vulnerable. Her personality, her char-
acter, her makeup, all were opened to her honest inspection.

There was no running away from the insecurities and the questions
any longer. Hard as it was to face this with her longing for Wander, the
truth that was reflected in her loneliness could not be denied. And above
all the other questions echoed the continual refrain, *Who am I, really?*

She fell asleep with that question unanswered, drawn into the overly
active dreams of nervous exhaustion. She spent uncounted hours chas-
ing down hallways without end for answers she could never find.

Then she started awake with a gasp so explosive it drew her upright.

She flung aside the covers, swung her feet to the unseen floor, and
searched for a trace of what she had sensed. Desperately she hoped it
was not just a dream. It could not have been. It was too real, too powerful.

Then it came, an image and a message and a flavor that was all his
own. She felt his nearness even while knowing that the space between
them was immeasurable in earth-bound terms. The message was vivid,
a picture without words, given only with a single wafting note of his love
and his yearning for her. Intense and demanding and precious. As
quickly as it came, it departed, leaving behind a vacuum so dark and
empty that the scream felt torn from her throat.

"Wander!"

CHAPTER EIGHT

She was looking at a box of space.

The image floated above the desk, square and stationary and dark. Dunlevy lifted a silver rod tipped with light, handed it to her, and said, "Press that little button on the side when you have the correct position. I will reorder the intensity once we have the coordinates. Try and remember as carefully as you can. This could be what we're looking for."

The captain interrupted, "You're absolutely positive it was Wander?"

"Yes." Consuela cut off further talk by closing her eyes. Arnol had alternated between excitement and doubt ever since he had been summoned. Dunlevy, on the other hand, had shown no hesitation whatsoever.

As soon as she cleared away the impatient pressure she felt emanating from the others, the image popped back into her mind. It remained as clear and as prescient as before. And still it carried that faint trace of Wander.

She opened her eyes and began to draw.

The image made little sense to her. But there was no questioning the feeling of rightness as she pressed the button and saw stationary points of light appear within the dark box. It did not take long for her to finish.

She handed the control back to Dunlevy, pointed in and said, "This one is very bright, a burning blue-white globe." She watched him make an adjustment by twisting the back of the control, then touching the indicated light. Instantly it grew to dominate the box. "Yes. And these four don't have any light. They're just round circles." Again the adjustments, as though he understood what she meant almost before she spoke. "Okay, and this one is a really big star, but not a globe like the first one. Sort of reddish orange. Yeah, that's it. These two are smaller. And this one is really bright too, but almost completely white, like an arc lamp. No, brighter than that, but smaller. Like that. Oh, and there's another little globe right next to this one." It struck her then with chilling force. "That's a moon, isn't it?"

Dunlevy nodded impatiently. "What else?"

She closed her eyes, recalled three more distant lights, added them. Took a deep breath, forced herself to hold the memory as vividly as she could, opened her eyes, and tried to overlay her mental image upon the one in the box. "I think that's all."

Dunlevy looked at her with piercing gravity. "You're sure?"

She did the exercise once more, her forehead knotted with the strain. "Yes."

Dunlevy eased up from his crouched position, turned to Arnol, asked, "Do you recognize it?"

"No," he said, his craggy features holding a sense of wonderment as he glanced from the box to Consuela and back again. "Never seen an approach like that before in my life."

"Nor I," Dunlevy agreed. "And I have spent my entire adult life studying the skies."

"Excuse me," Consuela said. "But what is it?"

"A star chart," Captain Arnol explained. "It appears that your boy has managed to transmit a landing approach for a system neither of us has ever seen before."

Dunlevy leaned closer, pointed at the shining globe that dominated the corner closest to her. "I want you to think very hard. This is crucial. Did he give any impression as to which of the planets circling this sun was their destination?"

Consuela started to shake her head, but something nagged at the back of her mind. She closed her eyes once more, and there it was. The final part of the message, held in place until she was ready and able to both accept and understand. Sent to her with an appeal so strong and so full of frightened desperate panic that she almost screamed again. Instead, she opened her eyes and stabbed into the box, her finger pointed straight at the planet with the single moon. "Here! Wander is here!"

CHAPTER NINE

Grim did not begin to describe Wander's surroundings.

The castle walls were so thick that even the air seemed imprisoned, unmoving and lifeless. The halls and chambers were cold, stern, and utterly silent. The castle possessed a morbid quality, as though every vestige of energy and vitality had been sucked out.

It was the first time in memory that Wander heard no ethereal communication. Not even a whisper.

The planet itself was not just arid. There was no water whatsoever. It baked under a too-close, too-intense sun, holding its meager atmosphere at the temperature of a roaring furnace. Its single moon was overlarge, and swept up hurricane-force winds with each six-hour revolution. The surface was utterly flat and featureless, all mountains and other protrusions having been blasted into nothingness by the dry heat and the savage winds.

The castle stood at the base of a fissure ten miles deep and half as wide. Overhead there was no sky, only a continual raging fury of sand and dust and endless gales. The castle itself could hardly be distinguished from the surrounding crevasse, for it had been carved from the very same stone. Boulders sliced from the cliff sides had been shaped into great blocks as tall and thick as ten men, erected with such precision that no mortar had been required to hold them in place. The few windows were mere slits through which little could be seen, only craggy stone and jagged cliffs and furious flaming red clouds roaring overhead.

"Enough of this time-wasting," said his escort, an impatient youth with dark, pinched features and an aggressive manner. "Let's get a move on."

Reluctantly Wander retreated out of the narrow tunnel leading to the corridor's single window. Although the outside view offered little, still there was a sense of expanse. But no freedom. The slit-window was imbedded in a stone tunnel fifteen paces long, the outer wall's thickness. Beyond the thick glass was a vista more desolate and forbidding than anything he had ever seen or imagined. Despite their density, the swirling clouds at the top of the castle's canyon were illuminated by the over-bright sun. From underneath, the furious dust clouds looked like continual blasts of fire and brimstone, a flaming curtain shutting him from all space, all sky, all hope.

Wander allowed himself to be led down the silent stone corridor by the only person he had seen since his arrival. The corridor was lined by one closed door after another, tall and impenetrable. The castle appeared as void of life as it did of sound. Their footsteps scratched and echoed down a hallway without end.

Wander had been too weak to do more than protest against his kidnapping on Avanti, and the soldiers had paid his words no mind whatsoever. The diplomat had only looked his way once as they had made their final approach toward the waiting spaceship via floater. He had peered down at where Wander sat exhausted and feeble in the power-chair, and sneered, "You would do well to harbor what strength you have, Scout. You will need every shred soon enough. And more besides."

The diplomat's vessel was jet black, formed with some substance that seemed to suck up all light and reflect nothing back. They had not gone through the spaceport, but rather floated down directly alongside the mighty ship. The warriors had obeyed the diplomat's sharp command and had taken Wander to a featureless cabin, dumped him from the chair onto the floor, and left him lying there. His protests had meant nothing at all.

Wander felt as well as sensed the ship's gradual upsurge in power. He managed to drag himself into his bunk. He remained upon his back, as calm as he could make himself, knowing that he had to reach beyond his crying heart and his aching sense of loss, and *observe*.

To his surprise, the ship did not enter directly into interstellar transport.

The ship raced out beyond Avanti's double moons, then began powering up to full thrusters, racing faster and faster outbound while at the same time reaching toward null-space without benefit of an energy net. Wander had never heard of such a maneuver, had not even known that it was possible. Yet as the ship's thrusters continued to build up to peak power, he understood how such a maneuver would keep the planet-bound tower personnel from sensing exactly where the ship was destined.

Then time slowed to a crawl, and the transition hit him.

It was Wander's first full-fledged transition within a starship not bound to the relatively short distances of lightways. He felt an explosion of his awareness, and at the same time a sense of controlled caution. Near to him was someone else with heightened awareness, a trained pilot whose attention was tightly focused upon the destination ahead, and yet who was also observing him. How this was possible, Wander did not know. Yet his senses, expanded by the almost limitless moment of transition, were too clear to be denied. He was being watched.

So instead of extending himself outward as he desired, he held back, caution granting him the ability to hold his awareness to what he could see without being seen. He observed the ship's direction, watched as the ship made the instantaneous transition in and through n-space, and as the ship powered down after transition, he made a very exact identification of their destination.

Perhaps because the ship's power-up did not permit an exact destination, or perhaps because they were monitored by some interplanetary defense system, they did not push out of n-space directly on the planet's surface. Instead, they hovered above and outside the planetary orbit. As the amps powered down and the sense of expanded awareness was gradually lost, Wander's final view was of a fierce identification blast, a radio signal sent at hyperspeed so that it could not easily be caught and interpreted.

Wander struggled to hold on to his sense of expanded time, but failed. The signal shot away from the ship just as his own awareness was returning to the confines of time and his cramped little cabin.

He sat and waited for what felt like hours after the ship had landed, until the cabin door finally slid back to reveal the pinched-faced escort. He wore what appeared to be a scout's robe, but one laced with fine silver threads. "You are to come with me," the young man said sharply, and led him out of the now-empty ship, through the connecting tunnel, and into an empty, endless castle corridor.

"This is your chamber," the escort said, pushing open a stout door identical to all the others.

Wander walked forward and peered inside. Like the door itself, the room was functional and austere. "Why isn't anything powered here?"

The question seemed to catch his escort off guard. But he recovered swiftly and snapped back, "You'll find out soon enough. Your meals will be brought to you. Do not leave this chamber until you are summoned." With that he left, slamming the door behind him.

Wander surveyed the room more closely. Featureless walls, a steel-framed bed with a thin mattress, a single chair, a desk, a dim glow-lamp operating from its own battery source. It all hearkened back to some bygone era. There was a reason for this, he was sure, but at the moment he was too tired to care. Wander stripped off his robe, sprawled on the bunk, pulled the thin blanket over himself, and was instantly asleep.

He awoke uncounted hours later to find that a metal tray had been slipped through a slit at the base of his door. He ate swiftly, the rudimentary meal spiced by hunger. Obviously he was being watched, for the instant he set the tray aside, the door was pushed back to reveal the same young escort. "Here," he said, "put this on."

Wander accepted the gray-brown robe, felt the coarse material, and started to protest. But a glance at the escort's face told him the young man expected him to argue, and had already prepared a harsh retort. Instead, he turned his attention to a series of dark markings that extended out of the escort's sleeve and traced their way across the back of his left hand. "What is that?"

The escort looked down, smirked, and drew back the robe further. A tattoo of a three-headed serpent coiled up his arm, fangs bared, vicious and deadly. "It is the sign."

"Sign of what?"

"That I have challenged the beast and won."

Wander studied the pinched, hardened face. "The beast?"

"You will see soon enough." The young man drew himself up to his full height and intoned, "Are you prepared?"

Wander slipped the robe over his head and stood. "Am I what?"

"No, of course not. How could you be?" The young man spoke with the formal tones of one reciting something well memorized. "You know not what is to come."

Uncertain of how to respond, Wander stood and waited.

"You who were once a scout now have no position, for what was earned elsewhere has no meaning here. You who were once labeled and known are now nameless and of no account. You will regain your name only when it has been earned here."

Labeled. As though all that had come before was nothing. Wander felt the heat rise within him.

"Once you had friends. Now none except the one assigned this duty will show you his face, for you are nothing and no one."

Before Wander could respond, the escort wheeled about and passed through the open door. "Follow me. It is time for your testing."

Wander walked down the corridor in resentful silence. He was feeling much stronger now, and the anger surged through his frame. Kidnapped, torn from Consuela's arms, taken across the length and breadth of the empire, and now treated like a nameless nothing. Wander walked a pace behind the escort and bored holes in the young man's silver-threaded robe with his stare.

Without warning, the escort jinked and entered a tall open space. Wander hesitated, for in his befuddled state he could have sworn that an instant before there had been nothing to his left but more stone wall. The escort turned and stood waiting.

Wander stepped across the unadorned threshold and entered a chamber perhaps fifteen paces to a side, with lofty ceilings supported by great sweeping arches.

"Think you have already been tested?" The escort's words bounced back and forth within the empty chamber. "You shall soon think again."

The words sounded to Wander like a ritual chant. A thought struck him and he spun about, only to find that the opening through which they had entered was no longer there.

"Think you have a special power? A gift? Perhaps." The escort raised one arm, and slowly, silently, the entire chamber floor began to descend. Wander glanced up, saw the ceiling move farther and farther away. "Or then again, perhaps you have only the means to destroy yourself."

An initiation. He was being brought through a rite. But the understanding brought Wander no comfort. There was also a warning to the words. One which he did not comprehend.

"There are many paths to destruction," the escort went on. The floor upon which they stood descended at an ever faster rate, until the great stone walls blurred by on every side. "But there is only one to safety. Only one among the many."

Without warning the floor exited the stone passage and floated into a subterranean hall greater than any enclosed space Wander had ever seen. The walls were so far away as to be lost in shadowy haze. The floor descended across an expanse so vast, Wander's face was touched by a mild breeze.

He looked down and saw that they were headed toward a domed structure built like a ringed fortress wall, as high as it was broad. Lights flickered and raced back and forth through the ring's black depths. At intervals dark arms extended outward from the ring, like the multiple arms of some giant prehistoric sea-beast. They continued on and on until they were lost in the distance. Beyond rose what appeared to be several more of the rings, but because of the distance Wander could not be sure.

"You cannot hunt for the one right way," the escort droned, "for there is no time. You must simply *know*."

The floor settled inside the great black ring, upon a deck surfaced in the same yellow-gray stone as made up their subterranean cavern. From this perspective, the dark ring-wall with its endless flickering lights rose up to ten times the height of a man.

Beside their landing spot, in the center of the ring, rested two black chairs. Upon the table separating them sat two headsets.

Wander stared at the sets and asked, "How many fail?"

"Questions are for later," the escort replied. "But this one I shall answer. Of the six arrivals since I became the newest scout monitor, only one has passed into training."

Scout monitor. Wander followed him over to the pair of seats, knowing he had no choice. He accepted the headset, sat down, adjusted the set to his temples. No matter what, he would show these people no fear.

The escort sat down across from him, studied his face, and for the first time showed a flicker of reluctant approval. But all he said was, "Can you identify your home planet from the surrounding stellar systems?"

Wander looked at him askance. This was one of the simplest of initial tests for any apprentice scout. "Of course."

The escort leaned back in his seat and closed his eyes. "Then prepare yourself to do just that. Remember, it is your only hope."

Even before the power-up was complete, Wander knew what encircled him.

In an instant of shattering comprehension, he realized that the ring was a huge mind amplifier, larger and more powerful than anything he had ever heard of. It was powered not by a man-made source, but rather it tapped directly into the core of the planet itself. The beast his escort had spoken of was not an animal; it represented the harnessing of this tremendous force.

An instant's perception, a moment so swift as to be immeasurable, but this was all it took for him to understand the first snare. He recognized the desire to plunge into the amp, seeking to flee its awesome strength by burrowing downward.

Never to escape.

The outer measure of time scarcely ticked away a pair of seconds, but as the amp powered up, Wander's internal spectrum was caught in the same extension of time as when tracking an interstellar transit. He recognized the sense of time being split in two, one segment connected to his body and remaining fastened to the rigid structure of physical time. The other, however, was being expanded, further and more powerfully than he had ever experienced. Shattering in its power, yet familiar.

It was this that saved him.

Despite its awesome might, the amplifier worked along the same lines as a ship or control tower. Because of his innumerable forays to the spaceport, sitting and watching and being caught up in ships' arrivals and departures since the time he learned to walk, Wander was able both to allow himself to be carried along with this immense power-up and at the same time to hold on to his capacity to think.

"Seek your homeworld," the escort had said. Wander sensed the instructions were somehow the key, although he did not understand why.

The power-up continued, seconds ticking by externally while internally the vistas continued to open and broaden and extend.

And then he understood.

Before him spread out the entire Hegemony, a vast network of stars and planets interlaced by the golden paths of energy called lightways. Wander was approaching full power now, and there was no apparent limit to what he could see or where he could go.

And here, he knew instantly, lay the greatest danger.

Too easily newcomers would find themselves confronted with this power and simply expand outward with the amp's awesome reach. Undirected, unfocused, unbounded. Stretching out farther and farther until the mind simply shattered from the strain.

Search for the homeworld.

Wander began focusing the power, sectioning space into quadrants. His knowledge of star-charting was meager, but it was enough to do a roughshod partitioning. As he worked, he became aware of another mind, watching, viewing, keeping a safe distance in case Wander allowed himself to become overwhelmed. Wander forced this awareness and this threat from his mind and concentrated on the task at hand.

Then it hit him.

Did the escort actually know where his homeworld was located? With the unchecked swiftness of a mind amped to full power, Wander decided that it was a risk worth taking. The spatial segmenting continued, but now with a different destination.

The space around Avanti was identified, the star system located, the planet approached. Wander felt the escort's awareness move closer, check his own internal status, then retreat. Somewhere in the distance this second mind turned away for an instant, in order to begin the power-down procedure.

It was then that Wander acted.

In the instant he was not being observed, before the power-down commenced, Wander sent two messages. He could not seek out Consuela, did not even know if such a thing were possible. So he simply blanketed the planet with his messages, backed by as tightly focused a beam of power as he could muster, and bound with the unspoken words of his heart.

The retreat was swift and undeniable. Wander allowed himself to be drawn back down and into the planet's bowels. In the juncture before his return was complete, he was confronted with a final awareness. The escort's attention was turned back his way, and now there was intermingled a sense of astonishment. Of cautious disbelief.

Wander kept his eyes closed as the world reformed into physical focus and knew that somehow he had done more than was expected. This was not a place where he wished to draw too much attention to his abilities, not until he was more aware of the dangers. So instead of opening his eyes, he slumped to one side and moaned. The reaction was only half feigned. He still felt the weakness from his time in the hospital. The escort moved over to him, and Wander let off one further moan.

"So you're not as special as you first seem," the escort said, poking Wander in the chest. Wander rolled his head to the other side and gave an open-mouthed groan in reply. The escort snorted. "You may be the first to have accomplished the task on his premier journey, but still the beast made you pay."

The escort tilted Wander's chair back and dragged it over to the waiting platform. As they began their ascent, the escort said formally, "Welcome to your new home, scout monitor, the only home you will ever know." As the great chamber was left behind, the escort muttered almost to himself, "May your chains not chafe you as they do me."

Chapter Ten

Consuela found the whole thing utterly baffling.

Ever since she had rejoined the crew, Rick had crowded her. It felt as though he was watching her every step. At first she put it off as just one more confusing notion in a difficult time. But with each conversation, with every passing hour, his feelings became clearer.

If she had not so much else to worry about, she might have even found it funny.

There would have to be a reckoning, she knew that. But she also knew that in all this alien hurry and commotion, Rick was the only link to her home. And she did not want to break this link with a careless word. So for the moment she did her best to keep her distance and hold at least one other person between them whenever possible.

Right now it was Dunlevy. The pilot sat on the airship seat next to hers, blocking her from the aisle. Rick was directly behind her, kept from trying to crowd in by the chancellor and captain, who occupied the next row forward. Dunlevy leaned forward, concentrating intently on their conversation. Consuela watched the world drift by outside her window and welcomed the relative solitude.

So much was happening. For two days now the crew had scurried with frantic haste, trying to prepare for their departure. The ship was ready, the new crew members as well trained as they could be while still on the ground. Every passing moment increased the risk of their secret coming out. Of some hidden glitch slowing them down. Of Wander being . . .

No, she wouldn't permit such thoughts. Consuela gave her head a violent shake and strived to focus upon the scene outside her window. They passed over a harsh desert landscape, not of sand but of mountains. Ochre hills fashioned by wind and heat and eons into sharp-edged peaks. There was not a single cloud, just limitless blue sky stretching from horizon to horizon, and overhead the dual suns with their eternal rainbow arcs.

Dunlevy leaned across her, squinting into the distance, frowning with concentration, shaking his head at something the chancellor was saying. Then suddenly all the crew was crowding over to her side of the vessel, leaning close to the windows, filling the air with their exclamations. Consuela searched the distance, wondered at what the excitement was about. She spotted the mining ship and was even more confused. It was the least impressive structure she had seen since this entire experience had begun. It looked like an overlong, skinny metal ice-cream cone, with a dark glassy dome for a top. The long tail was pierced with holes. What was more, the workers had apparently not even bothered to paint the outside. It had the raw, unfinished look of junk steel. She was in the process of turning toward Dunlevy to ask him if the ship really was ready for space, when she was struck by a half-formed notion. She turned back, leaned her forehead against the window, squinted, and gasped aloud.

The *size*.

From their altitude, it was easy to forget that these were true mountains they crossed. The ship had been erected in an open-ended valley and stood taller than the peaks to either side.

A *valley*.

As they began their gradual approach, Consuela saw how the cables strung from the two opposing peaks were not thin spider webs as she first thought, but actually were bridges large enough for trucks to drive back and forth upon. Which meant that the holes opening along the vessel's length were massive, larger than the ship they now traveled in. Which meant, which meant . . .

Consuela looked down at buildings rising from the valley floor, counted six and seven stories, measured them against one of the holes, and gasped a second time.

The ship was over two miles high.

Dunlevy glanced at her face, smiled, and said, "This is known as a gas miner, used in processing liquefied metals found in the high-density atmosphere of the gas giants. You have heard of these?"

Consuela nodded. "We have two in our own system, maybe more. Jupiter and Saturn."

Dunlevy frowned. "Again you mention planets of which I have no record." His face cleared as attention returned to the giant vessel they were approaching. "No matter. This is a perfect cover for our operation, for the gas mining ship must be both large enough and strong enough to withstand enormous combinations of atmospheric pressure and heat and turbulence."

Captain Arnol chose that moment to raise his voice, speaking not just to her but to all the gathered crew. "The ship that we see below us has been named Avenger, an apt title given our aims. As most of you know, a ship of this make is designed to descend through the gas giant's outer atmosphere, and as it drops it begins to spin. The speed of revolutions becomes so great that it forms a sort of mini weather system, almost like a submerged whirlpool. Once it has this island of relative stability established, it continues sinking down to where metals are flowing as gaseous liquids, and begins processing."

"The central pillar rising up through the undersection contains laboratory, factory, and storage bins," the chancellor said, picking up the discussion. "The ship's power plant, anti-grav stabilizers, and thrusters are all located in the underbelly of the upper section."

"A highly specialized vessel, with ample space for hiding everything necessary for our actions." Arnol turned to the chancellor, his craggy features sharpened by proximity to his new command. "Although I confess I am baffled at how you could keep a full battle-ready weapons system a secret."

"Aye, sir," Guns spoke up from farther down the aisle. "This is not just ordinary defenses we're speaking of. Seems any basic inspection would uncover an attack system."

"We did so by separating them entirely from the ship," the chancellor replied as their airship began sinking down alongside the vessel. At such close quarters the ship's size became even more formidable. "May I suggest that we allow your crew to begin familiarizing themselves with the flight deck, and we will see to these other matters."

———

The black-robed diplomat was unable to hide his astonishment. "You say the new boy completed the initiation trial his very first time?"

"Powered up and began segmenting the quadrants without hesitation," Digs answered. "Almost as though he had been trained as a monitor before."

Beady eyes probed. "Why almost?"

"Because he didn't know the quadrants. He had a vague idea, but he was off by tens of parsecs. Like he was trying to draw along lines he had maybe glimpsed once in a book."

"And yet he knew," the diplomat murmured.

"What to do? Absolutely." Digs had been around long enough to have observed how the other monitors treated the diplomats, mixing disdain and caution in careful doses. He stood because he had not been offered a chair, but did so in an insolent slouch. He was doing well enough to be able to count himself as one of the inner circle, whether or not he still wore scout's robes. There would be no more bowing and scraping to the likes of this desiccated old prune. Not ever again. "He didn't fight the power-up, not for an instant. Just rode the wave, caught sight of the expanded timescape, and knew exactly what to do. Split space by quadrants, more or less anyway, and isolated his goal, and honed in. Focused, fast, and precise."

The diplomat rubbed his chin for a long moment before saying in dry undertones, "How fascinating."

"Sure is." Digs did some probing of his own, hid his keen watchfulness by idly scratching an itch he did not feel. "You act as though you wanted him to fail."

"It would have been more convenient," the diplomat murmured to himself, then stiffened abruptly and focused once more on the young man standing before his desk. "That will be all."

"What do you want me to do for his next stage?"

"Take the customary steps," the diplomat snapped, irritated by his momentary lapse.

"Sure you don't want to put him under something a little more intense?" Digs pretended to be the diplomat's ally. "I mean, you want me to break the kid or what?"

The gaze sharpened into a calculating beam. "You could do that?"

"Just say the word," Digs answered, and hid his loathing with the training of one trapped on Citadel for almost four standard years. "I can break him like matchwood."

———

Rick stood at the back of the little group traversing the cavern-way on their floater and tried to make sense of the confusion that surrounded every contact with Consuela.

As they had descended from the airship, he had moved up close and said, "We have to talk."

She had turned to him, not with the pleasant politeness he had expected,

PATH FINDER / 193

but rather with a keen glance that probed very deep. Down to the layers of himself where even he felt uncomfortable. "I'm not sure that's a good idea."

"What are you talking about?" He kept his tone overly casual. "I just have something important I need to tell you."

She had spent a moment in silence, which somehow lent extra weight to her gaze, as though she were measuring him. "Come to the pilot's station when you're back."

The pilot's station was the most public spot in the entire control room. In the ship for that matter. But something in her gaze had left him certain that nothing would be gained by protesting. Rick had simply nodded and turned away at the sound of Guns calling him.

It was only now, as they continued down the winding cave, that he wondered why she seemed so much in control. This was not what he had come to expect from women. Normally control was totally his, without his even asking for it. He felt furious at the way she was treating him, leaving him both unsettled and aching for her. He didn't even understand why he felt so attracted to her.

But he did. He couldn't deny the fact. And the way she treated him only seemed to feed the flames.

The natural cave through which they passed had been expanded into a vast series of underground factories and warehouses. Great passages opened up at regular intervals, the rock still bearing the blast-marks of hasty carvings. The air around them was filled with floaters, piled high with men and equipment and with the battering sounds of metalworking.

"We have worked under one watchword—secrecy," the chancellor was saying from his place at the floater's bow. "The same concept dominated our planning. To work on more than one ship would have aroused suspicion, but at the same time we sought to enter the battle with our identity unknown. We have arrived at, in my opinion, a rather novel solution." He nodded to the ground forces officer beside him, a stocky woman with eyes and hair of steel gray. "Take over, Engineer."

"Aye, sir." She turned to the gathered group and said, "Mining ships work on the pod system, scouting out prospective sites, ferrying men and supplies, establishing a moonbase away from the strain of gas mining. We registered this one as having a dozen multipurpose pods, then added some changes of our own."

"Battle pods?" Guns' voice rose a notch. "You armed pods?"

"To the teeth," the engineer affirmed.

The floater landed in an empty passage, unmarked save for a single pair

194 / T. DAVIS BUNN

of great steel doors. The engineer stepped down, said, "Now if you'll just come this way."

But Guns was going nowhere. He turned to Arnol, said, "Begging your pardon, Captain, but this has been tried before. Pods are suicide machines, good for bringing in a swift initial attack, but only with men deemed expendable. That's why all you see these days are robot pods, even though computer-driven actions are more predictable and the communication links slow down reaction time. With the small number of pods we're talking about here, I can't see us using them effectively against a heavily defended base, even if I were willing to see my own men go down in flames."

It was the chancellor who responded. "Your sentiments are most worthy, Weapons Officer. And I might add that they match our own exactly."

Guns turned a pained expression toward the chancellor. "Sir, I hope you'll believe me when I say I'm for this mission one thousand percent. But I'm a weapons man to the bone, and I need to go in knowing my men'll have at least a fighting chance."

"Weapons Officer," the chancellor replied, "we are hoping to avoid all casualties whatsoever."

"Then pods just won't work, sir, manned or unmanned." Guns clearly looked uncomfortable holding center stage, but his cautious nature forced him to speak. "The problems are well known. Weapons systems powerful enough to take on a pirate ship, much less a base, need a full-purpose power-pile behind them. Batteries and storage systems are dandy for a single blast, but there's no telling how many shots we'll need, nor how long a battle will last. That means sooner or later my men and I will be sitting up there, our shields down, with nothing but stout hearts to defend ourselves." He turned to Arnol in helpless appeal. "Sorry for sounding off like this, Captain, but I've got the success of this mission to think of."

Arnol looked at the chancellor and said, "When it comes to matters in their fields, I have every confidence in my men and their judgment. If Guns says a pod will not succeed here, I would be loathe to put him or any of his men in one and send them off."

But the chancellor did not appear the least perturbed by their concerns. Instead, he turned back to the engineer and said simply, "Tell them."

"We redesigned the power plant systems," she replied. "Shrunk them by a factor of thirty, worked out a different shielding, held them to almost peak power."

"I thought that was impossible," Guns said weakly.

"So does the Hegemony," the engineer replied.

"If there is anything that might assure you of our commitment to this project," the chancellor said, "it should be this and the material we used in constructing these secret pods. The resources of three planets have gone into this project."

"Now if you will please follow me," the engineer said, and ushered them toward the massive doors, which began to rumble open at their approach. Beyond the colossal portal, all was shadow and half-seen forms. But what Rick could make out left him breathless.

"Lights," called the engineer, and the sudden illumination drew a gasp from every crewman's throat.

A jet black flying saucer floated overhead.

That was Rick's first impression. But at closer inspection, he saw that the shape was more like the head of a spear. The leading edge flowed smoothly out into a flat knife-edged line, without sharp angles or any other evidence of construction whatsoever. It looked like some substance that absorbed light had been reduced to its molten state, then poured into a gigantic spear-shaped mold. There were no protrusions, no rough edges, no openings or closures or visible weapons.

Guns walked under the ship, back out, inspected how the center segment belled out both above and below in perfect symmetry, creating a central portion perhaps twice the height of a man. It was hard to tell exactly, for the curvature was so smooth and so gradual, and the material absorbed every particle of light. His eyebrows were almost in contact with his hairline by the time he turned back to the engineer. "How large a power plant did you say?"

"I didn't," she replied, clearly enjoying his reaction. "But it is capable of holding a force ten charge through three fusion bolts while maintaining full acceleration."

If possible, his eyebrows crept even higher. "For how long?"

"You would die of old age," she replied succinctly, "before your energy supply runs dry."

Arnol walked off the ship's twenty-pace length, his head upturned and brow furrowed. He turned back and demanded, "Where did you lay your hands on elemental trinium?"

"Another of our many secrets," the chancellor replied. "One of our allies is the planetary system that supplies this material for all diplomatic and battle-fleet vessels. They too suffer under the Hegemony yoke."

Guns demanded of the engineer, "What weapons?"

"Phasers, neutron missiles, improved stun-bolts, strafers," she replied proudly. "And a new form of energy lance."

"Not to mention the pod itself," the chancellor added, motioning to the engineer.

From an inner pocket she pulled out a small control console and fingered in a command. Silently the ship began to tilt, until the nose was pointed directly downward. Another command, and the leading edge was brought within arm's reach.

"Careful," the chancellor warned.

Cautiously Rick reached out a hand, touched a substance that was neither hot nor cold. He ran his hand down the edge, drew back with a startled cry. He looked at his finger and saw that it was bleeding.

"We did not know if we would be facing an atmosphere world or not," the engineer explained. "Elemental trinium can be shaped like a sword, and that is exactly what we decided to do. You will find, if you are ever forced to attack through wind and storm, that there is virtually no drag or buffet whatsoever."

Guns examined Rick's hand, gave him a handkerchief, said with eyes agleam, "The lad's bloodied the ship. I say it's his by right."

"A dozen well-armed individual battle pods," Captain Arnol said to Guns. "Split into four groups of three, attacking in utter secrecy and without any warning whatsoever. What say you, Weapons Officer?"

"A challenge worthy of our finest effort, Captain," Guns said, excitement racking his voice up taut. "A battle to go down in history."

"So say I also." Captain Arnol turned to the chancellor and gave a formal bow. "Sir, I accept the commission and the challenge."

"The hopes of our three worlds will go with you," the chancellor replied in equal formality.

"Battle pods are an ungainly name for such a fine vessel," Guns observed, his eyes still on the upended ship.

"We thought the same," the engineer agreed, "and have come to know them as Blades."

CHAPTER ELEVEN

"It looks like a Formula One race car from the twenty-third century."

"What are you talking about?"

"It's incredible." Rick could not think of what he had seen and stand still at the same time. He paced about the pilot station, ignored the stares and smiles cast his way, and talked with his hands. "I mean, the thing is a racer's ultimate dream come to life. I asked what the thing would do, you know what the engineer said? Thirty gravities. Zero to thirty gravities instantaneous acceleration. Do you know how fast that is?"

"No."

"Neither do I." His laugh had a frantic quality. "But I bet it's faster than I ever thought I'd be driving. Especially something that doesn't even have wheels."

Consuela sat, calm and untouched by his excitement. "You realize I don't have any idea what you're talking about."

"A fighter," he exalted. "The best fighting ship you've ever seen. It makes the F–14 look like something the Wright Brothers designed. This baby is a dream."

"A dream," she said, "or a nightmare?"

That stopped him. "What do you mean?"

"We are doing this to save people from years of oppression and being ravaged by pirates," she replied quietly. She sat with hands folded in her lap, her features composed in a mixture of sorrow and youthful beauty. "The hopes of an entire planetary system go with us."

"Sure, I know that," he said, but had to wonder why he felt so ashamed by her words.

Consuela eyed him with that same sense of unspoken wisdom that had so unsettled him earlier. "What was it you wanted to see me about?"

"Oh, yeah." It was with a vague sense of disappointment and defeat that he sank into the seat next to hers. "I went back last night."

"Back?" Her dark eyes opened in surprise. "Back home?"

"Yeah. Your mom's in the hospital. But she's okay, and Daniel's there with her." Swiftly he recounted his experience of the night before, glossing over the disquiet he felt from Daniel's words.

But Consuela noticed his discomfort and demanded. "Are you telling me everything?"

He hesitated, again caught by her seeing more than he was comfortable with, then went on, "He talked about some stuff."

"Good," she said quietly. "Maybe Mom will listen to him." A fleeting shadow passed over her features, then quietly she added, "Maybe I should too."

He opened his mouth to ask what she meant, but was stopped by Dunlevy hastening up the broad stairs to the pilot station. "Ready to continue with your lesson?"

"Yes," Consuela replied, and then said to Rick, "Thank you for going by to see her. I know it meant a lot."

He did not try to hide his disappointment over their lack of intimacy. "I doubt if she even noticed it."

"She did, I'm sure of that." Her gaze pierced deep. "I'm very grateful, Rick."

He nodded, turned away, and made his way back down to the weapons station. Her reaction was not what he had hoped, but clearly there was nothing more coming. Not now. It would have to do.

———

Consuela lay in the darkness of her cabin, surrounded by the scents of newness. The quarters were very generous, far larger than what she had been given on the last ship, and on the same level as the control tower. She had been accorded full pilot's status, at least as far as her cabin went.

She should have felt pleased.

The cabin's only light came from the console by the door, ever alert to react to her voice commands. She sighed and rolled over, tired but not ready for sleep. So much had happened. So much.

The ship's departure had been set for the following day. That afternoon, the chancellor had formally handed over the ship to Captain Arnol and wished the crew success. That evening, Consuela had heard the crew discuss the Hegemony's surprising willingness to let Arnol transport the ship. They had agreed among themselves that Arnol was granted permission for this voyage only because the Hegemony never intended him to reach his destination.

Even so she found it both pleasant and comforting to return to the disciplined routine of ship life. And there were familiar faces surrounding her, both in the control room and through the ship at large. Chief Petty Officer Tucker unbent enough to smile at her every time their ways crossed. And Adriana had come aboard as assistant to the ship's doctor.

But the same troubling doubts continued to fill the darkness. Her own honest introspection refused to give way, regardless of all the new pressures that surrounded her. Consuela found herself returning to the dilemmas and insecurities and unanswered questions about herself every time she was alone. This sense of flagging confidence made such problems as how to handle Rick even more difficult to face.

Again she drifted into sleep almost without realizing that she had made the passage, but instead of returning to an endless maze of frustrating tasks, this time she found herself back home. There, but not there. Standing outside the apartment building in bright afternoon sunlight, yet knowing that she was not seen.

Knowing that something needed doing. Knowing that she was there and observing for a purpose.

She moved forward, both of her own will and guided by some invisible force. Through the doors and up the stairs and down the hall and stopping before her apartment door. Sensing that what Rick had said was correct, her mother had indeed been in the hospital, but was now back home. Then hearing a sound that had been all too scarce in Consuela's home life, a sound so rare it almost frightened her.

Laughter.

The door moved aside as though opened by an unseen hand, or perhaps it did not move at all, only she found herself passing through what was for her no barrier. As Consuela entered she wondered about that sound she had heard, for there was little in her mother's life that brought happiness to others, and she was sure she had heard two voices sharing that strange yet beckoning sound.

And then she passed down the narrow hall and entered their living room and saw Daniel.

His jacket was draped over the back of his chair, and he was leaning forward in intent discussion with her mother. Consuela moved closer, knowing that somehow this was the key, the purpose behind this dream that was more than a dream.

Her mother's eyes were fastened intently upon Daniel's face. She was lying on their sofa, a blanket tucked around her. She looked thin, but more alert than it had been in a long time. Consuela searched her mother's features and realized with a start that they did not hold the slackness of alcohol. Which meant she had not been drinking.

Her gaze still held a hint of the laughter, which was now past, but her voice was solemn as she asked, "But how am I supposed to start praying?"

The question had a devastating impact upon Consuela. She felt shaken to the very core of her being. First that her mother would ever come to a point where she could ask such a question. And secondly because her own heart seemed to respond by asking the same question. Mother and daughter speaking as one. Asking a question that felt as though it shattered the final illusions Consuela held about herself.

"First of all," Daniel replied, his voice quiet and gentle yet intense, "you must enter into prayer seeking to know God. This does not mean that you cannot ask for things. But to pray just when you want something, only because you need something you can't obtain for yourself, is a lie. Do you understand what I mean?"

Consuela understood exactly. And she understood more than just that. She looked at her mother there on the couch and realized just how much her own transitions through life had been propelled by her hidden anger and pain and frustration. Consuela had always thought that if she kept the feelings down deep, away from where even she could see them, they really did not exist at all. But in truth the emotions had always been there. And they continued to affect her every action.

"I'm not sure," her mother said slowly, but the guilt in her voice suggested that she did.

"All of us have needs that we cannot answer ourselves," Daniel told her. "It is part of the weakness that makes us human. And these very same weaknesses help us to find God, because we come to recognize that our own strengths are not enough. That we need more than what we can give to ourselves. That we cannot find the answers on our own."

Consuela felt the winds of change blowing through her heart, clearing away the dust and the cobwebs from chambers of her memories and emotions that she had thought locked away forever. It was not by self-imposed blindness that she would find true freedom, she saw that clearly now. It was not by running away, by refusing to confront the pains that had filled her young life, that she would know happiness. It was by accepting that she could never find the answers on her own.

Daniel leaned forward, his earnestness carrying a weight that was heightened by his gentle tone. "But to turn to God *only* because of these needs is wrong. It is denying God His rightful place in our lives, while at the same time asking Him to give us what we want or feel we need. We are refusing to accept Him as Sovereign Lord, while trying to draw from His strength and wisdom."

Consuela watched her mother take in the words and felt them sink deep within her own mind and spirit. Since Wander's disappearance she had thought of praying. But she had done so only in order to have things made better. Not for God. For her own sake alone.

Yet here in this moment of devastating truth, she understood that healing did not come by asking God to do some specific thing for her. It came from *surrendering*. It came through seeking Him and knowing Him and living for Him. It came not through directing and limiting and pushing away, but rather through *accepting*.

"In prayer," Daniel went on, "our foremost aim should be to know God. To know His will, His love, His wisdom. To humble ourselves before the Maker of all and enter into His glorious presence. To accept our place as members of His family, brought to Him through the eternal gift of Christ's salvation."

He leaned back, his eyes shining. "Then the Father of all creation returns us to His fold, where we have always belonged. And in His keeping, we may ask not only for the wishes of our heart but for the gift of a peace so wonderful it truly surpasses all understanding."

Chapter Twelve

"I don't understand," Wander said. "You *offered* to destroy me?"

"You're right," Digs replied. "You don't understand anything." He heaved a self-important sigh and leaned closer. "Look, anybody who makes it through the first initiation is one of us, got it?"

"I hear what you're saying." *First* initiation?

"Take it from me, anybody who meets the beast and survives is a monitor. The rest is just time and training."

Wander's new chambers were the largest he had ever had by far— sleeping quarters with geometric wall-hangings to mask the cold stone, and deep furs to cover his bed and floor. A bath large enough to swim in. And yet another room, the size of a small hall, with great sweeping ceilings and ornate bronze chandeliers, where he and Digs now sat.

And according to Digs, these were nothing compared to how the full monitors lived.

His escort, his pinched features split by an unaccustomed grin, had arrived soon after Wander had awoken. He had led Wander down a baffling series of hallways, each corridor more lavishly decorated than the last, until finally he opened a door and announced that here was to be Wander's new home.

Then he had shut the door behind them, brought a bulky apparatus out of his pocket, and swept the walls and fixtures and ceiling. He had then announced that they were safe for the moment, since Wander had not been expected to move so quickly. He had introduced himself as Digs and proceeded to tell Wander of his meeting with the diplomat.

Wander listened with a growing sense of astonishment before demanding, "Then why did you tell him you would break me?"

"Because if he thinks I'm doing it for him, he won't go looking for somebody else, see?" He examined Wander's baffled expression and snorted with impatience. "Look, you're not the first sensitive who's gotten on the wrong side of a senior diplomat. There's only one hope when it happens."

"Which is?"

"Make yourself indispensable. The diplomats may rule around here, but the monitors hold the reins. This means you've got to learn as much and as fast and as hard as you can. Which shouldn't be too hard for the likes of you. You're the first one who's ever made the whole trip from Citadel to the home planet the first time out. No wonder you collapsed. What you've got to do now is work, harder and faster than you've ever worked in your life."

"I think I see," Wander said slowly.

"Sure you do. You're a sharp kid. I'll be pretending to push you over the edge, which would really be happening with somebody else. But not you. What will then happen, sooner than later, I hope, is a senior monitor will catch wind of what you're doing and what you're learning and how fast you're coming up. When that happens, they're going to claim you as their own prize."

Digs leaned back, thoroughly satisfied with his plan. "After that, the diplomat and his minions will back off. There's always a few of the monitors who suck up to the Dark Couriers—that's what we call them, but never to their face, mind. These monitors are the ones we've got to keep you away from, see, and the only way to do it is to make them think I'm doing their dirty work for them." Digs bounced to his feet. "Ready?"

Wander found himself reluctant to face the amplifier again so soon. "You mean now?"

"It doesn't get easier by waiting," Digs replied, understanding him perfectly. "There's only one way to conquer the beast, and that's head on."

———

"One hour and counting," came the helmsman's droning call.

"Pilot powered and ready," Dunlevy responded in turn as the final check swept about the flight deck. He then turned back to Consuela and asked, "Are you sure you want to do this?"

"I have to," she replied quietly.

"For you to power up to such a level is a risk. Not just for you, but for all of us and our mission. We can go nowhere without your help."

She looked at him with eyes open to the sad determination at heart level. "I have to," she repeated.

"Very well," he sighed. He keyed his console, said in the whisper-voice used when speaking to others trained in his skills, "Pilot Dunlevy to Watch Comm."

"Communicator here, Pilot. All systems go, skies reported clear."

"Have special request. Please power down for five minutes."

A moment's pause was followed by, "Repeat that, Pilot."

"Our Talent needs to scan," he said, doing as Consuela had requested. "She needs to scan at full power. Do you read me? At full sensitivity. All the weapons and transport amps must be powered off, and all high-level communication ceased. Otherwise we might fry her ourselves."

"Ah, right." The watch communicator's tone became crisp. "Anything for the Talent, Pilot."

"My thanks. Five minutes to commence in sixty seconds and counting."

Dunlevy took off his headset, turned to Consuela, pointed at the switch in her lap. "Don't let go of that power-off control. And don't hesitate to use it."

"Thank you," she said solemnly. "I am so grateful for this."

Dunlevy cracked a nervous smile. "I think I would worry less if I really understood what you were planning to do."

"I'm not sure I understand it myself." She turned her chair a quarter-circuit so that she looked out and over the control room, signaling that she needed to be left alone. Dunlevy subsided into watchful silence.

It had come to her at the end of a restless night. Consuela had returned swiftly from her half-dream and spent many hours tossing and turning and struggling with the night's message. It was only with a sense of battling against herself and her pride that she finally gave in, exhausted and afraid, and prayed.

She had slept then, not long, but enough to awaken refreshed. As she had slid from the bed, she had realized that somehow she needed to make Wander aware of her departure from Avanti. And at the same time as she thought of the problem, she conceived the solution.

"All right, Consuela," Dunlevy said quietly. "It's time."

She adjusted her headset. "Is the amp on full?"

"Yes," he said, his voice registering his concern.

"I'll be fine," she said, hoping it would be true. She reached for the dial at her right temple and slowly began to turn.

As the power began surging in, she found herself recalling those earliest times of expansion, when there in the unfathomable distance she had sensed her own heart's yearning. As though it were out there beyond her reach and within her at the same time. Consuela shifted the dial another notch and realized that perhaps the answer was in accepting her own need for God and His strength at times such as these.

Another notch, and her mind began its expansive journey beyond the ship's confines. She shut her eyes and ears to the flight deck's humming excitement, increased the power another notch, then another, and another. Refusing to follow the easiest path, out along the lightway and removed from this planet's continual noise. Turning instead so that she raised unsheltered and unfettered into the planet's higher atmosphere, and there she hovered, pushing the dial up one notch after another, until she knew that if she increased the power by a single degree further, her mind would literally explode.

Then she let her heart cry aloud.

No words could be contained in the message, she knew that. Nothing that some monitor might overhear could mention anything about their mission, or who she was, or to whom she sent this message. It could only be her heart, and it had to be so clear that Wander, if he did somehow manage another mind-journey, would have no doubt that it was she.

She sang the tragic heart song of her yearning for him, her loss over his departure. Her wordless missive was a silver cloud of emotion, spun within a finest web of love. A shimmering veil was left hovering above the planet's surface, a wordless appeal for him to come, to return, to be with her. All of this wrapped about a single thought, an anguished announcement that they were leaving the planet, saying nothing more, terrified of having someone else detect the message and endanger his survival.

Robbed of the chance to speak in comfortable words, driven to ultimate risks by her own leaving, Consuela sang to him with the open helpless vulnerability of her growing love, of her yearning to be together, and of her hope that her departure would lead her to him. She gave it all to him, her awakening passion, her unanswered longings, her undying need.

Somewhere in the vast distance of physical reality, she sensed more than heard as Dunlevy whispered the five-minute mark. Consuela let the veil go spinning away, drawing from herself one final note of love, rising higher and faster and swifter than all else that her heart had sung, flying with all the force her love could give, soaring out into the uncharted depths of her loneliness, filled with the hope of a tomorrow shared with him.

And as Consuela returned, empty and hollowed and scared and weak, she felt the silent clarion call rise both from without and within, and sensed that somehow, even in that moment of greatest solitude, she was ever comforted, and never alone.

CHAPTER THIRTEEN

Consuela left the flight deck and returned to her cabin, drained but pleased. She had done her best. What was more, she was comforted by the sense of *presence*, the same feeling she had carried with her since her defeat at dawn.

She halted, her hand on the door-control. No, it had not been a defeat. Rather, her pride had been forced aside, and she had accepted her need for something more. She had been compelled to accept that her insecurities and her pains could not be solved by herself alone. But this was not defeat, not if she were accepting the truth. Consuela keyed her door open, certain that it was indeed the truth that she was finally facing.

"Consuela! Hey, great, just who I was looking for."

She turned, and the moment of internal honesty granted her the wisdom to know that it was false—both the surprise that Rick played at and the great smile with which he greeted her. He was nervous, he was uncertain, and he was ready to push their friendship over the brink of his own unfettered pride.

Consuela started to thrust him away with an excuse—she was tired, she had just come off a difficult watch, she needed a moment's rest before returning for lift-off. But before she could speak, she saw the need to confront this now. The realization was not something that came from herself. It was a gift of wisdom from somewhere beyond herself, clear and quiet and certain.

She smiled back. "Hello, Rick. Are you settling in okay?"

"Sure, great. Too much to do. Guns has assigned me a squadron, a pair of former airship pilots. They've never been in space at all, never flown anything bigger than the craft that brought us here." He grinned, less self-consciously this time. "Listen to me. As though I've had years of the stuff, right?"

"Come in." She stepped over the threshold, called for chairs, heard the ship's monitor sound the forty-five minute mark. "Would you like to sit down?"

"Sure." As he lowered himself, his nervousness returned. His hands played on his knees, with his belt, his cuffs, and his eyes were just as active. "Look, what I've wanted to tell you is—"

"Rick," she said softly, leaning forward and catching his hand with hers. The unexpected action froze him solid. She looked into his eyes, and in that moment she understood both why it was time to face him and what she should do. The open vulnerability caused by her message to Wander was still there for her, and this allowed her to show him not the pride and defensiveness that he usually brought out, but rather the truth. The only truth that might, just might, still his headlong rush and permit their friendship to remain intact.

She saw the hope kindle in his eyes and responded with the wisdom that was still being gifted to her, a sense of knowing beyond time and self-interest, a giving of what was truly her. Her gaze steady, she said softly, "I am totally in love with Wander, Rick."

The light in his eyes dimmed as fast as it had risen. There was too much truth in her words and her voice and her eyes for him to doubt. He looked down at his hand in hers. "Then there's no hope?"

"None," she whispered. "My heart is his."

There was a long, aching silence before he sighed and straightened. The barriers were back in place now, his eyes glinting with hurt pride and anger and vanquished desire. "So what is it about him that makes him so much more attractive than me?"

Consuela found herself unable to respond with anger. She looked at Rick and saw him and his distress through the pain in her own heart. She saw how his pride had been pierced by the fact that despite his looks and his abilities and his strength, she preferred another. Someone with whom he could not compete. Someone he could not overcome, and thus win her affection. And he had lost for reasons he did not understand.

So her answer was gentle, despite his wounded rage. "Because he needs me," she said, her voice soft.

Her words penetrated to a level so deep that his own anger dissolved. "So do I," he croaked.

Slowly she shook her head. "You rely on nothing and nobody except yourself. This is the perfect setup for you. Finally you're away from your parents and everybody else you ever knew, so you can stand totally alone and be the strongest and the best. The champion."

"And that's not enough for you?"

"Wander has a different kind of strength," Consuela replied. "He is strong enough to know how much he needs me."

"I don't understand that," Rick said. "Not at all."

"I know," Consuela answered. "But it's true just the same."

Even though it hurt his pride to do so, he had to ask once more. Give it a final fighting shot. "Couldn't you give me a chance?"

Again there was the sense of knowing more than could have ever come from herself. "You don't love me, Rick. Not really. You see the love and the connection between Wander and me, and *that* is what you want." With a gentleness she would have never thought possible, she stilled his voice before it could be raised in protest by raising one hand and placing it against his lips. "Don't say anything, please. You're hurt and you're angry, and you might say something that could keep us from being friends. And I need your friendship, Rick. Do you see what I'm saying? I *need* this."

"But not my love," he muttered.

"I know you don't believe what I'm saying now, but if you'll please, please just give it a little time, I think you will see that it is the truth. You are attracted to me because I am learning what it means to be completely open and give my heart and my mind and my love and my life to someone else."

She had to stop there, almost blinded by Wander's absence. She swallowed, took a shaky breath, and saw that even this was somehow intended, for her open confession had the effect of shaking Rick out of his pride-filled self-remorse. She swallowed again, and went on, "I hope and pray that you will find this same love for yourself someday, Rick. Because you are truly a special person. I'm not just saying that. You are strong and incredibly handsome, and I need you to lean on just now."

Again the heat pressed up against the back of her eyes, and a single tear slipped through. "But Wander is so much a part of me that loving him is as natural as breathing. And his absence is a wound that almost

210 / T. DAVIS BUNN

cripples me. So please be my friend. I need a friend, Rick. Especially now."

———————

"Four minutes and counting."

"Power up," Captain Arnol commanded, his face set in lines of granite.

"Power to redline crest," the power controlwoman confirmed.

"Cast off all bonds," Arnol intoned.

"Ship free and floating," the helmsman responded.

Through the vast stretches of open transparency, Consuela watched the massive cables fall with lumbering slowness toward the distant earth. The ship was now balanced upon the tight beam of its own power.

"All instruments tracking," the navigator stated. "Departure path confirmed, destination recorded."

"Avanti spaceport control grants us leave," the signals officer announced.

Dunlevy glanced over to where Consuela sat beside him, making sure she was following the exchange. The ship would travel along well-established lightways for at least the first portion of this journey, as the presence of a pilot on board remained a tightly monitored secret. Only the chancellor and a few close allies, including the officers in charge of Avanti's main spaceport, knew Dunlevy was on board. As there were no formal duties for a pilot, Dunlevy stood as back-up watch communicator and Consuela's tutor.

"Three minutes thirty seconds," the helmsman intoned.

The ship's flight deck stood upon the ship's crest like a vast crown. The chamber was far larger than that of the ship that had brought her to Avanti, as many of the mining functions would also be controlled from this point. For that same reason the interconnected vision system, which granted them the sense of having a window to the outside, was not restricted to just the ceiling overhead. Instead, the seamless view continued down around them, with bright brass handrails marking the chamber's boundaries.

"Three minutes."

What was more, the room was circled a second time, two paces in from the handrails, sectioned to coincide with the control stations, rising like concentric circles, giving views down through the floor itself. Yet instead of seeing the next ship's level, cameras fitted at the base of the broad dome granted them the sense of looking down the vessel's vast tubular length. Steps leading to and from the flight deck stations spread out between these floor-based visors like segmented spokes of a carpeted wheel.

"Two minutes."

"All officers," Arnol intoned. "Sound by station."

As Consuela listened to the final station-by-station check, she looked down and through the nearest floor-visor. Faint dust clouds were stirred up along the distant desert valley floor. All human activity had vanished from sight.

"One minute and counting. All systems green."

She looked around, saw how the ship was surrounded by giant serrated peaks. Overhead gleamed a pair of suns connected by gleaming rivers of light. She strived to take it all in, to imbed it deep within her, to treasure the memory for all her days to come.

"Thirty seconds."

A voice crackled through the ship's intercom. "Avanti spaceport, watch commandant speaking. Signing off, Avenger. Good luck, and good hunting."

"Roger, spaceport. Spaceship Avenger, Captain Arnol at helm. We will restore contact when we have news worthy to report."

"Five, four, three, two, one, lift-off. We have lift-off."

"Time to amp up and begin charting," Dunlevy said quietly.

Consuela fumbled for her headset's power control. Her attention remained held by the arresting vista surrounding her. Slowly, slowly, the ship rose from its valley, picking up speed with such grace and silence that it was hard to realize, except that now the peaks were far below her, and the sky was racing through darker and darker shades of blue.

"Consuela."

"Just a minute." Through the floor visor she watched as the dry ocher patch that had once been the surrounding desert shrank and shrank and shrank until it was just one small island encircled by great fields of white clouds. And then the clouds fell farther and farther behind, until she could look and see the entire great globe with its gently curving surface and seas and snowcaps and lights where cities were adjusting to the coming night.

Night.

The double suns with their shimmering rivers of light now rested upon a backdrop of utter black. And stars. If she turned away from the dual suns, everywhere she saw stars. Great blazing ribbons of silver light streaking across the depths of space.

"Scout, it is time."

"Right with you." She spotted the pair of moons then, rushing up and past on either side, their pitted surfaces glowing with every hue imaginable, the mountains and plains and exposed minerals reflecting the multitude of shades flaring down from the dual suns.

Consuela made her feeble fingers fit the headset to her temples, glanced over, found Dunlevy staring at her strangely. "What?"

"You have never seen a lift-off before, have you?"

"On television."

"Your homeworld did not have airships, spaceports, floaters, or regular contact with the Hegemony?"

"My homeworld," Consuela replied, "did not have any of those things and a lot of other stuff besides."

"I had heard," he said, his mind busy adjusting to this new information, "that there were frontier stations out beyond the Rim that had been lost during turmoil after the Great Transition. Planets that had reverted to primitive states and forgotten that there even was such a thing as the Hegemony." He looked at her. "Your homeworld was such a primitive?"

"That pretty much sums it up."

"So how then were you discovered?"

"I guess you could say," Consuela replied, and looked down at the swiftly shrinking globe below them, "that I just got lucky."

———

As per standard instructions, Digs pushed open the stout door and approached the diplomat's desk to report, "A ship blasted off from Avanti at the start of the current watch. Calls itself Avenger. Strange name for a giant gas miner, if you ask me."

The diplomat kept writing, his attention only half caught by the scout's report. "The sooner we're done with that blasted . . . " He caught himself and glared at Digs. "That was your report? You disturb my routine to tell me that this ship carries a strange name?"

"The planet is permanently flagged," Digs reminded him. "We are ordered to report anything out of the ordinary. The ship is headed offworld by lightwave transport, and not headed directly to their final destination. According to the manifest, they plan to test all systems before making a jump. And they are carrying a shipment destined for a nearby star system."

The diplomat's irritation subsided. "You say this is a new vessel?"

"First time outbound," Digs confirmed. "Never even made an interplanetary trial. Seven months behind schedule, according to our records."

"Then it seems a reasonable plan." The diplomat mulled it over. "Is this the ship that man, what is his name—Oh yes, Arnol. Is he commanding this Avenger?"

"I'd have to check the manifest," Digs lied, without understanding why, masking the fact that it was there in his pocket. Hiding his surprise that a diplomat would be interested in one particular ship's commander. "But I think I saw that name somewhere."

The diplomat showed a flicker of interest. "Any idea what cargo they will be delivering locally?"

Digs shrugged. "Usual Avanti cargo, far as I could make out. High-tech stuff, a lot of things I couldn't identify. Lot of high price tags, that caught my eye."

"Let me have a copy of their trajectory and manifest," the diplomat said, his voice lowering to an overly casual tone.

"Right." He took that as dismissal and started for the door.

"Just a minute." When Digs had turned back around, the diplomat demanded, "Just exactly what is a scout doing monitoring a flagged planet?"

"Monitor Damien handled that quadrant until this morning," Digs answered. "But he had a sudden attack of the screaming jeebies."

"Don't be insolent," the diplomat snapped.

"I don't know what else to call it when a monitor tears off his headset and goes into a weeping fit right there in the cavern." Digs' voice was overly harsh, but he was beyond caring. He and Wander had just been checking in when it happened. His skin still crawled from the memory, and the fear that it might happen to him someday. "Besides, since it was Wander's home planet and we're working from that point anyway—"

"What?" The diplomat half rose from his seat. "Avanti is *not* that boy's homeworld."

"It's not?" Digs was caught flat-footed, something that rarely happened. "I thought—"

"Go get the boy," the diplomat snarled. "Bring him to me. Now."

CHAPTER FOURTEEN

"I can direct the ship through transition," Pilot Dunlevy was saying. "I can chart the course. But only you can tell us where our destination lies."

Consuela studied his face, saw that he spoke in earnest. "You can't see the shadowlanes?"

"I knew of them only through rumors, until I met you."

Their pilot's station formed the uppermost portion of the flight deck's right-hand ring, or starboard deck as it was known. Light came both from the stars overhead and from soft illumination encircling each ring as well as from the flickering lights on each station's control panels. The effect was both to unify the flight deck and to offer each station a sense of comfortable isolation.

Consuela continued to gaze at him. "No one else can see them?"

"No one that I know. No one with whom I have ever spoken. No one I have ever heard of before." He let that news sink in a moment, then continued, "There is endless speculation wherever pilots gather and speak freely. But never have I met someone who claims to sense them as I do a lightway."

"It's all so natural to me," she said.

"I believe you," he said somberly. "Listen. A lightway is a carefully measured route, used by Hegemony ships since the dawn of interstellar travel. They are anchored by power satellites, great banks of prisms and mirrors and focusing instruments in permanent solar orbits."

"Wander told me about that. Part of it, anyway," she said, glad she could say his name without the catch in her throat.

"For those who truly believe shadowlanes exist—"

"They exist," she said. "Take my word for it. Please."

"The best explanation I have heard for their disappearance," he corrected himself, "is that they were *made* to disappear. There was a period called the Great Transition, brought on by the training and deployment of pilots, when in the course of fifty years the empire underwent a tenfold expansion. Imagine. Ten times the number of stellar systems and perhaps five times that number of new transport lanes. A complete restructuring of the known universe."

Dunlevy raised his eyes to the stars overhead. "At such a time of upheaval, with careful planning, any number of things could be made to disappear."

"But only if the Hegemony was behind it," Consuela offered.

"Exactly," Dunlevy agreed. "By locating the shadowlanes, your friend has uncovered one of the Hegemony's darkest and most ancient secrets."

A keening pierced her along with the sudden fear of what they might do to Wander in return. She pushed it away by asking, "So what is it I am sensing?"

"Traces," he replied. "Traces so faint and so old that they are beyond the ken of every other pilot I have ever met."

Captain Arnol swiveled about and addressed Dunlevy, "I am waiting your first report, Pilot."

"Aye, Captain." Hastily Dunlevy fitted his headset into place, said loud enough for Arnol to overhear, "We'll continue your lessons off watch, Scout. Now hook in and power up."

Consuela did as she was told. They were still a full day's acceleration from the first point where the Three Planets' records showed that a ship traveling upon this lightwave had sent its final message. She knew for certain that she could not reach that far, not yet. But Arnol wanted a constant check made of the path they flew, running forward as far as she could manage. Which meant that she would never be off the flight deck for more than a couple of hours at a time. She did not mind, not really. She was busy, she was needed, and she was moving toward her love.

But scarcely had she begun to turn the dial on her headset when the entire flight deck seemed to vanish beyond the power of an incoming message.

Before she knew it, she was on her feet, screaming at the unseen ceiling overhead, "Wander! I can hear him! *He's here!*"

———————

"Forget her!" The diplomat slammed his fist down on the desk. "Accept that for you, she no longer exists!"

"I can't do that," Wander replied quietly.

His subdued state calmed the diplomat somewhat. "You must. Be forewarned, Scout, your life hangs by the slenderest of threads."

Wander kept his eyes downcast, afraid that if he looked up, the diplomat would detect the love and the yearning and the stubborn hope radiating from his heart.

His first warning that something was amiss had come with shocking suddenness. Earlier that same day, Digs had guided him not down to the training ring where all his other watches had taken place, but over a segment of the great cavern to where a second, far greater ring rose from the yellow stone floor. This was one of seven monitor stations, Digs had explained, from which the empire was kept under constant surveillance. One of the senior monitors had already heard of Wander's success in the first trial and had wanted to meet him.

But as they had floated down inside the ring, one of the three men seated at the central station had suddenly let out a bloodcurdling shriek, flung his headset up and over the ring, and started clawing at his robes. "Home! I want to go *home!* Take me away, I can't stand it! No more, I beg you," and then the young man had collapsed into a sobbing heap.

The two other monitors, both older and gray-bearded, had ignored the arriving pair completely. With disjointed movements they had risen from their stations and moved toward the fellow.

One knelt beside the sobbing young man, looked at his mate, and asked, "You felt it also?"

The other man, the eldest of the trio, nodded back. "It shook me to the core, I can tell you that."

"What was it?"

"No idea," the elder replied. "None whatsoever. I have never experienced anything like it, and hope I never do again."

"I felt as though somebody had attacked my heart," the kneeling man whispered, allowing the sobbing young man to rock within his arms. "Torn it open. Told me things I never-"

The elder noticed them then. He frowned, then nodded as his addled mind struggled to focus. "You're Digs and that new trainee."

"Scout Wander, Senior Monitor," Digs replied for him, his own eyes never leaving the crumpled form.

"We have an emergency. I need you to assume monitor activities for this watch while we take care of him."

"Yes, Senior Monitor." Digs accepted the sudden promotion with no elation whatsoever.

"You are currently operating your training techniques within Vector Two, yes, of course, that is how I heard of you. Very well, carry on." He started to turn away, then stopped. "No, wait. There is a message on the table there for the diplomat. Along with a manifest. A ship left Avanti by lightway at the start of our watch. It's all there. Report in when you finish your watch." Then he turned away in dismissal.

As Digs directed their floater back toward the training station, Wander asked, "What was that all about?"

Digs shrugged miserably. "It happens sometimes, or so I've heard. The beast gets the better of somebody and tears him apart. First time I've ever seen a senior monitor break, though."

There was none of the banter that had come to signal their growing friendship as they hooked in and began the power-up routine. The training task was simple, though Wander did his best to mask the fact. Each training period, they directed their attention back to Avanti, then began working outward, tracing the lightways, learning the myriad of interconnecting lanes and stellar configurations that made up the inner Hegemony star chart. Avanti was ever the starting point, an anchor for their work. Yet because Digs was always there and vigilant at the onset of each training period, Wander had been unable to leave a second message.

This time, however, was very, very different.

The power-up complete, they made what was now a swift and steady approach to Avanti. But just as they arrived and turned away, Wander found himself overwhelmed by Consuela's love.

There was no mistaking the fact that it was she. Words were not necessary. He felt it was Consuela, knew it was she, knew it was a gift for him. A gift of her heart. And a single, fleeting, urgent message.

He felt the passion of her awakening affection, the sadness over his departure, the determination to find him, the longing hope that they would soon come together once more. All of it was there, bound together by the indelible strands of her love.

Wander felt his own heart fill to the bursting point at the same time that Digs was jerking away, pulling back, powering down. He allowed himself to return to the training station, knowing that she was no longer on Avanti, certain that he would carry her gift forever.

Digs tore off his headset, asked, "What was *that?*"

Wander found it surprisingly easy to play at calm. "What was what?"

"You didn't feel that?"

"Feel what?"

"Nothing." Digs's hands were shaking as he set the headset down on the table between them. "Are you sure you're all right?"

"Yes." Wander watched him rise unsteadily to his feet and felt a faint glimmer of hope. "Aren't we going to train?"

Digs looked at him in disbelief. "You really want to go back?"

"Sure. You said I needed to work as hard as I could. I'm ready."

"Maybe you are," Digs said, looking askance at his own headset. "I couldn't do it again now."

As calmly as his stuttering heart would allow, he suggested, "Then let me go alone."

"What?"

"It's got to happen sometime. I've seen how you order the power-up. Why don't you let me give it a try?"

Digs appeared to be having difficulty focusing on what he was saying. "Sure, if you want. I think, yeah, maybe I'll go report to the diplomat about . . . " He glanced at the papers given to him by the monitor. Color was gradually returning to his face. "About this ship. Flagged planets are supposed to be kept on constant watch, and, anyway, what better way for him to think you're getting blasted than to send you off so early on your own." He stopped and looked down at Wander. "Sure you can do it?"

"Don't see why not." Almost there. Almost. "I just go back to Avanti, right?"

"Yeah, and stay there. We'll start mapping again next watch." Another disturbed glance at his headset, then Digs moved toward the floater. "I won't be long."

Wander watched as the yellow stone platform flew up toward the distant roof, holding back as long as he could manage, before fitting on his headset. His heart thundering with anticipation, Wander did the mental reach as he had observed Digs make, and gave a silent shout of exultation as the power-up began.

With eager swiftness he reached out and forwarded himself to Avanti. The task was relatively easy. The system only had four lightways radiating outward, and the monitor had said that the ship had left on that very watch. They had to be somewhere nearby. They *had* to.

He raced down one after the other, identified the ship on the third lightway he scouted. Felt his pulse soar as he centered in, focusing upon the ship, and sending the single word message.

Consuela?

The sudden response was all he could have hoped for, and more. The scream of joy and heartache and love and passion almost shattered his heart. He reached down, focusing as tightly as he could manage. *I'm here.*

Wander, Wander, Wander.

We may not have much time. I need to do this first. Did you get my co-ordinates?

A second voice broke through the emotional flood from Consuela, a clearheaded response to his query. *Pilot Dunlevy here. Yes, she heard and recorded. Perhaps you could repeat for safety's sake.*

Swiftly Wander recoded the star chart location, then added, *The transition ended just beyond lunar orbit, not on land. There was a hyperspeed radio squeal sent just after we came out of n-space. I assume it was an identification signal. I did not get a chance to identify it. Sorry.*

Can't be helped. There was a pause, filled with the sweet scent of Consuela's longing, then Dunlevy was back. *Captain Arnol asks what can you tell us of surface defenses.*

Swiftly Wander described what he had seen of the raging storm and the castle's canyon. *I know nothing about other defenses, but if I can I will try to check. This palace and power chambers are beyond huge. I am working from a cavern big enough to hold a city.*

According to Senior Pilot Grimson, it used to house an entire battle squadron.

Wander took great comfort from the sound of the familiar names. *Where are you headed?*

Take note, came the crisp response. *Here are our trajectories as close as can be identified, given the likelihood of battle and perhaps pursuit.* Quickly Dunlevy imprinted what they knew of the pirate's stronghold. *This is at present a best-guess only. Afterward we shall make a delivery at Selanus, a planet with the following coordinates.* A swift image was passed on, showing a star system farther along the same lightway which they traveled en route to the pirate stronghold. *From there we are scheduled to deliver this vessel to Yalla. Do you know the system?*

Negative.

It is a star system not too distant from your coordinates. We have a possible buyer for our vessel there. Here is the star chart. After it was passed over, there was another moment's pause, then, *Arnol suggests you give us seven days for identification of the pirates and attack. We cannot take longer than that and maintain our cloak of secrecy. After that we shall make our delivery on Selanus, then head for Yalla by direct transition.* Another pause, then, *Now that we have contact with you, Captain Arnol has decided to wait in silent orbit one-half parsec beyond the Yalla system's outermost planet for a standard day. If we hear nothing further from you, we will make directly for Citadel.*

Citadel, that is truly the name of this place?

As far as we can tell. No record exists of the star chart you have passed on. Have you recorded our coordinates and time plan?

Affirmative.

Arnol emphasizes that we may make better time than stated. If you are unable to make further contact, expect us when we arrive. Scout Consuela will attempt to make direct contact as soon as we break from n-space, but there will be no chance to wait and try and contact you once we arrive at the Yalla system. Our only hope is to maintain surprise. We shall attack without delay.

Understood.

Then I shall break contact. A brief pause, then, *I look forward to making your acquaintance in person, Scout Wander. Until then.*

A moment's silence, and they knew they were alone. Then Consuela said, *I never knew what hope meant until now.*

Or love. He reveled in her intimate presence, then asked, *Can you try to leave me more messages?*

Yes, oh yes.

Wander sent images pinpointing places where he would look. *If there is anything more you can tell me, include it there. But be careful. Others can sense your communications.*

I'll try.

He felt her reaching out, sent his own heart surging across the immeasurable distances, wasting not a second with hesitation or self-conscious doubts. There was no time. His imprisonment had never felt so complete or so void of meaning. Their hearts touched because their lips could not. They yielded to each other with a grace and a passion that left words far behind. They soared in joyful union, a new heart song lifting them beyond space and time and distance and separation, one borne by the ecstasy of shared love.

Then Wander sensed the approach of another, and reluctantly, sadly, gently, he separated himself. Needing no words to convey how he felt or what he thought. Allowing himself to be powered down, away, out of the heart's embrace.

He opened his eyes to find Digs looking down worriedly at him. "The diplomat wants to see you. Now."

Wander raised himself with a sigh, walked to the floater, watched the cavern floor disappear into the distance, yet seeing almost nothing at all.

She was with him still.

CHAPTER FIFTEEN

The diplomat glared at him across the expanse of his cluttered desk. "Every day, every hour I am tempted to rid myself of you and the risks you represent."

"I'm not a risk to anybody, Diplomat," Wander replied quietly, his eyes still on the floor at his feet.

"Of that I'm not so sure." He inspected Wander coldly. "Was there some design behind your being sent to Avanti?"

Wander's surprise was genuine. "I didn't even know the planet existed until we arrived there."

"Perhaps, perhaps not. Even so, why did Grimson choose that particular training flight for you?"

"You'll have to ask the senior pilot," Wander replied feebly, recalling their panic-stricken departure.

"Indeed I shall. But in the meantime you will forget this girl you left behind on Avanti and watch yourself very carefully. Another such maneuver and you will find yourself terminated in the slowest and most painful manner possible. If you wish to survive this day, you must accept that the outside realms no longer hold anything for you. You have no family, no lover, no friends except those made here. In the meantime, you will be watched constantly, your actions carefully assessed. Is that clear?"

"Yes, Diplomat," he answered miserably, realizing that his chances of communicating with Consuela again had just been destroyed.

"Very well. Now get out of my sight."

————

"Who'd have thought it possible," Guns said cheerfully. "Me, traveling with a pilot and scout both and liking it. Not to mention risking my hide to rescue another. Times surely do change, eh, lad?"

"Yes," Rick said quietly. Up one moment and down the next. A hero on Avanti, lauded by his shipmates, but nothing to Consuela. Her friend. The consolation prize offered a loser. Her friend.

They traveled the transport tube down the vessel's vast central channel toward the weapons hold. They passed level after level of factory chambers and storage holds, any one of them large enough to swallow the ship that had brought Rick to Avanti and have room left over for more.

Guns caught sight of Rick's face. "What's eating you?"

"Long story."

"You had a perfect run first watch, that should be enough to cheer anybody up." Guns eyed him keenly. "Still pining over that scout?"

Grimly Rick nodded his head.

"Well, I've changed my mind about the likes of her, and I'm man enough to admit I was wrong. But I still say a warrior's got no business messing about with scouts or pilots either. They've got their world, lad, and we've ours. A man's got to hold tight to his duty. Especially before a battle."

He caught the sudden edge to Guns' voice, felt the sudden adrenaline surge in response. "You're right."

" 'Course I am. Watched too many good men go down because their minds weren't on their weapons. Wouldn't want to see that happen to you, lad."

Their own hold came into view through the transparent tubing, and instantly Rick felt his burdens lighten. Spread out before them were an even dozen of the jet black fighters, their attendants busy with last-minute adjustments. "I'll be okay."

"Sure you will." Guns clapped him on the back as they stepped from the tube. He raised his voice and called across the vast hold, "Now where is that lazy good-for-nothing Tucker?"

"Lazy, my granny's back teeth." The beefy senior petty officer came stomping up. "Been down here drilling my boys into line and waiting for you overpaid sky divers to roll your carcasses out of your bunks."

Rick ignored the glower Guns gave in return. Their skirmishing was well known, and mostly show. His attention was already caught by the sight of his ship. *His* ship. He walked over to where his two other squadron pilots stood waiting. "Everything okay?"

"Ready and waiting," they confirmed. Both were seasoned airship jockeys and had a good ten years on him. But neither seemed eager to disagree with his promotion to squadron leader. His battle with the pirates upon the approach to Avanti was well known throughout the ship, and from what he had heard, continued to improve with each telling.

"Mount up," he said, echoing the order he had heard from Guns.

Rick walked under his own ship, which hovered effortlessly just above head-height. He nodded to the deck supervisor, who gave him a cheery thumbs-up. He then looked up and said, "Open Blade Three."

A split appeared in the formerly seamless surface, and from this new portal sank his seat. Rick climbed on, felt the surface mold to his form, then said, "Load Knight Three."

It was Guns' idea to call the Blade officers "knights." Any battle squadron worth its mettle needed something to bind them together, he had insisted to Arnol. Something that would set them apart, make them feel special. As if they needed anything more than a Blade to make them feel special, Rick had thought, but said nothing.

The squabble between Guns and Tucker had erupted that very same day.

The Blade cockpit was more than spacious for one man. The view was spectacular. He was encased in what from the inside appeared to be a transparent bubble, which melded into the sweeping dark Perspex of the Blade's nose and sides. His controls were ranked on padded armrests which could be withdrawn or brought forward as required. Everything was functional, efficient, and thrilling.

Once again, his sense of prescient knowledge was there to help steer him through the vast array of new technology. Rick had caught on so fast Guns had assigned him as a training instructor for both his squadron and the third, taking on the other two himself. His run of the earlier watch had been the first for all of them operating as a team, and his two squadrons had far outshone those operating under Guns. The senior weapons officer had been as proud as if he had invented Rick himself.

Guns' voice sounded over the intercom. "Power up, Knights. Arm for blanks and seal your firing circuits. Then count off."

Rick fired the ship's main drive, leaned his seat back to a forty-five degree angle, drew the weapon console up and over his head. He keyed the console for blanks, which meant he would have every sensation of actually going into full battle, but all weapons would be blocked from firing. He heard his two fliers acknowledge, then reported, "Squadron two, powered and sealed."

"Same drill as before," Guns ordered, once the count off was completed. "Target is the aft hold. Squadrons One and Three, adhere to me. Two and Four, take orders from Knight Three. Lift off in thirty seconds. That is, if the battle squadrons think maybe they can shake the lead out."

Tucker's response came growling through his intercom. "Just be glad we're on the same side, me boyo. Else me and my boys'd make mincemeat of you and them fancy machines."

"Thirty seconds it is," Guns said, the smile clear in his voice. "All together now, let's make this one count."

Outside, the safety light shifted to green, signifying that all the deck-hands were behind safety doors. Rick felt his pulse hammer faster still, both from the sight of the great outer doors rumbling open to reveal the vastness of space and because of the surging currents of power that permeated every shred of his being. The Blades were wired similar to standard weapons consoles, with the extra thrill of being keyed directly into a main transport power-board. Not to mention the additional excitement of *flying*.

The two squadrons under Guns started forward. Rick checked his six Blades, was satisfied to see them conform to pattern. Behind them rested the bulky cargo transporters, refitted internally to become ground-troop carriers. All of them operated under Tucker's command. Rick thought the squarish transporters looked like oversized city busses, minus paint and wheels.

"Waiting for you, lad," Guns said.

"Squadrons Two and Four," Rick responded. "Move out."

Steadily he glided across the hold, through the vast steel portals, and into space.

———

"I wonder if I could have been mistaken about the girl's sensing abilities," the diplomat mused aloud. "What if that blasted transport skipper was lying?"

The battle-hardened guard captain shrugged disdainfully. "Have the local emissary bring the captain in for questioning."

"Impossible. Captain Arnol blasted off with a new mining vessel scheduled for delivery." The diplomat smiled, a chilling grimace. "I've arranged for them to have a little accident en route."

"Smart," the guard captain approved. "Tie up all the loose ends. No need to have our little attack on Avanti shouted around the spaceways."

"Besides which," the diplomat continued, "that emissary is a fool. The only reason he holds that post is because of allies within the Hegemony court."

The two were sealed within the diplomat's quarters, the papers and consoles shoved aside to make room for a flagon of wine and two goblets. The warrior poured them both another tumbler of the amber fluid. "How much trouble could one girl be?"

"I wonder." The diplomat drank from his heavy crystal glass. "Could she have left this Wander a message? Is that why he has been returning to Avanti? Something in that quadrant has been wreaking havoc among my monitors. Two of them are under heavy sedation at this minute."

"So I heard." The guard captain was a grizzled warrior, a man of many skirmishes and wars and medals. He was utterly pleased with this present berth, keeping sky-bound weapons poised and armed, an occasional off-planet exercise to keep his men on their toes, everything they could ask for to keep them content in their hole, and far enough away from the Hegemony to remain untainted by court intrigue. "But I thought sending such an unattached message was impossible."

"For standard pilots and communicators, certainly. But for a full Talent?" The diplomat sipped at a drink he did not taste. "There are so few of them that what they can and cannot do remains a total mystery."

"The girl?" The guard's eyebrows lifted a notch. "A Talent?"

"I was so sure it was impossible. The boy shows the potential. He did, after all, detect the shadowlanes as they passed." Another sip. "I never thought there could have been two of them together. Never. That was why I was so quick in believing that blasted Arnol when he dismissed her as a mere parasite. May the pirates soon make dust of him and his new vessel."

His scars and his years of service had earned the captain the rank of diplomatic courier, which meant he carried many more secrets than he ever wished to know. "So what now?"

The diplomat pondered a moment in silence, then turned and said, "I want you to go back for the girl."

"To Avanti?" The guard captain pursed his lips. "Difficult. Maybe impossible."

"It wasn't before."

"Ah, but this time me and my men, we'll be robbed of the element of surprise. They'll be ready and waiting for us."

"I don't care." The diplomat raised himself to his feet, indicating dismissal. "Contact the emissary through our channels and find out where they're keeping her. Make sure you mark the communication urgent, priority one, otherwise he might take months to reply. Once you've gained the information, make a midnight run. Avoid the spaceport entirely. Take all our available ships and the entire detachment of dragoons if necessary. But find that girl and bring her to me unharmed."

CHAPTER SIXTEEN

It was a painful night.

Without fully understanding why, Rick knew he was standing at a crossroads, and it had nothing to do with whether or not he chose to return home.

This choice involved his heart.

He knew how easy it would be for him to become the callous lover. It called to him with a plaintive familiarity. He was strong, he was handsome, he was a hero. He could have any girl he wanted.

Almost.

That he had offered his heart to Consuela and that she had turned him down was all the invitation he needed to never give himself in love again. He saw it all with instant clarity. He would become the man who gave his heart to none, who took and took and took, and gave nothing in return.

It was so attractive, this invitation, so very easy to accept. He would have a life filled with conquests, with women eager for his summons, with pleasures he could scarcely imagine. He would rise in the ranks, be showered with honors, and with them would come ever more beautiful and cultured and eager women. He would have riches. He would have fame. He would have it all.

And never be hurt again.

It called to him, this vision, and all he had to do was simply accept. The life was there for the taking. He knew it with a certainty that went beyond all earthly logic.

Yet it was with this very same clarity of vision that he knew such a choice would leave something unanswered. Some essential hunger would always go unfulfilled.

He lay there, tempted to shove the troubling visions aside and simply accept what he could so easily come to consider his due. But he did not. The quiet call of his own heart spoke to him, awakened by the love he saw in Consuela's face and gaze, a love destined for another and ever denied to him.

Yet was it really?

His pride would certainly like for him to think so. That if he could not have this woman's love, he would give his own to none. Yet the night's crystal clarity, fueled by his heart's soft yearnings, left him knowing that in truth it was not so. That were he to learn how to open his heart, he could have all, but only if he were willing to give all.

And this thought terrified him.

All his life he had made it by being tough, by holding back and striving for the top, being the loner who was constantly struggling for success. To be the best. At whatever cost. Even the cost of true affection.

Could he do it? Could he learn to accept someone into the innermost parts of his being, sharing all the hurts and the angers and the blackness that had fueled his scramble for the top? Rick struggled to push aside the eager temptations for just a moment and to examine himself with honesty.

And with honesty he realized that he could not do it alone.

It was this simple truth that troubled him most of all.

———

Two standard days later, the strain was showing. Consuela ate all her meals in the saddle, and left the flight deck only for three-hour snatches of sleep. Her rest was never long enough to be truly satisfying. Without actually ordering her to stay, Arnol continued to make it clear that he needed her there as much as possible. It was not enough to search for shadowlanes. She needed to set up a continual sweep of surrounding space, their only hope against surprise attack.

Dunlevy matched her hour for hour and never allowed her to sit a watch alone. He had numerous years of spacing experience behind him, yet he did not carry the burden of the search. The pilot did not show the pressure, save for a gathering half-moon of darkness under each eye.

Still, their searching had paid off. Three shadowlanes had been identified and marked on their computerized charts. Consuela had then powered-down long before they actually crossed the shadowlane path, thus saving herself the strain of making contact again while amped.

But they had found no pirates.

Dunlevy sat with his plate perched in his lap and a glass making a chilled puddle on the edge of the pilot's console. "I confess I felt some of the private exchange between you and Wander back there. For that I am sorry."

"It's okay," she said, too tired at the moment to feel shame over their intimacy being sensed by another, especially one she was coming to see as a friend.

"I have never heard of anything like this ever happening before," he said, shaking his head at the memory. "It is one thing to transmit a mental message formed into concrete images and words. But emotions. Never would I have thought such a thing could be done."

"Wander is a very special man," she said, blushing with the pleasure of such a claim.

"Yes, he is," Dunlevy agreed. "I am only now beginning to understand just how special." He drained his glass, gathered the remains of her meal, stacked the dishes and set them to one side. "Shall we commence?"

She made a face. "Do we have to?"

"No," he said calmly. "But if you do not, who will?"

She sighed, accepted her headset, fitted it into place, leaned back and began turning the power dial. Gradually her awareness shifted away from where she sat, moving beyond the flight deck, extending out and away from the lightway. Each time she pushed herself a little farther, extending her reach, trying to see how far she could manage to sense forward and around without losing her sensory anchor upon the ship.

Then she found it.

"Shadowlane!" Consuela called, sitting upright, not bothering to mask the tension that shot through her body. "And a ship!"

The flight deck was catapulted into action. "Yellow alert," intoned Captain Arnol, bolting from his casual stance at the rear of the control room directly into his station. "All hands, prepare for action."

The helmsman sounded the alarm, the flight deck shone with the pulsing yellow glow, then all tensed and waited. Every eye in the flight deck was upon them as Dunlevy leaned toward her and said quietly, "Are you sure?"

Consuela checked again, a swift in and out that left her nerve ends screeching. "A shadowlane and a stationary ship," she confirmed.

"Power Control Officer," the Captain intoned softly, now unwilling to shatter the moment. "Move to full shield."

"Full shield it is, Captain."

Dunlevy asked quietly, "Can you show me?"

She nodded, accustomed now to his following her out, leading him to a place he could not see himself. He in turn had the training she lacked to pinpoint the timeline.

"All right," Dunlevy said. "Let's go."

"On the ready, Navigator," Arnol ordered.

"Aye, Captain, ready to take the mark."

The incessantly angry buzzing struck her with the force of a billion metal bees. "There!" Consuela cried.

"Four hours, fifteen at . . . " Dunlevy paused, then shouted, "Mark!"

Arnol looked at the navigator. "Anywhere near the point where other ships have vanished?"

She inspected her charts. "Aye, Captain. Nine have sent their last recorded message before that point. And it matches the information Avanti supplied from the captured pirates. The pirate base should not be far off."

Though it cost her tremendously, Consuela did not back away. She had to be absolutely certain. She extended out, out, searching one way, then the other, and found it. "A second ship! They are sitting on either side of the intersection."

"Helmsman, full stop," Arnol commanded.

"Aye, Captain." A long pause, then, "Ship is stationary."

Arnol keyed his console. "Guns, there are two targets, not one."

"Two ships, aye, Captain."

"I am giving you three hours for a final trial run. Make it count, and make it good. Nothing fancy. Follow your orders."

"To the bitter end, Captain."

"Red alert in three hours and counting." Arnol switched off and turned to the pilot's station. "Join me aft for a coffee, both of you."

CHAPTER SEVENTEEN

"I want you to tell me what it is like," Arnol said. "When you traverse the shadowlane."

Consuela sipped at her cup, then set it aside. Her stomach could not accept anything just then. "Awful. Like termites eating inside my skull."

Arnol glanced at Dunlevy. "That does not sound like a simple trace of leftover energy belonging to an ancient shadowlane, Pilot."

"No, Captain, I agree."

"Whatever it is, it's powerful," Consuela confirmed.

"Then it makes it doubly difficult to ask this, but ask it I must." Arnol's face was grave. "We have two choices in attacking the pirate stronghold, assuming we are successful with this first skirmish against the two pirate vessels." His hands drew star charts in the air between them. "We can travel along the shadowlane, which was our original plan. Ride down the line until we come within Blade range."

Stationing his arms as intersecting points, he went on, "Or there is a second option. Once we have completed our attack on the ships, we could reverse back down the lightway. We could then cut through open space, traversing a line charted by our navigator. That might give us an extra advantage of attacking the base itself from an unexpected quadrant."

"Oh no," she murmured, the captain's request coming clear.

"I'm afraid so," he replied somberly. "The only way this is possible is if you would first cross the distance yourself, giving us a specific mark for where the pirates have their hideout."

"I would be there with you the entire way," Dunlevy assured her. "There would be no need to make the traverse but once."

"It could mean the difference between success and failure," Arnol told her. "Between losing half our Blades or more, and having no casualties at all."

He had hit her with the one argument she could not refuse. Consuela nodded once and started back toward the pilot's station, knowing she could not live with herself if she did nothing and something then happened to Rick.

Dunlevy settled into the saddle beside her. "All the way," he said quietly, "I'll be there beside you."

She nodded, her eyes already closed and one hand tuning up the headset dial. "Just hold my hand, okay?"

It was harder than anything she had ever thought possible. To begin with, the range was extreme. And traversing the shadowlane was like trying to focus at the limits of her ability with a drill biting into her brain. But Dunlevy was as good as his word, not simply traveling alongside her, but striving constantly to surround her with his confident strength. The pressure on her hand was matched by the sense that he walked with her, unaware of the way she traversed, but always there, ready to draw her back if the strain became too great.

It almost did, before she hit upon the idea of not remaining upon the shadowlane at all, but rather skipping along like a stone jumping across water. Touching it just often enough to hold to her course, then speeding along through empty space, allowing her mind and extended senses to recover from the shock. Passing farther and farther beyond what she had thought would be her maximum range.

Then she found it. "There!"

"Mark!" Dunlevy's voice was saber sharp. "Eleven hours, eleven minutes, and thirteen seconds." Instantly he began pulling her back.

"No, wait." Much as she wanted to go, to escape, to return, she had to be certain. She scouted as swiftly as she could, almost overwhelmed by what she found. Knowing she needed to discover everything possible, knowing she could not stand much more. Then, "All right."

Back more swiftly than she thought possible, but not swift enough to suit her. Returning to an almost blinding headache and a weakness so great she could hardly strip the headset from her temples. She turned to Arnol, winced at the lance of pain caused by the movement, whispered,

"An ice planet. Something around it, I don't know what, a horrible buzz-ing." Each beat of her heart tightened the band of pain around her skull, bringing the darkness that much closer. "Four ships, I'm pretty sure. One of them is big, not as big as us, but still very large. Two banks of weapons on the surface. I don't think . . ."

She did not feel Dunlevy's arms envelop her and lift her from the seat. Nor did she see the crew rise to their feet in silent salute as he carried her from the deck.

Chapter Eighteen

"Do you sense anything else out there besides planets and light-ways?"

Although the question was asked in the most casual of tones, Wander was instantly on alert. "Like ships? Sure."

Digs' tone turned impatient. "No, something else."

"Like what?"

"Nothing." He seemed angry that they were having the conversation at all. "I'm supposed to ask you that, but I don't know why."

Wander turned from his examination of the distant cavern floor. Watching the floater descend and ascend through the vast subterranean hall granted him his only sense of freedom. He had stopped looking through the narrow windows. Viewing across the lifeless landscape to the raging storm overhead left him with the sense of living in a prison with flames for walls.

"He's always so concerned about what you see," Digs went on, scuffing his foot across the floater's stone floor.

"Who?"

"The Dark Courier, who else?" He shot an angry glance Wander's way. "He asks a lot of questions about you. Whether you see things that aren't there. Every day he asks. I tell him you do good work, that's all I know."

Wander inspected the wiry young man, his pinched features, his darting eyes. "You're a good friend," he said slowly.

Digs raised his head, returned the gaze. As the floater settled into the ring, he said softly, "You're hiding something, aren't you?"

Wander continued to meet his gaze but said nothing.

Digs went over to the station and sat down. "I want to try something."

Wander followed him over, seated himself, settled his headset into place, remained silent.

"It's the only way you're going to trust me. I decided that last night. If you're the sensitive I think you are, I think it ought to work." He settled back, closed his eyes, said, "When we power up, just follow my lead."

With the surging force, Digs held them both anchored to the cavern. Instead of extending themselves out and into space, he turned *inward*.

Wander resisted the compulsion to push away. Instinctively he understood what Digs was attempting, and allowed himself to be drawn forward, down, into the other young man's mind.

He saw the turmoil and pain of a hard life. A family even poorer than his own, tied to a scrabble-earth farm on a distant outworld, the first candidate scout his homeworld had ever produced. Sent terrified and alone to a distant world, trained for less than six months, before being uprooted once more and sent here. Trapped and lonely, one of the few lower-class outworlders to be trained as a monitor. Hating his life, yearning for a freedom that could never be his. Chained and trapped and chafing in his stone-walled prison.

Wander allowed himself to return, and opened his eyes when the power-down was completed to find Digs watching him with those darting eyes. "Did it work?"

"Yes." He did not know how to express his feeling at this sudden gift of confidence, so all he said was, "Thank you."

Digs made do with a single self-conscious nod. Clearly he was feeling very raw. But also very determined. "I was right, wasn't I? You're a Talent."

"Yes," he said quietly.

"All the monitors are extreme sensitives, of course. But I don't know if more than a handful are real Talents. Maybe not that many." He eyed Wander swiftly, then turned away. Afraid that his gift of trust would be rejected. Forced to ask, nonetheless. "Do you see that stuff he's asking about?"

"Shadowlanes," Wander said. "All the time."

Digs' gaze fastened upon him, his eyes glittering with the excitement of knowing the barriers were down. "And the thing at Avanti that shook up the other monitors?"

Wander took a deep breath and committed. "A gift from my girl. Her name is Consuela. She's a Talent too."

"Amazing," Digs breathed. "She's on Avanti?"

"She was." The risk was tremendous, but he had to take it. This was his only chance of communicating with her again. "She's on a ship now."

"The Avenger. Yeah, I reported to the diplomat about that." A worried frown. "I think they're planning something."

"They're in for a surprise," Wander replied.

"Yeah?" A fierce light came and went. "They coming to rescue you?"

Another breath. "They're going to try."

Digs leaned across the table, his white-knuckled hands striving to etch furrows in the polished surface. He rasped, "Take me with you."

CHAPTER NINETEEN

"Consuela."

The soft voice filtered through the fog in her head. She rolled over, groaned as the thumping pain resumed in her temples.

A gentle hand raised her up, fitted a cup to her mouth. "Drink this."

She accepted the syrupy liquid, allowed the hand to ease her back down, taking none of the strain herself. She waited, coasting in the half-asleep state, until she felt the pain begin to subside. She opened her eyes to find Adriana smiling down at her, with Dunlevy standing behind her.

Adriana asked, "Better?"

"Much." She nodded, glad to find the movement did not cause the pain to return.

"I would have given it to you sooner, but we thought it best to let you rest. Would you like coffee?"

"Oh yes." She struggled upright, rubbed her face. "How long have I been asleep?"

"Almost twelve hours," Dunlevy replied. "We decided it was the best thing."

"Twelve hours." She struggled to make sense of the jumble in her head. "But that means—"

"It was a total success," he replied. "Our ship heaved to out of range of their sensors and sent the Blades and transports out and around for a surprise rear attack. The stun-bolts were as effective as the Avanti engineers promised. The troopers boarded while the pirates were still unconscious and captured both vessels without losing a man or a Blade."

She accepted the cup of coffee from Adriana with a grateful smile. "Where are we now?"

"According to the navigator's best estimates, less than two hours from the pirate base. They need you on the flight deck, Consuela. We must be sure our ships are on target. And we have to get a better fix on what their defenses are."

She forced herself to her feet, ignored the wave of fatigue that rolled over her, asked, "Ships?"

Dunlevy gave her a tired but satisfied smile. "We have a little surprise in store for the people up ahead."

———

"Final open communication," Guns said, his voice barely above a whisper, as though unseen ears up ahead might already be listening. "By the count, Knights. Run through your ops."

"Blade Three," Rick replied when it was his turn. "Take out the northern generators at mark minus fifteen seconds. When the shields go, hit the upper battery after Blade Six, then strafe with stunners at full bore."

He listened to the other leaders sound off. Each Blade was acting as a separate force, spread out thin in order to blanket the entire planet. Not really a planet, more a giant ball of ice and rock and iron, probably a comet that had strayed too far from some distant sun. Now parked in permanent orbit, haven to a pirate force that formerly had six ships by present count.

Two of them were now in their hands.

"Hit on the mark, Blades, and hit hard," Guns ordered, when the sound-off was complete. "Tuck, ready at your end?"

"Aye, armed to the teeth and champing at the bit."

"You know your attack points."

"We'll be hitting them on the money, don't you worry."

"Right." This close to the mark, neither professional had time for rivalry. "Captain, all systems are go."

"Strike hard and fast," Arnol said. "Good luck, warriors."

"Thank you, Skipper. Full alert, Blades. Silent running from here on in. Senior Weapons Officer signing off."

Warrior. Rick focused on trailing the second captured pirate ship, holding himself in tight position just clear of its blast. The captain had called him a warrior. He felt the surging power of guns armed and ready,

240 / T. DAVIS BUNN

the Blade's energy tuned to the maximum and connected to him through circuits so tight he could truly call the enormous force his own. All questions and doubts were put aside in the adrenaline-surging moment. Warrior.

Through the transparent visor he made visual contact with the target. It was a top-heavy globe, glinting black and evil in the starlight. The pirate ship he used as a shield matched it perfectly, an awkwardly constructed battleship never meant to leave deep space, with weaponry jutting from every imaginable portal. The pirate crew were locked in one of the Avenger's lower holds, the transfer made after the vessels had been secured and the enemy's controls powered down, so that none of the foes ever saw who had attacked and overpowered their vessels. Tuck's ground troops were now being transported in the requisitioned ships, armed to the teeth and prepared for null-grav battle.

Rick flew in perfect tandem to the enemy's ship. His relatively tiny Blade nestled between two massive cannons, he watched the ice globe approach. He checked his chrono, counted off the seconds, then on the timepoint shot forward like an impatient greyhound. He sensed more than marked the other Blades surging forward in tight array.

He had the generators locked on target when his internal alarm squealed as a ground-based cannon began tracking him. But too late. He fired the first phaser, powered up, fired again, shouted as both blasts struck home and the globe's shields shimmered once, then disappeared.

The cannons faltered in their tracking, then resumed hunting using alternate power. But Rick's squadron was in place, and the cannons were melted with two neutron missiles before they could get off their first shot.

Then disaster struck.

The largest of the pirate vessels entered into combat with Guns and another Blade, but while struggling to deflect the attack and launch missiles of its own, a rear hold disgorged a dozen misshapen robot attack-pods.

"Enemy pods!" Rick broke formation, raced forward as the first sent a bright flame shooting toward one of the Blades. "Knight Four, disengage and help Guns!"

"Busy," came the gasped reply. "Cannons located aft of Tuck's attack point."

"Blade Seven here," came the terse reply. "Engaging mother ship."

"Engaging pods," Rick said. There was too much risk of striking another Blade to launch a phaser or missile. He channeled all his power to the energy lance and roared to the attack.

A flaming sword seared the blackness ahead of his ship, a continual beam of fiery power. Without pause or hesitation he rammed straight through the first robot pod, scattering wreckage in every direction. A sharp swerve, turn, and another pod became a cloud of expanding metal.

"Blade Three!" Guns roared at him. "Rear shield!"

He canceled the lance, sent all power surging into a second protective barrier at his back. A single instant later he felt something slam into him with such force his Blade was sent spinning uncontrollably. Rick struggled to pull back into controlled flight, and realized he had spun in too close to the mother ship. Instead of trying to disengage he refocused the secondary shields forward, rammed the drive to full power, and struck the ship with the full force of thirty gravities' acceleration.

There was a shrieking blast of friction energy as the two shields collided. Then he was through, his Blade slicing the vessel like a knife through butter. Out the other end, no time to turn and inspect his handiwork, no time, for ahead lay two further drones, lances at the ready.

Rick shouted in defiance, switched power back to his lance, and raced to the attack.

The first robot pod's operator clearly did not expect the outnumbered single vessel to charge, and hesitated just long enough for Rick to mount over its sword and dive. But the second was cagier, operated by a seasoned fighter through comm-link, who raced forward and would have made a kill had Rick's reactions been a millisecond slower. But he managed to deflect the first thrust, slammed forward in an attack of his own, then made the mistake of wincing as the lances engaged in a deluge of fiery sparks.

The pod had intended this, for without an instant's hesitation it continued the swing, around and around and accelerating to a force that would slice Rick's Blade in half. But as the lance descended with terrifying force, another Blade appeared from nowhere, lance blazing, and smashed down upon the pod, blowing it away.

A breathless Guns demanded, "You all right, lad?"

"Yes," Rick panted. "Thanks."

"Tuck here," came the growled report. "Station secured. Communications destroyed. Ships under guard. Call in Avenger."

"Avenger here," Arnol said, his voice clipped with tension. "What are our casualties?"

"Ground troops report all intact."

"Blades, sound off," Guns ordered.

One by one the ships responded, their exultation louder with each man. There was a moment's silence before Guns said, his voice ringing with pride, "All hands accounted for, Skipper."

"Arnol here. Outstanding, warriors. You have just made history. Congratulations."

CHAPTER TWENTY

Consuela had the flight deck almost to herself. The skeleton crew, the only others in the control room with her, remained at their stations with little to do. They were two days from landfall on Selanus, and no further shadowlanes had been detected crossing their path. At Selanus they would halt long enough to deliver their load of trade goods, just as their manifest declared, and then make the n-space jump, guided by Dunlevy, for the Yalla system.

They had made good time since returning to the lightway, and would arrive at Selanus well within their margin of believable error, especially for the vessel's maiden voyage.

The pirate vessels had been crammed to the brim with every person found on the ice-bound globe. The Avenger crew had made the transfers through sealed passageways so that none of the prisoners could identify the attacking vessel. Then their drives had been melted down. They had been linked together, and were now being towed to the intersection with the lightway by two of the Avenger's sturdy troop carriers. Avanti had been notified and was sending one of its few remaining vessels to make the pick-up.

Then the globe had been mined with its own stash of weaponry and blown to smithereens.

Consuela checked the chrono. Three hours until the ship's brief downtime came to an end. In the meanwhile, most of the crew enjoyed a sleep approaching coma. But she had slept all she needed to. Besides, another task awaited her.

She fitted the headset into place and gradually began increasing the power-gain. She allowed her senses to expand outward, then focused upon a single point on the lightway, the next juncture where Wander had said he would search for a message.

There she began weaving another heart song, but this one was very different from the first. There was triumph this time. And determination. And righteous anger, and fierce pride in both herself and all the others with whom she had struggled. And longing. And yearning. And hope. And love.

And three words.

I am coming.

PART III

Heart Chaser

CHAPTER ONE

Eleven days had passed since their successful attack on the pirate stronghold. Eleven days of powering along the lightway course, headed for the Solarus system. Eleven days without another contact with pirates or a single message from Wander.

The silence took its toll on Consuela. She kept up steady watches, searching the darkness of space with her heightened sensibilities. Yet in truth the danger of pirates did not keep her in the control room as much as the hope of another word from Wander.

Sleep did not come easy to her during that eleven-day voyage. Her dreams were filled with images of Wander crying out to her, the message lost because she was not listening. She remained tired much of the time and gradually became more withdrawn.

On the last day before their arrival at Solarus, Consuela remained at her station for hours after her watch had ended. Captain Arnol had warned her that as Solarus contained a Hegemony military base, she would not be able to search far afield. There would be too great a danger of being detected. So she stayed and she searched until her weariness rose and fell like great waves and she stumbled out of the control room and fell into her bed.

The dream that came upon her then was so vivid that she felt as though she had returned home to Baltimore. And yet Consuela knew she was dreaming. She stayed locked in this in-between state until she was awoken by the chiming of her communicator.

She did not want to wake up. The dream was both powerful and radiant. But the chiming refused to go away, until she managed to rise and key the switch and hear the order for her to report immediately to the control room.

Consuela arrived just in time to hear Captain Arnol sternly announce, "It appears that we are faced with the unexpected."

Consuela settled into the chair beside Pilot Dunlevy and fought to bring herself to full alert. Under ordinary circumstances their pilot station was spaciously comfortable, yet now five chairs encircled the console. Guns and Rick sat on Dunlevy's other side, their gazes as focused as rifle barrels.

"You're saying we've hit trouble," Guns, the senior weapons officer, said.

"Not yet," Arnol responded. "Not necessarily."

Consuela struggled to set aside the lingering remnants of her dream—or had it been a dream? She was not sure. She had seen little that she recognized, but the experience had been so vivid that she wondered if she had actually been back on Earth.

"It could be a routine garrison inspection," Dunlevy agreed. But his tone did not match his words.

Consuela swept sleep-tousled hair back from her face. The summons had carried such an urgent note that she had leapt from her bunk, slipped on her robe, and rushed to the pilot station. But still her mind was caught in tendrils of the image she had left behind.

She glanced over at Rick, who responded with a grin. Her only companion from Earth was as reckless as he was handsome and possessed the courage required of a good combat pilot. That was the position he held now. Back home, he had been a local football star. She seldom thought of those things nowadays, what with everything that was pressing on her here. But the dream still lingered, and with it all the memories of Earth and her life before the sudden transition.

Guns leaned his elbows on the console and said, "Are you talking about Imperial troopers?"

"If it were only dragoons, we would have little cause for concern. Solarus is home to a substantial garrison, so we would expect to find them everywhere," Arnol replied. He turned to Dunlevy, the ship's chief pilot. Captain Arnol ordered, "Tell them."

"When we came out of n-space I made the standard check-in with the watch communicator at the Solarus main port," Dunlevy told them.

"We had decided, Arnol and I, that it was time to announce formally that a pilot travelled with the Avenger. Otherwise we would not be granted permission to transport direct from here to Yalla."

"The tower's making trouble," Guns muttered.

"Not as we expected. Just after I made the report, suddenly there was absolute panic in the tower. The communicator went berserk and started babbling like a novice scout. I was able to linger and listen in." Dunlevy's face looked as though it had aged ten years. "Two Imperial battleships appeared out of n-space directly above the port, with no notice whatsoever, and demanded immediate docking."

"We do not yet know whether our arrival and theirs are connected," Arnol reminded them.

"Captain!" the watch officer sang out. "We are now within range of their local communications."

"Request assignment of a parking orbit," Arnol ordered. And to the group, "We need time to plan."

A moment's delay, then, "Request denied, Skipper."

Arnol swiveled his chair fully about. "Remind Solarus port that Avenger is a ship designed for mining a gas giant, and that our dimensions will totally dwarf their port."

Their spaceship was indeed a mining vessel, one shaped like a top and as tall as the valley where it had been constructed was deep. But it was also a battleship, secretly designed and armed to fight the pirates that had been ravaging the planet of Avanti. An on-planet inspection could not be risked.

After another moment's delay, the watch officer reported, "Solarus port acknowledges message and says it is relaying orders for us to make for Docking Station Five."

"*Relaying orders*, is it," Guns muttered. "And with two Imperial battleships just landed?"

"Not good," Arnol agreed worriedly.

"Never heard the like," Guns went on, "not within the empire's center and this far from a trouble spot."

"No, nor I," Arnol agreed. He turned back and said to the officer, "Confirm receipt of orders. And thank them. Make it sound as though we are pleased with the *offer* of landing space. Request as swift a turnaround as possible. Inform Solarus we wish to off-load cargo and immediately make way for Yalla." He started to turn back, then checked himself. "And maintain constant watch over all comm-links. Let me know of any unusual traffic."

"Aye, Captain."

The control room's main doors slid open, and the bearlike form of Chief Petty Officer Tucker appeared. "You sent for me, Skipper?"

"Yes. Come join us." Chairs were slid about, and Tucker eased his great bulk onto the station railing. He listened as the captain gave a swift overview of what had occurred, and his face grew graver by the second.

Consuela tried to concentrate, yet part of her mind still was held by the dream, if that was what it had been. She had found herself standing in front of a red-brick church, one she vaguely recognized but could not place. The broad stairs rising to an entry ringed by great columns and crowned by a towering steeple. The doors had been closed, and somehow she had known that the church was locked shut. She had stood there, a soft wind blowing against her face, no one else around, and sensed that there was a message waiting for her. Something important.

Then Dunlevy had rung for her, and the urgency had pulled her away so swiftly that she felt as though she straddled two realms, the one of her dream and the one before her now. And the message still eluded her.

"I have to agree with Guns, much as it pains me to do so," Tucker said, when Arnol was finished with his recounting. "Two Imperial battleships arriving and demanding landing space is not the mark of an ordinary garrison inspection."

"I agree." Arnol reflected momentarily, then turned back to the officer manning the center console. "Do we have the in-system flight coordinates?"

"Just coming in now, Skipper."

"Let me have them."

There was a tense silence as Arnol reviewed the flight data. He looked up. "Petty Officer, you served time in the Solarus system, if I recall."

"Aye, Skipper." Tucker grimaced at the memory. "Duty officer on their rust bucket of a satellite refinery, promoted to master of the lunar landing station. Two of the longest years of my life."

"What do you recall of the inner moon?"

"That's where I was based." Tucker's broad features creased in a rueful grin. "Closest to a frontier port you'd ever care to find inside the Hegemony. Solarus mines turn out a high grade of iridium ore. There are also a few veins of gold, rich enough to send the rumors flying like sparks off a miner's drill. Strikers from all over the system make for here, hoping to open up the lost lode and make their fortune."

"A dangerous place, then."

"More like wide open, if you see what I mean, Skipper. Dangerous only to the unwary. A wild place, that moon. Handles a lot of secondary cargo traffic for ships not willing to pay Solarus landing fees. Lot of coming and going."

"That settles it, then." Arnol's tone took on the solid definition of command decision. "Guns, Tucker, I want you to ready your men."

"Sir?"

"Our approach takes us within close range of their moon. On our convergence, we're going to stray a bit closer still."

Guns and Tucker exchanged astonished looks. Guns said, "You're planning on off-loading us, Skipper?"

"We are supposed to be an unarmed mining vessel," Arnol replied, his tone crisp now that the decision had been made. "We have to be prepared for an Imperial inspection. That means most of our warriors and our weapons must immediately be made to disappear. Tuck, a vessel our size will look odd without a transporter of its own. So you'll take one and leave us the other. I want you to hand-pick your most seasoned troopers, Petty Officer. And fill the hold with weaponry. To the brim."

"Aye, Captain."

"Guns, you're going to have to disguise those attack pods. Will paint adhere to their surface?"

Their attack upon the pirate stronghold had been successful largely because of these fighter pods, or Blades, as they were known among the warriors. Constructed of the rare substance that was supposedly used only on Imperial battleships, the pods had cut through the pirate's defenses like a knife through butter. But to have the Blades discovered on a supposedly unarmed mining vessel would have meant the doom of everyone on board, and seal Avanti's fate.

"I can't say if it would work or not, Captain," Guns replied slowly. "I've never heard of anyone trying to paint elemental trinium before."

"Do what you can. It is essential that all prying eyes see nothing more than an in-system transporter with a contingent of simple guard pods." He inspected the two men, making sure they understood what he intended. "Just exactly what a mercenary outfit would possess."

Guns nodded slowly. "You want us to pretend that we are hiring ourselves out."

"Maybe to one of the outlying miner asteroids," Tucker offered.

"If worse comes to worse, yes." Arnol hesitated, then went on slowly, "We must prepare for the off chance that this is more than coincidence, gentlemen. I want you to see if there is an alternate means for your traveling on to Yalla."

Astonishment mounted to alarm. "Without you?"

"You will proceed without us only if necessary," Arnol replied. "Still, it cannot hurt to prepare for the possibility. And see if an alternate means of getting our forces swiftly and secretly to Yalla might exist."

They mulled that over in silence, until Guns pointed at Consuela and asked, "What about the lass here?"

"A good thought," Arnol agreed. "She must go with you. Her presence on this journey is a secret. As you know, all records show her remaining as a guest of the Chancellor on Avanti. Try and keep it that way. And mind you keep your troopers on their best behavior."

"No worry about that, Skipper," Tucker agreed, with a wink for Consuela. "The lass here is their prize mascot."

"Brought us the first successful attacks against pirates ever, far as I know," Guns agreed. "She'll be handled like spun glass, or I'll be knowing the reason why."

"I seem to recollect seeing a portable pilot's training station among the stores to be transshipped on Solarus," Tucker added.

Consuela brightened at the news. A pilot's station was required to focus. Her special sensitivities allowed her to communicate with other stations. Equipping the transporter with a portable station meant she would be of some real use during this expedition.

"Excellent," Arnol said. "You have my permission to appropriate it." His gaze shifted from Consuela to Dunlevy and back. "For reasons of security, you two will be our only link. Even so, you must hold yourselves to minimum contact. I shall expect you to do everything possible to elude any monitoring."

"Aye, Captain," Dunlevy responded for them both. "We'll make arrangements."

"Very well." He stood, drawing the others with him. "And be ready. There may very well be unwanted eyes watching us already."

Be ready. The words seemed to explode within Consuela's mind. *That* was the message she had been searching for within the dream. Again the image of the church with its closed doors loomed within her mind. But what did it mean?

"Only if they are really after us at all," Guns added.

"We must hope for the best and prepare for the worst," Arnol replied grimly. "Ready yourselves and your equipment. On the bounce."

Chapter Two

Hours later, Consuela found Rick collapsed in a sweaty heap beside a pile of paint-covered rags, a steaming mug in one hand, a thick sandwich in the other. He scarcely had the strength to raise either arm. He watched her approach and said, "You almost look like one of us."

Consuela raised her arms to show off the one-piece suit of pearl gray mesh. "It's been so long since I've worn anything except scout robes that I feel a little, well, exposed."

Guns chose that moment to walk over and deflate onto the pile of rags beside Rick. "If I have to look one more minute at what they're doing to our babies I'm going to shoot somebody."

"I thought of that too," Rick said, "but I didn't have the strength left."

Consuela looked from one to the other. "What are you two talking about?"

Guns accepted Rick's offered mug, then cocked a thumb and said to Consuela, "Just have a gander around the corner there, if you've got a strong stomach."

Consuela walked over, peeked into the main hold, and gaped. "What in the world?"

"Paint wouldn't stick," Rick said tiredly. "We tried."

"Aye, they'll be scraping gray gunk off the gunnels for ages to come," Tucker agreed, walking over. The chief petty officer was coated in gray paint and sandy goo from head to toe. Even so, he managed a tired smile for Consuela. "Hello, lass. You look the proper spacer in that getup."

But Consuela could not take her eyes off the Blades, the attack pods they had to camouflage. "But they look *awful*."

Guns nodded once. "I think that about sums it up, don't you, lad?"

"Sounds right to me," Rick agreed.

Tucker explained, "A ship made of elemental trinium and not bearing Imperial Hegemony markers would raise the alarm from here to the Outer Rim."

"I know that." Consuela raised a protesting hand toward the Blades. "But that is—"

"A proper subterfuge," he finished. Though he shared their fatigue, Tucker *was* obviously pleased with his handiwork. "We mixed up a batch of the same plasteel we use for sealing holes and building temporary supports, see, and then we blew it hard and fast over the pods. The stuff dries in seconds, so even though it didn't stick to the surface, it formed a shell." He glanced at the nearest Blade and amended, "Of a sort."

"Sort of, is right," Consuela agreed. The sleek black one-man attack ships were gone. In their place were sickly gray blobs of what appeared to be dried mud. They cascaded in frozen glops toward the floor, forming teardrop shapes. "How do the pilots get in?"

"Oh, we drilled a hole down toward the base." Tucker could not completely hide his smile. " 'Course, some pilots have more trouble climbing aboard than others."

"I didn't see you offering to play the space monkey," Guns snapped.

"Ah, Guns, me lad," Tucker said, letting his chuckle loose. "I wish you could have seen yourself wiggling in that first time, truly I do."

Consuela pointed at the shape and demanded, "How do they *see*?"

"Ah, now, that's not a problem, I'm happy to say." Tucker turned back and gave the Blades a look of pure admiration. "They may be small, but those pups were built proper, I can tell you."

"Nice to see you finally admitting to that fact," Guns said.

"I've never had a problem with the Blades," Tucker said, not turning around. "Just with some of the flyers."

"When you put the shields on full, they stop everything." Rick spoke to Consuela from his bulkhead perch, ignoring the banter of his superiors. "I mean *everything*, including light from the visible spectrum. So when they designed the viewing system, they figured out some way to extend the 'eye' out beyond the shield. Don't ask me how, but they did. And the shields are farther out than that, that . . . "

"Disguise?" Tucker offered.

"Monstrosity," Guns responded.

A voice from the central lift-well chose that moment to snap out, "Ten-hut!"

Despite the fatigue which had etched its way deeply into their features, Guns and Rick rose to their feet and stiffened as Captain Arnol strode into view. He glanced at their paint-spattered forms and said, "At ease. Do we have success?"

"Of a sort, Skipper," Guns replied glumly.

"Aye, sir," Tucker responded proudly. "Come have a look."

Arnol marched around the bulkhead, looked into the main hold, and winced. "Was that necessary?"

"Afraid so, Skipper," Guns said, his tone morose.

A flicker of mirth plucked at the edges of the captain's mouth. He struggled for a moment, then managed to bring it under control. "Well, there is one thing for certain. No one is going to mistake them for Blades."

"There are all sorts of craft used in-system where there are mining jockeys at work," Tucker agreed. He waved a hand at the lumpy vessels and explained, "A fellow trying to hunt for gold or iridium on a wish and a tight budget will buy whatever is cheap and works. Oftentimes this is nothing more than a chunk of asteroid. They'll hollow it out and fit it with a power plant, drive, and shields, and off they go."

"Then you gentlemen should fit right in." Another hint of a smile, then the captain's habitual grimness settled back into place. "I have some news."

"Can't be good," Guns said. "Not if it's brought you down here."

"It's not, I'm afraid." He turned to Tucker. "Have you selected your men?"

"Aye, Skipper. Everyone who's got full warrior status or seen enough battle duty so it would appear on their records. Nineteen in all."

"What about that portable pilot's console you found in stores?"

"Just finishing with the hookup now, Skipper."

"And the weapons?"

"The transport holds are crammed tight," Tucker replied. "Everything else that would look odd on a vessel being transported across the Hegemony for delivery is netted and ready for jettison, if it comes to that."

"It already has," Arnol said crisply. "We have received another communication. We are ordered to prepare to receive an official delegation from Imperial Command as soon as we land."

The news settled over the group like a somber sheathe.

Guns was the first to speak. "Any idea why?"

"None."

Guns nodded slowly. "We'll need to be pushing off, then."

"In a moment. Are the men gathered?"

"Ready and waiting, sir." Tucker amended, "Though a mite worse for wear, if you know what I mean."

"A weary and dirty appearance would not be bad in itself, for a team coming off mining work." Arnol nodded toward the main hold. "Call them to order, Petty Officer. I want to say a few words."

When the men were assembled, Arnol inspected them one at a time. He possessed the leader's rare quality of making each man in turn feel singled out. "By now, you have heard why this operation has been required," he began, his voice sharp and reaching to the farthest corner of the hold. "We have unwanted visitors approaching even as we speak. I do not know what this entails, nor what will happen once we make contact with the Hegemony commander. But this I do know. Whatever happens, the Avanti system is counting on us. Her people have invested years of work and a great deal of their dwindling wealth to get us this far."

He stopped there, allowing the echo of his words to ring through the great hold. Again there was the searching of each face in turn, then, "Guns, Tucker, stand forth."

Infected by the moment's solemnity, the two grizzled veterans marched forward two steps, turned smartly, and saluted with identical sharp motions. "Guns, I am placing you in command. Tucker, you are acting number two." Steel gray eyes bore into each man in turn. "I am also hereby ordering you both to set aside whatever contest there has been steaming between you, is that clear?"

There was a fair amount of coughing in the ranks as the two veterans snapped off, "Aye, aye, Captain."

"I want you all to understand how serious this is. We have the hopes and needs of Avanti and her sister worlds riding with us. Make no mistake, we are their last chance. Even if the resources were available, they could never duplicate the secrecy that has surrounded this mission. The Imperium would be watching too closely."

He waited through another silence, then snapped out, "Guns!"

"Aye, Skipper."

258 / T. DAVIS BUNN

"If for any reason we and the main vessel are diverted, I hereby order you to do whatever is necessary in order to successfully carry out your dual missions: Attack the pirates wherever you find them. Rescue the Talent Wander and return both him and Scout Consuela back to Avanti."

"But Skipper—"

Arnol leveled a gaze at Guns that would have melted steel. "Did you hear me?"

Guns snapped back to attention and cracked out, "Aye, Captain. Loud and clear."

"Very well." Arnol turned back to the team. "Whatever happens, whatever we face, you are hereby commanded to carry out your orders. And make heroes of us all."

CHAPTER THREE

The transport was a big bus with tiny side-windows and no wheels. Consuela kept telling herself that, and it helped. Otherwise she thought at times her heart would leap from her chest with excitement.

They had set up the pilot's console alongside the communication officer's station. The barrier separating the cockpit from the bus proper had been removed in order to make room for her. She sat directly behind the first officer. Her post was elevated slightly, as her chair was bolted to the console's portable amplifier, and it to the floor. The perch granted her an uninterrupted view through the front portals. The spectacle unfolding before her was truly awesome.

The first officer swiveled around and said, "Coming up to the first mark, Scout."

"Thank you." Consuela tore her eyes away from the rising vista and fitted on the dampened headset. She swivelled the miniature control-console toward her and ran through the conning sequence as Dunlevy had explained.

The portable console was, according to Dunlevy, a rudimentary affair, meant only to assist in training more scouts than could be accommodated at some pilot's station. It was common enough in larger ships and active ports, as many pilots did not have the patience to stand full watches with trainees. They now intended to use it for communication between Dunlevy, who had remained back on the main vessel, and themselves.

Yet when she powered up, she grimaced as the squeal of an almost unbearble noise filled her head. She placed two fingers to each temple and leaned over, striving to concentrate enough to send the proper message.

"Is something the matter, Scout?" Tucker shifted his bulk about in the second officer's seat and gave her a look of concern.

Consuela raised one hand to silence him and sent out the words, *Scout checking in.*

Pilot here. Dunlevy's tone came back calm and reassuring. *How are you?*

Hurts. Consuela lowered the power gauge down to where the myriad of voices was reduced to a constant shrill static. *So many voices.*

Amp up, Scout. Can barely read you. As Dunlevy had suggested before departure, they refrained from using names. There was no way of telling who might be monitoring, or how closely.

Consuela increased the power and repeated her words. The background noise had the persistence of a dozen dentist drills working in her skull.

Dunlevy thought a moment, then said, *I assume you can hear me all right.*

Consuela responded, *Affirmative.*

Then power up only to send. Dunlevy showed astounded humor behind his words. *Ask the flight lieutenant for his ETA.*

Consuela twisted down the power fully and looked up, only to realize that every eye in the transport was upon her. "The pilot asks when we are expected to arrive."

The first officer checked his chrono, and responded crisply, "One hour ten. Are you all right, Scout?"

"Yes, thank you." Consuela wiped at the sweat streaming down her face, then smiled as Tucker passed her a hand towel. She powered up and sent the time, then instantly cut back the comm strength.

The Imperial Hegemony has arrived in the form of a battalion commander, a senior pilot, and a fleet admiral, Dunlevy informed her. *Not to mention a contingent of twenty fully armed dragoons as escort. They seemed pleased to find me on board, which is troubling. They then insisted on a formal inspection of the entire ship.*

Despite the strain and discomfort, Consuela felt a shiver run through her. *They were searching for something.*

My thoughts exactly. They were most angry by the time the inspection was completed. And confused. They have been closeted with the captain ever since. Dunlevy's concern came through loud and clear. *I fear the worst. Best you inform the others. Check back this time tomorrow.*

And this noise?

You are picking up on Imperial traffic, Dunlevy replied. *Even I can catch segments of it now and then. This is good for us, as so much traffic will mask our own communications.*

Until tomorrow, then.

Consuela powered down, stripped off the headset, and leaned back against the seat. She felt exhausted.

"Here, Scout." A cool cup was pressed into her hand. Consuela looked up to see Tucker leaning over her. "Is there anything we can do?"

"I'm fine, really. It's just . . . " She struggled for a way to explain. "There's a lot of confusion."

Tucker kept grave eyes upon her. "From the console?"

She shook her head. "From the Imperial battleships."

The entire transport braced at her words. Consuela took a breath and explained what Dunlevy had reported. When she was finished, there was a long silence. Consuela was content to wait and sip at her cup. Then the communicator asked, "Should I relay this to the pods?"

"It can wait until we are safe on the ground." The first officer, though young, bore the same grim determination as Captain Arnol.

"Too much chance of being overheard, this close to a base," Tucker agreed.

Consuela took another sip and glanced through the front portals. She caught sight of a rock-shaped pod floating off to their left and wondered if it was Rick's. For a brief instant, she found herself envying Rick's easy way with these newfound friends. But she knew it was simply not her nature. She had always been reserved. The gift she had found waiting for her here in this realm, this extraordinary sensitivity, conformed to who she already had been on Earth. As though the gift melded to her reserve and granted it meaning.

She kept her gaze on the front portals. Despite her time in space, nothing had prepared her for this approach to a lunar landscape. The eerie vista drew her away from both her thoughts and her discomfort. She had never imagined that anything could look so utterly alien, so totally void of life.

The sky was made even blacker by the moon's silver-white scenery. Stars rimming the horizon grew ever more distant at their approach. The

262 / T. DAVIS BUNN

horizon itself was brutally jagged, as the moon's mountains had never known the wearing power of wind or rain. Even from this height, the peaks looked impossibly tall.

Directly beneath them spread out a great valley, the floor scarred with manmade domes and rutted tracks and circular meteor craters. Against the lunar backdrop, all man's efforts looked puny.

A sudden shaft of light pierced the blackness, forming a brilliant curtain toward which they floated. Consuela gasped and drew back involuntarily. Tucker grinned and said, "First lunar sunrise, lass?"

"First time on any moon, ever." There was none of the fresh wonder of an earthbound dawn. Instantly all was either burning brightness or impenetrable shadow.

"Just stay close," Tucker said, "you'll be fine."

"We're getting a signal from below," the comm officer said. "Wants our details."

"Here, let me handle that. Switch the signal to the overhead, will you?" Tucker accepted the hand mike, and when static hissed from the intercom, he said, "Come again, matey, we didn't catch you."

"Then open up your ears," snapped the speaker. "I don't like repeating myself, especially for rock hounds asleep at the wheel."

Tucker leaned back with a relieved sigh. "Happy, don't tell me they haven't given you a one-way ticket to the asteroids yet."

There was a moment's hesitation, then, "Tuck! You old scoundrel, is that you?"

"None other," Tucker replied jovially. "Good to know you're as full of smiles and laughter as ever."

"Full of spit, you mean. What brings you back to this forsaken hole?"

"I hear there's a mother lode just waiting to be dug out and delivered to market. Figure I and my men are the ones for the job."

There was a phlegm-filled laugh. "Then you're not the Tuck I know. He was always too smart to fall for that one."

Tucker shared an easy laugh, though it did not reach his eyes. "You've caught me out, mate. Truth be known, I got tired of the spit-and-polish routine. Put together a group of like-minded fellows, adventurers to a man."

"Mercenaries, you mean."

"I won't quibble with you, Happy. Know of any likely profits to be had?"

"Could be, could well be." The tone turned wheedling. "You'll remember your old mates if something comes up?"

"Always good to stay on your right side," Tucker replied. "You find us something, part of the proceeds will certainly find its way to your pocket."

"That's my Tuck," Happy said, suddenly eager. "You know where the north pit used to be? Sure you do, that was part of your old bailiwick. Been closed down, ran dry as a miner's graveyard close on five years back. It's our second landing field now."

"A second field," Tucker mused. "Things must be booming."

The old voice cackled. "You won't recognize the place, Tuck. See you when you've grounded."

Tucker spoke to the communications officer. "Make sure the off-riders caught all that."

"Off-riders, I like it." Guns' voice crackled over the intercom speaker. "You came through loud and clear, Tuck. We'll be following you in."

"Right you are." Tucker handed back the microphone, and as he did the jollity slid from his features. He turned to face the silent transport. "You've all heard what we're up against here, and what our story is. Stick to it. Anybody asks where you're from or where you're headed, tell them to see me. Keep a sharp eye, a tight lip, and trust only your mates." He cast a solemn gaze over the group, then added a final warning, "Folks in these parts have the habit of staying loyal only so long as nobody else offers them more."

CHAPTER FOUR

Wander stood alone in the floating station's corner as they descended into Citadel's great cavern. No matter how often he made this journey, he had never grown accustomed to the sight. The underground hall contained the mind generators, which used the planet's core as their energy source. Through these, Sensitives scanned the Imperium's vast reaches, a secret overview of the entire galactic regime. Wander stood by the railing, looking out to where the colossal chamber's edges were lost in haze and shadow.

As he stood, he paid careful attention to what was being said by the others going on watch with him. Wander had learned never to show how much he knew or what he found of interest. And their present discussion was fascinating indeed.

"They searched the mining ship Avenger from stem to stern," the senior monitor was saying. "And they did not find a thing. Nothing whatsoever out of the ordinary. It was just as the authorities back on Avanti had declared on the manifest—a brand-new gas planet mining vessel, outbound for Yalla."

Avenger was the name of Consuela's ship. Ever since the day Wander had received Consuela's message of hope and promise, saying she was coming to rescue him from his fiery prison, the Hegemony-wide monitoring station on this planet called Citadel had known constant commotion. Watches had been doubled, with little reason given. Urgent and confusing orders had been received from Imperial Command, only to be countermanded hours later. The diplomat was seen raging in the halls, shouting at the guard sergeant responsible for the contingent of Imperial dragoons.

Rumors abounded. One said the Hegemony was being invaded by outworld forces. Another contended that pirates had been detected, proving the accusations of numerous planets. Yet another suggested that a strange new weapon had suddenly appeared out of nowhere, attacked an Imperial vessel, taken it prisoner, and vanished without a trace. Such hearsay flashed and sped through the stone corridors, only to wither and fade when no confirmation was received. In truth, the monitors knew nothing at all.

Wander had learned that the monitors longed after information from the outside. They remained bound to their work and their station, thrilled by the incredible power of Citadel's mind-amps. Yet they spent long hours of every watch listening in on communication between Hegemony pilots, garnering every last shred of Imperial gossip.

The practice was officially frowned on, but in truth no notice was taken. To have restricted the custom would have resulted in a riot. Though only a handful of people, including the emperor himself, knew of the Citadel's existence, senior pilots were continually calling upon the monitors' services. Supposedly, the monitors were simply attached to Imperial Command, a vast space-bound organization that contained the emperor's official residence.

The monitors searched the far reaches of space, plotted unknown courses to newly discovered worlds, checked for dangers and possible attackers, watched over the turbulent outworlds. In return for their services, the monitors demanded nothing but a continual flow of news and gossip.

To have their news suddenly cut off, to be unable to determine what was happening, had every monitor on Citadel in absolute turmoil.

Digs sidled up to Wander. "Have you—"

Wander stopped him with an upraised hand. Although his talents had brought him to the attention of Citadel's three senior monitors, and his place was now much more secure, Digs remained his only friend. Digs understood the gesture. Realizing that Wander wanted to hear what was being said, he turned and faced out over the vast cavern beside his friend.

One of the monitors behind him demanded, "So they still do not know what was behind the attack?"

266 / T. DAVIS BUNN

"We still do not know," the senior monitor responsible for their watch replied, "if there has truly been an attack at all."

Wander kept his face turned resolutely toward the distance. The cavern's light was supplied by the transparent power line that ran through both the floor and the distant ceiling. They shimmered like brilliant veins. He struggled to keep his expression bland and listened intently.

"But the message from Imperial Command," another protested. "I heard it myself. They declared that an outstation had come under sudden attack, and that we were to monitor—"

"A message that was instantly countermanded," the senior monitor reminded him. "And a message for which there is now no record whatsoever. I know. I have checked. Twice."

There were three such floating stations interspersed throughout the great cavern. Yet since the disquiet began, all the monitors had begun gathering at the beginning and end of each watch to travel upon the central station with the senior monitor. This meant a very long walk for the lesser monitors and scouts such as Wander, as their stations were farther out toward the periphery, but he did not mind. It was vital that he hear and learn all he could. Especially when the talk was as today's.

"It is outrageous that we can be held to double watch-time with no explanation of what it is we are supposed to be searching out," complained another monitor.

"You are to search out anything unusual," the senior monitor answered. He attempted to be stern, but the fatigue in his voice drained his words of strength. "Anything at all."

"That is nonsense, and you know it as well as I," one of the monitors complained. "Forty thousand parsecs, more than seven hundred systems, not to mention the outworlds, and nothing specific to guide our search. I have a good mind to complain to the diplomat."

"You would be well advised to stay as far from the diplomat as you possibly can," the senior monitor replied dryly.

There was a moment's silence, then a quieter voice asked, "Any word on what's causing the ruckus between the diplomat and the dragoons?"

The senior monitor sighed, and his answer carried a resigned weariness. "The dragoons are against leaving Citadel, and I must say with all this confusion I agree. But the diplomat has this girl, this young scout, so firmly fixed in his mind that he has overridden the guard sergeant's strongest protests. Protests which I must say I agree with, though you never heard those words from me. How a young, untrained scout stranded on Avanti could possibly be a threat to the Hegemony is beyond me."

Wander's grip on the railing tightened until his knuckles turned white. They were talking about Consuela.

"In any case," the senior monitor continued, "protest or no, the dragoons are ordered to Avanti. They are to ferret out this scout and bring her back here."

"And us?"

"We shall simply have to trust in our own monitoring skills, and in the Citadel's mystery." The station touched down with a gentle thud. "And now, to your stations."

Wander and Digs were starting down toward their secondary amp when the senior monitor called them back. He inspected them with tired eyes. "We are stretched to the limit. I hereby raise you to full watch status."

Digs and Wander exchanged startled glances, then chimed in together, "Thank you, Senior Monitor."

"Thank me when this is over. For the time being, you are assigned to, let me see . . . " He raised the keypad attached to his belt, read for a moment, then decided. "The seventh quadrant, yes, we've left that sector unattended for nine watches now. You understand the drill?"

"Report anything unusual," Digs repeated. "We understand."

He managed a weary smile. "It is admirable to see the eagerness of youth. This will look good on your records. Now to work, and good hunting."

As they hastened down the corridor between the two main amps, Digs hissed, "Freedom at last. You can't imagine—"

"I have to get a message to Avanti," Wander whispered.

Digs gave him a look of total alarm. "You can't be serious."

"I *have* to."

Digs slowed, stopped, inspected his friend. "It has something to do with our escape?"

The idea hit Wander with the strength of a thunderbolt. Instantly he knew the answer was a definite "Yes."

"Then I suppose we have to do it," Digs said, resigned. "But fast."

To either side of their passageway towered the great mind-amps. Their dark surface was translucent. Within their depths sparkled and flowed the power drawn from the planet's core. Usually Wander found their patterns mesmerizing. But not today.

"You two certainly took your time arriving!" The monitor stripped off his headset and pushed himself from the seat. "It is outrageous, scouts forcing a monitor coming off double-watch to hang about! The senior monitor will hear about this, mark my words!"

"It was the senior monitor who held us up," Digs replied, trying for quiet submission, but unable to keep his pride from getting in the way. "We've been assigned to stand full watch."

The monitor was so disconcerted he could not hold on to his anger. He glanced at Wander and protested, "But this scout's not been here long enough to learn his way around."

"I guess the senior monitor thinks we can handle it," Digs said loftily. He waited as the monitor gathered his things and left muttering. When they were alone, his nervousness returned. He whispered, "You really have to try this?"

"Right now," Wander replied firmly.

"All right, then, this is what we'll do." Digs bolted for the central station. "I'll power up the amp and take my own sweet time hooking in. I've got to do the paper work for the new shift, that sort of thing. You contact Avanti, then *immediately* head for the seventh quadrant, got it?"

"I won't stay an instant longer than necessary," Wander agreed, seating himself and fitting on the headset.

"If anyone catches wind of what you've done, we'll say you started off on your own and used Avanti to position yourself." Grimly Digs shook his head. "Which they'll believe for about a half a millisecond."

"Thank you," Wander said quietly, fitting on his headset. "Okay, I'm ready."

"Here goes, then." Digs hit the power switch, and as he receded into the temporal distance, hissed, "Remember, in and out *fast*."

With that first thrust of power, Wander sped outward, coming faster into focus than ever before. His concentration was made diamond-sharp by urgent need. He rode the expanding force as if it were a great ocean wave, although it was normally not until the power expansion was completed that monitors began their own outward reach.

Avanti came into sharp focus. He followed the faint port signal straight down, tightened onto the tower, and signaled, *Urgent, Urgent, Avanti Port, Tower Control, come in.*

Immediately there was a response of total consternation. Then a shout of pain came across the way. *Watch Communicator here. Sorry. Spilled coffee in my lap. Who is this?*

Urgent, Urgent, Wander replied, almost shouting with the strain. *Have message for highest level. Can you record?*

There was a moment's delay, less than a few seconds, but long enough to make Wander want to scream with frustration and fear. Finally, *Ready to receive. Repeat, who is this?*

Friend of Avanti, Wander replied.

The reply became frantically excited. *Is this the Scout—*

Hold queries. Urgent, Urgent. Imperial dragoons are being sent to capture the Scout Consuela. Cannot give arrival time, but know they will be underway soon. Do you copy?

Copy. Finally, finally, the reaction he had hoped for, crisp and sharp. *How large an invasion?*

Can't say, but rumor is it will be guards from Citadel only. Could be reinforcements from Hegemony, but there is much confusion, so perhaps not. Do you copy?

Message received. We will be ready. Many thanks.

Wait. Message continues. Repeat, these are Citadel guards. It would make my rescue much easier if you can hold the attacking force there. Copy?

We will do our best to tie them up in knots, came the delighted reply. *Glad to be of service to Avenger. Speaking of the ship, we have word that—*

Not now. Must depart. Message ends. Instantly Wander retreated and circled and powered out. He sensed Digs moving in alongside, and began reaching toward the seventh quadrant. Listening, searching as he did so, detecting no signal of his move having been monitored. Only when he arrived and began the normal routine did Wander take what felt like his first breath in hours, and feel the release of the steel band of fear that had been wrapped about his chest.

CHAPTER FIVE

Consuela watched through the front portal as two figures in space-suits moved toward the transport. Together they dragged a chest-high accordianlike hose over and fastened it onto their airlock. As soon as the seals were in place and the double doors opened, a bandy-legged stranger pulled himself through and exclaimed, "Tuck, you old scoun-drel! If you aren't a sight for sore eyes, I don't know what is."

"Likewise, Happy." At the back of the transport, Tucker straightened from his task of sorting. There was a narrow open space where the seats ended and a wall sectioned off a small 'fresher and a cabin with a half-dozen bunks. The space was now littered with weapons from the Av-enger's aft hold. Tucker's bulk crowded the area as he waved the port official toward him. "Come have a seat. How you been keeping?"

"Can't complain, though I do anyway and all the time." The man was stubby in every respect—short legs, short jerky motions, a jutting chin upon a head that barely came to Consuela's shoulder. He wore a well-patched suit with port emblems so worn that she could make little out. His face was as seamed as a freshly plowed field, with all the furrows pointed downward, and he had the sourest expression she had ever seen. He made his way down the transport's crowded aisle with the ease of one long accustomed to the moon's lower gravity field, taking the stretch in easy leaps. He clasped Tuck's hand in a fierce grip and de-clared, "Whatever the ill wind was that brought you here, you'll live to regret it."

"Profit, just like I said," Tucker said briefly, and gave the trooper beside him a single nod. "Looks like everything's shipshape. You can repack."

"Right you are, Tucker."

Happy cast a shrewd gaze over the warrior's rigid stance and said, "Got yourself a packet full of ex-dragoons?"

"Not on your scrawny neck," Tucker replied, lifting one of the portable blasters and running his hand idly down the barrel. "But all have seen off-world duty of sorts."

"Planetary soldiers who wanted to see a bit more of the realm," Happy interpreted. "I like it. Seasoned soldiers are hard to come by for guard duty." He ran his gaze over the mass of weaponry set carefully out for his inspection. "Looks like you made off with the better part of somebody's arsenal."

"Picked up a bit of this and that, you know how it is," Tuck replied easily. "What was this you said about guard duty?"

Happy caught the interest and turned cool. "Oh, nothing much. Couple of caravans making for border worlds."

Tucker's tone matched Happy's pretended nonchalance. "What would a bunch of second-rate ore vessels need with guards, especially if they're staying within Hegemony boundaries?"

Happy tossed him an ancient gaze. "Where you been hiding, Tucker?"

"Here and there. Why do you ask?"

"There's changes on the wind, matey. None of them good. Solarus garrison is growing all the time. You know as well as I how cargo convoys would just as soon stay out of the way of dragoons and their commissars. Whatever is bought by the Imperium these days is paid for in Hegemony scrip, which is fine if all you're wanting is wallpaper. A lot of the upper-grade caravans have been forced to use us for their staging point."

"So that's why you needed the second landing station," Tucker mused. "Been wondering about that."

"Second and third and before too much longer, a fourth in the planning stages as well."

Tucker stretched his bulk in an easy yawn and said, "Caught some traffic about Hegemony vessels landing down on Solarus as we were pulling in."

"Don't know anything about that, and don't want to." Yellowed eyes

272 / T. DAVIS BUNN

turned shrewd. "You and the boys on the run?"

"Clean slates, the lot of us," Tucker replied, holding to the easy tone. "One of the requirements for signing on."

"Well, if that's the case, then you'll be having caravans crawling over each other to hire you on as guards."

Tucker turned to the listening crew and said, "That's the sound of profit if ever I heard it."

"You'll be remembering your mateys when it comes time to seal the bargain," Happy cautioned.

"If pickings are as good as you say," Tucker replied, "we'll be heading back this way again. We'll need to keep you on as permanent eyes and ears."

Happy showed as close to a pleased expression as he could manage, then leaned forward and said conspiratorially, "Something's got their wind up."

"Who?"

"The dragoons, the dark couriers, all the Hegemony parasites."

Tucker could not fully mask his surprise. "Dark couriers? Here?"

"Not here, no. On Solarus, or at least so go the rumors." Happy pretended to spit in disgust. "Rumors, you wouldn't believe how they're spreading. Word is, something's hit the Imperium and hit them hard. They're swarming about like crazy. Got everybody worried, especially the outbound caravans. You'll be in prime demand, especially if you can be ready to depart soon."

"Got nothing to keep us here, if the price is right."

"I'll see to that," Happy assured him.

"Of course you will," Tucker said. "Oh, by the way, as you were speaking of borderlands, keep your ears open. We've heard rumors of rich pickings out around Vector Nine. Any caravan headed toward that quadrant would be our first choice."

"Can't hurt to check," Happy said doubtfully.

Suddenly a voice came crackling over the intercom, "You plan on jawing all through the lunar day?"

"Guns," Tucker explained to Happy's startled expression. "Our number one outrider."

Happy squinted through the front window, then widened his eyes. "Those ugly suckers are guard pods?"

"I'm liking this man less and less," Guns said sourly over the intercom.

Happy shook his head in amazement. "I thought you mateys were towing some likely looking rocks, wanted to play at ore-hounds in your spare time."

"Why don't you string out a passageway," Guns barked, "so I can tell you personally what I think of your jokes."

"If they caught you unawares," Tucker said, "think of what they'll do to any incoming attackers."

Happy glanced back at the massed weaponry. "They well armed?"

"To the teeth," Guns snapped over the intercom. "Now hows about letting my boys and I out for a stretch?"

Happy turned back to Tucker and displayed the worst set of teeth Consuela had ever seen. "You're right, matey. There's the smell of profit in the air."

"Vector Nine," Tucker repeated, his tone as easy as his heavy-lidded eyes. "And a planet out there called Yalla. That was the world on everybody's lips. Just something for you to keep in mind."

CHAPTER SIX

Rick crawled from the claustrophobic tunnel, rose to his feet, and gave an enormous sigh of relief. It had felt more than strange, creeping along the flexible tube, nothing but the thin walls between him and utter vacuum. The tunnel was so narrow it had squeezed him from every side. The low gravity had not helped, for each scramble had pushed him up against the top, making handholds hard to keep and leaving his reflexes feeling out of sync.

"Rick." Consuela moved over in little airy steps, hands searching for the overhead holds. She stopped in front of him and began bouncing up and down, quick thrusts of her toes enough to send her several inches into the air. Her brown hair was caught back in a dark ponytail, which rose and fell in slow motion. "Can you believe this?"

He was about to say how good it was to see her smile, when a hand clasped his shoulder and Guns said, "That tunnel was something to remember."

"I felt like I couldn't breathe," Rick agreed.

"These middling trade moons are all alike, skimping on the basics." Tucker moved forward and stopped before them. "The upside is, the only way to the pods is first through the big passage here and then our transport."

"All it would take is one person in the know to clamber through the plasteel shell, look up, and see what the pod's belly is made of," Guns agreed. He glanced back at the small tunnel's branching and shuddered.

"Though I can't say I'm looking forward to the return journey."

Tucker asked, "Ready to set up watches?"

Guns looked up at the burly man. "I'd say you can handle that as well as I."

"Arnol put you in charge."

"Aye, but the skipper's a good ways off just now." Guns kept a steady gaze. "My suggestion is we hold to equal status for the time being. Especially here, where you know the lay of the land. Then, if there's trouble, we go with the captain's orders."

Tucker held the wiry weapons officer's gaze for a long moment. "Nary another man I'd have to guard my back in a battle, Guns."

"Likewise."

Tucker turned to the transport, cramped now with the Blade flyers perched alongside the troopers. "Three watch shifts. We're all weary from the preparations and the journey. Still, we need volunteers for first watch. Whoever stays will have to keep on their toes. Nobody but nobody gets through the transport to the pods."

Consuela raised a small hand. "I just sat around before we left. The others should get a rest."

To Rick's surprise, Tucker did not turn her down. "It may be best for you to hold back until we've got the lay of the land. Mining towns can be rough places. Plus you'd be earning our thanks." He raised his voice. "Six more. No flyers, you boys have already done double duty. Who else?"

Rick stood isolated by his fatigue and the disappointment of not being able to stay with Consuela. He started when she touched his shoulder, leaned forward, and said quietly, "I went back to Earth again."

"What?"

"At least I think I did. It was a dream. But it seemed vivid enough, just the same." Swiftly she described the red- brick church with its great pillars and tall steeple. "Does that sound familiar?"

Rick's attention was half-held by the bustle which surrounded them. "Maybe, I'm not sure."

"I felt like I knew it, but while I was there . . . I don't understand it." She seemed genuinely disturbed.

Tucker's voice brought them both around. "All right, those not assigned first watch, let's be moving out. Draw hand blasters from stores, but keep them strapped down; they're for show and not for use. Stay close, watch your mates, keep a sharp eye for trouble."

"Perhaps we can find a quiet moment later," Consuela said.

Rick nodded, grabbed his small pack, and allowed the crush to push him toward the transport's main exit. As he passed through the portal, he turned back, caught sight of Consuela's face, and saw her mouth the word, *Friends.*

CHAPTER SEVEN

Rick stepped through the moonbase's massive airlock, looked around, and declared, "Party time at the OK Corral."

"I don't understand what you said, lad," Tucker responded. "But I agree with the sentiment."

The airlock door was as large as a bank vault. They gathered to one side in order to gain their bearings and allow the crush to pass them by. Rick glanced up, astonished at the cavern's size.

The only way to grasp its dimensions was to count the levels ringing the central open space, which itself was the length of five football fields. Rick started at the distant floor and counted up, was around halfway and at the number twenty-three when his sleeve was pulled and a voice said, "Got a berth, mate?"

Rick found himself staring down at an undersized man of leathery skin and ancient eyes. "What?"

"Frankie's is the place. Guaranteed clean, airtight, and secure as—"

"We're fresh caught, but not first-timers," Tucker rumbled easily, stepping forth. Then to Rick, "Check and make sure your pouch is still intact, lad."

"Hey, what kind of . . ." The man's backward progress was halted by Guns sidling up behind him. The voice became more plaintive. "This is a legit hustle, mateys."

Tucker's eyes remained on Rick. "Lad?"

"Everything seems intact."

278 / T. DAVIS BUNN

"Best sling it under your poncho until you're used to the ways around here." Tucker's stubby fingers dug out a coin. He held it up so that it caught the light. "Dusty still running his hall?"

"You been gone awhile," the weasel replied, his eyes held by the coin. "Dusty don't do much but sit by the fire and spin his tales. His daughter's handling the trade. Good lass, name of Stella. Take you there, if you like."

"I know the way." Tucker flipped him the coin. "For your troubles."

They started off, Tucker at point and Guns holding the rear. All the group were tense, all eyes nervously scouting every shadow. Rick had trouble holding to the brisk pace. The moon's low gravity made walking a genuine effort. Plus he was as tired as he had ever been in his life.

Guns noticed his discomfort and moved forward to ask, "Your first time at low-g, lad?"

"Yes." Rick stumbled and kept himself upright by grabbing hold of Guns' shoulder. "This is a lot harder than it looks."

"Don't think of it as natural walking, that will help. Push yourself forward, then hold and wait for the ground to reach you." Guns repeated the instructions slowly, pacing him through the gait. "You're doing fine. Not long now."

Their walk took them along the same level as the airlock, perhaps a third of the way up the cavern. Below was a full-scale market, selling everything from foodstuffs to mining equipment. There were drills three times the height of a man and ending in an stubby black muzzle; Rick did not need to ask how he knew it was a drill and not some giant weapon. The flow of information remained available whenever he required something. It had been the same since their coming.

Rick flinched as they passed a great doorway. The noise from within the bar's shady depths was deafening. Once past, he slipped up to Tucker and asked, "Was that music?"

"Of course." Tucker showed mock surprise. "It wasn't to your liking?"

"It sounded like a dozen chain saws chewing on nails."

"That was fairly tame for these parts," Tucker replied.

"Whatever you do," Guns added, moving up from behind them, "don't enter any such place alone."

Tucker directed them down a tunnel, five times Rick's height and as crowded as everywhere else. Men and women pushed along, the crowds thick and boisterous. Clothing was beyond weird—animal skins and chains and heavy boots, or shiny robes that billowed with each step, or tattered space suits minus helmets, or ancient uniforms with faded medals—a hodgepodge of colors and forms. The noise was continual and overloud, battering at him.

As though a switch were abruptly thrown, a wave of stillness passed through the throng. With the suddenness of an involuntary shudder, people pressed themselves up tight against the walls. Rick felt arms grasp his shoulders and ease him back, just as a figure came into view. It was an old woman, dressed in a robe so black it drank in the light. She was followed by men obviously matched for size and girth, so large she scarcely came up to their waists. The men wore golden uniforms that shimmered like a liquid field with each step.

"A dark courier," murmured the trooper next to him.

"What is a—"

Guns hissed a command for silence. The woman's gaze flitted over them. Rick felt the air freeze in his chest. He had never seen a gaze so cold. The soldiers wore gold helmets with blaster shields pulled down over their eyes. Their massive weapons were carried at parade rest, across their chests, and their gaze was constantly on the move.

Only when the woman and her entourage passed did the tunnel gradually come back to life. "Okay, let's move on," Tucker said, his voice subdued. "Not far now."

Rick moved back to where Guns watched their rear, and asked quietly, "What was that?"

"Dark courier," he said, his voice crisp with unease. "What the common folk call a senior diplomat."

"But who—"

"The Emperor's hounds. Wherever they go, doom and destruction soon follow." Guns cast an anxious glance behind them. "I'll be glad when we've left this system behind us."

"Those soldiers were something."

"Aye, Hegemony dragoons. Bloodthirsty lot. Imperial household guards, from the look of their uniforms. Though what the emperor's chosen few are doing on a minor outpost like this one is beyond me."

Rick recalled the moment that old crone's gaze passed over him, and shuddered. "That woman shook me up."

"Aye, anyone who says they're not frightened by a dark courier is a liar and a fool to boot." Guns pointed ahead to where a grim-faced Tucker was motioning them through a narrow portal. "Looks like we've arrived. Don't know what I want most just now, a meal or a bed or a ticket out."

———

Rick awoke to the sound of low voices. He rolled over, and it was only his swift reflexes that kept him from falling from the narrow bunk. He unfastened the curtain, opened it a crack, and blinked at the bright light. When his eyes adjusted he saw that the central table of their chamber was now occupied by Tucker, Guns, and two strangers. A pair of guards—not theirs—stood at alert by the portal.

He slipped into his clothes, pushed the curtain wide, and dropped down. He slid his feet into his shoes, made his way to the 'fresher, and upon his return spotted a side table heavily laden with breakfast.

They had paid extra to have a private rock-walled chamber all to themselves. The chamber's only color was from the curtains shielding the floor-to-ceiling alcoves that lined three walls. Rick heard gentle snores coming from those nearby. He filled his plate, then turned to find Guns waving him over.

"This is one of our pod flyers," Guns said proudly, making room for him on the bench. "Rick, Mahmut here runs a caravan headed for Yalla."

"The desert planet is known for the beauty of its gems," the merchant offered, his voice as oily as his dark hair. His eyes were as black as onyx and as unreadable as the night. Mahmut offered Rick a smile that meant nothing at all and said, "Firestones are coveted throughout the Hegemony, even adorning the emperor's crown. Alas, the merchants of Yalla are well aware of the jewels' value, and charge us the moon and stars and sun and wind. It is very difficult for an honest merchant to make an honest living, much less pay the exorbitant amount requested by guard-captains."

Rick saved himself from needing to respond by keeping his mouth full. Tucker fired back, "We have requested a fair wage and not a penny more. Even the landing station's supervisor, the one all know as Happy, has said our price is low."

"And I say there is no need for further guards at all." The young cohort shared the merchant's slender build and dark complexion. His eyes blazed as he challenged each man in turn. "We are armed, our guards are well trained, and what's more, their trust has been earned over years."

"You must forgive my son," Mahmut purred. "He does not share my anxiety rising from this spate of rumors."

"There are always rumors in third-rate hovels like this," the young man said, his voice almost a snarl. "If we take them on, we'll have to assign our own guards to guard *them*."

"True, true," Mahmut grumbled, stroking his thin beard. He wore a gray belted robe over a singlet of black silk, simple yet clearly of finest quality. His single ornament was a ring with a stone the size of Rick's thumbnail, a jewel that seemed to flicker with a light from within. "It is indeed a dilemma. Perhaps if the guard-captains were to lower their price a trifle . . ."

"The price is fair and firm," Tucker replied tightly. "As to whether or not we are trustworthy, there are a dozen people and more around these parts who will tell you who I am."

"And profess to your honesty, yes, Happy has already brought several of these people for us to speak with. A most impressive show." Dark eyes flitted swiftly about, making it hard to get a fix on what the man was thinking. "Yet I am also wondering what argument you can make to my son's concerns."

"We won't argue with anyone," Guns replied. "But we also don't need access to your caravan or your goods."

The young man snorted. "That goes without saying."

"Abdul, please," the father murmured. "It is a fair offer. Hear them out."

"We are being hired as outriders," Guns persisted. "Your first line of defense in case of attack."

"Not to mention my trained soldiers there to help your men stand guard wherever you ground," Tucker added.

"The planets we shall visit before and after Yalla are indeed lawless lands," Mahmut agreed.

His son objected, "And what if the pirates are using them as a first line of attack?"

"Pirates?" Rick pushed his plate to one side. "You've heard something about pirates?"

"Ah," Mahmut said. "The young flyer's interest is piqued at last."

"And not just his," Guns said. "We'd give our eyeteeth for another go at pirates."

It was Mahmut's turn to show a keener gaze. "*Another* go?"

"We're not sure what it was," Tucker said, shooting Guns a warning glance. "But we know something's out there, and we've tangled with them before."

"And not just you," Mahmut confessed. "Several of our merchant friends and their caravans have vanished without a trace. And, as I said, rumors abound." He glanced at his son. "Especially now. Especially here."

Sensing the argument going against him, Abdul chose another course. "I have seen these guard pods of yours," he snorted. "What makes them so special? It is certainly not their looks."

"A solid weapons system," Rick replied. "And training."

"Not to mention finely honed reflexes," Guns added.

Abdul's eyes glittered like a big cat hunting prey. "Ah, reflexes. How very interesting. They have a sport here that requires good reflexes. They call it ground-flying. Perhaps your pod flyer would be willing to have these reflexes of his put to the test."

Tucker's brow scrunched together in unexpected worry. "I know this diversion. It's a suicide sport."

"The lad has never been on a low-gravity planet before," Guns added, "much less here."

"Our last journey was my own first visit," Abdul swiftly countered. "It was only then that I learned the sport myself. As to suicide, I have no intention of departing an instant earlier than necessary."

"Several of our guards have become passionate about this little game," Mahmut added, a flicker of humor deep within his gaze. "I assure you, gentlemen, I would not risk my valuable defenders at such an unstable time. The game has risks, yes. But so does life itself."

"And what better way to test these so-called reflexes," Abdul sneered, "than with a game he does not know?"

"I still would advise against this, lad," Tucker warned.

"Ah, of course, if your gallant flyers are afraid to have their courage tested as well," Abdul taunted, "we of course understand."

Rick met the son's flat gaze and replied calmly, "I have no problem with a contest."

"A wager," Mahmut cried. "Your young flyer will accept the challenge. If he succeeds, I agree to your price and terms. If not, you agree to mine."

"If not," Abdul corrected angrily, "we do not use them at all."

Mahmut hesitated, then waved his hand in agreement. "So be it."

"So the game is to beat you, is that it?" Rick watched the son and decided it would be a pleasure.

Abdul barked a laugh, his face taut with eagerness. "The game, fly-boy, is to survive."

CHAPTER EIGHT

"I still don't like it, lad," Tucker repeated for the dozenth time. He was cramped into the narrow seat beside Rick, his broad features furrowed with concern. Their transport was little more than an oversized pod, and jammed to the gills with people. "There are risks here you can't imagine. And the one who travels with you wants to see you lose."

"Too late to turn back," Rick said, glad his nerves did not show in his voice. "Guns and you have both been checking, and there aren't any other caravans headed anywhere near Yalla. We're committed."

"Aye, I suppose so." Tucker sighed past his objections. "All right, then, here's what I know of the contest."

Rick was overtall for the transport, and his knees were jammed hard into the seat in front of them. He glanced down at the helmet in his lap. Like the others around him, he wore a space suit as tight fitting and supple as a downhill skier's. Yet where his was a uniform gray, the others crowding the pod wore suits decorated with wild designs—racing stripes, angry masks, ferocious beasts, serpents weaving up and around their entire bodies. "Who am I up against?"

"This is not a contest against others," Tucker replied. "You fly against yourself."

There was no worry of their being overheard. The noise Rick thought of as chain-saw music raged from the overhead speakers. The shouted conversation among the other passengers was almost as loud. Tucker went on, "I had several mates who became hooked on ground-flying. It was a thrill like no other, they said. And the only way to survive was to be fully committed."

"Survive?" Rick examined the older man's somber features. "They used that word?"

"*Commit*. That is the word you need to concentrate upon." Tucker's expression was as fierce as Rick had ever seen it. "There is no safety in seeking control through slowing or stopping. The way makes any such movement unstable. You must *commit*, and stay committed to the end."

A slender figure, dressed in a suit of silver with purple lance-heads crossed upon the chest, bent over them. It was Abdul; he sneered at the pair and shouted, "Trying to give your mate a final lesson in courage?"

Before Rick could respond, wild cheers and shouts and war whoops rose until the music was drowned out. When they died down, Abdul shouted, "Too late for that! We have arrived!"

Rick let Tucker fit his helmet into place, waited until Tucker had adjusted his own, then joined the crush moving toward the portal. The din in his ears was overwhelming. Once outside, the view was so sudden and so shocking that Rick stood numb, immobile, until Tucker gripped his arm and drew him to one side of the platform away from the others. Instantly the din diminished. "Can you hear me?"

"Yes." But it was hard to concentrate on Tucker's words. "This is *awesome*."

But Tucker was too worried to pay Rick's excitement any mind. "The radios have a range of only a few feet. The authorities insisted on it, as noise from the ground-flyers was interfering with work. The flyers accepted it as part of the game." He sounded disgusted by the idea. "Which means you will be utterly on your own once you start. Do you understand?"

"Yes." Rick did a slow pirouette. The transport had landed upon the highest peak in the lunar range. The crest had been leveled into a broad platform. As far as Rick could see in every direction was sky of jet-black, with millions of stars flowing like great silver rivers. And directly overhead hung Solarus, so close he could actually see the globe's curvature, a vast sphere of cloud-covered blues and greens. Beyond and to his right hung a second moon, a bright silver orb too brilliant to be so still.

"Ah, there you are." Abdul sauntered up, his derision coming loud and clear over the radio. "Sorry, nothing gained by hanging back, there's only one way off." His steps were turned into a mincing dance by the low gravity, his head a silver globe set upon the gleaming silver suit. He stopped a halfpace from Rick and added, "That is, unless you would like to withdraw now, and let us be done with you."

"I'm ready," Rick replied. This sort of banter was nothing new. Taunts like these were part of every line of scrimmage of every football game he had ever played.

"That's what you think." Abdul held out what at first glance appeared to be a broad plank. It was half Rick's height, with curved edges and a slightly uplifted nose. "This is your flyer. And your last chance to withdraw."

"I'll take that," Tucker said. He bent the board over his broad knee and began checking the edges and the foot straps. Finally he straightened and said, "It all appears to be in order."

"Of course it does. I do not need to resort to subterfuge," Abdul announced. "The course will see to that for me. That is, unless you—"

"Let me have a look at that," Rick said, reaching for the board.

"See you on the crown. That is, if you make it down at all," Abdul taunted. "Fly-boy."

"The crown," Tucker said, once Abdul had moved away. "Now I remember. They used to talk about that. The course enters a long straightaway—there are several, but this is longer and straighter than all the others combined. They call that the safety stretch. The flyer has two choices. Most do slow sweeping turns down the straightaway, bleeding off their speed. And remember, until you reach that last stretch you will need all your speed to survive. So make sure it's the last stretch before you start slowing down."

Tucker breathed heavily, worried beyond words by what was about to take place. He collected himself and went on, "At the end of that final stretch there is a broad overhang. Use the last of your speed to swing up the side and over the top. The transport will collect you there."

Rick kept his eyes upon the board in his hand and had difficulty not to laugh out loud. "And the other choice?"

"Danger and disaster," Tucker replied. "The craziest of the ground-flyers used the straightaway to build up speed, because beyond the crown is a chasm. So deep, it is said, that those who did not have enough speed to reach the other side have time to die a thousand times from fright before ever reaching the bottom."

Tucker's reflective helmet turned around to watch a pair of the pod's passengers begin wild maneuvers to take them toward the platform's edge. They used the low gravity to jump high, doing backward flips and twists, the boards attached to their feet flickering like helicopter blades. Most of the boards were painted with designs to match their suits. The flyers weaved and danced, amping themselves up, preparing for the descent.

"If a flyer makes it over the chasm," Tucker went on, "the course continues all the way down to the main lock. It's a mark of prestige throughout the tunnels when someone makes it over the chasm for the first time. The trouble is, once they taste the thrill, they keep at it until they're eaten by the gorge. Lost a couple of good mates that way, I did." He observed the other flyers continue their wild antics and warned, "Do not allow them to tempt you into foolish games. Your task is to arrive, and to do so in one piece."

"Listen, it's okay, really." Rick patted the big man's arm. "Once football season was over, I used to go snowboarding every weekend."

Tucker turned back toward him. "I don't understand a word you have just said. Nor do I understand how you can be the one standing there, offering comfort to me."

"Let's go," Rick said. "I'm ready."

Tucker walked with him to the platform's edge and watched as Rick bent over and fitted his feet into the braces and tightened the straps. "How do you know how to prepare your ground-flyer?"

"I told you, I've done something like this before." Rick did not face forward, but rather stood with his front to the board's side. He straightened up, glad no one could see his grin. "A *lot* like this."

Another flyer hopped over and demanded, "You a first timer?"

"He doesn't need anybody's help," Abdul lashed out, moving up beside them. "He's a brave pod-fighter."

"Stay as close to the pack as you can," the flyer told him, ignoring Abdul's jibe. "There are guide markers at each side of the course, but you'll see your way clearer if you can keep up and watch what we do."

"Leave him alone, I say," Abdul snarled.

The flyer turned toward Abdul. His suit had a fanged beast painted across both back and front, with long claws reaching down over his hands and feet. "I remember another first timer," he said, his voice tinny over the suit radio. "He was so scared we had to put his board on for him. Then he had to crawl to the edge, and we all heard him scream—"

"Lies!" Abdul reached the edge with a fierce hop, grabbed hold of the rails, and launched himself high up and out. "May you . . . " The radio died to a faint hiss.

"Just keep as close to the pack as you can," the flyer told Rick. "Ready?"

"Yes," Rick said, holding back, not wanting to look over the edge until he was committed. "And thanks."

"Hey, anybody who can stay on his feet the first time he comes close to the edge is okay by me." The flyer hopped back over and joined his mates, waved once in Rick's direction, and dropped over the edge.

"I have to go." Without waiting for hesitation to slow him down, Rick took a hopping leap to the railing. The jump took him just high enough to let him have his first glimpse straight down. He gripped the rails, knowing to wait even an instant would be to freeze him solid with fear. "Thanks for coming up and seeing me off."

"Lad, you're one of the bravest—"

"Save it for the end," Rick said, and pushed himself up and over the edge.

The drop was sheer, a straight descent without any contact at all, as the cliff ducked back upon itself. Rick saw the three nearest flyers hunched over their boards, bodies twisted so as to face forward and down, one hand gripping the board's edge. Rick crouched and did the same, refusing to think of what he was actually seeing. *So far down.*

Finally the cliff moved out to greet him. With contact came sound, passing up through the board and his boots. He heard a quiet sighing as the board cruised over the super-fine silvery lunar silt. Rick passed an outcrop then and realized that the low gravity altered things mightily from what he had known before. His descent was far slower than the speeds he would have already achieved while snowboarding. He was just gradually building up speed now, even after the first long drop. And the slide did not have the same feel as a descent in higher gravity. What would have been impossible on earth was now a thrill.

The flyers before him began a series of sweeping turns, weaving back and forth in complicated patterns of joining and separating, their hands reaching out to trace finger patterns in the thick lunar dust. Rick followed suit, fashioning impossibly steep angles, almost standing upright and yet still continuing downward, his shoulder barely inches from the surface. The silt was finer than the lightest snow, streaming through his fingers like water.

It was then that he gave his first shout of joy.

The descent continued, faster and faster, the path broadening into a great sweeping bowl. At the bowl's lip was a slight rise, and the flyers ahead of him formed a single file, taking the lip in a series of great bounding leaps. Rick saw one break off to the side, slipping over the edge and simply moving into a descent, and he saw from the suit's design of purple blades that it was Abdul who had chosen not to jump.

He did not hesitate an instant. The lip swung up and he was over, leaping up higher and higher. The swooshing noise ended, no air or wind to slow him now, the only sound that of his breath. Rick looked up and saw that the transport pod hovered overhead. He waved both hands and shouted with a strength to cross the void, "This is *great!*"

He landed, pushing up a cloud of dust that shimmered like a billion tiny mirrors. Then he was beyond, swooping into the bowl and up the far side, his speed bleeding off as he crested the rise, and again there was another drop into nothing, as though the mountain had simply disappeared.

He did not hesitate, but simply launched himself forward, knowing now to grip his board's edge and raise his free hand, using it as a marksman would his gunsight, keeping himself straight and in line with the flyers up ahead.

Again the cliff came up to greet him, and he was down and running. But this time he was headed straight toward a field of huge stone fangs. The tall cliffs to either side of the run compressed like a funnel, aiming him straight for the stone spears. The razor-edged rocks crowded up to both sides of the narrowing cleft, leaving him no room whatsoever to maneuver. They looked far too tightly clustered to weave through.

Rick swallowed his sudden bile and followed the others' example, crouching low, making no turns to slow himself down, committing to a full run straight toward the rocks and their jagged knife-edges. Faster and faster until the narrowing walls became a silver-gray blur. Just as he was beginning to wonder how he would survive the impact, he saw the first of the flyers begin drifting up the cliff side, higher and higher, hanging at an impossible angle, glued to the side by speed alone.

Rick did not think, did not hesitate, did not even consider what he was about to do, just slid his weight to one side and let his board leave the silt-clad floor and begin climbing up the wall. The soft sighing was instantly replaced by a loud clattering, driving up through the soles of his boots and filling his helmet, a rattling, driving noise that seemed to push him up and up, higher on the cliff, until he was above the flint blades, then past them, then sliding back down, then swooshing back onto the floor, and screaming like a madman with the thrill.

On and on it went, his confidence growing until he was ready to move up and join the others on the straightaways, molding into their weaving patterns, mingling his shouts and half-heard cries with them. The noise rose and fell as they passed one another in their weaving dance. He obeyed their hand signals and backed off when the straightaways narrowed, watching and following their example through each of the challenging stretches.

Then they came to a straightaway that did not end, but rather broadened and continued, on and on and on. Rick knew it was the safety stretch, and part of him was beyond happy that it was almost over, while another part wished he could continue on for hours more.

Then he spotted Abdul's suit up ahead, not turning back into another sweeping curve, but rather allowing his slowing speed to lift himself up and off the stretch and onto a broad tongue of stone that flowed up and out and over the straightaway.

And Rick knew instantly what he was going to do.

The vast majority of flyers followed Abdul's example, but the flyer who had spoken with Rick swept over and shouted, "Last chance, first-timer!"

Rick did not even bother to reply.

"All *right!*" The flyer straightened from his curve, came up alongside Rick, and said, "What's your name?"

"Rick!"

"Okay, Rick, lower yourself to bring your center of gravity down . . . that's it, now start pumping. Harder. Yeah, speed's the only way, push and push, keep straight, don't let any of the speed go, hold on and push *harder*."

The voice took on a steely edge. Rick held the flyer in focus as everything else blurred into a silver-gray whirl. "That's it up ahead, ready yourself, see the ledge? Behind me, ready? Now *jump with all your might!*"

Rick did as he was told, moving in close behind the other flyer, crouching lower still, hitting the long steep ramp with such suddenness that he almost missed the chance, catching the last moment and pushing as hard as he could.

His speed was so great that on the steep rise it was harder than he expected to jump, but his adrenaline was enough to add steel to his legs, and he leapt up and out and over.

Farther and farther and farther, the jump endless, nothing below him but shadow. A darkness untouched by the stars and planet overhead, empty looming nothingness, so black it seemed to draw at him, seeking to slow him down and drag him in, never letting him go.

Just as the panic rose like bitter heat in his throat, the chasm's distant edge floated into view. The other flyer ahead screamed with the ecstasy of release. Rick held back another moment, scarcely believing he would make it to safety. Then he was so close he could see the crumbling edge, and he was still aloft, flying over and beyond and into safety, screaming himself now, landing and halting and pummeling the other flyer's back, so excited and exultant now he felt that for sure he was about ready to jump out of his own skin.

"They're not going to believe this!" the flyer crowed. "A first-timer who leaps the chasm! Don't know if it's ever been done, not even tried before. Wait till we get in, you'll have a name throughout the tunnel world."

Rick shook his head to clear the sweat pouring over his eyes. Now that it was over, his heart was pounding, his breath coming in such great gasps that he could scarcely get out the words. "I don't think I can stand."

"The weakness passes," the slender flyer assured him. "Always happens the first flight over the gorge, after you look down and know the mouth is waiting there, ready to swallow you whole."

Rick felt the words hit him square in the gut, and would have toppled had the flyer not reached out a hand to steady him. "Take a couple of deep breaths, that's it. Look around, see the stars. Ain't it great to be alive?"

Gradually his breath came under control, and strength trickled back to his shaking legs. "Great."

"Okay, steady now, time to head on back. Stand tall, now, 'cause there's a whole world who's gonna be watching you fly home."

CHAPTER NINE

Wander returned to his quarters, stripped off his robe, and collapsed onto his bed. His exhausted mind refused to slow down. Twelve hours he and Digs had remained on watch, longer than either had ever before been hooked to the amp, until even Digs had become so weak he could scarcely pull himself from the chair.

And found nothing. Six times during this past watch alone, messengers from the senior monitor had raced in, ordered them to search another sector, looking for something that was never specified.

The fifth time, Digs had lost control and screamed at the man that the nonsense was pushing them all over the edge. Either tell them what they should be hunting for, he had shouted, or let them stop.

The sixth set of orders was delivered by the watch's senior monitor, a wise old graybeard who had the power to calm the stormiest waters. He had spoken with a mildness that stilled even Digs, saying that he could not specify what to search out, because he himself had not been informed. Well, maybe the dark courier needed to be told off, Digs had said, speaking from exhaustion.

The senior monitor had hesitated at that, his silence a warning. Then he had replied simply, "Do your best."

Wander tossed in his bed, his body taut with unrelieved tension. His mind buzzed with the static of thoughts that would not come together. His heart ached with worry and with the emptiness of no outside contact. He yearned for Consuela. There had been no chance to send a message. Nor could he check to see if Consuela had left him another communication, another gift of hope. Every time he had been tempted to ask if he could reach out and check, Digs had met him with a look of desperate appeal, a fear so great that Wander knew it was wrong even to make the request.

Hope. There was so little of it. He felt as though the tension and the yearnings and the overlong watches were all mashing him down, straining out every last vestige of hope. It would be so easy to give in, to believe that the Avenger had been captured by this Hegemony-wide search, that the quest had been abandoned, that he was trapped upon Citadel for the rest of his days.

The fear of never being released, of never seeing Consuela again, threatened to snap him. He did his best to push the fog of painful loss away. But all he could manage was to keep it at arm's length, a shadow that never left him free to manage a full rest. Though his body ached with fatigue and his mind seemed stretched to the breaking point, still his worries hovered. Each time he began to descend into deep sleep, they returned to whisper and freeze his heart with nightmarish doubt. He would jerk awake, not knowing exactly why his eyes had opened, but filled with the dread of hopeless longing.

Wander extinguished the lights and closed his eyes to the darkness that sought to wrap around his heart. He slid his head under the pillow and pushed with all his might against the fears. He had to rest. He had to hope. There was nothing else.

CHAPTER TEN

Consuela fitted on the headset, flicked on the amp's main switch, and watched as the chrono ticked down the seconds. Across from her, Guns and Tucker sat in alert tension, their eyes watching the chrono with her. Guns droned, "Five, four, three, two, one, now."

Instantly she powered up and sent out, *Scout here.*

Must move swiftly. There was more tension to Dunlevy's response than she could ever recall hearing before. *Have a Hegemony pilot and senior diplomat in control room. Where is Guns?*

Here. Wait. Her wrist swung down the power dial, and she said, "We have contact, but something's wrong. There's a pilot and senior diplomat there with them."

"Another dark courier." Guns rubbed his chin. "Never heard of two of them lurking about a system like this. Not without a reason."

"A major one," Tucker agreed. "Consuela, ask him if they're all right."

A relative term, Dunlevy replied, the words taut. *The captain wishes to know your status.*

"He didn't say, not really." Consuela felt Dunlevy's tension pushing at her own words. "Captain Arnol wants to know what is happening with us."

Guns and Tucker exchanged glances. At a nod from Guns, Tucker responded, "Tell him we've found passage with a caravan headed for Yalla. We're to act as outriders and guards for the cargo."

"It'll be a roundabout journey," Guns added. "They have no pilot, so we'll swing from one system to the next, following the lightways. Two planetary stops between here and there, so we should arrive within seven to ten days."

"That is," Tucker added, "unless Captain Arnol thinks this storm is going to blow over, leaving us with the chance to get back on Avenger where we belong."

Impossible, Dunlevy answered, even before Consuela had finished relating the final words. *Even as we speak, we are taking on a battalion of dragoons.*

Tucker jumped out of his seat at the news. "The Avenger's being way-laid? Why, I've a mind—"

Consuela held up one tense hand to stop him as Dunlevy continued, *I am authorized by Captain Arnol to order you to Yalla. The caravan sounds as good a cover as you are likely to find. Take it, and proceed on from there.*

But how? Consuela's heart and mind could scarcely conceal her wailing fright. *The avenger won't be following the course we gave Wander. He won't know where to reach us, and I don't—*

No time. We're scheduled to depart in less than an hour. Tell the others we are ordered to transport the battalion back to Imperial Command. A ruse only, as they could easily have fitted on the two battleships here at Solarus spaceport. Even though they found no weapons on our ship, we are still under suspicion. Expect no further communication from us, the danger is simply too great. Dunlevy's anxiety rose another notch. *The pilot is headed this way. Get to Yalla, then hover outside the planet's orbit as we said we would. We'll hope Wander will continue to look beyond the time limits we set. Do you still recall the system approach that he gave us?*

Yes, but—

Then go, and may your course be true, your vision clear. Dunlevy off.

Consuela's numb fingers fumbled with the headset, her hair spilling forward as she pulled it off. She looked from one alarmed face to the other. "He's gone."

———

Consuela sat and listened to their planning as long as she could, hoping they would say something to reassure her, offer some guarantee that they would be able to renew contact with Wander. But though they sensed her distress, they refused to belittle her concerns or her station by offering empty words.

When sleep finally demanded her attention, she excused herself.

Guns rose with her and asked, "Would you like to go to our place in the dome?"

"Too tired," she said simply, feeling the worry weigh down her spirit, that and the strain of filtering Dunlevy's words from the continuous mental noise. "Maybe tomorrow."

Consuela moved back to the tiny alcove alongside the storage area. There a rudimentary 'fresher abutted a row of floor-to-ceiling bunks. She closed the door on their muted discussion, flung herself down, and was instantly away.

Not just asleep. *Away*. No sooner had she closed her eyes than she felt herself coming awake in that strange, eerie clarity. There, but not there. Asleep, yet awake.

Once more she faced the red-brick church, the plaza it fronted as empty as before. Yet this time the doors were open. And this time she recognized the building. It was the First Congregation, the church where Daniel Mitchum served as youth pastor. She had been there several times as a child seeking comfort, back in the dark days of her greatest helplessness. They doors stood open before her now, a silent invitation. Swiftly Consuela climbed the stairs and entered.

The preacher was already into his sermon. Consuela hesitated at the back of the hall, until the sight of a familiar face spurred her forward. She slipped into the empty seat beside Daniel and turned to smile at him, eager for his surprised welcome. But it did not come. Daniel remained as he was, his face turned intently toward the pulpit. Consuela sighed her way back around, disappointed that she was unable to make him realize she was there.

"Be ready," the pastor was saying. "For we know not the day nor the hour. How many times have we heard these words? So often, I would imagine, that we have all but lost the ability to look beyond the clearest message, that of hoping for our Savior's return, and see what else might be there . . . what other message might be intended."

There it was again. *Be ready*. Consuela felt a rising sense of resentment. She was hurting, she was worried, she needed assurance that all would work out as she hoped. But instead, what was she hearing? A challenge. A call to do more. Her first reaction was to turn away, simply stand up and walk out. She did not need this. Not now. Yet something held her there, a quiet whisper beyond the borders of sound, spoken to her heart. A plea to remain, to listen, to learn, to *grow*.

"More than likely, every one of us has arrived at some point or an-

296 / T. DAVIS BUNN

other where we have turned to God and asked, Why is this happening? Where are we going? What is the purpose here?" He paused to gaze around the chamber. "Remember, now, the Lord has not promised to always lift us from trouble. Instead, He said that He would *be there with us*.

"So long as we are upon this earth, we shall know trials. But by bearing up under this burden, by showing the world that we meet these stresses and strains as Christians, we are granted the chance to become beacons. To show others, who continue to suffer in the darkness, that we have a gift of hope to share.

"Now think about what this means. God does not say, first I will make your lives perfect, and then ask you to go out and save the world. Not at all. He says, abide in me, and I in you, and be my servant. Where you are. Right now.

"Then you will be able to listen for the words that our Savior yearns to hear, using your ears and your heart and your mind and voice as His own. People may cry from their lonely darkness, I am confused. I am lost. Where am I going? Why I am being forced to turn down this strange road with all its pains and perils? And you, my brothers and sisters, can give to them the gifts of grace. The peace that surpasses understanding. A light that pierces the darkest night. A love that heals the greatest sorrow. As you yourselves have come to know."

He stopped then and seemed to look straight at Consuela, as though he and only he was able to see her. As though his words were intended for her. For *her*.

"Therefore, my brothers and sisters, *be ready*. It may be this very moment that the Lord is trying to gain your attention, to ask you to do as you have been commanded and allow His infinite strength to bear your burdens, and *be ready*. Be ready to listen. Be ready to speak. Be ready to *serve*."

CHAPTER ELEVEN

By the time the caravan arrived at the last stop before Yalla, Rick was beyond bored.

The merchant's son, Abdul, was chief of caravan security. He had responded to their presence by emptying the very back hold and ordering them all inside. He had then welded shut the only door leading to the remainder of the caravan, then sealed them even tighter with restrictions. No radio communication of any sort. No sorties outside the hold, unless the alarm was raised. No trial sorties whatsoever. Guns and Tucker had argued directly with Mahmut that the restrictions left them hamstrung and unable to do their duty. But Mahmut chose not to overrule his son, and they were left isolated and confined.

Upon his arrival, Rick had flown the caravan's length. It looked like a colossal floating junkyard. Vessels of every size and description were bolted together with thick steel girders. Thruster units jutted from long steel arms at odd intervals. It had seemed to Rick that the merchant had bought whatever had come cheap, then attached it wherever there was room. The result was a massive metal space-bound bug, as ugly as it was huge.

Most of the troopers were seasoned enough to know the universal pattern of soldiering—hours of boredom followed by seconds of sheer terror. They gambled and gossiped and lounged, storing food and sleep in limitless amounts. Rick had little money to begin with, and soon had none. He spent as much time as he could making dry runs on the Blade's

298 / T. DAVIS BUNN

weapons system. By the time they made their second halt at yet another minor system, the weapons fitted to him like a glove.

When not working in the Blade, Rick retreated to a private corner for quiet reflection. It was a hard activity, and one which seemed to do little more than bore holes in his confidence. But still it held him, as though there were actually some purpose behind his forced detachment. Their chamber was extensive, with numerous nooks and crannies that were quickly claimed by other troopers seeking a bit of solitude. He had chosen for himself a perch halfway up the side wall, an aerie from which he could view their metal-bound world.

"Rick?"

The unexpected voice made him jump. Consuela continued up the wall-rungs until her head came into view. "May I join you?"

"Sure." He pushed his bedding to one side, then slid over to make room for her.

"Thanks." She sank down beside him, looked out and over the edge, and said, "This is nice."

"It's okay, I guess."

She pointed down to where Tucker was loading his troopers into the transport. "Are you going with them?"

"I can't," he replied glumly. "They only let one pod out at each landing. My number didn't come up."

She nodded her understanding. When the caravan entered a parking orbit, Tucker and his men landed with the caravan's own transport and guarded during the off-loading. This much Mahmut had insisted upon, overriding his son's strident objections that their own men were sufficient. "From what I've heard," Consuela said, "you're not missing much. Tucker said the last landing was on a place so dinky he'd never even heard of it."

"What about you?" Rick asked. "Doesn't it bother you, not being let out of this cage for a week?"

She shook her head and confessed, "I've been too worried about Wander."

"You still can't raise him?"

"I can't *try*." Frustration creased her forehead. "I'm not a trained pilot. Even if I knew where he was, I couldn't find it alone. I have no way to track my way down some invisible pathway."

"What about Dunlevy?"

"There hasn't been any word from them since we left Solarus. They know our course."

"Maybe Dunlevy tried and missed you."

"I doubt it. I haven't done much besides sit at the console." She hesitated, then added, "That and pray."

The softly spoken word shook Rick to the core. It felt as though all the time and all the solitude had been pushing and prodding, preparing him for that moment, so that when it came, he would be open. Able to reach beyond his pride and confess, "I've been doing a lot of thinking. About home, and myself. Where I'm going, what I'm supposed to do."

Her gaze held the calm of one ready to listen for hours. "Do you want to go back?"

"I don't *know*." All the frustration and confusion of the past eight days boiled over. "It's crazy. I've got everything I could possibly ask for here. I love this life and the adventure, but something, I don't . . . " Rick let his voice trail off.

She waited until she was sure he couldn't finish for himself, then said softly, "Something is missing."

It welled up within him like a vast emotional bubble rising to the surface of his thoughts. As though just waiting for a time like this, for him to acknowledge, "All the success and excitement I've been having, it's as though I've been painting over something. A hollowness inside. And now, when I'm forced to sit here on my hands, I can't help but see that it's still there." He shrugged helplessly. "So I've been wondering if maybe I need to go back. Like maybe I'm not supposed to be here."

"Maybe what you're supposed to do is ask for guidance," Consuela said quietly.

There was something in her voice, a depth of understanding that made him feel ashamed to think of how he had tried to pressure her into a relationship. As though here in this rusty hold, her tender intensity was inviting him to a level of trust and friendship he had never known before. "Ask God, you mean?"

She nodded. "Maybe it's not the place or the activity that is the problem. But what you're doing it *for*."

Rick felt a harmony with her words, so strong it resounded through his being like the pealing of a great bell. The force shattered his shield of pride, leaving him free to admit, "That makes sense."

"Hard as it is to bow our heads," Consuela went on, as though understanding his deepest thoughts, "maybe that's what is called for here.

To accept that without the Lord, we are nothing, just empty vessels going through the motions of life. We need to confess our weaknesses, our sins, our emptiness. And turn our lives over to Him."

Our *weaknesses*. Again there was the sense of resounding force, so strong Rick was able to see and understand and say, "I feel like all my life I've had to be the strong one. Make the family look good. Do everything just right. Be on top."

"And all the while," Consuela offered softly, "hold inside everything that did not fit with the image. Every doubt, every failing, every weakness."

He nodded, his chest suddenly burning with the freedom of confession. "I didn't even let *myself* see those things."

"But they were still there." Her own gaze turned inward, able to understand because she had confronted the same truth within herself. "Making every success empty, turning every triumph into a lie."

They shared a long silence, one filled with a power as comforting as it was real. Finally Consuela said, "Would you like to pray with me?"

CHAPTER TWELVE

As Consuela and Rick descended to the hold's floor, Guns came bounding toward them. "There you are. Good. Need to speak with you both."

He started to usher them over to one side, but halted to watch the transport return and ground. When the portal unsealed, Tucker was the first to hop from the transport. His hands gripped two carry-sacks of purchased provisions, and his expression was dour. "A more miserable rock I have never set my feet on, and hope never to again." He raised one sack and shook it toward Guns. "Do you know what they wanted to charge me for simple bread?"

"It doesn't matter," Guns said impatiently. "We—"

"It may not matter to you, matey," Tucker said, still venting steam. "But I'll be switched if a flour-dusted thief is going to make off with my hard-earned gold. Not without a fight, he won't."

Guns planted hands on wiry hips. "Are you done?"

"Aye, I suppose so." Tucker tossed his sacks to a waiting trooper. "What's got you in a lather?"

"While you were off gallivanting, we had ourselves a visitor."

"One thing for certain, matey, there was little gallivanting going on by us or anyone else on that gloomy world."

"Listen up, will you? While Abdul went down with your lot, the father came a-calling."

"Old Mahmut showed up, did he?" Tucker was vastly unimpressed.

"I hope you told him we were going stir crazy in this tiny tin room."

"I did," Guns crowed, "and he said our waiting was over."

Rick and Tucker exclaimed together, "What?"

"Aye, I thought that would get a rise out of you." Guns grinned wolf-ishly. "It turns out, Mahmut let his son have his way only because our route up to now was pretty safe. The lightways we've been following have been almost totally empty routes, touching down on secondary planets."

"Secondary is far too kind, if you ask me," Tucker interjected.

"But it makes sense," Rick exclaimed, the thought of possible free-dom agitating his words. "That would also explain why Consuela's not spotted a shadowlane, much less any pirate activity."

"Aye, the lad has a point," Tucker agreed grudgingly, as though re-luctant to let go of his irritation. One of Consuela's constant responsi-bilities had been to search the way ahead, extending the tiny training amp to its limit, checking to see if there was any trace of a shadowlane.

"But here our course joins the most heavily traveled route in Vector Nine," Guns went on, his eyes sparking with excitement. "And there have been four ships gone missing in the last twenty days that he knows of."

"You don't say," Tucker murmured.

"Apparently caravans heading in to purchase these firestones on Yalla are full to the brim with trading goods. Not to mention the fact that a half-dozen routes all converge at this point," Guns continued. "Only reason this system is inhabited."

"Which means there are planet-bound eyes and ears just looking for news of rich pickings to pass on to the pirates," Tucker said.

Guns crossed his arms, his grin fierce. "Now tell me what those very same spies heard your boys grumbling about while they were down on that forsaken planet."

"Nothing much," Tucker said, returning the grin. "Just how they'd been hired and then crammed in a hold, left to sit on their hands."

"Just what I thought. Mahmut may not have realized it, but by keep-ing us in the dark, and giving our boys a reason to complain, he just might have let us set ourselves up for some action." Guns turned his gaze toward Rick. "Assemble the outriders. I think this news is too good to keep to ourselves."

"Right," Rick said, and bolted.

Tucker asked, "Does this mean you can get out there and train?"

"As much as we like," Guns replied. "Not to mention station outriders as we see fit."

"I imagine our little friend Abdul will fair explode," Tucker predicted, "when he hears his father is lifting the restrictions."

"Aye, it pains me that I won't be able to listen in on that discussion," Guns agreed, and turned to Consuela. "The practice runs are over, lass. We need you to be reaching out as far and wide as you can."

"I understand," Consuela affirmed. "Search out the shadowlanes and see if there are any pirates lying in wait."

"Same as you've been doing so far," Guns confirmed. "Only now, if what Mahmut says is true, this run is for real."

CHAPTER THIRTEEN

Rick bent over her sleeping form, reached out an arm, and hesitated. She looked so fragile, so tired, and yet so beautiful. Her hair was scattered over the pillow, as dark as her long eyelashes, making her skin look porcelain pure. It was strange, how he could look down at her now, and feel his heart twist at the fragile strength, and be content to be her friend. As though all the storm of conflicting emotions was suddenly gone, leaving him free to look and examine himself first, and others afterward, with an honesty he had never known before.

She stirred, rolling over, and he touched her shoulder. "Consuela, it's time."

"It can't be," she murmured, not opening her eyes. "I just lay down."

"Four hours ago," he said.

"Your chrono is off." She rolled back over. "Bye."

"Guns says to tell you that by his best estimate, we've already passed beyond the farthest point of your last search." When she did not move, he had to smile. "He also said he was brewing up one of his special cups, just for you."

"That's not fair." She drew the covers up over her head.

He felt for her, knew from the circles under her eyes that she needed a longer, deeper rest. But there was no alternate for her watch. Mahmut had informed Guns that he was doubling his normal rate of acceleration, burning fuel at a prodigious level in order to pass through this hazardous region as swiftly as possible. Rick urged, "We need you."

Consuela sighed her way back out from under the covers, opened her eyes, and managed a tired smile. "I was having the nicest dream."

The look in her eye told him all. "About Wander?"

She nodded, suddenly shy. "He didn't say anything. He just looked at me. And smiled. For a moment it was as though he was here with me." She looked at him. "Does it bother you, that I talk about him like this?"

He searched his heart and answered honestly, "Not anymore."

She brought the world and his face into clearer focus. "Have you been thinking about what we discussed?"

"And praying," Rick replied. "It feels nice. More than that. It feels *right*."

"I'm glad, Rick. Really, really glad." She rubbed her face and said, "Pray for me too, will you? Most of the time I feel so weak, and Wander seems so far away."

"It's going to turn out fine," he said, and for once truly believed his own words.

A few moments later she emerged from the 'fresher, accepted the cup from Guns with a smile, and entered the transport. As always whenever she was standing duty, a pair of troopers came to lounge around the portal. The chance of anyone entering from the caravan and spying her operating the portable console were slim. But it was a chance they could not afford to take.

It seemed as though she had scarcely had time to power up before her shrill cry brought all activity within the hold to an absolute halt. Rick raced over, a half step behind Tucker and Guns, in time to see her emerge from the portal. Her hair was disheveled from her having ripped off the headset, her eyes were frantic. "They're *here!*"

"How far," Guns rapped out.

"*Here,*" she repeated, her voice almost a scream. "Right ahead, not seconds—"

"*Blades!*" Guns was already running for his pod. "Red alert! Power up!"

"Troopers! By me!" Tucker's voice roared across the hold. "Grab your suits and to the transport! Flight Lieutenant, power up!"

Rick raced across the hold to his pod and tore his sleeve from shoulder to elbow in his scramble through the plasteel hole. He shouted the order to close the Blade's entry platform and started running through the power sequence even before he was fully settled in the seat. Even so, when he looked up and through the front screen, Guns was already up and headed for the portal.

"Knight Two here," Rick said, glad that his voice was crisp despite the thunder of his heart, gladder still to hear two more Blades counting out behind him.

"You heard the lass," Guns said, leading them though the first translucent energy-plate and then the second and into space, powering forward as soon as they were clear. Rick was tight on his tail. "They're right around here some—"

"Bandits at three o'clock high!" Rick cried, his voice rising a full octave at the sight of the dull black surface glinting in the starlight.

"Shields to full power!" Guns sped forward, clearing the front edge of the caravan. "Attack on my—"

Then the endless night of space was shattered by flickering stun bolts. Purple lances hit the merchant ship at a half-dozen points, the secondary force burning out in evil-colored lightning. One of the Blade flyers shrieked in Rick's ears, caught by an aftershock. Rick craned and saw the stone-covered pod go careening off.

"Conform to me," Guns snapped. "I've marked his trajectory. All right, it's up to us and us alone. I'm going for their power, Blade Three—"

A second voice shrilled, "Transports peeling off, three, no four, I count four headed this way. Attack pods to either side!"

"They're mine!" Rick headed straight for the unsuspecting invaders.

"Blade Six here, I'm with you."

"Right." Guns' voice held the sharp clarity of a seasoned warrior. "The rest with me, fire together, go for their weapons, count down from five, four, three, two, one, *now*."

Three of the enemy pods spotted their fire and peeled off toward them. Rick roared with the adrenaline surge of coming battle and powered up his energy lance.

"Four here, the enemy's primary vessel was only partially hit. Their defenses seem to be holding."

Rick's attention remained fixed upon the nearest attack pod. The instant his energy lance was activated, his Blade's stony cover exploded outward, shattering in a million bits, leaving the Blade exposed for all to see. The pod tried to veer, but from the sluggish response Rick knew it was radio controlled. Where the flyer should have sat was filled with a larger energy pack and more weaponry. But the pod had chance to use neither, for Rick flew in at full power, raging straight through the attacker and heading for the second.

"Aye, they were alerted, no question, prepare to receive incoming fire." Guns' voice was a fiery roar. "Evasion tactics and fire at will!"

A second cannon bolt seared the space nearby, temporarily blinding Rick, the immensity of the power telling him he was drawing fire from the mother ship. Through the dancing sparks in his vision he spotted smaller flickerings of energy bolts; though he could no longer see the pod, he headed straight for the source of the smaller fire and knew he had struck home when a grinding, rending crash filled his small cabin.

"Get that cannon," Guns roared. "They may go for the caravan!"

"Can't," came a breathless reply. "Winged me, lost tracking."

"Their defenses are strongest around the weapon," came another voice. "I've hit it twice straight on."

"Do it again!"

"More pods! Out the aft portal, six, no seven!"

"Forget the pods. *Hit that cannon.*"

"I'm going in!" Before he could reflect upon what he was going to try, Rick switched all power to his lance and forward shields. His rear totally exposed to fire from the attack pods, Rick swerved away from the dogfight and aimed straight for the mother ship and its deadly ring of weaponry.

The blaster cannons formed a circle of malignant snouts halfway down the ship's length. One swiveled about and began tracking him. Instantly he swerved, but not far, because it was only straight ahead that he was protected. The cannon fired, but his visor was down, and instead of being temporarily blinded, he saw how the near miss outlined his forward shield, now extended almost as far as the energy lance itself, layer after layer of cover, a series of golden lances formed one within the next. Rick took heart from the sight, hunched his shoulders, and powered straight for the ship.

There was a great shrill shrieking as the two shields met, a squeal so high he felt it more than heard it. His skull hummed like a tuning fork, his vision blurred, and for a moment of sheer panic he thought he had failed, that the Blade would shatter from the rending force. Then he was through, and the first cannon was chopped apart by his lance, then the second, the space now filled with spinning fragments of molten metal, the air in his cabin swollen with the crashing clamor.

He continued around the ship in his destructive circle, the cannons ahead firing in futile fury, the energy bolts shooting out in every direction, unable to strike him. One by one the snouts fell like great metal trees until the circle was complete and the space about the mother ship was littered with ruddy red bits of steel. And the cannons were silent.

The mopping-up procedures were swift and sure. Under Guns' command, all their fire was directed aft to the thrusters, which soon glowed fiery red, and melted into a sullen heap. At that point the remaining attack pods traversed to the pirate transports and attached themselves in silent surrender. The two wounded Blades were returned to the hold, lines were attached to both the mother ship and the invading transports, then Guns rapped out, "Going to open channel." There was a short pause, then, "Senior outrider calling the Merchant Ahmet and his Caravan Desert Queen."

There was a long moment of silence, then through the hiss came a feeble voice. "Desert Queen here. Our flight deck took a direct hit, we surrender. Repeat, we surrender. Don't shoot."

"No need, laddie, the pirates beat you to it," Guns replied, a glint of dry humor coming through. "The bandits have been routed. We are sounding the all clear. Repeat, all clear."

There was a longer silence, then a very weak Mahmut himself came on and demanded hoarsely, "Can this be?"

"Just tell us where you want us to deposit the raiders," Guns replied, "and you can see for yourself."

CHAPTER FOURTEEN

"Firestones are more than a simple jewel," Mahmut explained. "For some, it is almost a religion."

Tucker shifted his weight on the cushion, and instantly Guns was alongside. "You all right, matey?"

"Just slide that pad up a notch, will you?" Tucker grimaced as Guns eased him more upright. The big man had been stepping into the transport when the stun bolt had struck, and he had fallen hard, straining his back. "That's better, Guns. Thanks."

"I shall have my personal physician attend to you again tomorrow," Mahmut promised. "He reports that the massage has helped ease your discomfort."

"Aye, perhaps," Tucker reluctantly allowed. "But I can't say as I enjoyed the experience."

"You made enough noise," Rick observed.

"Seems a bit strange," Guns agreed, "a big fellow like you, being bested by an old fellow who couldn't weigh as much as a wet breeze."

"I'd like to see how well you manage," Tucker blustered. "That man has fingers of solid titanium."

"Easy, mate, I didn't mean anything by it," Guns said with a grin. "Anyway, it's good to see you up and about again."

"That it is," Mahmut agreed. He raised his cup and said for the dozenth time that night, "A toast to the gallant warriors and their magnificent victory."

Since their return from the battle, all had changed within the cara-van. The portal had been unsealed, and they had been granted free reign of the ship. Mahmut had loaded them down with gifts and declared that all money from the sale of the pirate vessel was theirs and theirs alone.

They were seated in Mahmut's private quarters, a sumptuous cham-ber lined with brilliantly colored tapestries and luxurious carpets of in-tricate design. They rested upon ample silk cushions, and before each person stood an individual hand-carved table, laden with goblets of fil-igreed silver and the remnants of a grand feast.

Guns stretched out his legs and asked, "How's your son getting on?"

"He rests easy, and the doctor promises that there will be no per-manent damage," Mahmut replied. A flicker of concern passed over his features. "If it had not been for your swift actions—"

"A stun bolt can knock the best of men for a loop," Guns said, doing away with the need for more thanks. "You were saying something about those firestones of Yalla."

"Of Yalla, indeed." It was Mahmut's turn to lean back, settle himself, and stroke his slender beard. Dark eyes moved from one guest to the next. "Do I perhaps detect more of an interest in Yalla than just that of mercenaries seeking their next posting?"

"We are honest men," Guns protested. "There'll be no thieving—"

Tucker cut him off with, "That's not what the merchant is on about, matey."

"Indeed." The eyes continued to probe each of his four guests in turn—Tucker, Guns, Rick, and finally Consuela. They lingered long upon her, until he said, "You will forgive me for saying how strange it seems, that at the banquet to celebrate the victors, you choose to include a young lady who only today has regained her strength."

"I'm fine," Consuela said, misunderstanding him. And she was. She had powered down, but remained at the console with the damping headset in place in case they wanted her to search farther out. Instead, when the stun bolt struck, the headset had the effect of damping out much of the bolt's effect. She had experienced the mental agony of a harsh electric shock but had not lost consciousness, and had been one of the first to recover. "Really."

"I am delighted to hear this," Mahmut said gravely. "And yet, still I fail to understand what grand role you have played in our rescue from the pirates."

Tucker and Guns exchanged worried glances before Tucker responded, "That's our secret."

Mahmut gave a grave nod. "And I, in turn, am not in a position to refuse you anything. Yet I must warn you that if I tell you all that I know of these firestones and of Yalla itself, my life and all my possessions would be delivered into your hands."

"You want an exchange of secrets," Guns said slowly, "to know you can trust us."

"Family honor *requires* that I trust you now," Mahmut countered. "But the pirates, they will not stop with this one attack. I am not insisting, and yet, as a merchant plying the hazards of space, I would ask to know what your secret is."

Guns and Tucker exchanged a second, longer look, before Tucker finally nodded and said, "Fire away."

Guns turned back, sighed, and said, "We can only tell you what secrets are ours to share."

Dark eyes widened in surprise. "Mercenaries who carry the secrets of others?"

"We're not," Tucker said quietly, "what you might consider your ordinary run-of-the-mill mercenaries."

"The lass here," Guns said, "is what they call a Talent."

The merchant's eyes became round in astonishment. "The legends come alive, one after another. First the pirates become more than myth, and now a true Sensitive shares my table."

"You hold more than our lives in your hands," Tucker warned.

"By the head of my only son, these are secrets I shall share with none other," Mahmut promised.

Guns turned to Consuela and said, "Tell him."

So she explained the shadowlanes and the pattern of searching down the lightways. Mahmut listened in a silence so focused and intense that she could literally feel the strength of his gaze upon her. When she stopped, he sat and sipped from his goblet, digesting the information, before turning to Guns and asking, "And these remarkable attack pods of yours?"

"That," Guns replied, "is not our secret to share."

"Someone has equipped you to hunt down pirates," Mahmut breathed.

Guns and Tucker responded with faces of stone.

"I understand," Mahmut said, and set down his goblet. "Very well. It is now my turn.

"Among merchant caravans, Yalla is known as the impenetrable world," Mahmut began. "It is a world of secrets and levels. I have known success there only because my mother was a Yalla native, from a chieftain's family. She fell in love with a merchant trader, my father, and agreed to exchange the desert reaches for his life of spacing. Because of this, I have been granted leave to sit at the edge of the tribal fires and share in the bounty of firestones. Only a handful of traders carry the gems, and fewer still are ever permitted to land. Lifetimes have been spent transporting wares to Yalla and shipping the gems away, without once setting foot upon the golden sands."

"Why the secrecy?" Guns demanded.

"Ah, the mystery. Yes." Another sip to fortify himself, and then, "You understand, to say more places all that I have in your hands."

"We have already shown you," Guns said, "that we can both be trusted, and hold our secrets well."

"It is as you say." Mahmut leaned forward and said with quiet intensity. "It is said that the firestones do not come from Yalla at all, but rather from another system entirely. One so mysterious that no record of its existence remains anywhere."

Guns did not even notice that he spilled his goblet as he catapulted to the front of his cushion. "What?"

"Ah, I see that this interests you. Yes, this rumor has never even been whispered to me, one who has spent a lifetime trading for the Yalla chieftains, and who has traced his way through the secret caverns since he was able to walk. But I have learned the ability to sift through the sands of time and desert, and capture the hidden meanings. A word here, a shrug there, and over the years I have come to believe that this is why the chieftains are so reluctant to allow any visitor to set foot upon their globe. Because, in truth, there is nothing there."

"You don't say," Tucker breathed.

"Why else," the merchant continued, "would there be great dunes hollowed out, to conceal fleets of small, swift-running craft?"

"For planetary defense?" Guns hedged.

"Perhaps," Mahmut conceded. "And yet, not even the Hegemony is granted much leave upon Yalla. Firestones are coveted by the dark couriers, and it said that the emperor himself has been known to lose himself within the cabalism of firestone worship."

Consuela exchanged a glance with Rick, saw him blanch at the words. Guns said for them all, "Sounds a strange way for the ruler of all the Hegemony to conduct himself."

"My mother made me swear never to handle a polished firestone," Mahmut replied. "So I can say nothing from experience. But I hear from others that it is a rite as addictive as any drug."

"So the Imperium leaves the planet alone," Guns suggested. "These gems or whatever they are, they're too valuable to risk cutting off their supply."

"So do I think," Mahmut agreed. "And the tribes have spent centuries perfecting the art of guarding secrets."

"Have you ever," Tucker demanded, "heard the name of this hidden world?"

"There was once a word spoken," Mahmut replied, his voice dropping to a whisper. "A word murmured in the late of night, by one so old he did not realize what it was he said. After that night, I never saw the elder again." Mahmut looked from one face to the next, then finished, "The word was Citadel."

CHAPTER FIFTEEN

Tucker followed her across the oasis, back toward the cavern entrance and their transport, and asked once more, "Are you sure you want to keep this up?"

"I have to." Consuela massaged her neck with one hand, more tired than she had ever been in her life. "There's no other hope, is there?"

"Even so, lass, you've set yourself a killing schedule."

"It's not that bad," she insisted, trying for a light tone. But her voice sounded flat and drained even to her ears, and her eyes were gritty with more than just the desert sands. "All I do is sit behind the console."

"Anybody who looks at you knows you can't go on like this much longer," Tucker replied worriedly. "And without you we have no hope of finding Wander, lass. None at all."

Consuela had been resting beyond the last trees, where tall flat stones acted as a natural break-wall against the desert winds. Before her had stretched endless waves of golden sand, rising and falling in sweeping ridges to the distant horizon. Now as she walked back toward the looming entrance, a trio of ruddy peaks rose to her right. Other than these three lonely mountains, the desert reached out boundless and forbidding. Under the utterly empty sky, the setting sun glowed huge and orange, as though it were melting into the sands.

Already by this fifth day on Yalla, they had formed the habit of going aloft for the day's final hour. This was the hour of calm, so named because the heat and the fierce winds of day had dimmed, and the cold winds of night had not yet begun. One of the elders had told them at the feast marking their arrival that Yalla had a second name among its desert folk. They called it "The Place of Storms."

Consuela shivered at the memory of their arrival, the heat and huge sun and triple moons, the wind and lightning and desert sands. From the portal in Mahmut's quarters she had watched their descent and felt as though she were diving into a boiling yellow sea.

When they had passed the system's second gas giant, the ones that the ship Avenger had been intended to mine, a trio of Yalla battleships had arrived to escort them forward. Tucker and Guns had told Mahmut they would have preferred to stay aloft in the caravan, but the trader had nervously requested that they descend. He said that the tribesmen wanted to formally thank the ones who had saved one of their own from the pirates. Then he had drawn them aside and explained that the chieftains did not want to have leaders of such a strong fighting force out in space, and that even he and his son would be required to remain in their custody until negotiations and off-loading were completed. Never before had strangers been made welcome on Yalla, Mahmut had told them. Clearly the desert warriors were worried about allowing the leaders of such fighters to remain overhead, circling their planet.

Tucker and Guns had reluctantly agreed, then watched as Yalla guard pods came to station themselves about the caravan. A suspicious lot, was all Mahmut had said. If you want to keep your pods a secret, make sure your troopers stay on the alert, and weld your hold-doors shut.

Now as Consuela approached the vast cave entrance with its decorations of burnished metal and intricate carvings, the sun disappeared below the horizon. Almost instantly the first night winds began blowing their chill whispers of coming cold. Consuela shivered again, wanting to stay out of the stone-lined hall, knowing she had to go in.

"Aye, back where I come from, they'd call this a lazy wind," Tucker said, leading her around the last stand of stumpy trees, their short height sheltered from the worst of the storms by the ring of stone guarding the cavern entrance. "It can't be bothered to go around you, so it just blows straight through."

"You've never said anything about where you are from."

"That's because there isn't much to say." He nodded to the portal guard, who ignored them entirely. Since the feast marking their arrival, the desert clan had not spoken a single word to any of them. Even so, with each day the air of resentment over their presence grew stronger.

The desert soldier was dressed in traditional garb of robe and hood and cloak against the coming night, his blaster slung across his back. "The best thing I can say about my homeworld is I'm not there anymore."

"Do you ever miss your family?" Consuela entered between the tall stone pillars carved from the rock entrance and rising up to five times her height. The portal was large enough for even the caravan's transport to have entered through, and was flanked by a pair of great iron doors.

"My mother passed over while I was still a lad. My father was a good man, but he married again, and his second wife preferred her own children to the one from his first wife. She wasn't sorry to see the back of me." They proceeded across the entrance hall, a cavern that dwarfed the transports nestled at their center. Only one of the tribesmen they passed even looked their way, and that was to pierce Consuela with a look of bitter hostility.

This first cavern was as far into the tribe's underground hive as they had been permitted to enter. They skirted around the caravan's transport, a vessel large enough to contain both a residence for Mahmut and a large cargo hold. Beyond both rested their one guard pod, which remained encased within its plasteel shell. This was the pod that had been struck by the stunner and kept out of the battle. They had decided to leave the plasteel cover in place for precisely such a time as this. Rick waved to her from his station at the pod's base. One of Mahmut's most trusted personal guards kept him company. None of their own troopers had been permitted to land.

Tucker walked her over to their transport's portal and asked once more, "Are you sure you want to do this?"

"I have to," Consuela replied, and cut off further argument by entering the transport and shutting the portal.

She had spent every waking hour at the mind amp, even taking her meals at the console. Sleep had come in snatches, her dreams often ending in a burst of fear that she had missed a take-off, and thus lost her only opportunity to follow the tribal fleet to Citadel. In truth, she had not really rested for five days now, and the strain was wearing her down.

She fitted on the headset, powered up, closed her eyes, and began yet another search around the desert planet. The practice had become almost second nature now, sweeping out and around with growing confidence.

The space around Yalla was utterly silent, for the planet possessed neither true spaceport nor watch communicator. The desert chieftains preferred to keep themselves and their secrets under close control, and there was too great a risk that any communicator trained by the Hegemony would be an Imperial spy.

The first signal was so unexpected that she almost missed it.

Then it came again, startling her so that when she tried to bolt upright, she tumbled from her chair, ripping the headset from her temples. She gave a panic-stricken cry and righted herself. She struggled to refit the headset, her fingers made clumsy with haste.

Tucker clanged open the portal and demanded, "Is everything—"

Frantically she waved him to silence, hunched so far over that her forehead touched her knees. Her eyes were so tightly shut she saw stars. Consuela hunted, hunted, then quietly, the words almost a moan, "I've found strange ships."

Tucker moved with stealth, shut the portal, slid the bolts home. "You're sure?"

"Four of them," she whispered, wishing he would listen, say nothing, simply let her focus and use his silent strength as an anchor. "The size of our transport, no bigger."

"Then their destination can't be too far off."

"They're making course out of the system." For an instant she opened her eyes, fearful of what was to come, searching for the here and now. "But there's no lightway."

"Follow them, lass," Tucker hissed, crouching down beside her, reaching out a tentative hand, withdrawing it before making contact. "It's our only chance."

"I don't . . . " Consuela felt a tremor of fear course through her. Already the ships were reaching out beyond the system's limits, with nothing but black and empty space surrounding them.

"*Follow,*" he urged.

She sighed her way back down, one hand to her forehead, the other reaching out to be swallowed by Tucker's massive grip. She stayed with the ships.

Fighting off the terror of uncharted space, Consuela refused to worry that the return would be impossible, that she might stop and turn about and find herself lost, alone, to hurl forever in panic-stricken search for refuge. She offered a swift prayer for guidance, and gave herself over fully to the challenge.

The Yalla transporters continued to gain speed, streaming an energy trail far behind, burning fuel at an alarming pace. She watched them

318 / T. DAVIS BUNN

continue to accelerate at their punishing rate, then, "They've vanished."

"N-space," Tucker breathed. "And so fast. Either they've a pilot aboard—"

"No," she said, definite on that point, while still remaining outward focused and searching, though the terror of having no fixed point upon which to fasten threatened to swallow her whole.

"—Then they've got a system close at hand, and they know the jump backward and forward, so much they can make do with a line sight and old records." Tucker hesitated, then asked, "Do you see a system dead ahead of where they were last?"

"Yes. One of the closest to us."

"Go there."

"It's not that easy. I can't—"

"Do it, lass." His grip tightened. "For your Wander."

At the sudden sound of his name, she flung herself out, her hand on the console sweeping the power control up to the limit, not pausing an instant for thought, just going.

And colliding straight into the strongest focus of mind-amp power she had ever known.

Not directed toward her. Not yet. The force inundated space about the planet like a multitude of brilliant lighthouse beams, all directed far outward, searching, searching.

Again there was no time for thought. She did not need to inspect. She *knew*. Wander was *there*. She drew back a fraction and bundled together all the anxieties, all the yearnings, all the frustrations and fatigues and longings from those endless fearful days. She wrapped them with the cords of her growing love, shimmering bonds of heartsong, and *flung* them toward the planet. And in the same instant, though she longed to stay and see if they were received, she retreated. A leap across the limitless chasm of emptiness, wishing she could stay, wishing she could shout his name to the heavens, knowing to do so would draw down doom upon their heads, praying with all her heart that he would hear, and understand.

She raised up with an effort, opened her eyes, and found a round-eyed Tucker watching her with burning intensity. She nodded once and managed, "It's there."

CHAPTER SIXTEEN

The platform carrying Wander and the other watch monitors descended into utter bedlam.

The monitors riding the platform down with him were completely silent. They hung over the side rails, their faces blanching with each wail rising from below. As the platform approached the cavern's floor, figures began springing from their positions and racing over.

The senior monitor riding the platform waved those below back to their stations and screamed, "You're all going on report!" There were three senior monitors, one for each watch. Like all personnel, their own watches and subordinates had become hopelessly scrambled. The senior monitor leaned over the railing and shouted down, "Back to your stations!"

Someone down below shrilled, "We're being attacked!"

As the platform sank to the cavern's floor, several distraught faces came in line with Wander's. Their eyes showed white all around. "Something is coming!"

Another voice within the milling throng yelled, "It's not coming, it's here!"

As soon as the railing dropped, two monitors shoved their way onto the platform. More panic-stricken figures came streaming from the mind-amps. One cried, "Get me out of here!"

"Back, I say!" Bony arms protruded from the senior monitor's robes as he tried to stop the charge by will alone.

The senior monitor travelling upon the platform was thoroughly disliked. He was far older than the other senior monitors, and not up to the crisis at hand. He covered this by sudden outbursts and constant criticism. "Remember your duties!"

"I am hereby on sick leave," a monitor declared, shoving his way onto the platform. "I've done more than enough overtime to sleep my way through the rest of this."

One of those just arriving demanded, "What was it?"

"I don't know and I don't want to know."

"Did anyone else hear anything?"

"I didn't need to," came the reply. "I've had all I can take of this balderdash."

"I heard someone cry out," another offered.

Two more crowded their way on. One of them agreed, "It came from the mind-amp next to ours. Stood my hair on end, I can tell you that." From the safety of the platform, he glanced about and said, "Where are they?"

His compatriot replied, "Sprawled in the dust at the foot of their station."

The senior monitor whirled about, grasping at the robes of several scouts who were pressing themselves upon the platform. Then he realized that none of those who had descended with him were climbing off the platform and heading for their stations. He stared from one stubborn face to another, then raised his voice a full octave as he shrilled, "I'll have each and every one of you before the diplomat!"

"Good," one of the newcomers replied. "It's about time we got some answers."

"And stopped this nonsense of double watches and no clear orders," added another voice.

"We've overloaded the platform," someone else observed. "And there's still more coming this way."

A voice from the back cried, "Platform, mount!"

At the last moment before the rails slid up and the dais began its ascent, Wander grabbed hold of Digs' robe and pulled him off. Their move went unnoticed, as the platform's rise drew a chorus of shouts from those still streaming toward it. One monitor leaned over the rails and promised, "We'll send it right back for you!"

"Come down here!" The senior monitor was almost dancing with helpless rage. "You have watches to serve!"

"Serve it yourself," drifted back the reply.

In the tumult and confusion, Wander gripped Digs' shoulder and hissed, "Tell him we'll scout our own system."

Digs turned disbelieving eyes toward him. "Are you completely deranged?"

"Do it."

Reluctantly Digs slipped over to where the senior monitor was watching helplessly as the platform melded with the distant ceiling. "Ah, someone should be watching our own skies."

The senior monitor wheeled about, for a moment unable to focus on him. "Eh? What's that you said?"

"In case there really is something coming in," Digs said. "Just to be on the safe side."

The senior monitor peered at him, his ancient chest heaving. "What's your name, Monitor?"

"Digs, Senior Monitor. And we're just probationary watch standers."

"Not for long." He turned back to those waiting for the platform to return and shouted, "Here's what a true monitor is made of!"

"Give him time," said a grim voice. "He'll learn."

The senior monitor's shoulders sagged. Defeat transformed him into a tired old man. "Go," he said to Digs. "Serve your watch."

Digs waited until they had rounded the first mind-amp before declaring, "I hope you know what you're doing."

"It's a chance," Wander replied. "Only a chance."

"Right." The pinched-faced young man snorted as he raced to keep up with Wander. "A chance to get ourselves fried by some new mind-gun."

"My friends are ten days overdue," Wander said. "More."

Digs remained silent until they had arrived at the station, seated themselves, and began the power-up procedure. Then he glanced worriedly at Wander and asked, "Do you think maybe it's time to give up on all that?"

"I can't," Wander replied stonily.

"But this risk we're taking, what if we're—"

"If I stop hoping I stop living," Wander said. "Stay back here if you want. I'll go look."

"No, no." Digs sighed as he reached over and triggered the amp. "Guess I've got to hope with you."

There was the now-familiar surge outward, but instead of flinging himself headlong across space, Wander hovered, swung out and around the fiery planet, then stopped.

She was there.

Faint tendrils spun across his awareness, like wafts of some familiar perfume almost lost upon a rising wind. But it was Consuela. He knew it instantly. Her concerns, her fears, her struggle against a loss of hope, just like him. And her love.

Digs was there alongside. *I sense something.*

It's all right.

At least I think I did. It's gone now. It felt like, I don't know. A message? The awareness shifted and focused upon him. *Was it that girl?*

Consuela. Yes. There was no doubt. *She is nearby.*

I wonder . . . Digs floated free, his thoughts a jumble, then finished, *I wonder what it would be like to have someone care enough to search for me.*

Wonderful, Wander replied simply. *Will you cover for me?*

An instant's scanning, then, *We're alone out here right now. Make it fast.*

Immediately he sped outward, traversing the accustomed route to Avanti, and said, *Urgent, Urgent, Avanti Port, Tower Control, come in.*

A moment's delay, then, *Avanti Port, Watch Communicator here.*

There was something different, a crispness to the response, which made Wander hesitate before responding, *This is a friend—*

I know who this is. Go ahead, Allegro.

Again he was forced to pause. Allegro was the Avanti sister planet. Clearly the words were meant for someone else. A listener. *Request update on Spaceship Avenger.*

Avenger still detained at Imperial Command. No reason given. Arnol supposedly under suspicion of some crime, but nothing has been substantiated. The chancellor himself has lodged a complaint, as you have probably heard. As soon as the ship is freed, arrives in Yalla, and payment is passed on, your planet will receive its share for the investment made in its construction. How received?

Clear. But not possible. Consuela could not be there. She could not. Imperial Command was on the exact opposite side of the Hegemony. There was no way she could extend herself that far, much less compose and leave a heartfelt message.

Our chancellor has also notified Imperial Command that the invading dragoons will not be released until Avenger and all her crew arrive safely at their destination. How received?

Clear. That much was good. So long as the dragoons were in captivity, Citadel's defenses remained in a weakened state.

You had something urgent?

Wander reflected a moment, then replied, *Only that I am uncertain if my visitors are still expected to arrive.*

It was the watch communicator's turn to hesitate. *Repeat, please.*

Wander did so, then felt an urgent mental prodding from Digs. *Signing off.*

He powered back, slid the headset from his temples, and turned toward his friend. Digs looked frantic. "Someone's coming."

CHAPTER SEVENTEEN

Mahmut looked in astonishment from one to the other. "You want what?"

"It was just a question," Guns replied. "We were just wondering if your caravan might hold a copy of astrogation computations."

"We thought you might have had cause to travel off the standard course from time to time," Tucker added.

"But to travel anywhere away from Hegemony lightways without a pilot on board is strictly forbidden," Mahmut pointed out.

"Right," Guns agreed, despondent. "Sorry we asked."

They were seated in the caravan's transport, which held a private owner's cabin, a smaller version of the caravan's own luxurious setting. Rick drew his silk cushion to the gathering's edge so that he could sit with his back against a heavy wall-tapestry. Even from this distance, however, he could feel Abdul's gaze upon him. The merchant's son sat beside his father, his dark gaze glowering across the circle, boring angrily into Rick.

"Still, it is a strange request," Mahmut contemplated aloud. "For our companions to ask if we might keep astrogation texts within our records."

"Companions," Abdul said bitterly. "They are nothing more than hired help."

Mahmut turned his gaze toward his son. The side of Abdul's head was still swathed in bandages from where he had fallen and hit the control console when the ship had been struck by the stun bolt. "Such words, such an attitude," Mahmut chided gently, "for those who saved both your life and mine."

"No one is out to usurp your position," Tucker offered gently to Abdul, "as master of the caravan's guards."

Abdul flushed darkly as the words struck home. "A fat chance you would have if you tried," he snarled.

Guns sighed his way to his feet. "Forgive the intrusion," he said to Mahmut, keeping his gaze off Abdul. "We won't bother you any further."

"One moment, please," Mahmut said, motioning for Guns to resume his place. He spent a long moment stroking his beard, then mused, "Even if we were to possess such information, we could not give you access to our ship's computers. The chieftains have sealed Yalla tight."

"For how long?" Guns demanded.

Mahmut showed him open palms. "They did not say. They never do. Nor did they give a reason. It seldom lasts for more than a few days. But during that time, we are forbidden to leave the planet's surface. And any contact with the mother ship must be made through their communication system."

Abdul stared at his father, aghast. "You cannot be considering their demand!"

"Their *request*," Mahmut corrected. "A request from *friends*."

"They are not friends," Abdul spat. "They are mercenaries. They hire out to whoever has the gold to pay them."

"And yet they are honorable men," Mahmut said, "who not only saved us, but did not take advantage when we were offering surrender, and all we had was theirs for the taking."

"But, Father—"

"Hold," Mahmut said, showing sternness for the first time. "Go and ask our hosts if we might use one of their larger computers to tap into our shipboard records. Tell them it is a highly confidential matter and must be done on sealed circuits."

Abdul sat as one frozen to stone. "You cannot be serious."

Aquiline features tightened in a flash of sudden anger. "Dare you to defy your father and master of the caravan?"

Abdul blanched. "No, Father."

"That is very good," Mahmut said, his voice taut with quiet intensity. "I am extremely glad to hear it. Now go and carry out your orders."

"I hear and obey," the son said numbly, and forced himself to his feet.

He cast a final venomous glance toward Rick before slipping through the portal.

There was a moment's awkward silence before Mahmut sighed, "An only son, growing into a young man, granted his first true command on this very voyage."

"As guard captain," Tucker said sympathetically. "Only to see it taken away from him and the honor of battle go to someone else."

"It does not matter that rumors abounded, nor that one of our allies disappeared on this very route," Mahmut agreed, glancing at the door with dark sorrow. "He saw my decision to take on extra guards as an indication that I trusted your fighting abilities more than his own."

"And the fact that we were the ones who rescued the caravan," Guns added gravely, "only rubbed salt into the wound."

Mahmut managed a small smile. "You have growing sons of your own?"

"No, but I remember how it felt to be young and handling my first command station," Guns replied. "It's hard enough, without having a father to please."

"Then you will understand why I must apologize for my son's behavior," Mahmut said. "And why I tell you that nothing of our earlier discussion has been passed on."

"Including the true strength of our pods," Tucker said anxiously.

"Indeed. Your hold remains sealed by your own men. Your secret is safe." He looked from one face to the next. "I trust that your request for astrogation guidance is not an idle one."

Guns glanced at Tucker, who said, "Tell him."

"We think we have found the planet called Citadel," Guns said, turning back to Mahmut. "The lass here followed four ships out on an uncharted course this very morning."

"Just when the chieftains placed this planet on quarantine." Dark eyes peered at Consuela with fierce intensity. "Is this indeed the planet from which the firestones come?"

"I don't know," Consuela replied honestly. "I was looking for my friend. Nothing else."

"But it would make sense," Tucker offered. "There's no other reason for them to take such a risk."

"They're headed to one of the planets in that system," Guns added. "And we need to go there ourselves. Will you help us?"

Mahmut gave his beard another stroke, then nodded once. "Right now."

Chapter Eighteen

"What's this I hear of mutiny?" the diplomat demanded.

Wander and Digs had tried to lose themselves at the back of the crowd, but to their alarm, the senior monitor had ordered them to the front row. There they stood, unable to escape the diplomat's furious glare.

They had been summoned with the other few who had chosen to stand watch, after the panic and the fears of an invasion. For the first time that Wander could recall, the cavern was left utterly empty, the listening stations unattended. Wander followed the others into the meeting hall, and though his legs were quaking, allowed himself to be led down front.

A querulous voice from the back spoke up. "We were tired—"

"*Silence!*" At the front of the chamber, the diplomat's midnight robes swirled as he strode angrily up and down the dais. "It is unthinkable that what I have heard might be true. Especially when the emperor's own supreme pilot, the head of your sect, is at this very moment making way for Citadel."

A tight shudder passed through the assembly. Wander glanced to his left, where Digs met his eye and gave a slight shrug of incomprehension. Wander looked to where the senior monitor stood on Digs' other side, and felt a chill of unreasoned fear when he realized that the unshakable old man was gray and sweating.

"Ah," the diplomat said with satisfaction, surveying the assembly. "I see that some of the elders among us recall the last time the emperor's pilot graced us with his presence. Good. Take note of what they have to tell you. Tomorrow you will all have the honor of explaining your behavior in person. And be forewarned that all who do not answer satisfactorily will be invited to try a second time." The smile that suddenly creased the diplomat's features was perilous. "With Imperial dragoons there to assist you."

Wander shared the assembly's second tremor, but for a different reason. The emporer's pilot and more Imperial soldiers were to arrive *tomorrow*.

The diplomat turned his attention to the few monitors who stood alongside Digs and Wander on the front row. "Despite the fact that we were facing a possible attack, you were the only ones to stand to your stations. I shall allow the Supreme Pilot to determine your rewards. Except for you," he said, his gaze focusing upon Wander and Digs. "Stand forth, the both of you."

Wander took the step forward on shaking legs and waited.

"Our two youngest watch standers have shamed you all," he said to the assembly, his eyes remaining upon Wander. "You are both hereby awarded full status. Welcome to the ranks, Monitors."

"Thank you, sir," Wander said, his own voice a dull echo of Digs' triumphant response.

"It is traditional for a new monitor to be granted a boon. Name your request."

Wander did not need to think it out. "We'd like to return to duty."

He could feel Digs turning a dumbfounded gaze his way and shot a swift elbow into his friend's ribs. Digs jerked back to full alert and said, "The stations are unmanned, and we still don't know what's out there."

A gaze cold as space observed them a moment longer, then the diplomat said quietly, "Your request is noted. Dismissed. The rest of you, stand at attention as your betters depart."

Eyes upon the floor at his feet, Wander followed Digs through the silent assembly. As they approached the hall's main portals, a voice to one side hissed, "We too have made note of your request."

"Traitors," another seethed.

When the portals were closed behind them, they walked the empty hallway in echoing stillness until Digs said, "I hope your friends show up. Otherwise we may not have long to enjoy our new status."

Wander nodded and quickened his pace. "We have to hurry."

CHAPTER NINETEEN

They came in the late afternoon. A full contingent of Yalla guards marched up with Abdul, who stepped forward and announced, "We are ready."

"Is that so." Tucker rose to his feet from the gaming table. "You hear that, Guns? They're ready."

"Ready for what?"

"A very good question, that is. Ready for what, I ask as well, bringing along a full bevy of armed soldiers."

"You wanted to communicate with the mother ship," Abdul retorted. "It is a rare privilege to be permitted into the tribe's quarters. This is your honor guard."

"A privilege," Tucker repeated, his eyes casting doubt on all they touched. "Well, Guns, it looks like your predictions have come true after all."

"Aye," the grizzled veteran agreed, and demanded of Abdul, "Where's Mahmut?"

Flanked by the guards, it was possible to see how the desert blood flowed in Abdul's veins, in the aquiline features, the knife-edge to his chin and cheekbones, the glittering cast to his eyes. "Alas, my honorable father has been called to a meeting of the chieftains."

"How timely," Guns muttered, and motioned to Rick. "You completed that work I set for you?"

"Not yet," Rick said, his eyes still on Abdul.

"Then you'll just have to stay put and do your work."

"But, Guns—"

"That's an order, flyer!"

"Aye, aye, Guns." Rick turned and stomped off to the stone-draped pod.

Abdul watched the exchange in consternation. "But he is to come with us!"

"Why?" Tucker demanded, shifting his bulk up oppressively close. "A pod flyer's not required to draw information from your memory banks."

Guns stepped up alongside. "Just what is it you've got in store?"

"Nothing, he, I . . . nothing." Angrily Abdul gathered himself. "If you are coming, come now!"

"Right with you." Guns nodded to Tucker, turned back to the pod. "First I need to make sure the boy understands his business."

"No weapons. You will be searched," Abdul added.

"Of course we will." Guns disappeared as Tucker raised his arms and submitted to a rough jostling by the guards.

When Guns returned from speaking with Rick, he walked over to Consuela and said softly, "You mind coming with us, lass?"

"But you don't need me."

"Ah, but we do." He handed her the cloak he carried. "Might do best if you cover yourself a bit more."

"But I—"

"Humor an old man," he said, keeping his back to the suspicious guards. "Here, let me help you." He slung it over her shoulders, then fastened it at her neck with a glittering silver clasp. "There. Much better."

The robe's clasp was heavy, with a single blue stone at its center. She fingered it and asked softly, "What is this all about, Guns?"

"Nothing, I hope." He turned around and allowed himself to be thoroughly searched.

Abdul pointed at Consuela and demanded, "She comes with us."

"Wouldn't have it any other way," Guns agreed cheerfully. But when the guards moved toward Consuela, both he and Tucker stepped in close. They hovered over the guards as they searched her, and observed in menacing silence. The guards hastily completed their frisking and stepped back.

"This way," Abdul said, smiling fiercely.

"Hang on a second," Tucker said. He ducked inside the transport and came out with a small flat rectangle. He handed it over for inspection, saying, "Wouldn't help us to go unless we had a portable memory for storing the information."

Abdul accepted the box, flipped open the lid, keyed the console, nodded, and handed it to one of the guards.

"Just your basic portable set," Guns offered.

Clearly the guard agreed. His fingers searched out the catches, opened the back slot, checked everything carefully, then handed it back. Abdul rapped out, "We go."

The tunnel was large enough for the three visitors to be flanked on all sides. The few tribesfolk they passed refused even to look their way.

A hundred paces farther in, the tunnel opened into yet another cavern. They were led toward a series of small transport-platforms and instructed to step aboard. Instantly the railings slid up, the platforms lifted, and they were away.

Consuela did not try to hide her interest as they traversed tunnel after tunnel. This was not some impoverished series of underground dwellings, but a civilization rich in culture and tradition. Even at their high speed, she could make out how all the internal tunnels were decorated with brilliant murals of vibrant scenes. The caverns themselves were equally impressive. Far overhead, translucent skylights allowed in soft filtered light. They illuminated walled worlds of green, for each of the caverns was centered upon an underground spring. Water bubbled into lakes and carefully managed rivulets. Trees bloomed in gardens of flowers and vegetables and fruit vineyards. Birds with brilliant coloration flitted alongside their platforms, singing strident challenges to these other flyers.

They entered yet another tunnel, which took an upward slant. Higher and higher they climbed, leaving Consuela to wonder how they could make such an ascent and yet still remain underground.

Eventually the platforms landed in an antechamber whose vaulted ceiling rose to a high peak. Abdul alighted and brusquely motioned them forward. "In here."

They followed him through a pair of powered doors, which slid open at their approach. Consuela took a step inside and stopped with a gasp.

The room was ringed with communication and computing equipment. Above it rose great windows, which looked out over a billowing yellow sea.

They had climbed up inside the center of a mountain, she realized, stepping closer to the thick sheets of glass. They were now so high that

332 / T. DAVIS BUNN

the planet's perpetual storms were below them. The clouds of sand rose and puffed like ghostly yellow waves, churning and swirling in glistening streams.

"Of course," Tucker said. "Transmission would be better if they could stay above the worst of the gales."

"Enough," Abdul snapped. "Give me the memory console."

"Just a minute there," Tucker responded, and turned to Guns. "You know this rig?"

"Trained on one just like it," Guns affirmed.

Tucker turned back to Abdul and said, "The deal was, you connect us with the ship's onboard memory, then we are left alone."

"But I—"

"Alone," Tucker repeated. "Your father agreed to this."

Abdul looked from one to the other in helpless fury, then spun about and began coding in. He waited a second, then snarled, "Be quick about it," and stomped for the doors, signaling the guards to follow.

Guns stepped to the console, searched a moment, grunted when he recognized the configuration, and swiftly made the connections from the communicator to his portable set.

"Seal the circuits," Tucker reminded him.

"Just seeing to that," Guns agreed, pulling up a chair and working swiftly. "Okay, that's done."

Immediately Tucker moved up close to Consuela and said, "We're in. Stand at the ready."

Consuela took a confused step backward and asked, "Ready for what?"

"Ready for the coding," Guns replied.

Consuela looked from one to the other. "But I don't—"

"Here is the coding from Mahmut." Tucker drew a paper from his pocket, unfolded it, and began droning out a series of numbers and letters, giving time for Guns to punch them in. There followed a tense moment, until Guns announced, "Receiving."

"Make it fast," Tucker said.

Another span of a dozen heartbeats, then, "All done."

"Check for error," Tucker urged. "We won't get a second chance."

Another hesitation, then, "Up and running."

"Here it comes then," Tucker muttered, and stepped toward the portal.

Instantly the doors slid back to reveal Abdul and the guards. The merchant's son was smiling yet again, an evil grimace that stretched his entire face out of shape. The guards stood with blasters at the ready. "You are finished," Abdul announced.

"We were just about to tell you the same thing," Guns agreed easily.

"My father's orders have been carried out," Abdul announced. "You have received the secret information. But you will never have an opportunity to use it."

"What about the lass here? She's done nothing wrong." Tucker drew her close with a heavy arm on her shoulders, then said, "Alarm, alarm."

"What was that?" Abdul snapped.

"He said, alarm," Guns agreed. "And that's exactly what we think. It's *alarming* that you would think of dishonoring your father like this."

"I have done exactly as he ordered," Abdul retorted, his face flaming. "It is you who poisoned his mind with thoughts of honor, when you will take your coin and turn against him."

"The only one who's turned against him is you," Tucker said, risking a nervous glance around and out of the windows. He turned back, gave Guns a slight shrug.

"I am protecting our caravan!" Abdul rapped out. He signaled the guards forward.

Guns turned fully about, muttering, "What's going on here?"

"Maybe the storm stopped the signal," Tucker murmured and turned around as well, drawing Consuela with him as the guards moved to surround them.

"Yes, look well," Abdul said. "For you will never again see the light of day."

"Trouble," Guns muttered.

"The storm," Tucker agreed. "Should have thought of that."

"Too late for regrets," Abdul crowed. "You are now my . . . "

His words trailed off when one by one the guards murmured and pointed and cried out as a stone dot puffed up through the billowing sandstorm and shot toward them. Just outside the window, the guard pod stopped and hovered.

Tucker turned and announced, "Looks like the tables have turned."

"He won't shoot," Abdul cried, struggling to rally the nervous guards. "He wouldn't dare. He'd only be shooting his own people!"

"The lad," Guns replied, with his battle hardened grin, "doesn't have to shoot."

With an explosion so powerful that the windows quaked and the floor beneath their feet shivered, the pod erupted. The guards cowered and covered their heads, then slowly rose back when the windows held. They stared dumbfounded at a midnight black flyer shaped like the head of a spear.

"Lay down your weapons," Tucker ordered. "All of you."

"Shoot them!" Abdul screamed.

Guns leaned towards Consuela and rapped out, "Blade! Attack sequence *now!*"

Instantly a tongue of brilliant white energy shot from the front of the pod. Deftly the flyer maneuvered forward and sliced through window and wall as though they were butter.

That proved more than the guards had bargained for. They made for the portal in a mad rush. When Abdul tried to stop them, he was flung to the floor. Which meant he was the only outsider to witness the arrival of five other Blades from the depths of that deep blue sky.

Tucker swung around and said to Consuela, "Blade Three, go back and escort the transporter down."

Instantly one of the fighter-pods swung away and descended back into the billowing storm.

"Her brooch is a microphone," Abdul rasped, struggling to rise. "You tricked me."

"Stay where you are," Tucker commanded, hefting one of the discarded blasters.

"Don't hurt him," Consuela pleaded.

"I ought to fry him to a crisp," Tucker grated. "But it would be a dishonor to his father, who is a man among men."

When Abdul realized he was not to be harmed, he turned his attention back to the melted windows and the pods beyond. His eyes narrowed. "Elemental trinium," he said. "I wonder what the emperor would pay to learn that rebel mercenaries were operating attack pods of elemental trinium."

"I wonder how well you'd serve your father without a tongue," Tucker replied.

"Hold," Guns ordered, then said to Abdul, "You should be glad, matey. They're the only thing that kept you from sitting in the belly of a stinking slaver."

"Gratitude is one of the many traits his father failed to teach him," Tucker said, glowering.

Guns motioned toward the window and announced, "Our transport is here."

The first Blade to have arrived, the one piloted by Rick, switched off his brilliant power-lance. Gently Rick then nudged the outer wall, pressing in, shoving through rock and molten glass, sending dust and stones billowing inward. The communication equipment sparked and fizzled as it was pushed farther and farther back. The Blade shifted to one side, making a larger space where the transporter could move in and land alongside.

When the Blade's portal opened, Guns stepped forward and said, "You took your time about it, lad."

"I could scarcely make out a word," Rick responded. "It sounded like you were talking inside a machine shop. I finally decided it was better to be safe than sorry."

"You did right," Tucker said, motioning Consuela forward and into the transport. "Another minute and we might have been gone for good."

Rick stood in the wreckage of the communications tower, ignoring Abdul entirely. "Where do we go now?"

"Out and away," Guns said, the memory console tucked under one arm. "There's work to do, and not a second to lose." He patted Rick's shoulder. "You did well, lad. I'm proud of you."

CHAPTER TWENTY

"You have to sleep."

Wander pushed the hand away. "Power me up."

"It's not going to help your friends any if they arrive and find you flat on your back, your brain melted down."

"I'm all right, I tell you." Yet despite his best efforts, Wander could not fully erase the slur from his voice. His words seemed to slide out, melding together into a toneless tangle. "Hook me back up."

Digs looked pained. "You've been on three watches and more without a break."

"I have to," Wander replied stubbornly.

"You *can't*." Digs ripped the headset from Wander's hands. "Look, just pull your cushions off the chair and lie there on the floor. I'll stay hooked up the whole time."

Wander tried to argue, but he didn't have the strength. "I don't know what to tell you to look for."

Digs gave a humorless smile. "Sounds just like the orders I've been following for weeks."

Wander found it necessary to use both hands to push himself erect. When he bent over to lay out the cushions, he almost fell over. "It's less than six hours before the Hegemony vessel is due," he said, stretching out with a groan.

"I can read a chrono as good as you."

Wander suddenly found he could not keep his eyes open. "What happens if my friends don't get here before the Imperial ship and its dragoons?"

Digs was silent a long moment, his face growing steadily grimmer. Finally he said quietly, "I don't know."

But Wander was already asleep.

———

Tucker said to Consuela, "There's no doubt?"

"None." This close, Consuela did not even need to power up. The air seemed to buzz with static power. She pointed through the viewport and said, "The next planet after this one is where Wander is being held."

"All right, lads." Guns kept his voice to a low murmur, as though talking quietly would keep them from being detected. "Unhook the Blades."

Tucker gave a satisfied nod to the transport's first officer. "Well done."

"It wasn't me," the young man protested, and pointed to where Guns sat in the navigator's seat. "All I did was follow his instructions."

"Aye, well, congratulations to the both of you." Tucker stared out the front visor at the pitted surface of the system's fifth planet. Even at this close proximity, the sun was so swollen it blazed about the planet's edges, surrounding the globe with a fiery halo. "Wonder what possessed them to put a garrison in a red giant's system."

"I seem to recall the pilot Dunlevy saying something about this once having been the Hegemony's borders," Guns offered, unstrapping and standing up, massaging his back.

"Aye, well, I've served some miserable posts in my time, but this is one place I'm glad to have missed."

"You and me both." Guns patted the first officer's shoulder and said, "You'd best go ahead and plot our return course."

"Me?" The young officer showed genuine alarm.

"You saw what I did. The computer does most of the work. Make preparations for a swift departure for Avanti. We may be in a hurry when we return."

"Aye, aye, Guns."

There was a rough scraping through the transport's roof, and a pair of shadows flitted in front of the viewport. For the voyage across uncharted space, the Blades had melded their shields together and bonded tightly about the transport. A voice declared over the intercom, "All Blades but yours are freed, Guns."

"Prepare for action, but don't power up your weapons," Guns replied.

"We don't know what those boyos on Citadel can and cannot detect." He turned to Tucker and said, "I better be off, then."

Tucker offered him a meaty paw. "Good hunting, matey."

Guns met him with an iron-hard grip. "Aye, we'll give them a run for their money."

"More than that," Tucker said. "We'll be watching for your signal."

Guns nodded in Consuela's direction and said, "And I for yours."

When Guns had slipped through the portal and entered his Blade, Tucker said to her, "Time to hook up."

She hid her grimace, as all the troopers were watching her every move. Consuela slid behind the console, fitted on the headset, and powered up. Instantly the distant buzz rose to an angry swirl of power. But no voices. There was no communication, just an incredibly focused source of listening.

Thankfully, none of the focus was directed at her. In fact, everything seemed to be reaching so far out beyond the system's borders that anything this close went undetected. Gingerly she inched up the power dial, reaching out, ever fearful of being discovered.

When the signal rapped through her headset, it shocked her so that she leapt to her feet, jamming the seat back and over the edge. She kept one hand pressed to the headset upon her temple as she leaned over and powered back. She stayed like that an instant longer, observing, focusing more tightly about the source of the voices, and feeling all the blood drain from her face. Finally she powered off completely, raised up to face Tucker, and said quietly, "We have trouble."

CHAPTER TWENTY-ONE

Wander awoke to the smell of hot soup and a nudge from Digs. He opened his eyes, rubbed away the grit that matted his lashes, and saw his friend offering him a steaming mug and a sandwich. He struggled upright and said, "I feel as though I just shut my eyes."

Digs showed grim humor. "You've been snoring away for almost three hours."

"So long?" Wander rubbed a crick from his neck. "How did you get those? I thought you said you'd keep watch."

"I was only gone a minute." The grim lines deepened. "Besides, you'll be needing all your strength and wits."

Wander took a sip and felt the warmth course through him. "What's the matter?"

"The Hegemony ship has arrived early," Digs said, and a flicker of fear rose within his gaze.

———

"Await my signal," Wander said, fitting his headset into place.

Digs looked at him uncertainly. "You're sure you want to do this?"

"Unless you have a better idea." Wander settled back, took a deep breath, then another.

"I've never heard of anyone trying anything like this." Digs' hand hovered over the controls. "Probably because they knew they'd end up getting fried."

"My friends are risking their lives to come for us. At least I hope they are." Wander regarded his friend. "How can I do any less?"

Digs nodded acceptance and fitted his own headset into place. "Just be careful."

"Is your damping on full?"

"Don't worry about me," Digs replied, nerves turning his tone sharp. "Just go out, do it, and get back."

Wander closed his eyes. Took another breath. "Ready."

"Here goes, then."

There was too much risk of him getting out and not being able to make it back. He needed a back-up, someone to remain at the borders of his activity, watching carefully, ready to draw him home. That was Digs' task, to protect himself with a fully damped headset, observing both what Wander did and how he was, with one hand ever ready on the controls.

Even so, Wander was a mere hair's breadth away from sheer terror.

Digs did exactly as they planned, powering up just a fraction, enough for Wander to raise his awareness above Citadel's scarred surface, hover, and collect himself.

Then Digs rammed the power controls to full.

The force was enough to have sent Wander's awareness rocketing to the Hegemony's farthest borders and beyond. But he resisted, remaining exactly where he was, though the force threatened to split his mind into a billion shimmering fragments.

Finally he moved, harboring the force, riding it like a whirlwind, drifting up to the Imperial ship, seeking out the communication link. A silver thread of mind-amp power flickered outward, the Supreme Pilot and his two assistant pilots communicating with Imperial Command. Without making contact, Wander's harnessed force was sufficient for him to make the instant identification.

The pilot noticed something at the periphery of his extended awareness and began the turning. It was what Wander had wanted, a crack in their concentration. Immediately he pounced.

Releasing all the force that he had been holding back, Wander gave it a face of utter frenzy. He *screamed* out, using his focused power as a flashing mental fist, attacking down, forcing his way into the pilots' protected chamber, shrilling with all his might, *DANGER HERE. DANGER. CITADEL UNDER ATTACK. WITHDRAW. DANGER. WITHDRAW IMMEDIATELY. SAVE YOURSELVES.*

He stayed only long enough to see all three pilots retreat in gibbering horror, their minds stunned to insensibility by the suddenness and the force of his attack.

Then he moved away.

The power still coursing through him, unleashed and unchecked, he circled back and around the planet, stopping at each outward-focused lance of attention. One by one he attacked them with a diving force, a biting strike of unexpected fury, the words always the same. *DANGER. DANGER. ALARM. ALARM.*

The monitors' mind-amps granted him an unexpected advantage. They opened and focused the monitors' attention, which meant that his attack was met not with defense, but rather by focused and amplified openness. Instantly he realized that here was the reason for the Citadel's secrecy: *A monitor had no defenses other than concealment.*

One moment, the monitors searched the far reaches in utter certainty that they were concealed and thus invincible. The next, an apparition flooded directly into their minds, screaming alarm. By the time Wander had made one swift circle of Citadel, there was not a single focused monitor-beam remaining upon the planet.

Wander did not hesitate. Instantly he sent the signal to Digs and heaved a mental sigh of relief as the power eased back. He continued outward, but not far, extending only through the system, searching with open liberty and shouting in frantic haste another word now, over and over, calling out her name. *Consuela!*

One moment he was alone and lacerated by the fear that all was still in vain. The next, he was enveloped by a mind and heart as eager and yearning as his own.

They spun together for a half-dozen heartbeats, locked in the embrace of those who no longer have room nor time for barriers. Their love was as boundless as space, their joy as brilliant as the red orb shining overhead.

Gradually, reluctantly, Wander eased himself away. *I must hurry.*

Wander. Oh, Wander.

Listen to me, beloved. We must go, and now. He offered her a mental shake, in the form of a shimmering diamond that flashed toward her and exploded with a spark of unexpected power. She jerked away, relinquishing her hold. He asked, *Where is the ship Avenger?*

Gone, I mean, we are just the transport and the Blades. Consuela struggled to collect herself. There was an instant's pause, then, *I told the others you are here*.

Where . . . oh, I see now. He located the ships as they rounded the fifth planet and headed toward Citadel. The six Blades and the battered transport seemed so puny, set against the might of the empire. But there was no choice. He braced himself and said again, *We must hurry*.

We are ready. And she was. Quivering with taut eagerness. *Tell us what to do*.

Swiftly he sketched out his plan, stopping at intervals for her to repeat it to the others. When he was finished, there was a brief pause, then Consuela said, *They agree*.

It startled him, this military-like acceptance. No argument, no doubt, no hesitation. For the first time since the kidnapping, Wander felt himself thrilled by the sudden flood of unbridled hope. *I must go and prepare*.

Swiftly they embraced, a gift of closing together, moving beyond the realm of words, giving and receiving the rapture of love granted a future.

CHAPTER TWENTY-TWO

As the mind-amp's power receded, Wander felt his own physical strength drain away. He turned toward Digs without raising his head from the chair. "You'd better be going."

"Are you all right?"

"Fine," he said weakly, willing strength back into his limbs. He could be feeble later. "Hurry."

The concern in Digs' gaze was suddenly replaced by a blaze of hope. "You found them?"

"They're coming." Wander waved him away. "Hurry."

Digs leaped from the chair. "This should be easy."

"Why do you say that?"

His friend gave a genuine grin for the first time in days. "Can't you hear?"

Wander stilled his breath and listened as wails rose from the distance. "It worked," he said, vastly relieved.

Digs raced for the mind-amp's entry, then hesitated. "You won't forget me?"

"We are leaving this place together," Wander promised firmly, his energy returning. *"Hurry."*

Digs gave him a grin so wide it almost split his face. "Watch me fly," he said, and was gone. He raced down the aisle between the mind-amps, screaming at the top of his voice, "Alarm! Alarm! The amps are blowing! Out of the cavern, everybody! Hurry!"

344 / T. DAVIS BUNN

The call was swiftly picked up by others, and Wander heard the sound of racing feet and frantic voices scrambling by outside his amp.

Grimly he switched to Digs' seat, fitted on the headset, and reached for the controls. He had time for one brief hope that it would not be necessary to power up fully another time, especially not alone, especially when he was already so weak. Then he switched the amp back on and focused outward.

To his vast relief, the Imperial ship was retreating.

The great dark vessel was moving up and away from Citadel. It could not attain n-space transport, not without the pilots for guidance. But it could and did place greater distance between itself and what it thought was the source of attack. An attack unheard of in the Hegemony annals. An attack not made with standard weapons, but rather launched directly upon the piloting network, locking the ship down, holding it trapped within an alien system, without even lightways to guide it away. The captain was no doubt fighting panic among his crew.

Even so, Wander could sense the risk of pods being launched, Imperial dragoons pouring out, hunting the unseen assailant. He switched his attention and saw the seven tiny ships flitting toward him.

He turned and reached out. *Consuela?*

Here. The response was immediate. Terse with eagerness.

Your course is correct. Hurry.

Guns sees the Imperial vessel. Are they attacking?

Not yet.

We are passing through the fire storm. No, I see, it's your atmosphere. A pause, then a subdued, *What a horrible place.*

Yes.

Strike in thirty seconds. Wait, wait. Rick sees the canyon! And the fortress. Yes! There it is! Oh, Wander, we are coming!

Wander felt a hand on his shoulder and knew it was time. *We are leaving now.*

We?

Oh. I forgot. He felt Digs shake his shoulder again. *There are two of us.*

CHAPTER TWENTY-THREE

"Attack mode!" Rick powered his weapons systems to full and steadied his course to skim just above the canyon's scarred and pitted floor. Overhead swept a perpetual storm covering, not of clouds, but of fire. "By me, Blades!"

"Blade Four, in formation."

"Blade Six, roger that."

"First Officer here. We are adhering to your track. Remember we need a hole large enough for the transport."

"Target in sight," Rick announced, his voice a knife edge. He popped the guards off his foregun triggers, sighted, and shouted, "Firing one!"

The bolt seemed to drift down, impossibly slow for an energy missile, giving notice to the gallons of adrenaline that pumped his heart rate to overdrive. Then the missile struck, followed swiftly by a second, and, "We have an opening! Prepare the troops!"

"Roger that." It was Tucker. "Guns, any sign of the dragoons?"

"All clear. Just don't hang around."

"Not an instant more than necessary."

Rick tucked his shoulders in tight, as though trying to draw the Blade in narrower. At his speed, the hole seemed impossibly small. But he entered with room to spare, as did the transport. Then he stopped. He had to.

"Incredible!" came Tucker's hoarse exclamation. "What are they?"

"Power-amps," Rick said. "They have to be."

Stretching out as far as they could see was a cavern of impossible size. Their energy bolts had both sucked out all the air and filled the space with dust. Through this maelstrom they could see the dark flickering rings below, and the veins of light planted in both floor and ceiling.

It was Tucker who broke the frozen tableau. "On to the center, Blades. Move."

They dropped to the cavern floor, hunted, found the first platform near their entry-point, kept moving, and finally Rick shouted, "Central platform dead ahead!"

"Guard our flanks, Blades," Tucker said, and then went on, "Set her down easy."

"Like a baby," the transport's flight officer agreed.

The transport drifted over and down, settling at the platform's center. Over the internal communications system and all-channel radio as well, Tucker shouted, "Platform, mount!"

Instantly the rails rose up, and the platform began its gentle descent.

Chapter Twenty-four

The explosion rocked the floor of Wander's compartment. Digs showed no fear whatsoever. Instead, he raised his fists to the ceiling, his robe falling back to expose the dragon tattoo swirling down his right arm. His neck so taut the muscles stood out like cords, he shouted, *"Yes!"*

"I hate this waiting," Wander said. Somehow the tension left him quieter, more focused, counting the seconds like endless days.

"Your plan is a good one. You're sure they know which chamber?"

"I gave them the clearest instructions I could."

"Then they'll be here any moment."

But they weren't. Instead, there was only silence. Alarms sounded in the distance, then halted, then started back. Nothing else. The waiting stretched out so long Wander felt his nerves were snapping, one by one, threads as taut as the chamber's atmosphere, splitting under the unending strain, leaving him tottering on the brink of—

Through the heavy portal there came the sudden chinking of metal on stone. Wander leapt up and shouted in a voice not his own, "Open!"

Chief Petty Officer Tucker stormed in, eyes blazing, weapon at the ready. "Time to fly, lad."

Another trooper fitted through the portal, spotted Digs, and raised his weapon. "Wait!" Wander shouted. "He's a friend!"

Tucker eyed the stranger and demanded, "He's coming?"

"Yes," Wander and Digs said together.

"Let's be off, then."

Together they raced down the corridor, around one bend after another, until the transport came into view.

The portal opened, spilling out a brown-haired figure in a gray spacesuit who came racing over, her arms outstretched and hair streaming, eyes wide and filled to overflowing. She flew into Wander's embrace, holding him with a force that promised never to let him go, saying things to his ear that he could not hear for the pounding of his own heart. A heart that shimmered with the fullness of hope and promise.

Tucker let the reunion continue for a brief moment, then said gruffly, "Into the transport. Hurry, now. We're not out of this yet."

The transport lifted and started before the last trooper was settled, heading back to the platform chamber. The chamber's door lay shattered upon the corridor floor. They entered the chamber, hovered above the floor, and Tucker said, "Everybody fixed down tight? Take a good grip." He then said into the microphone, "All right, Rick. Easy does it."

For a moment there was nothing, then the floor below them began to glow. Stronger and stronger, until there was a rending tremor, which rose until the very air seemed to shake.

Then the Blade's energy lance came into view, prodding a hole that grew and grew, and with it came a shrieking wind, powering through the chamber's destroyed portal, pouring air from all the corridors, a hurricane of air and dust and moisture. It streamed through the hole where the Blade had been, pulling the transport down through the ceiling and into the mind-amp chamber.

"You're sure about what you told us," Tucker demanded, "all the monitors' private chambers have airtight doors?"

"It's a fact known by most," Digs confirmed. "When I first arrived, they still held regular safety drills, everyone going into the nearest chamber and sealing it down. But then the new diplomat arrived, and all that was stopped. The alarms sounded when you attacked. Even the ones who never practiced the drill will know to go into their chambers. There is emergency food and water in each. They will be safe."

A voice over the intercom said, "Shall I blast these amps?"

"No," Wander ordered. "It could crack the planet in half."

Tucker looked doubtful. "It would save us all a lot of worry in the future, lad."

"It's not necessary," Wander assured him, both his hands captured by Consuela's. "I've found a way to protect us."

"Eh? How's that?"

Wander shared a look of love and joy with Consuela, and replied, "I've learned the secret behind Citadel's mystery."

EPILOGUE

Rick stopped in front of the carnival entrance and said, "I sure hope I know what I'm doing."

It was here that their adventure had begun. An unexpected shift to new challenges came through the same roller coaster which glittered and soared just up ahead. Consuela looked up at him, her eyes shining. "You have prayed about this, haven't you?"

"All last night and most of today," Rick confirmed.

"And have you been given a sense of direction?"

"So clear and so strong," Rick hesitated, then finished, "I feel as though God has been waiting for me to ask the right question."

Daniel moved up to stand alongside Consuela. He said for them both, "Then you should do as you feel called."

"I will," Rick agreed. He looked upward at the stars, their light white and beckoning against the dark sky. "I just wish I could be sure I'm doing the right thing."

"Sometimes God's promise of blessings to come must be enough." Daniel said. "He urges us to set out upon His chosen road, accepting that there will be times when only He is able to see the way ahead."

Consuela looked from one face to the next, feeling sad and excited and happy and confused all at once. The carnival's jangling noise seemed held at bay by the same calm that reached through the unsettled storm and granted peace to her heart. And that defined her own path.

As though reading her thoughts, Daniel said, "God promises change. Just as He said to Abraham, He tells us, I will bless you. And in doing so, He opens up a future. A future of hope, of change, of renewal. Like Abraham, though, you may be called to a land whose name you don't even know. And if that happens, your trust must grow to meet the challenge."

Consuela shivered, half in anticipation, half in fear, and clutched her bundle tighter.

"You must realize," Daniel went on, "that in fully accepting the Lord as your God, you accept the future He has chosen for you."

"That is how I feel," Rick said solemnly.

"Me too," Consuela agreed.

Daniel turned solemn eyes to Consuela. "Then go. We will miss you. But our prayers will be with you always."

Rick offered her as much of a smile as the sadness in his eyes would permit. "It was great seeing you and your mom together like that."

"And to see her so well," Consuela agreed. The words brought another bloom of sadness and longing, and for a moment she faltered.

As though reading Consuela's mind, Daniel patted her arm and assured her, "Your mother has blessed your decision. She is well, and she is praying for you. That is a gift and a sign both, or at least it seems that way to me."

"Thank you." Consuela hugged them close, first Daniel and then Rick, trying to seal their presence into her heart for all time.

Together they turned and entered the carnival. The crowds and music and noise and lights flitted about them, leaving them untouched. The stillness and peace moved with them, granting the action and the moment a sense of rightness beyond thought, beyond words.

They stopped before the roller coaster. As Rick moved over to buy the tickets, Daniel hugged her a second time and said, "I will pray for you, each and every day."

Rick returned, and together they mounted the platform, handing the man four tickets so they all could go forward. But it was only Consuela who seated herself. Rick held her parcel until she was settled, then handed it to her before moving back to join Daniel. He called over, "Do you think I can ever go back to that other world?"

"If it is God's will," Consuela replied, as sure of that as she was of anything in her entire life.

The roller coaster started forward with a jerk. Consuela pulled the Bible from her parcel and wrapped her arms tightly around it, pressing it to her chest. As the roller coaster gained speed, she turned back and called out a single word to the two men who stood and waved her onward.

"Friends!"